FATE
and
Ms. Fortune

By Saralee Rosenberg

FATE AND MS. FORTUNE
CLAIRE VOYANT
A LITTLE HELP FROM ABOVE

FATE
and
Ms. Fortune

Saralee Rosenberg

AVON
TRADE

An Imprint of HarperCollins*Publishers*

This is a work of fiction. Names, characters, places, and incidents are products of the author's imagination or are used fictitiously and are not to be construed as real. Any resemblance to actual events, locales, organizations, or persons, living or dead, is entirely coincidental.

FIRST EDITION

Interior text designed by Elizabeth M. Glover

Library of Congress Cataloging-in-Publication Data

Rosenberg, Saralee H.
  Fate and Ms. Fortune / by Saralee Rosenberg.—1st ed.
    p. cm.
  ISBN-13: 978-0-06-082388-7
  ISBN-10: 0-06-082388-7
  1. Divorced women—Fiction. 2. Man-woman relationships—Fiction. 3. Parents—Fiction. I. Title.

PS3618.O833F38 2006
813'.54—dc22   2006004767

06 07 08 09 10 JTC/RRD 10 9 8 7 6 5 4 3 2 1

To Lee
Thirty years and still climbing.
Our fate has been our great fortune.

To Zack, Alex, and Taryn
Whom I love and cherish
Only the journeys you share are the ones worth taking.

Acknowledgments

Writing a novel is like being in labor. You feel anxious, excited, tense . . . and that's just the first half hour. By nine centimeters (the last chapter), you're cursing like a high school kid. Then, miracle of miracles, your beautiful baby is born (manuscript) and it's thank you, thank you, thank you . . . Sorry if I forgot your birthday . . . It's just an honor to be nominated . . .

So . . . I gratefully acknowledge those who gave so generously of their time and expertise: Dr. Mitch Shapiro, Adam West, Blaine Gorelik, Lisa French, Annette Ridam, Hinda Abramowitz, Frank Culotta, and Josh Gorelick. My characters learned from the best.

Without Alana Smithers, the beautiful, talented makeup artist to the stars, my heroine would have had zero to say and even less to do. Thank you for your wisdom and grace. You have the best hands and heart in the business . . . Arnie and Sheila Wexler, the founders of 1–888–LAST BET, are national treasures. Bless their determined souls for devoting themselves to getting compulsive gamblers (as young as twelve) back to living instead of losing.

My tenacious, don't-even-think-of-not-calling-me-back research assistants, Maya Dollerhide and Liza Jaipaul, hit the ground running and returned laden with information. Ladies, thank you. The best fiction always gets the facts right.

My kids swear I have the world's shortest buddy list, but I am lucky to have many friends and family with whom I am enjoying the ride. Thank you Judi Ratner, Pat Hanley, Fern Drasin, Ellen Gordon, Lenore French, Heidi Rosenberg, and Cindy Spodex for your decades of kinship and faith. Thank you Susan Kaufman, Sue Zola, Bonnie Hoffman, Ellen Wolfson, Cheryl Goldblum, and Denise Morris for insisting I come out to walk/play/eat sushi.

Authoring was a lonely gig until I pledged PPG (Power Punch Gals). Now I've got sixty sorority sisters who know from the thrill of victory (royalties!) and the agony of defeat (rejection). Love you all, but especially our fearless leader, Dr. Mickey Pearlman, the indomitable Erika Moore, and my dear, funny Long Island muse, Christine O'Hagan.

I say one semifunny thing to my sister, Mira Temkin, and there goes the conversation. She's laughing so hard she can't breathe. Thanks Mi, for a lifetime of sharing, caring, and shameless promotion. Between you, Darryl, Alison, Hilary, and Ari, is there anyone in Chicago who hasn't heard of me?

Talk about fate and good fortune. I lucked out when the gifted Lyssa Keusch agreed to be my editor. She always has the right words to nurture and inspire and she so gets my humor (thank God). I adore her style, her vision, and mostly her ability to turn messes into masterpieces. Ditto for getting plucked from obscurity by über-agent Deborah Schneider. This marks our tenth year in the trenches together, and without her compassion, wisdom, and don't-you-worry-about-a-thing approach, I wouldn't have such sweet dreams. I am also grateful that she brought Steve Fisher, the hardest working Hollywood agent, to the party. Thank you, Steve, for your unwavering faith, perseverance, and head-of-the-class intelligence. I am so proud to be represented by you both.

Jason Kaufman, founder of Ta-Da.com and webmaster extraordinaire, is a true original. His creative visions and business smarts are such a winning combo. Thank you, Jason, for outdoing yourself book after book.

How is this for amazing luck? My parents, Harold and Doris Hymen, and my second mother, Rita Rosenberg, are still working, playing, volunteering, and singing my praises. Did I mention they are all in their eighties? Their zeal, courage, and support inspire me daily.

My children used to fight like hell until they discovered a more entertaining pursuit. Making fun of me. Thank you Zack, Alex, and Taryn for your endless repartee of mom jokes that fill the house with laughter. But what I love most is that you conduct your lives with such grace, honor, and integrity. I am abundantly blessed to have you in my life and in my corner.

It takes great courage to say to your wife, "Sure. Quit your high-paying job to stay home and write. Who needs a second income?" We did. Thank you, Lee, for your unshakable belief in me and for holding down the fort all these years so I didn't have to put my dreams on hold. I promise I'll pay you back. Love you so much. Can't and won't do this without you by my side.

And finally, a word to every reader who took the time to e-mail me and wish me a long, happy career. Thank you for your generous praise and encouragement, though truth be told, I found far greater inspiration in *your words* than in my own. Please, please, please, keep in touch through my website: *www.saraleerosenberg.com*.

Continued good things to you and yours,
Saralee Rosenberg
February 2006

If I am not for myself, who will be for me?
And if I am only for myself, what am I?
And if not now, when?

—*Rabbi Hillel*
from Pirket Avot ("Sayings of the Fathers")

Why me?

—*Everyone*

A ♪ from Robyn

WHEN I WAS a freshman at Penn State, I took a class called Interpersonal Communications. It met every week at the library, and involved little more than moving from floor to floor observing other students' body language, study habits, and social behavior.

Easy A, I thought, until we were given our first assignment. Write a short essay on religion, sexuality, and mystery, demonstrating our ability to make a point while using the least number of words.

The professor informed the group that in his fourteen years of teaching the class, he had yet to give out a top grade. Still, he held out hope.

I submitted the following: "Good God. I'm pregnant. I wonder who the father is."

I got an A.

Inspired, I became a big fan of brevity, never imagining that one day, the shortest sentence I would say aloud would turn into the longest sentence of my life.

"I do."

Chapter 1

"SOMETHING IS WRONG with Mom and Dad," Phillip whispered.

"What?" I hollered over the blaring music and the din of a hundred kids running wild.

No matter that my older brother was an in-demand attorney who earned more in a billable hour than I did in a week, to me he was still a putz. Therefore, family bar mitzvahs were the perfect venue for conversation, as it was near impossible to engage in anything other than short, superficial chatter over an ear-pounding "Everybody dance now . . ."

Yet Phillip insisted we talk. He pointed to our parents, Harvey and Sheila Holtz, who were seated across our table, but obscured by a massive centerpiece. "Look at them." He leaned in. "Don't you think they're acting strange?"

"For about thirty years now."

"Don't joke, Robyn. They haven't said two words to each other all night."

I peered around the foam board cutout of hockey great Bobby Orr, and sure enough, they had turned their chairs to literally face the music. An unusual gesture for two people who wouldn't know Ashlee Simpson from Homer Simpson.

"Mom, how's your salad?" I yelled. "Great raspberry vinaigrette."

Everybody dance now . . . yeah . . . yeah . . . yeah . . .

"Daddy, how about those Mets?" I yelled louder. "Could be our year."

Come on let's sweat, baby. Let the music take control . . .

"You guys want anything from the bar?" our server asked. "It's free."

"What?" I cupped my ear.

"The drinks are free. What can I get you?"

Free drinks? Really? Because we are having such a blast at Brandon's Hall of Fame, we thought we were at Madison Square Garden, not a sixty-thousand-dollar reception hosted by our cousin Barry and his wife, Rhonda, in honor of their thirteen-year-old son, who learned to read from the Torah in between ice hockey clinics. "Diet Coke, please."

"I'll take an Absolut," my brother said to our white-gloved waiter, who seemed to care as much about French service as Paris Hilton. "And bring my wife another cosmo. Thanks, buddy." He leaned closer so I could hear. "I'm just saying I've never seen Mom this well behaved. She didn't even do her usual   take-the-bread-off-Dad's-plate-and-hand-it-to-the-busboy stunt."

"Don't worry. She's still up to her old tricks. I heard her go up to the Connecticut cousins and ask if they're all so rich, why can't the men afford socks? . . . Uh oh. Possible host alert. Look happy for Rhonda. Remember. Everything is beautiful."

Phillip faked a laugh. "Then yesterday I called the house to remind Dad not to write a big check today because Barry and Rhonda stiffed us for Marissa's bat mitzvah. I think they gave seventy-five a plate, or some ridiculous number . . . like they didn't know what a Saturday night black-tie affair on Long Island costs . . . Anyway, Mom picks up and says Dad's busy, so I said, Where is he? And she says, How the hell should I know? Am I his parole officer?"

"Ten bucks says he was in the basement studying a map of the former Czech Republic."

"He never called me back."

"Oh, so that's where it comes from? You never call me back either."

"Funny. Then this morning at the temple I said to Dad, Why didn't you call me back yesterday? and he looks at me. So I said, Mom told you I called, right? No answer."

"Well I'm glad they're too busy to talk. Otherwise they'd be killing each other."

"They took two cars here."

"No way."

"I know their license plates, okay? They both drove."

"But Dad would go by mule before he'd fill up two cars going to the same place."

"Exactly."

Phillip's wife, Patti the Whip, slid into her seat reeking of nicotine, certain her spearmint gum would baffle even us *CSI* fans. Like we'd never have guessed that she'd just spent the last ten minutes outside with her sisters in smoke.

"I need another, hon." The former cheerleader pointed to her glass. "Where are the kids?"

"I'm on it . . . Em found a friend from camp, and Max is hanging with some boy whose father owns three homes . . . He asked Max where we winter."

"Love it." I laughed. "Kids comparing vacation destinations . . . We bought in Arizona. Mel and I don't mind the dry heat . . . Dry shmy. A hundred and ten is an oven."

Patti ignored me as usual and turned to her husband. "Where's Mariss?"

"Oh. She just called from the Mario Lemieux table to say

Evan is picking her up now, so I said like hell you're leaving early. This is a family bar mitzvah. We're here till the bitter end."

"I thought her cell died."

"Apparently it's born again, but that didn't stop her from bitching she needs a new one."

"I'll take her after school on Monday." She held up a soup spoon to dab on lip gloss.

"It **is** a new one, remember? You replaced the one she left at the mall without asking me."

"Fine. I'll bring it back to see if they can fix it."

"It's not broken, Patti. She never gets off long enough to charge it."

"She's fifteen. What do you want her to do? Play house?"

I found out the other day that my brother and sister-in-law have signs of Holtz Disease. It's a degenerative disorder in my family in which every conversation ends in an argument. My parents are carriers, so of course the odds were that an offspring would inherit the gene. Fortunately, they just came out with a new pill called Damnit-all . . . You take it, and everyone around you goes to hell for eight hours. . . . Side effects may vary.

Thank God for the wet-kiss intermission from Aunt Lil and Uncle Sol. How was I doing since my divorce, and what a shame that David left me in debt, and didn't I know he was a compulsive gambler, and what happened to my beautiful long hair? "We almost didn't recognize you, dear. You look like that nice lesbian on TV. The one who dances."

"Ellen DeGeneres?" I sighed.

Since making the rash decision to go from long and brunette to short and dirty blond, I'd heard this a lot. But it wasn't just my hair. Having recently met Ellen at work, I discovered we were both a boyishly trim five-seven, with sky-blue eyes and jawbreaker cheekbones.

"Yeah, what the hell were you thinking?" Phillip made a face. "It's so . . ."

"Short." Patti studied me from every angle. "But it'll grow."

"Well, I love it." I fluffed it up. "It's so much easier in the morning."

"Aunt Lil is right." Phillip gulped his drink. "You look gay."

"Mom," I whined. "Phillip is picking on me again."

My mother had no problem commenting on everything from my choice of nail polish ("Didn't I drive a Buick that color?") to my poor taste in swimwear ("The tag says you'll look ten pounds thinner. With whose glasses?"). But if Phillip dared insult me, beware the wrath of Sheila Holtz. Until tonight, as if someone finally hit her mute button.

Lil and Sol took their cue. "You kids take care." Kiss kiss. "And don't be such strangers. Let us know next time you're down in Boca. We'll take you to lunch at our club."

"You bet," I answered. *Because there is nothing we love more than watching slow, out-of-shape seniors ordering lunch with little golf pencils and then eating like it's their last meal.*

"Talk fast." I said to Phillip. "The DJ is supposed to introduce me after the main course."

"You're doing your comedy routine?" Patti sniffed. "Here?"

"That's right," I said. "The accordion-playing juggler on stilts backed out last minute."

"No offense." She coughed. "But aren't you still in training?"

"Yeah, but comics are like hookers. Even the new ones get paid for their time."

"Would you two stop?" Phillip cracked his knuckles.

"I thought you were bringing a date tonight." Patti leaned over him.

"I never said that."

"Yes you did. You said you invited that radiologist from Lenox Hill."

"He was a cardiologist from NYU, and we didn't hit it off."

"How come?"

"How come?" I sighed.

"Are you sleeping with anyone else?" I asked him.

"Sex is part of dating. I would never promise monogamy."

"Not even if we became very close?"

"I'd have to be inspired to offer that. And you'd have to be willing to do anything."

"Uh huh . . . do you even like me?"

"Yeah. You're great . . . but maybe you should look into a boob job."

"Leave her alone, Patti." Phillip said. "She's been divorced like what? Six months?"

"It's fine. Much as I'd like, I'm too busy for dating or root canal."

Frankly, I was too busy trying to hold on to my job as the exclusive makeup artist to two-faced network news star Gretchen Sommers. Too busy staving off the dozens of creditors demanding what little money I had left thanks to my gambling-addicted ex-husband. Too busy selling off our wedding gifts on Craigslist so I could contribute to the Help Robyn from Being Homeless Fund. Too busy trying to starve so that my depressed, après-marriage ass would never again look like an IKEA couch cushion. Too busy trying to break in to stand-up comedy in New York, probably because my life was a joke.

"Robyn, when do you do your little act?" My mother finally turned around.

"In a few minutes . . . Everything okay, Mom?"

"Perfect." She turned back around.

"See?" Phillip whispered. "When does she ever say that?"

In spite of my brother's perfect SAT scores and a law degree from Princeton, most days you could post your thoughts on a lighted scoreboard, and he'd still miss the point like a rookie place kicker. But had Phillip, King of Clueless, finally gotten the story right?

Whereas our mother was like Mama Bear on party patrol

("This music is too loud . . . that food is too salty") she could always be counted on to keep conversations lively by picking up juicy morsels of family gossip at the cocktail hour and dropping them like puff pastry time bombs by dessert.

And whereas my dad preferred to spend his free time pondering the wildlife indigenous to within fifty miles of the equator, he would still be a good sport and invite my mother to dance.

But like the first question asked at the Passover Seder, we wondered why this April night was different from all other nights. For on this night, my parents were glued to their seats.

"Please tell me you're not doing that whole bit about how lame they are," Phillip said.

"Have to. All my other routines are R-rated."

"Then cut out all the curses," Patti offered.

"It's not the curses. I don't think Barry and Rhonda want the kids going home telling their parents about my talking dildo."

"You have a talking dildo?" Patti giggled. "Does he have friends?"

"Okay, we have a problem here," Phillip, the senior partner, held up his hands. "You must know other jokes, Rob. You've been cracking them your whole life."

"Comics aren't just joke tellers, okay? It took me months to develop a solid routine. There's a lot of nuance and setups and—"

"I don't care what you do up there. Leave Mom and Dad out of it."

"Robyn," my mother interrupted. "After your little show, we need to talk."

"We do?"

"Oh why wait?" she said to herself. "I should tell everyone right now."

"You're pregnant?" I laughed, though no one else did.

"Sheila, zip your lip," my father yelled. "You want her to bomb up there?"

"Thanks for the vote of confidence, Daddy. What's going on with you two? We noticed you still had your bread."

"Don't tell me when I can and cannot talk, mister." Sheila jabbed his shoulder.

"Go to hell." He shook her off.

"Mom. C'mon. Please don't make a scene," I said. "Save it for the coatcheck girl."

"Fine. We'll discuss this later . . . I'm going out for a cigarette."

"But they're introducing me any minute."

"I'm sorry. I can't listen to one more word of your father's nonsense . . . Why do you think I'm leaving him?"

Having grown up with a mother whose words were usually code for something else, I knew exactly what Shakespeare meant when he wrote, "Methinks she doth protest too much." *Would that it be William's mother was like thine own?* The more she insisted everything was fine, the more I knew she was lying.

If I asked her what was wrong and she answered, "nothing," that meant everything was wrong, but she never wanted it said that she was a burden to her children. If I asked permission to do something and she said, "Do want you want," it meant "Don't you dare, or I'll never let you forget the terrible choice you made." Sentences that began with "I'm very sorry" meant that for whatever reason, I was about to be very sorry. And her favorite, "We need to talk," meant that not only was something wrong, it was about to get ugly.

On the up side, after years of decoding mother's mixed messages, my interpretive skills were among the best, which had proven helpful since returning to the dating game. I didn't need He's Just Not That Into You. I already knew that "I'll call you" meant "I've deleted your number from my cell." "You're great" meant "I'd prefer someone with boobs." And "Let's get together sometime" meant "I'd rather sleep with a lunch lady."

So how was it possible that guess-what-I-mean Sheila was suddenly coming in loud and clear? And what had happened since Wednesday when everything was fine? The real question, however, was how could I handle my parents' marital storm if I was still reeling from my own? A storm in which the wind gusts uprooted me from a luxury co-op on Central Park West and deposited me in the heart of the Maclaren Mommy Mafia: Park Slope, Brooklyn.

"Mom, what the hell is going on with you?" I followed her out of the ballroom.

"I've had it. That's what's going on." She headed for the front entrance. "We're together forty years and do you think maybe once in all that time he'd put a plate in the dishwasher or pick up his socks? Not Dr. Big Shot . . . He's too busy studying maps of places he's never going . . ."

"Sorry, but if you're busting up a marriage, the law says you need one good reason."

"I have plenty, starting with the man is crazy!"

"Then it's a perfect match!" I quoted Yente the Matchmaker.

"Make jokes all you want, but I'm moving out of the house and moving in with you."

"Ladies and gentlemen. Friends of Brandon. We have a very special treat for you this evening. Here to perform live is a great new comic. She's headlined at Catch a Rising Star in LA, and Caroline's in New York . . . Let's give a big round of applause for Brandon's cousin, the one, the only Robynnnnnnnnn Fortune!"

I'm walking. I'm smiling. Now what? Of all times for her to spring this on me. Oh God. Daddy's right. I'm going to bomb.

"Thank you and good evening. [bow] Hey, you know what? Let's give DJ Johnny a warm round of applause too. Isn't he doing a fantastic job? [clap] And let's thank our hosts Barry and Rhonda. [clap] Guys, this is the greatest bar mitzvah party ever! I don't know how you did it. Free food. Free drinks. Free music and entertainment. . . . okay, anyone here get in for less than five hundred dollars?"

Yes! They're laughing! Okay. Do the bit on young girls wearing Tiffany. Good to know babysitting pays more than prostitution. No! They'll smack me with their Prada bags . . .

"Thank you everyone. Okay, first thing I have to tell you is that I cannot tell a lie. Actually I can. And I do . . . Yeah. Truth is overrated. Life is so much easier when you say whatever it takes to get you out of trouble . . . Robyn, have you been drinking? No Dad. Good. Go to your room . . . Robyn, is that your picture in the paper holding up the 7-Eleven? No Dad. Good. Go to your room . . . So that's my philosophy. Lie and no one gets hurt.

"You know when DJ Johnny said I've headlined at the top comedy clubs? Never happened. I mean I've been to Caroline's. Isn't that the one over on Broadway and Forty-ninth? Now see, what harm was done by telling a little lie? [spots woman at table] Oh wow, ma'am. May I say how much I love your dress? I bet it's a designer gown. And you paid like what? Four thousand dollars? [turns away] Designer, my ass. She got it at Kohl's. Seventy-nine dollars less the coupon . . . See how easy that was? She's happy, I'm happy . . .

"Of course, you ladies all know lying is the key to survival. You buy something really expensive, go to the trunk of your car, take out the bags from Target and Marshalls, do a little switcheroo, one, two, three, dumb husband sees the bag, asks if you remembered to pick up deodorant and chips, and boom, you're in. [crowd laughs]

"Okay, where's Brandon? [looks out] Come on up here Brandon . . . let's give the bar mitzvah boy a huge round. Didn't he do an amazing job today? No really. I'm being totally honest. You were super. [shakes his hand] And there was no lip synching involved, right? 'Cause I wasn't sure. I thought

I saw your mouth moving after the tape stopped . . . Oh, that was the rabbi?

"Okay, well now that you're a man, let me give you some manly advice. Do you always tell the truth? [he nods yes] Really? You always tell the truth? [nods yes] You're gonna have it very rough in high school my friend . . . Brandon, is that vodka in your Poland Springs bottle? [I move his head from side to side] Excellent. Now you've got it. You get good enough at this you can run for president . . . [crowd applauds]

"All right. Let's talk careers. You like playing hockey? [he nods yes] And I bet you think you're pretty good. [he shrugs] Well here's a little reality check and I'm not making this up. It's a statistical fact. Less than one percent of all Jewish boys grow up to be professional athletes. Ninety-nine percent of the time they grow up and buy the team . . . Write that down. Grow up. Buy a team.

"Got it? Okay, go sit down. It's all about me now. Deal with it . . . Let's give Brandon a big hand. . . . he's a future owner of a hockey team!"

They love me! Only now I'm out of untested bits . . . Sorry Phillip.

"Remember being thirteen? You had friends, you had fun, you could use your allowance for drugs . . . No. Just kidding, kids. Don't go home and tell your parents this lady at Brandon's bar mitzvah told you how she saved up to buy these special plants you could smoke.

"But really. I had a great childhood. Grew up in Jersey. And I'm telling the God's honest truth now because my parents are here tonight . . . My father is a retired dentist whose passion is cartography. Yeah. Map collecting. Very exciting. Other dads used to stuff *Playboy* magazines under the bed. Mine had maps of the thirteen British colonies . . . Funny thing was, he could tell you the exact distance between Peking and the Gobi Desert, but when I needed him to give directions to my friends' parents, he'd say, 'Sheila? What's the street after Harrison?' And she'd say, 'You mean the one we live on?'

"And my mom? Now there's a great lady. Taught violin for years. My dad said she could have been a been a concert performer but had to be realistic about how much they made. Translated: She never heard anyone say, 'Wow. Look at the violinist's Mercedes!' But she was a wonderful mother. She'd call upstairs and say, 'Kids, what do you want for dinner?' and I'd yell back, 'What are our choices?' She'd say, 'Yes or no.' And talk about great teachers. She taught me about envy. 'Pity the millions of less fortunate children who don't have a wonderful mother like you.' She taught me about religion. 'You better pray your father doesn't find out.' And justice. 'If there is a God, one day you'll have a daughter just like you.' But mostly she taught me about luck. 'Of course there's luck. How else do you attribute wealth to people you hate?'

"Yeah my parents are great . . . just not great with all the new technology. Bought them a cell phone a few weeks ago. Big mistake. My father tried to tune in to Radio Free Europe. My mom kept looking for the little answering machine that takes all the messages . . . They ended up bringing it back . . . damn thing couldn't get a dial tone . . . and yet they want to look like everyone else so now they walk around with the garage door openers clipped to their belts . . ."

Crap! Mommy is leaving, Phillip looks like he's going to kill me, Daddy looks like he's going to kill Mom, Patti is gloating . . . Sorry you guys. You know I don't mean any of this stuff . . . It's just a comedy routine . . . You do remember how close I live to the Brooklyn Bridge now . . .

Chapter 2

"OKAY, THANKS GUYS. That wasn't at all humiliating." I found Patti, Phillip, and my parents in the parking lot. "My whole family walking out in the middle of my act."

"I could have sworn I told you to leave them out of it." Phillip puffed on Patti's cigarette.

"Oh, so this is all my fault? Sorry. But this, whatever this is"—I pointed to my parents—"has nothing to do with me . . . Will you two please tell us what's going on?"

"I told you inside." My mother blew smoke. "Your father and I are through. Over and out. And don't try talking me out of it. I'm not changing my mind."

"Nice of you to sit us down like adults," Patti groused. "Show a little respect for the family."

"Oh hello Carmela Soprano! I wasn't ready to talk, do you mind?"

"Well, I knew it!" Phillip kicked a stone. "I said to Robyn you've been acting strange."

"And I said, Really? How can you tell? . . . Now Daddy, tell us what's going on." I shivered. "There must have been something that—"

"It's nothing . . . Nothing is ever right, nothing is ever good enough . . ."

"Oh, please." My mother squished the butt. "Like I'm the only one who complains? You carry on plenty. The neighbors are too noisy, the kids are too selfish . . ."

"Whoa . . . I am not selfish," I said. "Phillip may be, but I am a very good daughter."

"Like hell I'm selfish." Phillip puffed out his chest. "Who takes them to Shea Stadium for the Mets home opener every year? Who sends them Omaha steaks?"

"You get all that stuff from your clients," Patti said. "It's not like you actually pay for it."

"Ladies and gentlemen. The model child." Phillip turned to her. "You haven't even seen your folks in six months."

I wish I could say that after a few more minutes of Family Fireworks Night, cooler heads prevailed and we all went back inside and enjoyed the rest of the party. But no. It was as if someone had thrown a lit match at a stack of hay, and there went the whole damn barn.

My dad handed his stub to the parking attendant, which shocked me. The only time I remembered him leaving before dessert was served was when he had his heart attack. And even while being carried out on a stretcher, he was yelling for someone to save him a piece of strudel.

Patti and Phillip went inside, I assumed to fetch their kids, while I ended up seated next to my mother on a stiff loveseat in the ladies' room, listening to her complain about her loveless marriage, and how unromantic it was to be in bed with a fat man who made the same noises as the coffeepot. "Honey, the Messiah will come before I do!"

At that point I realized all eyes were on us. And nothing like sharing your personal drama with a bunch of rail-thin Long

Island girls in Mommy's high heels who thought they'd tuned in to an episode of the *OC*, instead of the real-life unraveling of a forty-year marriage.

"Would you girls please excuse us?" I looked desperate.

"I had to wait for the right time to tell you," she said when we were alone.

"And this was the perfect moment? In the ladies' room of the Sands at Atlantic Beach?"

"I'm sorry. You're so busy with your day job and your night job . . . Plus, how could I upset you while you were in the middle of your own divorce? At least now you're settled, thank God."

"This isn't happening." I closed my eyes. "What did Daddy say when you told him?"

"How should I know? When does he ever listen?"

"I can't believe you're doing this . . . All I hear is how much your widowed friends miss their husbands."

"Now they can have mine."

"Just tell me why now? It's not like Daddy was ever any different. He's always driven you nuts."

"This may be hard for you to understand," she whispered, "but all I think about is sex with a younger man."

"Mental image, Mom . . . Not good."

"I'm sorry, but I'd like to think I'm still young enough to enjoy a man's company . . ."

"Don't you know the only time you want a man's company is when he owns it?"

"I thought you of all people would understand . . . because you've been through a divorce."

"This is different. I was only married for three years. You and Daddy have been together for a lifetime."

"Exactly. And now it's time for me to get out there and live my life while I can still catch a man's eye . . . Do you think I'm attractive?"

"I think any sixty-four-year-old woman who can still wear size ten jeans is hot stuff. And all my friends who saw *The Notebook* said you reminded them of Gena Rowlands."

"I hear that a lot." She fluffed her lemon souffle hair.

"But how do you just suddenly decide to throw everything away? Life in Fair Lawn, New Jersey, is all you've ever known."

"No, not all . . ."

"What?"

"Nothing."

"Yeah, but if you don't have a house and Daddy to take care of, what will you do? Teach violin again?"

"Are you kiddin' me? These kids are crazy today with the volleyball this and the community service that . . . Setting up lessons, then canceling last minute."

"Fine. So then what's the plan?"

"Maybe I'll be your assistant."

"My assistant what? The only thing you know about makeup is buy one, get one free. And trust me, you do not want to spend every morning with Princess Gretchen, the Royal Ass."

"Then I'll help you with your comedy work. Do you need costumes, because I still have my Singer sewing machine?"

"Mom, you've seen my act. I don't dangle from the high wire in sequins and tights . . . Okay look. I know Daddy is very moody, and I'll give you that he's not the most exciting creature in the sea, but this little escape plan of yours is not going to work."

"How do you know? You haven't even thought about it."

"I'm primal. I survive on instinct. Besides, we both know my place will never be clean enough for you, my extra bedroom was actually a closet in a last life, and what if I want to bring a guy home? Don't mind my mother? She's blind and deaf."

"Well I'm sorry you feel this way, because you have no idea what I'm going through."

"Look. I want to be supportive. But you still haven't given me one good reason to—"

"Oh believe me. I have plenty." She sniffed.

"Daddy isn't . . ." I leaned in. "He's not having . . . is there someone else?"

"I wish! Then maybe every once in a while I'd see a little fireworks. Instead it's every morning with the green tea and the Shredded Wheat. Every night with the gargling and the toenail clippers . . . I tell you, Robyn, I can't take it anymore. I wake up thinking, Damn. Still here!"

"Then let me help you find a good therapist."

"But I'm not crazy. Did you know that according to the AARP, more and more women over the age of fifty are leaving their husbands? Remember your friend Susan's mother? She left Hal six months ago, met a man on that Internet, and now she's going on cruises and—"

"That's what you need. A cruise. You and Daddy had such a great time when you went to Mexico. Remember? You came home with all those great little ceramic bowls?"

"Ceramic bowls do not save marriages. Great sex saves marriages."

"Okay. That's it. I can't take the chance that you and I are about to start competing for men on JDate. We'll have a family meeting. Daddy will hear what you have to say, you'll hear what he has to say, you'll both go for counseling, I'll take you shopping for thongs . . ."

"I tried those, dear. Very uncomfortable. I don't know how you gals walk around with two pieces of thread and a loincloth."

"Don't look at me. I donate money to raise awareness for big, cotton underpants."

"I don't want new underwear. I want a new life. One that doesn't have me married to a man who likes the bathroom better than the bedroom."

I couldn't believe what I was hearing. Not that I'd grown up confusing my parents with Bogie and Bacall. The only romantic getaway my parents ever took was that Mexican cruise, and come to think of it, my father invited his cousins from Toronto to join them.

It was also true that growing up, there was endless bickering about home repairs, vacations, and, every Passover, whose turn it was to make the Seder—my mother, or my dad's sister Fran, the lazy ganef who catered half the meal and asked her guests to bring the rest.

But at least Phillip and I never woke up to find broken dishes on the kitchen floor, or worried that finding our father asleep on the couch meant he'd lost admitting privileges to the bedroom. Frankly, his snoring rattled the teacups, so we assumed his sleeping in the den was out of pity for our mother.

And though there were times I wondered why he never lavished her with expensive gifts like my friend's fathers did their wives, I figured it had more to do with his frugal nature than a plot to withhold love. For years he drove an old Toyota, rather than fall into line at the Cadillac dealer like the other doctors and dentists he knew.

Besides, he knew that anything my mother ever wanted she bought for herself. In fact, he often joked that her three favorite words were not "I love you," but "Sale starts Saturday."

And even when they did argue, we never felt threatened. Somehow they raised two nice kids, paid their taxes, and kept the lawn so perfectly groomed, we could have hosted the running of the Kentucky Derby.

And unlike the neighbors who spent the seventies getting high on everything but life, at least my parents weren't the ones trying to break the marital monotony by exchanging keys, partners, and the names of clinics where one could be discreetly tested for syphilis.

Clearly they were meant to stay together, like swans who

mated for life. Come to think of it, swans were just like my parents—aggressive and territorial, but in it for the long haul. Only difference between the two species was that humans understood guilt.

"Daddy could have another heart attack over this . . . He loves you very much you know."

"Ha! The other day I'm in the shower and he starts singing, 'Mrs. Brown you've got a lovely walker.' "

"That's cute. He still wants to make you laugh . . . Maybe you need more time to think."

"Are you kiddin' me, Toots? I've done nothing but think."

"You're serious about this."

"Dead serious. And stop looking at me like I'm ruining your life. You're my inspiration."

"Me? What did I do?"

"I'm just saying I thought you were all washed up, and at such a young age. But you got right back out there and now look. Everything is hunky-dory."

"Mom. Stop. You're wrong. My life's a disaster."

"What disaster? You're busier than ever . . . but maybe if you're weren't running around like a lunatic day and night, you'd have time to call and know the things I'm thinking about."

"Okay, you know why I don't call? Because I don't want you to hear that I'm living on four hours of sleep, my headaches are back, I have no time for friends, my boss is the biggest bitch . . . Plus, I've got Teri Hatcher Disease. I haven't been laid in—"

"I thought you were seeing that nice doctor."

"He was an asshole."

"Well I'm sure there will be others."

"Assholes? Definitely. Today the only difference between the circus and a bar is at the circus, the clowns don't talk."

"I don't care. Let's make a deal. You help me, I'll help you . . . I'll pay your bills."

"Really? The ones on my desk or the stack on the dining room table? Correction. I sold the table."

"No," she gasped. "But that was an antique. A—"

"Way to pay my maintenance until the end of the year. I got a card table instead."

"Fine. I can still play mah-jongg."

"Mom. Stop, look, and listen." I reenacted her hand gestures from her days as a volunteer crossing guard. "You cannot move in with me."

"Not move in. Visit awhile until I can get my bearings."

"No. Visits last four hours and include a meal. You're talking suitcases and mah-jongg tiles . . . Look I'm sorry, but you know how fast we get on each other's nerves. You don't know a soul in Brooklyn, my hours are insane, plus you'd miss all your friends . . . your theater group."

"I'll start a new one. I was getting plenty sick of listening to Mimi Adler kvetch that we never take in musicals anymore."

"But don't you think you'd be much happier with Phillip and Patti? They have a huge house. And Long Island feels more like Jersey. Shopping centers on every corner."

"Oh no thank you. I could never live under Patti's roof with her ridiculous food rules, and Max's five A.M. hockey practices and Em and Marissa slamming doors all day . . ."

Speak of the devil.

"Hey you two." I hugged my nieces. "I swear you are both so grown up now, I can't stand it." I eyed Marissa's pocketbook. "Oh my God. That's the Juicy bag I wanted so bad. But it was like two hundred dollars."

"Two fifty." She yawned. "I have it in pink too, but I let the little dipshit borrow it, and she got gum on it."

"Did not!" Emily smacked her arm.

"Girls!" my mother yelled. "Zip it!"

"You spent five hundred dollars of your own money on pocketbooks?" My jaw dropped.

"Hello? My mom buys things for me if I like get good grades. But at least I'm not spoiled compared to all my friends. Oh my God. They get everything they want and they don't do crap . . . I can't believe my dad is so cheap . . . Like don't move us to Dix Hills then."

"You think he's cheap?" I said. "I was happy when my dad threw me an extra ten in my allowance . . . And I was out of college before I got a really good pocketbook . . . this black leather Coach shoulder bag. Remember, Mom? I wore that thing to death."

"Sucks to be you, Aunt Robyn." She eyed herself in the mirror. "God, what is up with my bangs? They are so retarded."

"We thought you left," my mother said to the girls.

"I wish." Marissa rolled her eyes. "But my dad said if we leave early, we'll never hear the end of it from Rhonda, so I said, Yeah, then how come you never care about that when you want to go play golf, and he like started bitching at me in front of all these people. He is such an asshole."

"Marissa! The mouth!" my mother yelled. "That's how you talk about the man who buys you all those nice things? And what's with your puss?" she asked Emily.

"The girls at my table are being mean to me . . . They said I need an extreme makeover because my teeth stick out."

"Get names!" I hugged her. "I'll do a bit on how they fart in their sleep."

"Okay." She laughed. "Oh I forgot, Aunt Robyn. Some man wants to talk to you."

"Me? About what?"

"I dunno." She shrugged.

"Is he cute?"

"He's hot." The worldly Marissa snapped her gum.

"How hot?"

"Brad Pitt hot."

"But his wife is fat," Emily added.

"She's pregnant, dumbass."

"Well what did he say exactly?"

"Something about Showtime." Marissa yawned.

"What about Showtime?" I jumped.

"He knows someone you can call about your act."

"Oh my God! Girls, make Grammy feel better." I tore out of there. "Sing to her."

"We're not five anymore," she yelled.

"Fine. You're right. Then explain to her about hooking up."

Chapter 3

UP UNTIL THE MOMENT I raced into the ballroom looking for hunky Brad Pitt and his pregnant wife, I realized I had given about as much thought to the role of fate in our lives as I had the status of my parents' relationship. Zero.

Frankly, when Rhonda called to ask if I would be willing to do one of my comedy routines at her son Brandon's bar mitzvah, I said not a chance. It was one thing to humiliate myself in front of drunken frat boys who cared as much about me as they did their statistics professor. It was quite another to stand before family who remembered me in diapers, and who would rather not hear how I accepted twenty dollars from a guy at a bar to whisper three dirty words in his ear. A true story, actually. I grabbed the money and said, "Wash my car."

Anyway, in spite of my reluctance to bare my comic soul, Rhonda was persistent. No, desperate. Anyone could hire a great DJ. She needed to do something inspired to impress Barry's Wall Street buddies and Brandon's friends, all of whom had been to forty other bar and bat mitzvahs by then, and would rather steal martinis off the adult tables than be subjected to yet another parent-approved game of Coke and Pepsi.

She confessed that she was way over budget and that Barry would kill her if she spent another dime, but if I said yes, she would make sure that it was worth my time. Though she had yet to explain how, out of compassion for the party pauper, I gave in.

Now as I scanned the crowd, it occurred to me Rhonda might have meant there was an important producer or an agent on her guest list. And wouldn't that be a beautiful thing? For the past two months, I'd spent many a night trudging from one Manhattan comedy club to another in the hopes of finding the holy grail. An open-mic night with somebody influential sitting in the audience, who with one roll of the dice could play Chutes and Ladders with my career, allowing me to whiz past other less fortunate comics, and zoom all the way to a paying gig. Or even better, a chance to audition for a producer.

If someone of that stature was here tonight and had seen me perform, I would start to think a great deal about fate and its role in my often futile life. Unfortunately, no one fit Marissa's description.

Turns out I'd rushed out of the ladies' room so fast, she never got to tell me the man was waiting for me in the lobby. It gave me a minute to get details. Did he say who he knew at Showtime, and was she sure that was his wife, not his sister?

For a girl who was in all AP classes, Marissa had no street smarts when it came to ferreting out important information. All she knew was he was there because he grew up with Rhonda's brother.

Marissa pointed him out just as her cell rang, and off she went before I could commend her for her exceptional taste in men. Working for a network news division, I saw tall, dark and handsome all day long. But this guy was a standout. The Italian knit suit, the expertly cut hair draping his baby face . . . Ten bucks said he drove a BMW that cost more than my parents' first house.

Correction. Having just divorced an in-denial gambler who couldn't even bear to watch reality shows, the only thing I would bet on was that I would say yes if he offered me sex.

Meanwhile, it struck me that in the seconds leading up to an introduction that could possibly alter your destiny, you think of the most random things. The underwire in your bra that is poking your right breast. The hideous jobs women do applying their makeup. The prospect that your parents might call it quits and sell the house in which you grew up, decimating the contents of your youth one garage sale at a time.

It was in the middle of that scary thought that I found myself shaking hands with the man, and though it's common courtesy to greet a new acquaintance with a smile, particularly if one of you is a comic, I must have looked as if I was about to cry.

"Seth Danziger," he said. "Are you okay?"

"Hi. Robyn Fortune," I smiled. "Sorry. I'm good. How are you? Nice to meet you."

"Usually women have that confused look after I start talking. You must be psychic."

Damn! He's charming and *gorgeous.* "Busted. But let's be clear. I do the jokes."

"Yes you do . . . Anyway, you were great. You remind me of Ellen DeGeneres."

"Thanks. I get that a lot. Which is great. I love her too . . . I understand you have a connection at Showtime."

"Wow. Do you like have one week to live? You went right for the close."

"Sorry." I laughed. "Aside from the thrill of being called up to light a candle, it hasn't exactly been a great evening. Let's start over. Hi, I'm Robyn. I'm a stand-up by night and Gretchen Sommers's makeup artist by day. I'm thirty-three, back in the single world, and hoping my mother was just kidding about wanting the name of my divorce attorney."

"Is there going to be a test? Because that was a lot to absorb."

"No test." I laughed. "You're pretty funny yourself. Let me guess. You also do—"

"No. I'm a lawyer, but spare me the jokes. I know we inspire you guys . . ."

"Guilty, your honor . . . Any chance you're a divorce attorney?"

"I'd be making a lot more money if I was. I mostly do bankruptcies."

"Oh. My brother too . . . I should take your card in case I end up going that route.

"Wouldn't you use your brother?"

"Why do you think I'm in so much trouble?"

"Never operate on family." Seth laughed. "Wait. Isn't your last name Fortune? Or was that just part of your act?"

"I wish it was a joke, but it's my ex's real last name. Ironically, he left me in deep financial shit. I mean it's so bad, even PBS thinks I'm too high risk."

"So basically the fortune cookie crumbled." He laughed. "Sorry. I'll let you do the jokes . . . Anyway, if you ever want a second opinion, here's my card."

"Thanks."

"Speaking of brothers, I was wondering if I could talk to you about mine."

"Let me guess. He wants to do stand-up."

"No. Although he is very, very funny. Or was."

"Was?"

"Look. This is weird for me . . . my brother is a great guy. I think you'd love him. He's smart, he's successful, he's got a wicked sense of humor . . ."

"Wait. You want to fix us up?" *By any chance are you twins?*

"Not a date or anything. Just coffee. Or even a phone call. He could really use a laugh."

"Oh. My niece said you had a connection at Showtime. I thought . . ."

"I do. Or, I did."

"Hi." A perky pregnant woman sidled up to Seth. "I'm Madeline, Seth's wife. Nice to meet you. You are sooooo hysterical, I thought I'd pee in my pants." She patted her belly.

"Nice to meet you, Madeline. Thanks. Oh, and congrats on the baby."

"Baby?" She looked down.

"You're not pregnant?"

"God no. I just overdid it a little at the smorg. Who can resist pigs in a blanket?" She howled. "No, just kidding a kidder. Of course I'm pregnant. It's a boy. We're so excited . . . I just love your makeup. I noticed it before. You city girls are so lucky. So many great places to get it done."

"Thank you. It's what I do . . . I'm a professional makeup artist."

"She works for Gretchen Sommers, the one on *Daybreak*."

"Oh I just love her." Madeline clapped. "Is she sweet? Please tell me she is. I hate it when I hear about these big celebrities who are so mean to everyone."

"We love her," I gritted. *We're raising money to take out a contract on her life. Can I put you down for the Thin Mints?*

"Well good. Restores my faith in humanity . . . Did you ask her yet?" She turned to Seth.

"I'm trying." he laughed. "You girls are always in such a rush . . . I'm sorry, Robyn, is it?"

"Yes."

"Let me do it," Madeline said. "Kenny was adorable, smart, successful, a great skier—"

"I don't mean to be rude, but are you trying to hook me up with the deceased? Because as much as I tell men to drop dead, I still prefer that they start out breathing."

Seth and Madeline looked at each other. "She's perfect!"

"Look, I'm sort of in the middle of a family emergency right now," I said. "Could you maybe connect the dots for me here?"

"Sure. Sorry." Seth nodded. "It's just . . . you could say we're in the middle of a family emergency ourselves."

I just don't get people who always have to do you one better. You mention you're vacationing in Europe, they tell you about their trip to Prague as a guest of the ambassador. You live in a co-op in the Village. Theirs overlooks the Hudson River and was used for a movie.

But when it comes to bad luck, everyone has a story they think can't be topped. Me especially. These past few years have been hell, and not even AAA could have found an easy path out of the mess, for when your journey is doomed, the hard road is the only one on the map.

But as I listened to the litany of tragedies that had overwhelmed Seth's kid brother, Ken, hands down he'd won in the lightning round called, "My life sucks worse."

Here was a star who had it all. Tall, good-looking. ("A stunning, stunning man," Madeline sighed.) High school salutatorian. Made law review at Columbia. Married a beautiful young woman doing a pediatric residency. ("We loved Nina to pieces.") A world-class skier. ("The U.S. Olympic Committee so wanted him.") And then as if somebody upstairs pointed a finger and said, "He's our guy," it all fell apart.

It wasn't just that his oldest childhood friend died in the attack on the World Trade Center. Or that two years later, Ken's bride decided that although he was great guy, he had more problems than she realized, and with all the late hours at the hospital, she'd met a fellow resident with whom she thought she'd have a brighter future.

Or that four months later, Ken would accept an invitation to ski Zermatt in the Swiss Alps with a friend, and in a heroic act to save her from hitting a tree, he crashed instead and had to be airlifted to a trauma center in nearby Visp, where he lay in a coma for weeks. He'd been home recuperating ever since.

"And then a few months ago we found out my dad has prostate cancer," Seth said. "They think they got it in time, but it's been rough on the whole family."

"Oh my God," I said. "So wait . . . Who's your connection at Showtime?"

Two pairs of eyes bugged out.

"Just kidding . . . I'm sorry. Sometimes I say the worst things."

"No, it's our fault." Seth laughed. "We dumped this whole, God-awful story on you."

"We just thought you'd be willing to call him." Madeline said. "Who knows? Right?"

"Yeah. You did this whole thing about dating jerks, and here we know this great guy."

"Who's only slightly beaten up and broken," I replied.

"He's much better now," Madeline followed. "Almost good as new."

"Gee, I don't know," I said. "My life is so complicated right now, I'm not—"

"He's a top guy in the legal department at Showtime," Seth blurted.

"Oh?" I smiled.

"Well, he was. He's been out on disability since this happened."

"Oh."

"But they still love him over there," Madeline rubbed my arm. "I'm sure he would be happy to make a call for you."

"And he's very well connected," Seth said. "He's good friends with Billy Crystal."

"Yeah right." My heart raced. "What's Billy's wife's name?"

"Janice."

"What's the daughter's name?"

"They have two. Jennifer and Lindsay. Jen is a filmmaker."

"Okay. I'll call. But no promises. I have signs of Holtz Disease. I can repel people on contact."

I'm a comic, so I often encounter situations I find hilarious, only to discover I'm the only one laughing. But standing in the lobby at Brandon's bar mitzvah, I was struck by a thought that any woman would appreciate.

You get an invitation in the mail, mark it on the calendar, and though it's months away, you don't think about what you're going to wear until a day before, and by then it's too late to buy something that will camouflage the damage done by those late-night visits to Wendy's.

Nor does it dawn on you when you say yes that you've made a date with destiny. Which is just as well, for if you had an inkling that on that day, events would unfold that would alter your landscape, who'd be crazy enough to RSVP?

Would I have said yes if I knew my mother would drive herself to the bar mitzvah? Or that her trunk would be loaded with suitcases, pots and pans, two boxes of books, her prized mah-jongg set and a photo album from her days at Queens College?

Did I expect to be approached by a couple who hoped that what my life was missing was a man who, like me, had inadvertently enrolled in the school of bad luck and was hoping not to graduate with honors?

For sure I never expected that five minutes later I would get a call from Simon Kaplan, the executive producer of *Daybreak*, informing me that with the passing of Pope John Paul II earlier that day, didn't I know they would be doing live feeds throughout the night, and that Gretchen would carry on that she looked hideous whenever the weekend girl did her makeup, and how soon could I get to the studio?

For sure I never imagined that I'd be driven to the studio by my mother, and that when I mentioned this Madeline person's plea to go out with her brother-in-law, she would act downright giddy. "We're talking about a blind date," I said. "Not the *King and I.*"

"So what?" She smiled. "You never know."

And for damn sure I never expected that my techno-phobic, what-do-I-need-that-for mom would mention that she was very interested in learning how to use the Internet.

"Great," I said. "What would you like to do first? Learn how to e-mail? Surf the Web?"

"Which one is better at helping you find people from your past?"

Chapter 4

ON A NORMAL BUSINESS DAY, a network news operation is a hub of chaos that works itself into a deep-fried frenzy until the anchors bid adieu, and the director and the team of producers, stage managers, technicians, and camera crew put away the Tums.

But when catastrophe strikes, a plane blowing up over Scotland, the collapse of the World Trade Center, the death of the pope, terror clutches the hearts of even the most hardened news-gathering professionals. For the effort, talent, and luck required to get on the air with all the facts and footage, and most important, before the other guys, brings the normal behind-the-scenes craziness to a whole other level.

At *Daybreak*, however, it didn't take shortened deadlines to ignite already short fuses. Gretchen and cohost Kevin O'Shea so detested each other, staffers seemed less worried about the broadcast than a boxing match. In fact, right before air, the goal was to keep the prizefighters in their corners until the bell rang.

Ultimately, it was the job of Simon Kaplan, executive producer and twenty-year veteran of the Century Network, to make sure that once the show was in progress, there was no sparring between the opponents, let alone any come-from-behind knockout punches.

Like the time *Daybreak* did an investigative report on the dangers of tanning booths, and at the end of the segment, Gretchen turned to Kevin to ask if he'd ever had a tanning treatment. He sputtered, then froze before Simon cut to commercial.

Gretchen claimed she had no idea that his sun-kissed glow came as a result of his being a part owner in a chain of tanning salons. She was simply engaging in friendly on-air banter.

No wonder dear Simon had facial tics, and spent the entire two hours in the control room chewing gum, cracking his knuckles, and muttering his oft-used phrase, "Oh fucking well."

So how best to describe the woman for whom I awoke before God each weekday morning so that when she greeted viewers, she looked not only polished and professional, but good enough to screw (her words, not mine)?

Well, she once asked me to wipe her ass because her manicure wasn't dry (I said sorry, wet polish made me sick). She used to call me Tweety Bird because Robin was the name of her ex-husband's cat (until I started calling her ma'am because Gretchen was the name of my ex-husband's bookie). And her latest edict was that I wear a pager, like a prisoner's monitoring bracelet, so that I could be summoned should her stubborn rosacea peek through the powder.

Though she was an award-winning broadcaster, and the best in the business at excavating the truth from guests with informational treasure, the mere sound of her heels clickety-clicking across the studio floor made me shake. In fact, so great was my inner loathing, the only way I could stand in her personal space day after day was to imagine her either being dissed by fellow diva Katie Couric, or being sent back home to local affiliate WCNC-TV in Charlotte.

In fact, from the moment I began cleansing her southern-belle pores to when I applied the last of the loose powder, I had to hold my tongue and also my makeup brushes so I didn't accidentally jab a handle into her neck.

Tonight, especially, I would earn my keep, as three people informed me that Gretchen spent the day slugging tequilas at her Westhampton beach house, then fell asleep in the sun. Now her face looked like a farmstand tomato.

But before I could take the Gretchen challenge, I had to find a place to park my mother.

I was bringing her down to the greenroom when I ran into one of the stage managers.

"Oh thank God you're here." Benitez stopped me. "Simon needs you."

"Hey Benny Boy. This is my mom. Mom? Benny. So he's freaking?"

"Hi Mom. No. He's having a massage. Of course he's going crazy." He looked at my fancy attire. "What did they get *you* out of?"

"A bar mitzvah on Long Island. You?"

"What did they get me out of?" He laughed. "Angelina."

"Oh my God. You are such a perv! Did I not just tell you this is my mother?"

"Oh yeah. Sorry ma'am . . . Anyway, Simon's in the control room . . ."

"Let me get Gretchen in the chair first."

"She's in hair. Go. I'm not kidding. He's chewing his cheek."

"So much excitement." My mother clapped. "I'm so glad I'm here."

"Oh me too." I sighed. "Okay, you know what? Follow me." I grabbed her hand and brought her into Gretchen's dressing room. I'd find out what Simon wanted, take her back to the greenroom, fetch Gretchen, and, God willing, the two would never meet.

"This is where you work?" My mother beamed. "It's so clean. Not like your apartment."

"Didn't I tell you when it comes to my job I'm very neat? Everything has a place. See all the bins and baskets? I can reach for cotton balls, moisturizer, whatever, without even looking."

"Too bad you can't live like this at home. You'd be a much happier person."

"Oh I know . . . I'd still be divorced, but I'd know where I left my scissors."

"Funny. Now what can I do to help? Answer the phone? Organize drawers?"

"Not unless you join the union or the circus, although around here, it's the same thing."

Just as with the party invitation I never would have accepted had I known how it would turn out, I wouldn't have rushed off to find Simon if I'd had an inkling what he was about to ask of me.

I knew, of course, that he was just back from his honeymoon with wife number three, socialite Adrian Hughes, and that people were already betting on how long the marriage would last. Not that I would wager on another couple's union. Hell, I hadn't even bet on my own.

Meanwhile, it turned out that the pressing matter was a personal favor, which for someone with my training meant only one thing. "Of course I'd be happy to do Adrian's makeup," I said. "Does she have a special event coming up?"

Although he was sure Adrian would love to take me up on the offer, this favor was, well, bigger. Seems her daughter was interested in learning the makeup trade and Adrian would be so grateful if I took Sierra under my wing for a little while. "Sierra?" I winced. "As in Madre?"

Thing about being asked a loaded question by Simon is that

it is never multiple choice. More like fill-in-the-blank with only one right answer. Whatever Simon says you do. Still, he couldn't expect me to say yes without clarification. Were we talking a few days? A few weeks? Did she have experience? Did she understand she'd have to be at work before dawn?

Given the chance, I would have marked his answers wrong. Sierra was a twenty-two-year-old college dropout who moved to New York with her mother only because the judge at her bail hearing remanded her to parental supervision due to her inability to function outside rehab.

"Look, I'm shooting straight with you Robyn. Adrian and I could really use your help here, so I'm bringing her in tomorrow. We gotta get this kid off the party wagon."

"The party wagon." I gulped. "Tomorrow . . . Wow. So when did she become interested in makeup? Was she working in the business out in LA?"

"That's a no. She's never worked."

"So much for comparing medical plans."

"What can I say? The family's loaded. But don't misunderstand. She's got a lot of enthusiasm for this. You know kids. They love being around celebrities. It's glamorous."

"Not at five A.M."

"She's cool with it." He cracked his knuckles. "It's probably when she gets in anyway. Oh, and one other thing. She has to be called by her full name."

"Fine. I can't really think of any nicknames for Sierra."

"No, I mean her whole full name. Sierra Paige Mather."

"Wait. What? Why?"

"Must be a California thing. Who the hell knows."

"But that's crazy."

"I found if I say it really fast, Sierrapaigemather, all three names blend together like one of those long Indian names."

"Simon, some mornings I can barely say my own name . . . I'll just call her cutie."

"It won't work."

"Why not? Who doesn't like being called cutie?"

"Wait until you see her." He puffed out his cheeks.

The buzz from Gretchen's dressing room made my stomach churn. At first I thought it was hunger pangs, as I'd been so nervous about my performance at the bar mitzvah, I hadn't eaten a thing. But that wasn't it. The nausea stemmed from recognizing two familiar voices.

"Oh my God." I walked in on my mother slathering pink lotion on Gretchen's face. "What are you doing?"

"I wasn't sure how long you'd be." Gretchen's eyes remained closed.

"Not you. I meant my mother. Mom, step away from the talent . . ."

"Relax, Robyn. I'm very much enjoying this refreshing treatment . . . I understand your mother taught you everything you know about makeup artistry."

"That's right." My mother winked. "Dear, I noticed you're out of witch hazel. Remember I told you, always keep an extra bottle on hand. It does wonders for—"

"Thanks Mom. Really. You've been a huge help . . . Do you remember where the greenroom is? I think you'll be more comfortable in there."

"Don't be silly," Gretchen said. "We were just chatting about mah-jongg. I haven't played in years . . . used to love the game."

"I was just saying how I'm moving in with you. Temporarily, of course. But as soon as I can find two other people who want to play, we'll make it a foursome."

"Perfect!" I grabbed the bottle from my mother. No! She'd just covered Gretchen with insect repellent. Please God. Not the one that made her break out in hives when we did that remote from the Everglades. The only way she'd be able to go on the air was if she wore sunglasses and a hat from the Camilla Parker Bowles collection.

But no time for an anxiety attack now. I had less than twenty minutes to get her ready.

"Mom, do me a favor." I started wiping thick, greasy globs off Gretchen's face.

"Sheila Holtz. Beep beep. At your service."

"Open this roll of paper towel and split all the sheets up so they make a nice, big pile."

"What for?" Gretchen peeked with one eye.

"It's an idea I read in one of my journals," I lied. "Paper towels make great test palettes."

"We need Gretchen in fifteen." Benny returned, now in uniform: headset, microphone, clipboard. "Hey Gretch? As long as you're here, can we get you to do the local promos?"

"Go to hell." She threw a tissue box at him. "Do you see what I look like? Get Kevin Kiss Ass to do them . . . Who was that little man?"

"Who? Benny? We're going to his retirement party next month, remember?"

"Hey Gretchen," Jay, a line producer, bounded in. "Okay, so here's how this plays out for now. Because the Holy Father just passed, we're keeping it low key. For twenty-six years Pope John Paul II has been a great religious and moral leader who traveled the globe in the name of peace, he helped bring about the end of communism, he took on Castro, yada yada yada . . ."

"And don't forget he was the first pope to ever step foot into a synagogue," my mother added. "That's very important."

"Mom. Shhh."

"What's O'Shea working on?" Gretchen sneered. "Oh wait. I bet he's on his way to Rome as we speak . . . another *Daybreak* exclusive. Kevin O'Shea kisses the pope's ass . . ."

"No, he's here, Gretchen . . . but Simon wants you to handle the Farrell Carew interview. He's the author who wrote the book about how the pope only named bishops and cardinals who opposed masturbation, birth control, and premarital sex, so now the next pope is coming from a group that may not be the brightest or the best, he just bought the program . . ."

"Jesus Frank Christ!" Gretchen bellowed from the chair, knowing if she jumped and smudged her makeup, it would cost us precious minutes we didn't have. "He's only dead for a few hours and people are screaming, '*Santo subito*, sainthood now!' Why the hell are we giving airtime to some writer who got lucky with a publishing contract?"

"Although the author makes a good point," my mother said. "Maybe if all those priests got a little hokey in the pokey every once in a while, they wouldn't be molesting little boys."

"Mother!" I led her outside.

"The guy's not a definite yet." Jay cowered. "Let me get back to you . . ."

"Don't you love it?" Gretchen seethed. "You've got all these liberal New York Jews running the news division . . . no respect . . ."

"What did she say?" my mother gasped.

"Nothing. She's letting off steam . . . Prebroadcast jitters."

"Robyn, get me ready this instant! I need to see Simon mas pronto."

"Coming, Gretchen."

"If you ask me," my mother whispered, "you should make her look a little orange."

"Good thinking," I whispered back. "Because I can afford never to work again."

I couldn't remember the last time I pigged out, but if ever I'd earned the right to eat a pint of Chunky Monkey, tonight was it. And shame of it was, it had started out great.

I'd gotten a no-hassle ride to the bar mitzvah with a teacher friend of Rhonda's. I looked svelte in my new, little black dress that cost more than my zipcode (actually, it was my friend Julia Volkman's old, black dress, but she's so rich, she wore her clothes for a season, then gave them away), I killed with my comedy routine, and then got the number of a guy who could line up a meeting for me at Showtime.

If only the God of Favors hadn't decided I'd reached my quota. Sorry, Robyn. Four is the limit. Now we return to our regularly scheduled torture:

My mother wanting out of her marriage, leaving behind a husband/heart patient who was unfamiliar with major appliances, let alone minor ones.

My mother moving in with me and making me clean my room or be grounded.

My mother insulting my boss by telling her she was a big-mouth anti-Semite with a dingy smile who would be lucky to have a Jewish dentist give her a much needed set of veneers.

My job going from bad to worse now that Simon was siccing his spoiled brat stepdaughter on me. At least I couldn't blame my mother for that one.

Until we left the studio and I discovered that I most certainly could.

We had just gotten to the car when she slid into the passenger seat and informed me that I should drive because lately her night vision was bad. Not that her day vision was so great either.

"That Gretchen gal is one piece of work." She kicked off her shoes and lit up.

"Put that out. If I can't breathe, I can't drive."

"It's my car."

"Yes, but it's my life."

"I'll keep the window open."

"Oh my God," I groaned. "You're the piece of work. You do realize that was my boss you were unloading on."

"Not for long." She puffed away.

I slammed on the brakes. "What did you say to her?"

"Nothing. Why do you always accuse me like that?"

"Thirty-three years of history."

"I just heard her talking, that's all. She didn't know I was waiting for you in her room."

"Okay, but how do you know she was talking about me?"

"Are you Tweety Bird?"

"What did she say?" I gulped.

"Something about your contract expiring next month and she's thinking of hiring someone new."

"Oh my God! She actually said she wasn't renewing my contract? Did she say why? Who was she talking to?"

"Some other gal I think. I tried to listen good, but lately I miss a word or two."

No, it's called selective hearing and you've had it since I was born. I turned off the ignition and started to shake. Every weekday for six years, the first of my three alarm clocks went off at 3:15. And to this day I was still thrown by the darkness, the loud buzz, and the momentary lapse. "Fuck! What was that?"

But had I ever complained? Constantly. Still, I wasn't a fool. Working as Gretchen's personal makeup artist had been my ticket to decent pay, perks, and premieres. It had also given me face time, literally, with the world's biggest celebs and VIPs, most of whom were great. Save for the women who thought my blush brush was a wand, and the athletes who thought I got that close to their face because I wanted sex. *Note to NBA stars. You ever stick your tongue in my ear again, you'll see real balls bounce.*

And on what grounds could Gretchen fire me? I was the consummate professional. Talented. Respectful. Up-to-date on the latest antiaging techniques. Ready for the high-definition challenge. I played well with others. And most of all, I had never betrayed her confidence, though what I knew of her private affairs could earn me rent money for a year.

But if what my mother had heard was true, the timing couldn't be worse, as I had just renegotiated my debts with a credit counselor, and if I lost my main source of income, I'd have no choice but to declare bankruptcy. I'd have to live with my mother forever, and learn to play mah-jongg and listen to her bitch, and put up with her smoking and that awful hacker's cough . . .

"Now you know why I put insect repellent on that little pisher's face."

"Wait. What? You knew what you were doing?"

"Naturally." She laughed. "She was buggin' the hell out of me."

"Oh my God, Mother. You're insane. That alone could get me fired."

"Don't worry, darling. You have nothing to worry about."

"Why? Did you also poison her Evian bottle?"

"Don't be ridiculous. I stopped that nice Mr. O'Shea in the hall and asked if he'd heard the rumor that Ms. Sommers was leaving . . . because of the affair and all."

"No. Please don't tell me you really did that . . . Wait. How did you know?"

"You mean it's true?"

"Oh my God."

"Well, gals like her aren't hard to figure out. They're always *shtupping* the boss."

"She's not *shtupping* the boss, Mom. She's *shtupping* Kevin O'Shea."

"No! But you said they hate each other."

"It's all a big front so no one suspects anything. He's married with two kids."

"Oh. Well that's not good. He'll probably think you told me."

"Why would I do that?"

"Because I'm your mother. How should he know you tell

me nuh-thing! But look at the bright side, darling. If they get caught with their ding-a-lings a-linging, that doesn't look good for a family show. They'll both get fired."

"Mom, you don't know what you're talking about, okay? That will never happen . . . Unless . . . if word did leak out, then the other networks would jump all over the story. No, but that would only make our ratings go through the roof, but then later, viewers would be pissed at them and the ratings would tank and then, you're right, one of them would have to be reassigned."

"Sheila Holtz." She honked the horn twice. "At your service."

Chapter 5

As YOU KNOW, I recently dove off the comedy cliff. Though I'd secretly thought about taking the plunge for years, if not for friends blindfolding me and bringing me to the Gotham Comedy Club on open-mic night a few months back, I might never have set foot on stage.

So go figure that the adrenaline rush from performing would become my drug of choice, and that in spite of the worry that puking would become my opening bit, I had been pursuing stand-up with a vengeance.

Now every free moment was devoted to writing bits, studying the masters, and rehearsing in front of foreign tourists, especially after discovering that they laugh at everything and always ask to take my picture. "You Ellen DeGeneres?" "Yes." I give them a high five. "Yes, I am."

But I sure do pick 'em, right? Exciting jobs with the worst possible hours. Out of the house by 4:45. Then some nights it's midnight before I get my shot on stage, so do the math. Twenty-four hours in a day minus three hours to sleep equals no life whatsoever.

Saturdays are better. Clocks are set for seven A.M., allowing me to make it to Manhattan by eight-thirty, and be standing in front of my beauty school students by nine. Twelve young artists who aspire to have my job, no matter how honest I am about the pressure and the hours.

I share this so you understand that I never rush away a Sunday. It's my one day to wake up at leisure, take on the *Times* crossword puzzle, and actually eat breakfast not over a sink.

Which is why when I awoke to slippers shuffling, a tea kettle whistling, and fingernails tapping on the counter, I threw a sneaker at my bedroom door.

It was seven-twenty on the Sunday morning that followed the Saturday night roller coaster ride I took with some lady named Sheila Holtz. Not the Sheila Holtz I grew up with who dusted light bulbs, scrubbed tiles with toothbrushes, and baked cupcakes inside ice cream cones.

That Sheila Holtz would be home in Fair Lawn, New Jersey, yelling at the Merrill Lynch broker for missing a golden opportunity in tech stocks. Not pacing in her daughter's looks-like-a-burglary apartment, wondering if the mail in the microwave was incoming or outgoing.

"Mom, didn't you get the memo?" I yelled. "We sleep late on Sundays."

"So sorry." She was all smiles. "Did I wake you?"

"Yes." I opened one eye and noticed she was already showered and dressed. "Oh good. Are you leaving?"

"For bagels. Plain or poppy?"

"Oh my God," I groaned. "It's my only day to sleep, remember?"

"I'm sorry." She started to close my door. "Just tell me where you keep a spare key so I don't have to wake you when I get back."

"Shit!" I stubbed my toe. "I told you this was a bad idea."

"Not for me! I woke up feeling alive and excited. I'm going to—"

"—be on the front page of tomorrow's *New York Post*. 'Fair Lawn Homemaker Suffocated in Park Slope. Daughter Pleads Guilty with an Explanation.' "

I rifled through a kitchen drawer in the dark before realizing the counters were spotless, the floor was mopped, the garbage was emptied, and through some unexplained miracle, I now owned a broom.

"You feel like you won a contest, right?" She beamed. "I told you I could be a big help."

"You don't get it." I collapsed in a chair. "I don't want a maid. I want my mother."

"And here I am! I just can't be the one who stays in an unhappy marriage while the rest of the world is out there enjoying themselves. I want to try yoga. Oh and that new one . . . Plotzey?"

"Pilates." I laughed. "So wait? That's the reason you're leaving Daddy? So you can learn how to turn your body into a pretzel?"

"I am leaving your father because he only cares about three things—his *farshtunken* maps, food in the fridge, and toilet paper in the bathroom."

"And what about *your* obsessions, like cleaning? You haven't even unpacked yet, but already my apartment is spotless."

"No. Just the kitchen. Incidentally, you're out of SOS."

"I'm not out of it. I don't buy it. You know why? Because I never scour. You know why? Because I never cook. You know why? Because it's Brooklyn and we have free delivery."

"I was just trying to help. I know how busy you are."

"Which is why I don't give a damn about cleaning. Life is messy. I decorate accordingly."

"No need to yell. I am trying to make this a positive experience."

"Oh good. Positive experiences are my favorites. They remind me of all the times a guy broke my heart, and you'd say, 'But darling. It's part of life. Think of it as a positive experience.' "

"And was I right?"

"Not yet . . . oh my God . . . Did you line up all my shoes by the door?"

"Better I should trip and break my neck?"

"It's no use," I cried. "Here's a key. Make your bagel run. Just don't come crying to me when you see what they charge for lox."

"I wasn't always like this you know. Crazy with the cleaning and the organizing . . . I used to be the belle of the ball who loved parties and staying out late . . . used to drive my folks crazy."

"You?"

"Yes me. Everyone said it just wasn't the same if Sheila Marcus wasn't there."

"Really?"

"Yes. And I'll also have you know I wasn't a virgin when I married your father."

"Okay. Stop. You are not going to turn every conversation into 'true confession.' Unless you'd like to hear about the time Ricky Wexler took me to Radburn Park . . ."

"I just want to find the old Sheila again, dear. The one who woke up every day looking for fun and adventure."

"Well then you've come to the right place."

"I have?"

"No, but just because I don't have time to play doesn't mean you can't knock yourself out. Go. Check out the bookstores and boutiques. Oh and there's a great deli at the corner of Union and Seventh Avenue . . . Daddy would love their tuna."

"Then he'll have to buy it himself. I'm not going home. Now if this is too much of an imposition for you, just say the word and I'll find a nice hotel somewhere."

"Really?"

"No. But I promise I won't be in your way."

"This is a recording . . . You won't even know I'm here . . . Except for my cigarette smoke, my opinions, my need to rearrange the furniture . . . God, I am so screwed." I brushed past her. "I'm jumping in the shower. If I try to fall back asleep now, the nightmares will keep me up . . ."

"I think you should call him."

"Who? Daddy?"

"Don't you dare. No. That man who lost his best friend and had the skiing accident."

"Forget it. I'm sure he's a nice guy, but if I want one who is clinically depressed, I'll hang out at a pharmacy."

"I'm serious. I have a feeling about him."

"Me too. A bad one . . . He's an emotional cripple, and we know how that movie ends."

"Well, I think you should take a chance. I've been reading some good books about fate."

"Oh please. Last time fate showed up, I married a guy whose idea of fun was dropping thousands at a casino while the rest of our money was being siphoned by an offshore bookie."

"That wasn't fate. That was stupidity."

"Same thing, especially if you think the reason I did my comedy act last night was so some guy in the audience would notice me and say, hey, that girl would be great for my brother."

"So damn stubborn like your father . . . I'm saying who the hell knows why people come into our lives. Maybe there's a reason. You should be more open-minded like me."

"Open-minded? Aren't you the one who threatened to sue Penn State when I got a black roommate? What happened? Did you read *The Five People You Meet in Bloomingdale's*?"

"No smarty pants, I'm reading a wonderful book by His Holiness, the Dalai Lama. I brought it to show you."

"Here we go . . . extra allowance for doing book reports."

"And another one called *The Miracle of Mindfulness* by Thich Nhat Hanh. You should try his meditations. They help with self-awareness."

"I swear if you light a joint, I'm calling the FBI or whoever handles alien abductions."

"I once smoked marijuana." She giggled. "It made me hungry."

"I cannot believe I'm having this conversation."

"I told you I could be a lot of fun." She chucked my shoulder.

"A barrel of laughs . . . So wait. Now all of a sudden you believe in things like destiny?"

"I don't know what I believe. But my mother, pooh pooh, may she rest in peace, always said, 'Sheila, if fate comes all the way to knock at your door, the least you can do is open it.' "

Not only are Sundays my day to sleep in, it's the one time I try to stay off the phone so that my brain has time to reboot. But that morning, as word of the insurgent wife and mother spread, family and friends ignored my "don't call" policy.

It was as though Tinker Bell was flying through the tri-state area sprinkling pixie dust intros: "Robyn Fortune has all the latest details from Park Slope. Robyn, what can you tell us?" "Thanks Tinker Bell . . . Well, it seems that love does not conquer all . . ."

At least my brother apologized when he called my cell at eight o'clock wanting to ask if it was true that our mother was at my place, and to make sure I was trying to talk some sense into her. But it was his second call an hour later that was more pressing.

Seems he had taken it upon himself to be chief mediator, only to discover that negotiations might be more challenging than he thought. After talking to our dad, it was clear that neither party was interested in coming to the kitchen table. And as there was no deadline for talks to resume, the impasse could go on indefinitely.

"What are you going to do?" Phillip asked.

"Me? Why is this suddenly my problem?"

"Because possession is nine-tenths of the law. Mom is now residing with you."

"Whoa, white boy. She is not residing. She's crashing until she finds her own pad."

"She actually said that? That she wants her own place?"

"Basically. Seems Daddy refuses to make any changes, so there's nothing to reconcile."

"That's awful, Rob. You gotta do something. Make her understand it's not a good idea."

"I'm trying, but she's pretty adamant. She said she's been thinking about this for years."

"Is she crying her eyes out?"

"Actually, she's out shopping for bagels and a yoga mat."

Bingo! The tough-talking lawyer son wimped out. I had a better relationship with our parents, therefore this was under my jurisdiction. Oh, and to make sure that Mom didn't start talking about moving in with him and Patti because he'd gain a mother and lose a wife.

Apparently, family and friends concurred. As long as my mother was staying with me, she would be fine.

"Give her a week. She'll be on the Jersey Turnpike headed home."

"Take her passport. She mentioned something about wanting to see Sri Lanka."

"If she divorces Harvey, she can say it's for health reasons. She was sick of him."

Even Uncle Lou, my father's brother, called from Boynton Beach to ask if the story was true, and did that mean they weren't coming to visit him next month. How he had heard anything at all baffled me as he had Florida hearing: every third word, and only if it was very, very loud.

Uncle Lou:	*My new hearing aid is state-of-the-art. Cost me four thousand dollars.*
Harvey:	*Really? What kind is it?*
Uncle Lou:	*Twelve-thirty.*

Mystery solved. My Aunt Marilyn, my mother's sister, the Matt Drudge of Weekauken, had called both sides of the family. "Sheila finally walked out on him. Had it up to her eyeballs with his *meshuggas*. Serves him right. He practically forgot she was alive."

Ironically, the one person I didn't hear from was dear old Dad. I tried reaching him by the only means possible, a one-line phone in the house, but according to the operator, it was off the hook. "Not fair," I whined. The whole world is keeping tabs on one another through cell phones and the Internet. Why should he get to be unreachable?

Meanwhile, my mother was out *shpatziring*, the Yiddish term for blowing an entire day cavorting the neighborhood while accomplishing nothing. But at least it gave me a short reprieve.

Then, just as I started to tackle my beloved *Times* crossword puzzle, in walked my mother holding a bag of groceries, fresh flowers, a new pair of sneakers, and a blue yoga mat. The very one I returned after discovering it was a shorter version of my old Slip 'N Slide.

"I just love it here." She hugged me. "Prospect Park, the little shops, the bakeries . . ."

"That's great, Mom . . . Looks like you found everything you needed."

"Because everyone is so friendly. In fact, I met this nice young man . . . I think he was one of those homosexuals because he looked too thin to have a wife who feeds him. Anyway, he said he could come over later because he's very knowl-edgeable about computers . . ."

"Wait. You gave out my address? What if he was Mr. Stranger Danger?"

"Trust me. He was a *faigelah*, not a criminal . . . he had on a nice, clean shirt."

"Good, because you never hear about serial killers who shop at the Gap. He didn't happen to mention anything about being an altar boy?"

"We didn't talk religion, darling. He was getting something in the computer store and said he could help me set mine up."

"Are you serious? You bought a computer? What's wrong with mine?"

"I don't know. My friend Estelle said that's how you catch one of them nasty viruses."

"Estelle . . . Estelle . . . Isn't she the one who dries her un-derpants in the microwave? Trust me, the computer gets the virus, not the user. Besides, where the hell would I put it?"

"Not to worry, darling. I happened to notice your living room was down to a couch and an end table, so when I passed the flea market and saw this man selling beautiful antiques, I said to myself, Sheila, so what if they're reproductions? Better than having an empty room. Later today he's delivering a roll-top desk. No need to thank me."

Thank her? Thirty-three years of experience dealing with my mother had taught me one thing. Logic meant nothing once she made up her mind. Besides, who had time to argue? Round two of the phone calls had begun.

My dad finally checked in and threatened that if I was going to harbor the wifely fugitive, I was an accessory to the crime and should no longer expect financial aid from him. "And tell your mother, same for her. If she's such a big shot, let's see her do this all on her own."

Later we'd review the concept of community property, but

for now I had to convince him my mother didn't really want a divorce, just a chance to be heard. And that maybe if he paid more attention to her, she'd leave him alone about his map collecting.

"What's wrong with having a nice, quiet hobby?" he bellowed. "Better than playing mah-jongg every week. 'Ooh. Harvey! I won twenty dollars,' " he mimicked.

By now my cell was ringing nonstop. Fortunately, I was hearing back from my two best friends. Unfortunately, they weren't friends with each other, so I had to repeat the story. The good news was that they were so different from each other, I would likely get two opinions of the same problem, like doctors who specialized.

Rachel Waldman was my big sister at Alpha Epsilon Phi, and like a wise, older sibling, knew her stuff when it came to matters of the heart. It also didn't hurt that she frequented famous psychics, thereby increasing the odds that not only was her advice spot on, but divined.

Trouble was, Rachel had three-year-old twins and was not as readily available to rescue me now that she was (a) putting in fourteen-hour days on the partner track at Hellman and Gray LP, (b) fighting with her ex over custody, and (c) trying to hire a new nanny, as the last one was caught at the playground having sexual relations with another nanny.

Then there was Julia Volkman, the tall, geeky girl from down the block who predicted as early as third grade that I would be rich and famous because I was so brave and funny, unlike her, who cowered behind me and never thought she'd find anything at which she was good.

Go figure that she would be the quintessential ugly duckling who blossomed into a top fashion model turned designer for Ralph Lauren, and who could buy waterfront homes and horses where ever they were sold.

Though busier and more successful than anyone else in my circle, Julia was diligent about getting together to keep our friendship intact. Only problem? She kept lots of friendships intact, which was nice except that "Don't repeat this" was her signature phrase. So when you finally met her roommate's boyfriend's mother, you could forget first impressions. You already knew about her young lovers, and, no question, she knew about yours.

Bottom line? I had two dear friends, though neither could offer the kind of rabbinic wisdom that would solve this problem. But on this they agreed. If my parents didn't reconcile, I would have the only roommate in Park Slope who expected Medicare to pay for her vibrator.

Then came the knockout punch. A call from Madeline the matchmaker. You remember her. The pregnant wife of tall, dark, and handsome, who was certain that the man of my dreams was her brother-in-law, Kenny. A guy who used to be able to walk and talk on his cell phone at the same time. But don't worry. His prognosis was excellent.

Madeline wanted to know if I'd decided whether or not to call him because he seemed to be falling into an even deeper depression, and she was so sure that if I spoke to him, it could be just the thing to snap him out of his funk.

"But no pressure," I said.

"It's just a phone call, Robyn. Think of him as a guy who came back from Iraq and he's been badly wounded. He has nightmares. He can't hold a job . . ."

"Wow. Have you ever considered a career in sales?"

"You know, you seemed like such a nice person when we met."

"I am a nice person. It's just that at the moment, my mother is leaving my father and moving in with me, and because he thinks I'm on her side, he's threatening to cut me off, which is awful because in a few weeks I'm making a court appearance before a judge who doesn't care that my ex-husband is in jail and left me penniless. Oh, and when I show up for work to-morrow? I have one boss who needs me to babysit his twenty-two-year-old wacko stepdaughter, and another who might chop me into little pieces because she thinks I've been spread-ing rumors about her. So how can I possibly help a drowning man when I'd like to jump in with him?"

"What if I made this worth your while?"

"You mean pay me?"

"A thousand dollars."

"Are you serious? Just to go out with your brother-in-law? That's insane."

"Fifteen hundred. Final offer."

"I get it. *Who Wants to Be a Millionaire*, the home game . . . Look, I may be broke, but I am not going to prostitute my-self . . . Oh my God . . . that's it, isn't it? He's been laid up for months but hasn't been laid, and you thought, What the hell, he's horny, she needs cash . . ."

"I'm sorry. It's nothing like that . . . Okay, look. This may sound selfish, but I'm very worried about Seth. With the baby coming, I wanted this to be a really happy time for us, but he's so worried about Kenny, he's not thinking about anything else. So I thought, maybe if we fixed him up with someone like you who's really pretty and funny . . . it could turn everything around."

"You think I'm pretty?"

"Oh my God, yes. Don't you know that? The blue eyes? The high cheekbones?"

"To be honest, my life is such a mess right now, I don't know anything anymore."

"Really? I told Seth I thought you'd be great together. You have so much in common."

"Like what? We're both righties?"

"No silly. That you're both so funny . . . I'm sure you'll find lots of stuff to talk about. Where did you grow up?"

"Fair Lawn, New Jersey. Oh. But I was born on Long Island."

"Really? So was he. The family's from Oceanside."

"Are you serious? That's where I was born. But we moved when I was four."

"See? Okay, where did you go to school?"

"Penn State."

"Oh my God. Him too."

"Stop."

"I'm serious. But then he transferred."

"Really. When was he there?"

"Gosh, I don't know. But he's thirty-three now, so he would have been there in—"

"I'm thirty-three."

"Didn't I say you had so much in common?"

"Yes, but if he's so gung-ho about being fixed up, why can't *he* call *me*?"

"Oh, he's not gung-ho. I am. You know guys. Totally clueless."

"Then forget it."

"He's just nervous . . . he got dumped recently. He needs a tiny, little push."

"Let me save *you* some time and *me* some aggravation. Men don't like being pushed."

"I know. So when you call, don't say anything about a date. Make something up. Maybe you got his name from Penn State. Yes, that's it. You're on the reunion committee and—"

"You just said he transferred."

"Oh. Good point . . . But it's fine. He'll say there's a mistake and you'll just keep talking."

"Look, I may do a whole thing about lying in my act, but I'm a very honest person."

"Fine. Tell him the truth. Your ex is in prison, you are so in debt a judge might throw you in jail with him, you live with your mother, your job requires powdering people's faces, and to make ends meet, you stand in front of strangers making a complete fool out of yourself."

"Wow. My life does suck . . . Okay, I'll call. But I'm not taking the money."

"Why not?"

"Because, Madeline. These days I'm so broke, I have to return everything I buy."

Chapter 6

Woman: *I got this wonderful bottle of wine for my husband.*
Friend: *Great trade!*

I MARRIED DAVID FORTUNE on my thirtieth birthday, certain I had given myself the greatest gift ever. He was a six-four fair-haired lad with a resilient laugh and a strapping hug that could knock the demons from my soul. He was quick on his feet, fast with his wit, and deferential to all.

He was also a man's man, whether wearing his North Face jacket and jeans, or an expensive designer suit. And always, his cologne matched the moment. Testimony less to his Seventh Avenue savvy than his ability to remove expensive bottles from his father's dresser.

Everyone adored David. And why not? A room didn't come alive until he entered, his massive form sashaying through the crowd, always tendering a smile, a kiss, and an inquiry as to the well-being of others. For if there was one thing he understood, it was how to win people over. And winning, more than breathing, was the name of the game.

Call me naive, particularly as we met at a cruise casino, but in the two years we dated, I didn't know he was an addicted gambler. I knew he loved the night life, and the day life too. I knew he was upbeat and funny, and true to his last name, never without a wad of big bills.

But what did a Jewish girl from New Jersey know of addictions? The only thing my mother was compulsive about was cleaning, and my dad would rather have ridden a horse backward than throw money away on a bet that it could win a race.

I suppose that's why I fell so hard for the guy. He was nothing like my sullen, life-is-full-of-disappointments dad. In fact, David didn't just embrace life, he inhaled it.

Want to know his idea of fun? Getting up early on a Saturday, taking me out for a big breakfast, driving to Atlantic City in his little red Fiat, then spending the next two days enjoying the excitement, the entertainment, and, more than I knew, the gambling.

Precisely because my parents didn't understand the point of these excursions, I relished every invitation to join him. "Mom, c'mon. Where else can you see the Righteous Brothers and Yakov Smirnoff on the same bill?"

I never told them about the hours I spent throwing quarters into the slots while David parked himself in front of a card game that lasted two straight days. Or how much I hated the smoke, the boob-job waitresses sniffing around for big tippers, and the sight of drunks genuflecting before tables full of dice.

Yet did the little bell in my head go off? The one that would have said, Robyn, wake up. Your friend is losing thousands of dollars a day. Of course not. Because just like at home, I had not only turned off my alarm, I'd thrown it against the door to make it stop ringing.

I had fallen in love with Mr. Stranger Danger himself, and though there were things I saw with my eyes, I could not deny what I felt in my heart. No other man had made me laugh as hard, feel as loved, or experience such exhilaration. For David truly believed that life was one big grand opening, with amazing prizes awarded to the luckiest customers.

Unfortunately, at the point I was living in fear of creditors, phone calls, and goons knocking at the door, I had to face facts. My husband was a conniving, substance-abusing, gambler who could not function in a world that expected him to act responsibly. Or let a day pass without betting on a horse, an athlete, a stock, a playing card, or, to my disbelief, the score of a high school football game in a Texas town he couldn't even find on one of my dad's maps.

And yet after a year of the three Bs—badgering, begging, and bribing—he still refused to acknowledge his mounting problems, our runaway debts, and his inability to show up sober. Finally, after it became necessary for Nate and Arlene of Denial, New York, to hire a Park Avenue lawyer to defend their drug-dealing son, I retained legal counsel myself, and filed for divorce.

Now only six, painful months since that decree, I was holding the telephone number of Ken Danziger, a man who, like David, was supposedly handsome and charming, flat-out funny, but also, coincidentally, an emotional train wreck.

Could you blame me for crumpling his number? Madeline may have been right that we had a common bond, but it was that we were both so beaten up from our previous matches, neither of us was ready to get back into the ring.

You know how early I wake up. But guess when I go to sleep if I'm not on the comedy circuit or watching *Jeopardy!*? Seven o'clock. Yep. I have the bedtime of a two-year-old, though no one to read me a story or rock me to sleep until I stop crying.

So on that Sunday when my mother established that *mi casa* was *su casa*, by evening she was acting like the new camper who couldn't wait to find out the evening activity. Maybe dinner and a movie, she suggested. Or a walk through Prospect Park.

"Another time," I said. "I'm wiped out." *You know how some weekends just fly by? Well, this wasn't one of them.*

Sorry, but I wasn't one of those daughters who could spend the day with her mother and be sad when it was over. I was more the type who turned to Lamaze breathing to get through her painful zings, which, like contractions, came closer and closer together as the day progressed.

"Do you brush your teeth every day? Maybe have your father bleach them again."

"Is your left breast larger than your right? Aunt Marilyn's are lopsided like that, too."

"I saw this machine on TV that's good for flabby arms. I wrote down the number for you."

So you can imagine that after a disastrous Saturday night together, Sunday was hardly a reprieve, as I spent it dodging insults while looking for places to put all her belongings: her iron cookware (they would double as weapons should we return while a robbery was in progress), her books (did the fact that half of them were about sex tell you anything?), a planting from her rubber tree (I swore I killed that thing when I watered it with a bottle of Asti Spumante), a seven-foot high antique desk that she'd bought off a truck (hopefully nobody reported one stolen), and finally, her new computer, which came accompanied by a kid who thought he could make a quick hundred by hooking up four wires and a plug.

But out of pity for us both, I finally agreed to a two-hour dinner break, knowing I wouldn't be able to sleep with her yakking on the phone or watching TV. "We'll get a bite to eat, maybe share a bottle of wine, and then it's lights out," I said.

To my surprise, dinner was very pleasant, considering we were seated two tables away from a man I'd recently tried to pick up who rejected me on the observation that my wallet and my breasts were equally flat.

Man: *Why do you wear a bra? You've got nothing to put in it.*
Woman: *You wear pants, don't you?*

Granted, it was odd referring to an outing with one's mother as pleasant when she had just announced the breakup of her marriage. But it spoke to the consolation powers of brick oven pizza and a bottle of Pinot Noir . . . until the conversation clouds thickened.

"What do you mean you're searching for a man?" I nearly knocked over my glass. "It's too soon for that. It's like the handgun law. You have to fill out a permit and wait two days."

"Not a new man. An old man."

"You already have one of those. His name is Harvey."

"No. No. Someone I once knew."

"Like who? An old boyfriend?"

"Exactly. An old boyfriend . . . I was engaged to."

"I get it. You mean you want Daddy to be like he was when he first proposed."

"Okay, buckle up, Toots. This ride's a little bumpy . . . I was engaged before I met your father. A young fellow I knew at Queens College. We fell in love, he proposed, then he gave me this tiny little nothing of a diamond, but according to my uncle Mort, it was a perfect stone so who cared . . . Close your mouth or you'll catch flies . . . Right after that, he goes into the army and ends up serving in Cuba . . . Anyway, I was thinking it might be nice to find him, say hello . . ."

I looked to see if anyone else had heard this confession. "That so did not happen . . . did it?"

"Of course it happened. Who makes up a story like that?"

"Then why didn't you marry him?"

" 'Cause a year later he comes back to the States, and P.S., now he's got this Filipino gal he met at a bar in Miami, and he tells me they're in love."

"Oh my God. It's blowing my mind that I didn't know any of this . . ."

"You weren't the only one. I never told your father either. It all happened before I met him. I figured what the hell business was it of his?"

"Are you serious? Wouldn't you have wanted to know if he was previously engaged?"

"Get real, darling. Who else would have married him but me? He was plenty green in the bedroom, if you know what I mean. One Trick Harvey I called him . . ."

"Oooh. Oooh. Oooh." I covered my eyes as if avoiding seeing the scene of an accident. "May I remind you we're talking about my father here?"

"Sor-ree, darling. We're just old married women talking, that's all."

"But what was the big deal if Daddy knew? It's not like broken engagements were a sin."

"You didn't know my mother. She got herself all worked up that the rabbi wouldn't marry us and I'd end up an old maid like my cousin Ruthie. Although ask anyone. I was a hell of a lot prettier than her. I don't care how many hats my uncle Mort bought to cover her face."

"Okay, but other people had to know you were engaged. Aunt Marilyn, your friends . . ."

"Sure they knew. They swore not to tell."

"You're making this up. Aunt Marilyn couldn't keep a secret if you paid her in shoes."

"It's the God's honest truth."

"So you want me to believe the subject of old boyfriends never came up?"

"Oh, it came up. I just kept my mouth shut."

"Okay, now that I don't believe."

"What can I say? Times were different . . . Sometimes I watch that Judge Judy and I think, What the hell is wrong with people, telling the whole world where they have tattoos, and how they made love in an airplane lavatory . . . Do I need to hear this? Anyway, by the time your father and I got engaged, I wasn't exactly a spring chicken."

"How old was old?"

"Twenty-six."

"Jeez."

"Your father thought I was twenty-two . . ."

"You sound like a used car. Turn back the odometer or you won't get a second look."

"Exactly. In those days, a man wanted right out of the show-room, if you catch my drift."

"So wait. That would make you . . . sixty-six, not sixty-four?"

"Give or take." She coughed. "But what does it matter? You're as young as you feel, and people tell me all the time, Sheila, what's your secret? You don't look a day over sixty."

It was true. She didn't look her age, but now she wasn't acting it either, which was hard to fathom. This was Commander Inspector Drill Sergeant Holtz I was talking to. If she wasn't barking orders, she was clobbering me with life lessons.

This was not a woman who would abandon her parental post, let alone fit the description of a young woman in love, with all its requisite affection and giddiness. And for someone who couldn't keep her opinion to herself, how could she have hidden a secret past?

"I gotta tell you, Mom. I'm in shock. You know how many times I got grounded because I lied to you? And remember when you made me miss a whole month of *Knots Landing* because I forged your signature on my report card? Now I find out you're this big hypocrite."

"Who's a hypocrite? I didn't lie. I married your father and put the past behind me!"

"Are you saying you married him but you never loved him?"

"He wasn't the best-looking guy, but he was good to me, he was plenty smart, he worked hard, and oy, my folks were so happy . . . their daughter marrying a professional, which, believe me, was a big deal back then. Especially after my cousin Doris married a surgeon. We never thought we'd hear the end of that . . ."

"Stick to the story. You married Daddy but the whole time you were thinking of . . ."

"Marv . . . Marvin Teitlebaum."

"Marvin Teitlebaum? I'm sorry. That is not the name of someone who makes your heart beat faster. That's the name of your electrician, or someone from temple who runs bingo."

"Believe me, he was quite the catch. Very tall and debonair . . ."

"All right. I'm done listening. It's a helluva story, but this could all be a big waste of time. He could be dead by now."

"He's not dead . . . He lives in the Phoenix area . . . has two children, a son and a daughter, three grandchildren, maybe more now, I don't know . . . His wife died in a car accident . . ."

"Wait. You've spoken to him?"

"No. I hired a private eye. My friend Sonny's brother's next-door neighbor. He located Marvin in Scottsdale. Even took pictures, but I said he should hold on to them. Then a few months ago, I found out the spy guy died and his wife threw out the old files. But at least now I know where to start looking."

"This is crazy! You can't just walk out on Daddy to go chase a man who abandoned you."

"What do you always say? I'm like obsessed with the idea? He's all I think about."

"You're a married woman."

"It's not fair." She mimicked the fifteen-year-old me. "Everyone else is getting to go."

"I don't care what everyone else is doing . . . Under my roof you go by my rules. Now go to your room and don't come out until you've thought about the terrible mistakes you're making."

"I never talked like that." She laughed.

"Like hell you didn't . . . God, I can't believe what you're thinking of doing."

"See? And I thought for sure with all your craziness, you'd understand."

"But you already know the rest of the story. Marvin left you. He married someone else."

"I'd like to know if he ever thought about me . . . if he had any regrets . . . You read stories in the paper all the time about people finding their long-lost loves."

"Exactly. But he wasn't lost. He ran away."

"I don't care." She shrugged. "I want to ask him straight to his face. 'Marvin, why did you do it?' "

"Mom, c'mon . . . even you've got to admit you're not an easy person to get along with . . . He probably got scared and—"

"He said he loved me," she snapped. "Not like that nin-compoop who married you."

"Oh my God." I leaned in. "What don't you get? David loved me more than he ever loved anyone in his life."

"Then how come he couldn't stop himself from turning into a hoodlum?"

"We've gone over this. Gambling is a disease. A handicap."

"Oh that's a bunch of hullabaloo. If you don't want to spend the night at the craps table, you go to the movies. A cripple can't just decide to get up and head for the fridge."

"This isn't just my opinion, mother. Experts have proven that gambling is an addiction, just like drugs and alcohol abuse. Your body has a physiological need for the rush."

"So fine. You can't stop yourself, you get help."

"You know how hard I tried to get him into counseling. He wasn't ready."

"Then he didn't love you enough."

"No, he didn't love himself enough."

"Whatever it was, darling, you're lucky to be rid of him. Now you can look for a man who'll take care of you so you don't have to work all those crazy hours . . ."

"No! I'm done shopping for love. I'm much happier being alone."

"Who's happy being alone? That's nonsense. Of course you want to get married again."

"Why? So I can end up like you? Hunting down old lovers from forty years ago to see if they've still got tread on the tires?"

"I'm not saying your father and I didn't have a good life . . . I'm saying . . . Remember that movie I like, the one with Billy Crystal in the restaurant with that little blond girl? And she's showing him how she fakes—"

"*Don't you dare*," I whispered so loud, the people at the next table stared.

"What? I'm just saying. I'm tired of being treated like the old chairs in the den. You can sit on them whenever, so where's the thrill?"

"That's why they invented couples counseling."

"No! I'm done talking." She waved her finger in my face. "I'm like a movie director. I want action! Now are you going to help me find Marvin or not? I hear he has a very good-looking son who's a doctor."

"I wouldn't care if he was the goddamn surgeon general. How could you even ask me for help? Daddy may be weird and crazy, but he's my father and I love him."

"Fine. I'll find him myself."

"Just tell me this. After all these years, why now?"

"You know what the famous Rabbi Hillel said. 'And if not now, when?' "

"Nice quote, mom. But it's doubtful he was talking about divorce."

"You interpret it your way." She raised her glass. "And I'll interpret it mine."

Chapter 7

ONE OF MY FONDEST childhood memories was of spending summer days with my grandpa Danny, building miniature rocket ships that could be launched from his backyard in Brooklyn. I was maybe four at the time, too young to be able to do anything other than help Grandma Rita serve the cookies and lemonade. But my age gave me a distinct advantage over Phillip.

Since he got to help Grandpa with the assembly, I got to push the button that set the launch in motion. And nothing beat shouting out the countdown. "Three . . . two . . . one . . . blast off!"

As the rocket soared, smoke billowing from the base, Phillip and I would cheer, pondering the mission's fate. Would the shuttle reach new heights and the parachute open over Ocean Parkway, or plummet into Grandma's blackberry bushes?

Mind you, even at four I knew the rockets went no farther than the neighbor's backyard. Or perhaps the rare one traveled as far as the A&P parking lot. Who cared? It wasn't the rockets we loved. It was the fantasy.

Funny that for a memory so grand, it took thirty years to recall, and that the prompt came from my mother lighting a marital match, revealing her decades-old union for what it was. A steadily worn down vessel that was imploding due to hairline cracks in the relationship caused by extreme pressure in the master bedroom, and one partner not fully committed to the program.

It got me wondering. Was not every marriage born of heat and energy, launched with great fanfare in the hopes of assuring a long, happy trajectory? Yet who among the invited guests believed that love and passion were all it took to fire up a successful mission? If that were so, then why did so many marriages crash and burn?

It couldn't always be attributed to stress and disappointment. Both sets of my grandparents' marriages withstood war, the Depression, and disease, yet they orbited happily for decades until first one, and then the other, lost their spark.

And take Phillip and Patti. They began their wedded life on shaky ground, zigzagging through religious differences until finally wealth propelled them to their suburban sphere, where their biggest battles centered around kitchen renovations and which Lexus to lease.

On the other hand, for my friend Rachel, she of the Psychics-R-Right club, the score was a surprising ex-husband, one, her and her kids, nothing. And at work, it sure seemed as if everyone was divorced, except for Benitez, who had been with Angelina for thirty-two years (theirs would have been a great marriage if they'd ever exchanged vows). Simon was on his third wife. Gretchen was divorced from her first husband, though I'd heard rumors that she had been married once before him, to a high school sweetheart she dumped when the network discovered her doing the weather at a local affiliate in Charlotte. And now with she and coanchor Kevin riding the infidelity train, it was likely the next stop for Kevin and his wife, Anne, was divorce court.

My marriage, though accompanied by a lavish Manhattan sendoff and an all-expense-paid honeymoon to Aruba, clearly had fatal flaws. The relationship was shoddily constructed of dishonesty and recklessness, and anyone who examined the workmanship closely would have been able to predict our demise.

But of all marriages, the one I presumed would stay airborne forever was my parents'. In fact, they were together so long, they weren't on anyone's radar. Yet out of the blue, their raucous but stable relationship was hurtling to earth in a fast, downward spiral, and it didn't look good for survivors.

I wondered. Did marriage, like life, have a destiny all its own? One guided not so much by love and devotion as karma and fate? Because if the success of a marriage was predetermined by some mysterious, celestially scripted backroom deal, then my mother would be crazy to escape one marriage rocket, only to try to hop a ride on another, and frankly the same would be true of me.

On Monday morning, with my mother sleeping soundly on a pullout couch in my spare closet/bedroom, and no interest in checkout time, with whom could I commiserate?

I almost gathered friends for an emergency summit, but decided to consult with the one person who knew my parents as well as me and had as much of a vested interest in their marriage.

"What the hell time is it?" Phillip whispered.

"Four forty-five . . . I'm in a cab on my way to work . . . Gotta love New York. It's already rush hour . . . hold on . . . Excuse me. Sir? You have to take Ninth Street to Third and take a left by that big, ugly building for the Battery Tunnel . . . Yes I know what I'm talking about. I do this every morning . . ."

"Robyn, you just woke me out of a dead sleep. Is Mom okay?"

"Oh wait. Hold on. Sorry. I have to take this. It's Simon . . ."

"You're killing me," Phillip groaned.

"Relax . . . Hey Simon . . . No, I didn't forget. All three names. Sierra Paige Mather. Yeah, it'll be great. I can really use the help." *Maybe I should talk the driver into taking a different detour. A little trip over the Williamsburg Bridge. Literally.*

"I'm back. Sorry . . . So Mom slept in my tiny little guest room last night, which I thought would freak her out because she's not used to sleeping in such tight quarters, but instead she says, 'If Jane Fonda can leave Ted Turner and move into her daughter's place, so can I.' So I said, Yeah, but you don't own twenty-three other houses you can go to when you've overstayed your welcome."

"Is there a point here?"

"Yes. She had so much fun yesterday, I'm looking at a life sentence without parole."

"I'm sure this will blow over, Rob. She's just going through a phase."

"That's what I thought, but you don't know the whole story. She's been keeping a secret that's going to blow you away."

"You mean about the cancer?"

"I'm sorry?" I shivered.

"She finally told you about the lump in her breast?"

"Driver. Stop the car," I screamed. "Stop the car. Pull over. I'm going to be sick."

"Shit," Phillip said. "She didn't tell you? I thought that's what you were getting at."

"I kent stop, lady. Where you like me to pull over? This is highway . . . Look 'round."

"Oh my God." I leaned my head back and started to cry. "Oh my God."

"I'm sorry. She said she would tell you. If it's any consolation, she kept it from Patti and me at first too. But she's fine, and it probably explains where all this craziness is coming from."

"I can't even speak," I whispered. "I think I'm going to heave."

"Not in thi car, miss." He miraculously found a place to pull over. "Get out. Quick."

I crawled out of the cab and bent over a guardrail.

"Robyn, where are you?" Phillip yelled. "What are you doing?"

"I'm not six anymore. How could she have cancer and nobody tell me?"

"Because she found out the same week your divorce papers came through."

"Oh my God." I fell into a heap.

"Lady, if you're not enymore sick, get beck inside. I have plenty more pickups."

Ever the obedient one, I climbed back in and blew my nose.

"She's fine. I swear," Phillip said. "It was a little lump in her right breast. They removed it, she had three weeks of radiation, and now she's on this new wonder drug that seems to be working great. Trust me, she's got plenty more years to bug the crap out of us."

"When did she have the radiation?" I blew my nose. "Where was I?"

"Remember last summer when you went to Rome with the show? And then after you got there you decided to stay an extra week?"

"I stayed an extra week because my brother didn't have the decency to tell me our mother was sick. What the hell were you thinking, Phillip? I should have been there for her."

"Hey look. We were afraid you'd go off the deep end, okay? But at least now we're all on the same page, and you're going to make sure she goes home where she belongs."

"Believe me I'm trying," I choked. "But she's not listening. You talk to her. She knows you longer."

"I don't have time to deal with this crap right now. I'm up to my eyeballs at work, we're still in the middle of the kitchen renovation, God knows why Patti hired that dickhead contractor, you wouldn't believe the incompetence; Max made the division one ice hockey league, which is great for him, but it means even more shlepping for me; and you have no idea what it's like every day with the girls and Patti constantly going at it—"

"Phillip. Stop. I can't listen to you. You just dropped a bomb on me. I'll call you later."

I shut my phone and squeezed it in my palm, hoping that a tight grip would somehow placate the hand tremors. Cancer. Oh my God. The frightening six-letter word for malignancy. But no point asking how a tumor ended up in my mother. The statistical probability was way up there after a lifetime of inhaling noxious tar and nicotine. Both her parents smoked, she smoked, as did my father until his heart attack, and just about all their friends.

I flashed on me at four hiding cigarette cartons in my dollhouse. Me at ten coming home from school with pamphlets on the dangers of secondhand smoke. Me at thirteen telling my mother that a film they showed us said she would end up with black lungs and froggy voice if she didn't quit. Me in college calling to say that my roommate's mother was diagnosed with breast cancer and I had a dream she was next.

All to no avail. My mother loved the ritual of smoking, the smell of lit tobacco, the deep inhalations, the Bette Davis glamour with the dramatic swirl of smoke, and her favorite, the conversational stall, as she fumbled with her fourteen-karat-gold lighter from Cartier.

To hell with the surgeon general's report, she coughed. Or

the hacking morning phlegm. The stale odor on her clothes. Not even the threat of wrinkles. When the time came, she would have me show her a few tricks to camouflage the evidence.

But now what? Call her and say I told you so? Serves you right for not listening? Of course not. I would act as if her disease was a random act of God, like a tornado whose path was an equal opportunity destroyer.

Only trouble was, I didn't believe that she was a victim, any more than David was when he was prosecuted for dealing cocaine. Collateral damage brought on by self-inflicted wounds was just that. A loaded gun you pointed at your head. Could you really cry foul if the safety dislodged?

What was I saying? That my mother's cancer was no different than my ex-husband's addictions? Ridiculous. But then, the crisis did feel eerily familiar, like a movie I'd seen and remembered hating.

First reaction was to feel anger that a loved one had brought a pox on their own house. Next came resentment that their illness would consume my life. Finally there was dread that even if I came to the rescue, there was no guarantee of a happy ending.

Regardless, I would be there for my mother, just as I had been for my husband, and I wouldn't allow myself to pass judgment. Only the Xanax.

When you work someplace for a long time, you develop rituals. The way you greet the security guard with a high five. The way you kiss the cheek of the coffee man if he says you remind him of Audrey Hepburn. The way you ask the lady at the newsstand about her granddaughter's flute lessons (and hope she's too busy to talk).

So you'd think that after six years of bantering with the same cast of characters, one might notice I looked a little blue.

Maybe offer to bring me some tea when they went on break, or find a quiet spot in the dark, cavernous studio to sit and listen to my woes.

Not that I was trying to advertise my troubles. It just would have been nice if someone stopped and said, "Jeez. You look terrible, Robyn. What's going on?" And then I would tell them the whole pathetic tale and they'd say, "Wow. And you came in anyway? You're so brave."

Instead, three people passed me in the hall and waved hello. Finally, someone noticed I wasn't my usual perky self. "You look like death." An associate producer sped by. "Simon's asking for you. Don't stop to collect your two hundred. Just go . . ."

"Robyn, there you are." I heard Gretchen's shrill voice. "I seem to have misplaced those cucumber melon eye patches you left me. I assume you have more."

"I have plenty, but I'll be right back . . . Simon is looking for me."

"Well how long will that take? My lids are very irritated."

Not as much as me. "Two secs." I took a deep breath. "Why don't you use the green tea bags for now? They're in your top right drawer, left-hand corner next to the udder cream."

"Please hurry. I shouldn't be having to do these things myself. They pay me to—"

"Gretchen." I swallowed. "You will look amazing as always. In fact, I got a sample of that beautiful new foundation primer I told you about. It's super sheer but works great at covering sunburn. Now go look over your notes . . . I have to go do a small favor for Simon."

"What kind of favor? He should have gotten my approval first."

"It's not a big deal. He just wants me to show his new stepdaughter how I do makeup."

"No! I will not sit there and be your little demonstration girl."

"Fine. I'll just have her observe. I won't say a goddamn word to her."

Gretchen jumped. I was never abrupt with her. Never disrespectful. "I beg your pardon?"

"I'm sorry. I just got some very bad news . . . I'll go get the eye patches for you and then tell Simon to forget about—"

"No. It's fine. Maybe if you have a little assistant, you won't do such a rush job."

My cheeks turned crimson. "You think I do a rush job?"

"Well of course you do. You have to work fast. It's morning television."

"Oh."

"But clearly you can't wait to get away from me."

"I'm sorry you feel that way." *Bitch!*

"Oh please. You could give a damn how I feel . . . You're Hit and Run Robyn."

Hit and Run Robyn? It was like getting stomach-punched, for in spite of my personal feelings, I had never sacrificed her appearance. In fact, she had no clue how much thought I had put into creating a look that was not only flattering but circumvented her long nose, sunken cheekbones, blotchy complexion, and the normal signs of aging, which were exacerbated by binge drinking, smoking, and God knows whatever drug dependency had made her already tiny eyes droop.

"Let's talk after the show," I said. *I'd do it now, but I'm late for my nervous breakdown.*

"Yes, it's time we did . . . Oh damn it, Robyn . . . It's so unprofessional to resort to tears."

It's so unprofessional to resort to tears. I cried as I fled down the hall to the makeup studio. Hit and Run Robyn? Prick! I had been totally devoted. Never said a bad word. Well maybe a few, but nothing terrible. And what about getting extra credit for not having revealed the secret that could bring her down like the S.S. *Minnow*?

I flipped on the light switch and ran for the bin that contained my eye repair products when I thought I saw a shadow behind me. It had to be the way the sunlight was peeking through the curtains, or that my vision was now so blurred, I could barely see my hands.

"Scare the shit out of me why don't you?"

I screamed when a massive figure emerged from under Gretchen's down comforter on the couch. "Oh my God." I grabbed a can of hairspray in case I had to blind the intruder. "Who are you? What are you doing here?"

"Oh chill." A girl shimmied back under the comforter. "You know who I am."

I put down the can and placed my hand on my beating heart. "Sierra?"

"Sierra Paige Mather. Don't bother to curtsy. Where do you get Coke around here?"

"What?"

"Coke. Pepsi. Yoo-hoo. What the fuck. Something with caffeine."

"Oh. Um, the commissary is on three, but I'm sure you could check the greenroom."

"Whatever. Simon's looking for you. He needs to give you the rundown on me. You know, be nice, show her everything. All that shit. On the way back, get me two cans."

I tried to calm down but my temper was bubbling like a cauldron. For a moment all I heard were the sounds of a blob rustling and birds chirping. "Jump," they were saying. "It's all over."

"Dudette, are you just going to stand there?" She peeked out.

"I'm sorry," I mumbled. "It's been a terrible morning. You frightened me and I'm—"

"Boo hoo, Dorothy. Life's a bitch. Just ask the Tin Man."

I wanted to shake her like a can of Coke, but I didn't want word to get back to Simon that I had a bad attitude. "The pantry down the hall also has breakfast stuff," I offered.

"Great," she mumbled. "I'll take some Pop-Tarts, but not the ones with the fruity shit."

"Oh good." Simon walked in and put his arm around me. "You two have met."

"Not really," I said. "I was getting something for Gretch. Oh God. She's waiting for me."

"Sierrapaigemather, you have to get up now, dear. This is Robyn. She's the one who—"

"For God sakes, Simon, is this little conference necessary?" Gretchen blew in. "Can't you see my eyes are nearly swollen shut? I need Robyn this instant."

"Just hold on." He smiled. "This is my stepdaughter—"

"Hello?" The lump finally sat up. "We're not related, okay? You're just the latest fool bastard to marry my mother . . . God. Way to suck at life."

"Simon," Gretchen snapped. "Have your whatever she is to you hand over my comforter before it gets, I don't know, infested. That was given to me by the Duchess of York you know."

Oh please. Not the Fergie story. How many times did we need to hear about the two mad-dash shoppers reaching for the same Simone Astor sweater at Bendel's and having such a laugh, they ended up lunching together and becoming the most marvelous friends. "She's really quite lovely, you know," was Gretchen's patent-pending close.

Fortunately we were spared, as Gretchen was too busy trying to assess whether Simon's whatever she was to him had left any cooties on the couch.

It was hard not to laugh. For all her southern-fried, polite-to-your-face breeding, Gretchen was doing a lousy job hiding her feelings. And who could blame her?

Sierra etc. was a supersized goo girl who looked slovenly in a baggy sweatshirt and jeans. And unlike a true makeup artist, she knew nothing about the ground rules for eyeliner (read the directions—don't apply to lips). Her chopped/cropped hair was three shades of purple, and her black fingernails made her look like she'd just left the set of *Dracula II: Return of the Fat Ass*.

Hardly the image one would expect of the daughter of a Beverly Hills socialite.

"Which part of 'I need Coke' don't you two get?" She glared at Gretchen and me.

It was 5:30 in the morning. Who would believe me if I said it was already a long day?

Chapter 8

IN HONOR OF my twenty-first birthday, my father bought shares in Kimberly-Clark, makers of Kleenex. Though he had no idea how his wife, a stoic, had spawned a crybaby like me, he figured the family might as well profit from my overactive tear ducts.

How ironic, then, that my career would dump me smack in the middle of the news business, where not a day went by that I didn't hear reports ranging from bad to unfathomable. But did it desensitize me, or help me acquire some decent coping skills?

To the contrary, I was still awful at getting awful news, whether it be mine or someone else's. And even worse at getting a grip. Which was why as soon as the show was over, I retreated to Gretchen's dressing room, where I sat Indian style, frozen like a photo, sobbing without shame.

I realize it made no sense that as much as I despised my boss, I loved using her personal space to regroup. Especially at midmorning, when Gretchen was holed up in meetings, and the long hall leading to her private sanctuary was quiet and dark.

But at the moment, not even her scented creams and candles could steady my nerves, for I felt like an Egyptian David Letterman doing battle with the top ten plagues, with no hope for a commercial break, let alone the Red Sea parting.

My father was clueless, my brother was useless, and my mother was a walking time bomb. Gretchen wanted to get rid of me, Simon wanted to take advantage of me, and Madeline wanted to borrow me so that her mess of a brother-in-law would be off her hands. And as if there weren't already enough crazies in my life, please welcome Marv Teitlebaum and Sierra Paige Mather.

Did I mention that until payday on Friday, I had $124 in my bank account?

Frankly, not only was this too much to handle at once, but I was desperate for a culprit. Someone to whom I could direct my anger. Dear Mr. President. No. Dear Congressman. No. Dear David . . . no damn it! He was in jail.

Up until now I hadn't realized the speed at which I implicated my ex-husband as the source of all my grief, just as he had charged that gambling was the cause of his. But without him playing the role of villain, how would I survive the loss of my most reliable crutch?

Meanwhile, my mind was racing but my foot was falling asleep. And though the burning tingle was annoying, I couldn't get up, for fear it would mean that the self-pity party was over.

A call from Phillip forced my hand. "What do you mean you have no idea where Mom is? This is nuts, Rob. I don't have time to chase her. Get her a cell phone for God's sake."

Perhaps he'd forgotten the last time we went through this exercise, she refused to leave the phone on for fear the battery would die, then wrote nasty letters to Sprint. "Twenty-nine ninety-five a month? But I only used the phone twice last month and the ads say nights and weekends free."

Then came a knock at the door. Damn! The last thing I needed was to be found crying in Gretchen's room. This being a news-gathering operation, office gossip traveled at twice the speed of an instant message:

I took a deep breath before opening the door. Of all people, it was a security guard wondering if I'd seen my mother. Not him too?

"Or at least I think she's your mother." The embarrassed man cracked his knuckles.

"Can't be. My mother wouldn't know how to get here on her own."

"Short, little, blond lady?" He raised his hand to chest level. "Yells pretty loud?"

"Damn her!"

"She tried to get past the desk without clearance." He peeked in as if I might be hiding a stowaway. "You didn't give us her name this morning."

"I would have if I was expecting her. So wait. Where is she?"

"Can't tell you. That's why I came up here. Maybe you can help us locate her."

"Well I'm sure if you sent her away, she's probably out shopping or something."

"No ma'am. We reviewed the tapes and she never walked out the stage door . . . Means she's gotta be in the building . . . I don't want to lose my job . . . Can you call her cell?"

"She doesn't have one."

"Same with mine." He shrugged. "Gave my mom a phone for Christmas . . . only time she uses it is to prop the back door open for the cat."

Next thing we know, Runaway Mom gets off the elevator with the loathsome Sierra, unaware that (a) there was an all points bulletin out for her (or maybe both of them), and (b) her new friend was probably too stoned to care what she said.

"Yoo-hoo." She waved. "Found you."

"You are unbelievable," I cried. "How did you get up here?"

"It wasn't easy." She was all smiles. "I couldn't remember which floor you were on, and let me tell you, they were not at all helpful downstairs. Oh, you again." She sneered at the guard.

"Mom, you can't just barge in here without getting clearance," I yelled. "Innocent people get in trouble when you break the rules. Why didn't you call me before you came?"

"Calm down, darling. Remind me to get you that book *Don't Sweat the Small Stuff*."

Again with the recommended reading list. "Remember last night I told you I'd be on the run all day today?"

"I thought I'd surprise you and take you to lunch. Sor-ree if it's too much trouble."

"It's not too much trouble, but I have to get Gretchen ready for a taping at two, then I promised I'd help her get ready for this big media dinner tonight . . ."

"Don't you ever chill?" Sierra yawned. "She's just trying to be nice."

SHUT. UP. "I'm aware." I smiled. "By the way, what happened to you this morning? I thought you were supposed to be observing me."

"It's not like a job or anything . . . I hung out in Simon's office. He's got a better couch."

"Uh huh . . . So how did you get past the guards?" I turned to my mother.

"Are you kiddin' me? Security around here stinks. What good are all the fancy cameras if nobody's checking the side door where the smokers go . . . You fellas really oughta beef things up down there." She jabbed the guard's shoulder. "I coulda had a gun."

"Mom, stop. This isn't the Bellagio . . . By the way, how did you two meet?" I felt like I was asking a couple to share their first-date story.

"She bummed a cigarette from me," my mother replied. "And I got a light from her."

"Yeah. Then she told me who she was looking for and I said what the fuck, I know you."

"Mind your manners, dear," my mother reprimanded. "We're in mixed company . . . So what do you say. Time for lunch?"

"I told you I can't."

"Did you eat breakfast?"

"No."

"Then good thing I'm here. I'm saving you from being trampled when you faint on the street."

What part of "no" don't you understand? my mother used to ask. Only now I was asking the question, for in spite of my protests, she wouldn't take a no. So what if it was Pope week at work. She had come all this way to treat me.

Besides, what educated person would go a whole day without eating (it was only 11:15), and didn't I want to get to know Sierra now that we'd be working together?

Um, no. I already knew more than I needed. She was the spoiled, rich girl who knew the price of everything and the value of nothing. The girl who by virtue of her connections felt entitled to opportunities, preferential treatment, and a free pass when she behaved like a brat.

What do you bet her first words were directed to the hired help? "That will be all."

So how, you ask, did I find myself squeezed into a booth at a coffee shop having a lunch I didn't want, seated next to a girl I didn't like, with a mother who was driving me insane? Jewish guilt (you can run, but you'll die tired). What if these were my mother's last healthy days? What if she hadn't beaten the cancer and a year from now I was standing over her grave?

I shuddered at the thought until my reality check bounced. She and Sierra were ordering lunch and taking off for a cigarette break.

"Mother, what are you doing?"

"I need a smoke. Why don't you call your brother now and tell him I'm fine?"

"But you're not fine." I looked her in the eye.

"Yes I am." She pulled away.

"Really? And I'm thinking, maybe instead of reading all those books, you should be paying more attention to your oncology reports."

"Oh, I see. The big mouth couldn't keep his word."

"He shouldn't have had to. You should have been honest with me."

"You want honesty? I'll give you honesty. They found a little nothing in my breast. Like a peanut. They took it out. Now you see it, now you don't."

Sierra tugged at my mother's sleeve. "If you're not gonna go out, can I bum another smoke?"

"Jesus!" I went for my wallet. "You can't afford to buy your own pack?"

"I have money." She shrugged. "Just not on me."

Because you spent it all on drugs. "Fine. Here's four dollars."

"I need ten."

"For cigarettes?"

"And gum."

"That's crazy," I gasped.

"Tell me about it. It's nuckin' futs."

"No, it's insane that it's so expensive, yet you still keep smoking."

"So? We're paying over two dollars a gallon for gas," my mother exclaimed. "But do you see anyone giving up those big, *farshtunken* Humdingers?"

"Good point, Sheil." Sierra nodded.

Sheil? Oh that's good. You should be able to freeload at least a pack now. "You know what?" I got up. "I can't do this."

"Where are you going?" Sheil asked.

"I told you. I have to get Gretchen ready for a taping."

"You want one of my Zolofts?" Sierra bit a hangnail. "Take some of the edge off?"

"No. And when I get home," I said to my mom, "let's you and me have a nice long chat."

"Oy. Speaking of home," she said, "I forgot to tell you. You got an important phone call."

"Oh God. Please tell me you didn't pick up." *My luck you invited a collection agency over for cake and coffee.*

"What am I? An idiot? I just listened to the answering machine."

"Oh. Sorry."

"Then I picked up because it was that girl from the bar mitzvah who wants to fix you up."

"Are you serious? She's like stalking me."

"She's not, darling. She just wanted to tell you she spoke to him and it's okay to call. Here." She reached into her pocket. "This is home, this is his cell phone."

"Call who?" Sierra asked.

"A very handsome and successful man," my mother said. "And how's this for *bashert*? Melinda said he lives a few blocks from here."

"Madeline."

"Same thing. And what a co-inky-dink? It's right around where you and David lived, too."

"Thanks, because I'd forgotten my old address."

"What the fuck?" Sierra said. "Call him."

"Not for nothing." I glared. "But why do you care?"

"I don't. I just want you to stop talking so me and your mom can go out for a smoke."

*   *   *

It wasn't exactly the Red Sea parting, but in a way it felt like a miracle. Suddenly everyone who had made me miserable that morning scattered in all directions, giving me the first chance in days to make it to the Promised Land (the ladies' room) without feeling like I had to hide in a stall.

New pals Sheil and Sierra decided to get to know each other over Greek salads and a half a pack of Newports. But not before I whispered to my mother that if she so much as breathed one bad word about either my father or myself, she'd be looking for a new roommate by sundown.

From there, my mother planned to meet up with Aileen, a neighbor from Fair Lawn, who had recently convinced her husband, Arnie, that what their empty nest marriage needed was a little pied-à-terre in Manhattan so that they'd have a weekend place to rekindle their passion.

Only to discover that Arnie hated spending time in the cramped studio ("You call this a kitchen?"), much preferring their comfortable home where he was only a ten-minute drive from their country club, and his long standing tee-off times.

Lonely Aileen said it would be fabulous if my mother joined her for dinner tonight, and did she have any plans tomorrow, because it was so much more fun to shop the galleries in Soho when you had a friend with a good eye. And Wednesday, a ticket broker who lived in her building said he could get her front row seats for *Wicked*. What next? A sleepover with s'mores?

By the time I got back to the office, the only sign of Gretchen was a note she'd posted to her makeup mirror saying the taping had been rescheduled, as had the media dinner because everyone had left town to attend the pope's funeral mass. But not a word about us talking.

My busy brother didn't pick up his cell, so I'd have to wait for further instructions as to the next thing on *his* list that *I* should do for *our* mother.

A call to my dad found him in surprising good stead, as he was taking advantage of his newfound freedom to spread out his mapmaking tools on my mother's (her mother's) beloved dining room table. "And tell her I am *not* using the table pads!" the proud rebel bellowed.

And other than a call from my lawyer's office reminding me to submit the paperwork for my upcoming court appearance (like I could possibly forget the upcoming encounter with Judge Payup R. Else), I had not a single e-mail, voice mail, or text message.

Frankly, I couldn't remember the last time I wasn't bombarded with demands from lawyers, bosses, parents, friends, my brother, and a husband. In fact, of late, my life had been so much about answering to higher authorities, I'd forgotten how to spend a carefree day.

Yes, of course, there were things I should be doing, I thought as I uncrumpled the paper with Ken Danziger's numbers. But none that would cause the universe to blow up if I didn't. Besides, wasn't I entitled to time off for good behavior?

Avoid blind dates, the voice in my head said. At least with semisuicidal guys. On the other hand, Ken's brother was one of the hottest men I'd seen in a long time, which boded well for the gene pool. And I was curious if we had a Penn State connection.

But who was I kidding? The only connection I cared about was the one he had with Billy Crystal. A good word on my behalf could get my stalled-on-the-shoulder life back in the fast lane.

First, however, I'd use my phone-a-friend option to call Rachel, my relationship expert, to ask if she or her supposed gurus thought I'd go to hell for taking advantage of a disabled person. Not that it would stop me if they said yes.

Chapter 9

YES, I CALLED HIM. Well not right away. It took an hour to get through to Rachel, who first wanted to know how my dad was doing, not because she cared, but because it so happened that her mother was moving back to New York, and if my parents were splitting, maybe my dad and her mom could be introduced. "She is so done with the widows in Broward County," she said.

Was she serious? My parents were apart for less than forty eight hours, and already my father was prime meat in the AARP manhunt? "They're not splitting, okay? They're having . . . technical difficulties."

"Fine. But don't you think it would be a riot if we ended up stepsisters?"

"Hilarious!" I almost hung up.

Finally, Rachel was ready to listen. I mentioned Ken's name as if it was the answer on *Jeopardy* and waited for her to tell me what I won. Was she hoping for a sign from my deceased relatives? No, she was letting the name register, and to my surprise, she said she knew him.

"If he's who I'm thinking," she said, "we were on a panel to-gether at some Bar Association seminar and he was drop-dead gorgeous. Tall, dark, curly hair. Great body. But he was mar-ried, and the only reason I remember that is because he stopped talking when his wife walked in.

"She was stunning. Tall and thin like him with great hair. I loved her hair. Then he breaks into this huge smile and says it's his bride, the doctor. I'll never forget it. He looked smitten."

"Well, here's a late-breaking story," I said. "He and Nina didn't make it."

"Yeah. Nina. That was it. No! Really? He's divorced? Shit! I wish I knew. Are you sure?"

"Positive. I'll tell you everything later."

"Okay, well then you should definitely call him because he's a find. And if for whatever retarded reason you don't like him, give him my number, but don't say a word about my kids. Un-less you find out he's crazy about children."

"How can I call him now? I'm obviously not his type."

"You don't know that. How do you know that?"

"Because you just said his wife was (a) beautiful, (b) smart, (c) skinny and I'm (d) none of the above."

"Would you stop? I hate when you're all anti. First of all, it's his ex-wife, so lot of good (a), (b), and (c) did her. Besides, you're not only beautiful and smart too, you're hysterical!"

Yes, but being funny was not the same as competing with his ex in the swimsuit competition. Now I'd have to wow him dur-ing the talent portion of the pageant, and that would put a lot of pressure on me to be clever and bold.

For inspiration, I Googled him, hoping to see the words "No matches found." Then I could write him off as a loser no-body, not even worthy of bad press. Instead, I found several ar-ticles about his entertainment law career, and pictures from industry functions.

Since he was in group shots, the faces were tiny. But even

among a crowd, he was a standout. Just as Rachel remembered, he was tall, with dark, curly hair, an amazing body, and a great smile. Then my stomach knotted like after the first drop on a roller coaster. Rachel wasn't the only one who might know him.

Maybe it was his resemblance to his brother that made me think I'd seen him before. Or was it his resemblance to David? No. My ex was twice his size. But wait. Did he look familiar because we had met before? If I could just remember where.

I dialed his home number so fast, I forgot to rehearse a funny spiel. Not that it mattered. My best routine, along with a laughing gas chaser, wouldn't have warmed up this audience of one.

"Yeah, I heard you were supposed to call," he said with the same enthusiasm you'd greet a census taker. And yes, he was aware of Madeline's matchmaking plans, as she had done her little bit before. And yes, he agreed that if we didn't at least meet for a drink, she would never let up so we might as well get on with it. "But do you mind telling her I took you to dinner?"

Only if you don't mind telling her I know why she has to pay people to meet you.

Funny thing was, the chilly reception didn't bother me, or the heads-up that our getting together would be a waste of makeup. I didn't even care that I was wearing old clothes, no jewelry, and a Mets cap to cover my desperate-for-a-touch-up hair.

What did annoy me about his icy tone was that it meant there was merit to Rachel's theory, which held that fifty percent of the men you met were assholes. The other half were someone else's asshole (though if you were so sure psychics were right, why would you know any at all?).

Of course, for someone like myself who had sworn off men

and marriage, so what if the odds of finding a great single guy in New York were about as good as finding one-of-a-kind Blahniks on sale in your size? I was no longer in the market.

No, that wasn't true. I hadn't stopped shopping. I had stopped hoping. For once you've invested your heart in a man who bankrupts your soul, there is no going back to the broker and asking what else he recommends. You are spent in the truest sense of the word.

Trouble was, in spite of the dysfunction and disappointment, I missed David terribly. Naturally, I understood that everyone in my inner circle would rather duct tape my mouth than listen to me pine for the emotionally insolvent man who mortgaged my life for a winning hand.

And don't kid yourself. Even for marriages that ended in a heap of broken dreams, one thing couldn't be erased by a judge's decree. Your union was a declaration that at one time you were armed with purpose. Your ring, a universal sign that to someone you meant the world.

So yes. I would love to find another companion with whom I could wake up and inhale virile traces of soap and cologne. Of course I wanted to see the approving, desirous eye of a man when I walked into a room. It would be amazing to once again exchange glances with a partner and know so well the meaning of his expressions.

But what were the odds Ken Danziger could ever be that guy? They didn't call it a long shot for nothing.

Theory pants were one of those luxury items on my list of things I'd buy if money was no object. Meanwhile, the only way to get my hands on a pair was if they were hand-me-downs from Julia or borrowed from Gretchen.

Since I was within arm's reach of Gretchen's dressing room, the logical choice was to quietly steal through her closet to see if that new black pair I'd admired last week was back from the cleaner's. Along with that white man-tailored shirt from Barneys she wore for her interview with Faith Hill. And because it was only April, she'd not likely notice those fabulous Jimmy Choo thong sandals with the black beads were missing.

Hell! If she was going to fire me, I might as well give her cause, I thought as I tore through the closet. Technically, these weren't her clothes, I convinced myself. They were purchased by the news division, like any other line item in the budget. And since we both worked for the same network family, shouldn't she do the sisterly thing and share?

You'd think I'd have raided it by now. And I would have if not for gaining twenty pounds, which made me wish I was one of those infomercial space bags. ("It's easy! Just suck out all the air with your vacuum.") But since losing the weight, it was finally time to "shop" the magic closet.

Sure enough, the pants zipped, the shirt buttoned. And you know what they say when the shoe fits. And why stop there? I knew where she kept her Cartier watches and Tiffany studs. And would she really mind if I borrowed that black Chanel tote Simon gave her last quarter when we won our daypart for women twenty-five to forty-nine?

I admired my slender silhouette in her three-way mirror and felt like Cinderella. Half thief. Half ready for her close-up. God help me if my cruel step-boss spotted me at the ball.

"What do you mean you called and canceled on him?" Rachel yelled. "Are you nuts?"

"Yes . . . No . . . Maybe?" I was trying to hail a cab with my cell at my ear. "I saw him and I panicked. Or I think I saw him."

"What did you do? Peek through his window?"

"No. I saw him on the street. I was about a block from his apartment, and I don't know. It hit me that this guy limping in front of me with a cane was probably him . . . Taxi!" I waved.

"Would you stop trying to get a cab?" Rachel said. "I have a client waiting and you need to give me the short version. What made you think it was him?"

"Because he was carrying a bag from a liquor store, and like one from a gourmet shop or something . . . and he looked too young to be walking with a cane. Although I only saw him from the back."

"So wait. You just turned around and took off?"

"Yeah. I left a message on his machine that I was sorry, but my plans changed and I couldn't make it, and I'd call to reschedule . . . I'm sure he'll understand."

"Right. A handicapped guy shleps out to the store to pick up something nice to serve you, he has to hobble there and back, and you think he won't care that you blew him off?"

"Fine. I'm a terrible person. But it's not like he was very nice to me on the phone. Taxi!"

"I swear to God, Robyn, if you get in that cab, it'll be the last time we talk. You call him back right now, tell him your plans changed again, and you can still come over if that's okay."

"Why would I want to get involved with a guy who walks like my grandfather? He probably needs help in the bathroom too."

"Who said anything about getting involved? Be a good person and drink his wine and eat his cheese and steer the subject to talking about Billy Crystal."

"I guess." I put my taxi-flagging arm down. "It's just that this whole meet and greet thing is so hard for me . . ."

"Really? Would you rather be in his shoes?"

"No thanks. I'm already in Gretchen's and they hurt like hell."

I didn't need one of Rachel's I-swear-she's-amazing psychics to predict how my meeting with Ken was going to go. All hints of a disaster took place in the first thirty seconds when I buzzed from downstairs and his voice came through the speaker. "I'm one floor up. Door's open. Let yourself in."

Sounded like my shrink. Take a seat until I can summon the courage to listen to your whining. Except here I was greeted by a dog instead of a doctor. But at least I passed the sniff test.

"Hello?" I didn't know whether to heel at the door like the dog, or walk down the long hallway. "Yoo-hoo. Avon calling." *Oh good. Very original. Where can I get tickets to see you?*

"Where is he, boy?" In exchange for his answer, I had to let him sniff my crotch. Well, at least something with testicles wanted to go there, I thought as I followed him into the living room.

As brownstone apartments went, this one was not especially spacious, but given his disabilities, maybe he'd chosen it because he could manage better. And what was this? A *Daybreak* exclusive? A genuine eat-in kitchen unearthed in the middle of Manhattan?

Another eye-opener was that the decor was legal-leather brown, with an occasional touch of red and gold to break the monotony. Which could mean only one thing. His mother, his decorator, his ex, or all of the above, had descended to take charge of setting up the place.

The ultimate proof that the man of the house hadn't been asked his preferences? The missing recliner and big-screen television. For no guy is ever going to say, "Who needs a TV? Go for the reception area look. And don't forget the Steuben glass eagles."

Frankly, the place looked less like a home than one of those temporary residences for traveling executives. But at least there weren't dirty dishes and clothes strewn, waiting to be picked up by someone with ovaries and a mop.

"Anyone home?" I called.

This was crazy. Who expected company and then disappeared? Unless he was in the bathroom and it was a whole, embarrassing ordeal, I thought as I studied his choice of art-work, which was lame. One only adorned their place with shots of the city skyline if they were a newcomer, or so disin-terested in their environment, they left the choice up to a decorator.

Ah. Finally something personal—a huge collection of CDs and a group of photos. What better way to get a sneak preview of a guy than to check out his taste in music and find out who was important in his life. Oh. And in this case, to see if Ken was as stunning as Rachel claimed.

Whoa . . . Assuming he was the guy standing next to Seth and Madeline at their wedding, he was hot as lit coals. And what a cute one of Seth with his dad, and I assumed Ken stand-ing next to them. Such sweet-looking little boys, gap toothed and beaming, clinging to fishing rods.

Funny thing. My dad kept a similar shot on his desk of Phillip and me, taken on visiting day at camp . . . Wait. Why did the lakefront in their picture look like the one at Lohikan? Couldn't be. There were dozens of sleepaway camps in the Pocono mountains, all with glistening lakefronts and canoes. What were the odds that our paths had crossed as kids? Was that why he looked familiar?

At least now I had a good ice breaker. But that would be nothing compared to the conversation we could have about the photo I found tucked behind the others of three adorable young men locked arm in arm, hamming it up for the camera.

If not for the dog barking, I would have cried. "What is it, Lassie?" I said only half in jest.

Should I just walk into this man's bedroom? No way. What if he wasn't dressed? What if that was the point? Oh gross. If this was a Hugh-Hefner-in-a-silk-bathrobe stunt, I was defi-nitely taking the bribe money from Madeline.

But when the barking grew louder, obviously something was up. I just prayed it didn't involve blood. Ever since I fell out of a tree at camp, I was really bad with blood.

"Oh my God," I cried as I followed the dog into the bedroom. "Oh my God."

Ken was lying facedown on the terrace. First thought? If he had just taken his life, or even attempted to take his life, no shrink in the world would be able to talk me off the ledge now.

By now the dog was barking and jumping so furiously, it was as if he was mocking me. "Open the sliding door, asshole. He needs help."

I raced out to the terrace, saw blood spewing from Ken's head, and screamed.

Once again, the dog gave me the cue, as he tried to get the cordless phone from Ken's hand. "Smart doggy." I dialed 911. Fifteen hundred my ass. Madeline would owe me more than that.

Queasy me was afraid to look down, though I couldn't help but notice his crisp, white shirt, now covered in blood, and realized he was the guy I'd spotted on the street. And yet with his gaunt eyes and shorn hair, he no longer bore a resemblance to the sexy, bring-it-on guy in the pictures.

I felt his wrist, and at least he had a pulse, which was more than I could say for my last blind date.

"Help operator!" I said. "A man fell on his terrace. He's bleeding and he's not moving . . . I'm so scared . . . Wait. Now he's trying to get up . . . Yes, that's the right address . . . Second floor."

"I'm okay," he mumbled. "Help me up . . . hey boy." He tried to pet the dog.

"He's talking," I said. "He wants to get up . . . They said don't move. They're on their way."

"I'm fine. Just give me a hand . . . come here, Rookie. Come here boy."

"Are you sure?" I asked. "Ma'am, he's insisting he can get up . . . Uh huh. Okay. Right."

"Please." Ken reached for my hand.

"No wait. The lady said you could injure yourself worse if you move."

"I swear to God if you don't help me up, we're through."

"Wow. I thought my last relationship was short." I knelt down with the dog barking in my face. "Here. Try to grab on to my waist. No wait. I don't think I'll be able to lift you myself . . ."

"Robyn, just give me your hand. I can do this. I've done it before."

"You've tried to kill yourself before?"

"I wasn't trying to kill myself."

"Well that's good," I said as I slowly helped him off the ground and into the chair. "Usually men don't try to jump until after we've had sex."

An awful thing to say, but at least it got Sourdough Boy to smile. "What happened?"

"I was looking for my phone but guess I found the table first."

"Oh my God. You poor thing. You've been through so much."

"Spare me your sympathy. And call 911 back. I'm fine."

"No you're not. You're bleeding. You could have a concussion. Or a broken collarbone."

"Are you a doctor?" Rookie jumped on his lap and licked his face.

"No, but I dressed up as one for Halloween . . . Shouldn't we try to stop the bleeding?"

Ken touched his blood-soaked face and looked faint.

"Does it hurt to breathe?" I asked. "Are you in pain? Where's your Advil?"

"In the kitchen. Make sure to take them with food."

"Not for me. For you."

"I'm fine. Just get me a towel with ice."

"Good. That's good. A towel with ice. I'm on it . . . By the way. I'm Robyn Fortune." I shook his hand. "We went to the same college, and possibly the same camp."

"Well, that's better than the last girl Madeline fixed me up with. The only thing we had in common was a last name."

"She fixed you up with your cousin?"

"No. My wife."

Chapter 10

I'VE BEEN ON some first dates that involved unusual modes of transportation, like the time Rachel fixed me up with a Wall Street friend who thought I would be impressed if he took me for a quick spin over Manhattan in his twin-engine Cessna (I threw up after take-off and spent the rest of the flight writing out my will).

And last month I'd agreed to go out with an Englishman I met on the show, who showed up in a brand-new, 475-horsepower Porsche, then insisted he would get the hang of driving on the left by the end of the night (I jumped out before he got on the FDR).

But I'd have to say that speeding through the streets of midtown in an ambulance took the prize. Particularly since my date assumed we were strangers, and I now knew otherwise. The proof was in the picture of the three boys I'd seen in his apartment. A picture I had taken fifteen years earlier, though I hadn't known the subjects.

I would never forget the December afternoon that I walked out of my dorm at Penn State and had a camera tossed in my face. "Hey chickie, take our picture," one of them shouted. What jerks, I thought, until I looked through the lens and realized my cafeteria honey was in the shot.

I hadn't been much of an eater until I went away to school, laid eyes on this adorable guy who lived in my dorm, and realized I had three meals a day to run into him. Which explained how the Commons became my second home, and how I gained my freshman fifteen.

Sadly, in all that time, I never worked up the courage to say hello or ask his name. And that picture I took? It was the last time I ever saw him. So you can understand my excitement at getting this out-of-the-blue chance to solve the mystery of who he was and where he went.

But once inside the ambulance, an oxygen mask was placed over Ken's nose and mouth, making it impossible to study his face, let alone grill him with questions. Instead, I was being asked to focus my attention on the paramedic's questions. How did this happen? How long was he blacked out? Was he taking any prescriptions or did he have any allergies?

I tried to sound informed because if I confessed that I knew the patient all of twenty minutes, I couldn't very well pass myself off as his wife once we got to the hospital. And that was key, as I didn't want to be relegated to the waiting room for the nonfamily, you-don't-count folks.

Actually, selfish as it was, I wanted to stay by his side so that I could find out more about the picture. And more important, if, by some miracle, he was the eighteen-year-old boy/man for whom I ate rice pudding every day so I had reason to hang around a noisy dining hall.

It blew me away that I might be looking at the same person, though with the mask over his face, much shorter hair, a bigger body, and fifteen years since the last spotting, it was hard to tell if I was on to something, or if I was back to fantasizing, as I had during those few months I kept my eyes riveted to the hall entrance, hoping to see the tall, lanky boy swagger in with his friends.

"So you guys have any kids?" The medic wrapped a blood pressure cuff around Ken's arm.

Ken's shook his head just when I said, "Two. Breanna is three and Tristan is nine months."

From beneath the mask, Ken turned into Darth Vader, spewing ominous messages through an echo chamber.

"Aw, he misses them already." I patted his hand. "Don't worry, sweetheart. My mom will be fine with them. I just hope she lays off the vodka tonics until I get back."

The great thing about being a comic is you learn to ignore those who don't appreciate your sense of humor. "What happens when we get to the hospital?" I asked.

"Basically, they'll run him through a bunch of tests, look for internal injuries, broken bones. They may keep him overnight. But his vitals are good. I'm sure he'll be fine."

"Oh thank God." I sighed. "My poor husband has been through so much already . . ."

Ken squeezed my hand so hard I let out a cry. And though I could understand him being a bit annoyed that I was misrepresenting our relationship, he should only know how many times men had done that to me.

Speaking of the shoe being on the other foot, I looked down and freaked. In all the chaos, I'd forgotten I was Cinderella at the ball. If I didn't return Gretchen's things before midnight, I would wind up with a pink slip as a souvenir. Difference was, Cinderella didn't have bloodstains on her clothes and Jimmy Choos cutting off the circulation in her feet.

If only a fairy godmother was circling the neighborhood now. Preferably one who had connections with a twenty-four-hour dry cleaner and flip-flops in her bag.

Meanwhile Ken was air scribbling. He must have noticed I was concerned about my soiled clothes and wanted to suggest

I drop them off at his dry cleaner's, which was sweet. But after I handed him a paper and pen, I learned otherwise:

> *Cut the crap. Key under mat. Feed Rookie. Leash on hall door. Medicine on kitchen counter. Treats 1 brown 1 green.* DON'T CALL MADELINE OR ANYONE.

"Breanna and Tristan?" Rachel howled. "Weren't they on *General Hospital*?"

"I don't know, but you had to see the look on his face. He was so pissed . . . How do you know when a dog is done walking?" I asked as Rookie sniffed every bush along Sixty-sixth.

"What kind of dog?"

"How should I know?" I studied him. "He's white, he's small, he has four legs."

"That's very helpful." She laughed. "Show me on your camera phone."

"Don't have one. My cell is so old it has a rotary dial."

"Well did he do his business yet?"

"Did he do his business yet?" I repeated as if I was unfamiliar with the local customs.

"Did you bring his pooper-scooper?"

"No. That was not in my instructions . . . You know, he's not very nice."

"The dog?"

"Yeah. The dog. No, Ken."

"Oh c'mon. You're not exactly meeting him under the best of circumstances."

"I know, but I'm just saying. He's very snotty and he's got this whole anger thing going."

"Well, I can solve that mystery," she whispered. "I did some checking and oh my God, it's amazing he's not dating men yet."

"What do you mean . . . Rookie!" I pulled his leash. "Must you sniff other dog's poop?"

"Well first of all, his apartment isn't his apartment. It belongs to Showtime."

"That's a relief. Even the books looked fake."

"Exactly. Showtime keeps it for celebs when they're filming in New York . . . I found out they're letting him use it until he's more mobile."

"Who told you . . . Rookie, slow down, babe, or I'll put these shoes on your feet and see how fast you walk."

"I have my sources, but wait. That's not all . . . He also dated Mira Darryl."

"Are you serious? I love her. She was so amazing in *Fall of Pompeii*."

"Never saw it. But yeah. She dumped him for . . . are you ready? Kyle Rider."

"Oh my God. Can you blame her? Wow. I can't believe Ken actually knows Mira."

"Knows her? They practically lived together. I guess it was before his ski accident. Anyway, a few months ago she hooked up with Kyle at some charity thing, moved back to LA, and it was adios Kenny Boy. I heard he didn't take it well. Called her constantly, flew out to LA, the whole begging scene. No wonder he's a mess."

"I can't believe you found all this out in an hour. Oh wait. Call waiting. Maybe it's him. Call you later. Thanks for the poop. No, not you, Rookie. Yes, yes. You're a good boy." I petted him.

It *was* Ken, and who saw this coming? He was as crotchety as ever, for in spite of his protests, he was being kept overnight for observation. But good news. They weren't making him wear the I-See-You gown, so now I could pack him a bag and bring it back to the hospital. Oh, and then in the morning after work, I could swing by his place, take in the paper, then feed and walk Rookie. "And if you're there when UPS comes, it's fine to sign for any deliveries."

Um, hello? Was I a date or employee of the month? And didn't he have friends who could help him (although given his conduct, maybe not)? And what about my early curfew? A girl whose wake-up call was in the middle of the night needed her sleep. And I should really get home in case my mother hadn't taken a key. Plus I had to stop at my office to switch clothes, and please God, to get out of those podiatrists-love-'em heels.

And yet I mentioned none of this as the thought occurred to me that Ken would owe me if I cooperated ("Really? You'd call Billy for me?"). And too, the possibility that our lives had been randomly crisscrossing for three decades was starting to freak me out. I wondered at what point coincidence ended and karma began. *Hello Rachel's psychic? Do you ever have clearance sales?*

Yeah yeah. Curiosity killed the cat. But what harm could come from snooping around a man's apartment? Technically it wasn't even his apartment, and was it really snooping if I had his permission to put together a bag of personal belongings? Naturally this involved going through his closets, dressers, and the tell-all medicine chest.

Then again, how could I violate this man's privacy even if he'd never find out? And how would I feel if someone did that to me? Come to think of it, someone probably had. For all I knew, my mother had spent the morning sifting through my things and discovered that her precious daughter had two vibrators, an ounce of pot, and an addiction to La Perla bras.

Still, I was only human, and this might be my only chance to find out if beneath Ken's gruff exterior, there was a warm side. So I made a deal with myself. Given I was on borrowed time, and I wanted to believe I had some integrity, I'd only poke around a little . . . starting with the box on his closet shelf marked "KMD: Personal."

"Oh, don't look at me like that," I said to a barking Rookie as I carefully placed the box on Ken's bed. "You'd do the same thing if you could reach . . ."

As I stripped away the masking tape, I had to laugh. Only last week, Gretchen interviewed this actress, Claire Green, who was pitching a movie she made with her mother called *Claire Voyant*. She told a funny story about how she broke into a guy's apartment to use his shower and ended up casing the joint. Now they were married. So see? The story didn't have to end badly.

But minutes later I was not only shame-faced, I was bored. If the contents of this box held this man's prized mementos, he had the sentimentality of a gnat. All I found were science projects, a bunch of old letters, and a shoe box filled with baseball cards.

Maybe Rachel was right. Just because I worked in television didn't mean I had to watch it all the time. Not everyone lived on Wisteria Lane and had deep, dark secrets. Speak of the devil. She was calling to see where I was now.

"I'm back at his apartment," I said.

"Why?"

"Because they're keeping him overnight for observation and he needs his medication and things."

"Lucky girl. Now you can case the joint and he'll never know."

"I'm sorry, but a lawyer who condones trespassing should be brought up on charges. Besides, I would never do anything so . . . oh my God."

"What?"

"Oh wow. He was an adorable kid."

"What are you looking at?"

"I took a box down from his closet and found these old pictures."

"Robyn, did you or did you not just say—"

"Oh spare me. I was just looking for clothes to throw in a bag and I found it."

"Right. And don't forget to check out his medicine chest . . ."

"Did that . . . In two months they'll be forwarding his mail to Betty Ford . . . You should see the picture of him and his two little friends . . . so cute . . . Oh my God. They look familiar too."

"What?"

"Nothing. Long story . . . I don't even know what I'm saying myself . . . I found a picture of him and two friends at college, and now here's one of them as little kids. At least I think it's them."

"You lost me."

"Sorry . . . I'm a little freaked out. I'm saying I think I might know Ken."

"Really? How?"

"From Penn State, and maybe my sleepaway camp."

"Then how come you didn't recognize his name?"

"Because I never knew it . . . I only knew him by sight. Isn't that so weird?"

"No, it's perfect! The *Times* loves the wedding stories with all the destiny stuff going."

"Would you stop? I spent maybe twenty minutes with a guy who was not only mean, he was horizontal the entire time, so it's a tad too soon to interview florists.

"But don't you see? It's *bashert*." She laughed. "You were meant to be together."

"Because we might have gone to the same camp and college?"

"Because it's time you had someone to dream about other than David."

I call it a brain fart. My mother, *farmisht*. Either way, it's when you are on such overload, you can't think straight. Drop Ken's things off at the hospital, go to the office to change, then head home? Nope. Couldn't take one more step in these shoes. Take a cab to the office, a bus to the hospital, then try to reach my mom? Nope. She didn't have a cell.

I decided to walk to the office first and borrow Ken's size twelve Adidas slides. Didn't care that they were huge. At least they wouldn't send a blood rush to my ankles. And so what if I looked unfashionable, I thought as I charged into Gretchen's dressing room, turned on the light in her walk-in closet, and said hello to Gretchen and Kevin, who were screwing on the floor.

"Oh my God." I screamed. "Oh my God. I'm so sorry. I was just—"

"Christ!" Kevin rolled over, leaving both him and a panting Gretchen exposed. "Oh thank God it's not Anne . . . It's not what you think, Robyn."

You're right. You're better hung than the Mona Lisa and Gretchen would make a great spokesperson for Wonderbras.

"It's not what you think." A sniveling Gretchen reached for her shirt. "That's right. We're in here doing local promos."

"Well sorry." He looked at his watch. "Damn! It's late . . ."

"Robyn! How dare you just barge in here like this." Gretchen glared.

How dare I? Am I the one having sex with a married man in a closet at work? "I'm sorry. I was just trying to—"

"Are those my clothes? You little thief . . . And is that blood on them?"

"It's not what you think," I said without realizing I was mimicking Kevin.

"Look, I'm sure you girls can work this out." He zipped his fly. "You both owe each other . . . Robyn, we're counting on your discretion."

About your indiscretion? I almost laughed. "Of course . . . I didn't mean to . . . Let me just get my things . . . Gretchen, I'm sorry. I'll explain in the morning . . . I had this last-minute blind date . . . he ended up in the hospital . . . is that my digital camera?"

"Your what?" She pushed it under a pile of clothes.

"Ooh, ooh, ooh." I waved my hands. "You were photographing each other?"

Kevin grabbed the camera. "You'll have it back in the morning. I promise." He looked like he had signs of Bell's palsy as he tried waving to Gretchen. "Call you later."

For one fleeting moment, we were sisters in sympathy.

"Emergency dance party?" I did the hustle.

"What?"

"Ellen DeGeneres always does this little dance when she's in an awkward situation . . . It seemed like a good time."

"Oh . . . Tell me something. Why didn't you act surprised just now?"

"Are you serious? The last thing I expected was to walk in here and see—"

"No, I mean that Kevin and I are together. I would think that would shock you."

"Gretchen, I've known for a long time. You once asked me to hold on to your cell phone while we were at a shoot, and he kept leaving voice mails."

"Oh. But yet you never let on."

"Because it's none of my business . . . Nor have I ever breathed a word to anyone."

"Thank you. I appreciate your, you know, your professionalism." She bit her lip. "So we have an understanding?"

"Absolutely." *I understand that if you fire me, it's open season on news anchors.*

"This is, of course, embarrassing for me, but actually I'm glad it happened."

"You are?"

"Yes. Now Kev and I will have a lookout. Can you be here on Mondays and Wednesdays at three?"

Chapter 11

"GLAD IT'S NOT ME" is the universal refrain when you're whizzing by at sixty mph, while the cars on the other side of the highway are at a standstill. But that's nothing compared to the pity you feel for the unsuspecting motorists who are approaching and about to start cursing.

If only there was a way to warn them, like the hurricane trackers that alerted folks to run for higher ground. Come to think of it, why not a sophisticated warning system for life?

Boss Alert: Call in disillusioned. Management is freaked about third quarter earnings and looking for scapegoats.
Parent Alert: Don't go home . . . unless you really want to help clean out the garage.
Husband Alert: It's not your imagination. He's a fuckup. Bail! Bail! Bail!

Believe me, I would have appreciated the heads-up that in the span of forty-eight hours I was going to have to contend with so many people riding in the danger zone: a gone-crazy woman battling cancer (my mom), philandering bosses (Gretchen and Kevin), two lost souls (my father and Sierra), and now a broken man (Ken).

What had I done to end up on this highway to hell? I got the concept of things happening for a reason, but doubted anyone had ever inched along the road in heavy traffic, then said, Wow, that was life changing.

Come to think of it, what was Ken's crime, for which the penalty was lying in yet another hospital bed? From the looks of him staring out the window, bandaged and bruised, he had to be wondering himself. But at least his being lost in thought gave me time to scope out the situation before walking in, as hospitals were notorious for exposing visitors to a whole lot of ooeyness.

I waved to Ken as I tiptoed past the elderly man dozing with the TV on. "How are you?"

He waved back with zero enthusiasm, already succumbed to the weak, pale, get-me-out-of-here glaze. He'd been here what? An hour?

"Hey." I smiled. "What's the diagnosis?"

"The top specialists all agree," he grunted. "I'm a klutz."

"And the cure is charm school?"

"No time. I'll be too busy juggling between more physical therapy and sitting on my ass."

"Ouch."

"Yeah. I sprained my good ankle and bruised my coccyx."

"Oh that's awful . . . But wait. Why were you bleeding?"

"Because I also lost two teeth and put a nice gash in my cheek."

"Wow. You *are* a mess . . . You know, if you decide to go for a nose job, I know the showrunner on *Nip/Tuck*."

Tough audience. Not even a smile. You'd think he'd appreciate the no cover charge.

"Good to know," he finally said. "Must be great to be a comic. Everything is funny."

"I'm sorry. I know this has to really suck to be—"

"Spare me. I've had enough of people's sympathy to last three lifetimes."

"I'm just trying to be nice." I sighed. "It's not like I bought stock in Hallmark . . . Anyway, my dad is a dentist if you need someone to—"

"I'm covered on that front, thanks."

"Great! Here's your stuff. I did the best I could finding everything . . . Rookie picked at dinner but ate the treats. He peed, he pooped, he sends his best . . ."

"Thanks . . . Look, I'm sorry. You've been terrific . . ."

"Nope. No apologies necessary. The whole situation blows."

"You have no idea."

"Actually I do. I was talking about me."

Was that a chuckle?

"Well you may be having a bad day, but I raise you," he said. "I've had a bad year."

"Never bet a gambler's ex-wife." I sighed. "We're used to high stakes."

"Sorry. I didn't know."

"I'll fill you in." I threw down his bag and pulled the guest chair closer to the bed. How great was this? A captive audience who wasn't drunk or screaming for a stripper.

"Can you tap a kidney for us, Mr. Danziger?" A male nurse brushed past me, pulled the blue curtain around us, then reached for a bedpan. "Oh hello. You must be his wife."

"His wife?"

He propped the pan, picked up Ken's gown and exposed him.

"What are you doing?" Ken covered up.

"Oh my God." I jumped so fast the chair screeched across the linoleum. "I'm sorry." I turned around. "I swear I didn't see a thing." *I saw everything!*

"Newlyweds?" The nurse adjusted his ponytail while waiting for Ken to pee.

"Blind date." He glared.

"Yeah," I said. "So could we please have more than five seconds' notice for an enema?"

Finally a laugh. I couldn't believe this is what Ken found funny.

"Sorry, miss. The file said his wife accompanied him in the ambulance. I just thought . . ."

Oh. The ride with the paramedic. Who knew my lies would travel to the nurses' station?

"Good story to tell my wife." The nurse opened the curtain and carried the pan to the bathroom. "She loves the ones where I screw up."

You mean she's not sick of them yet? "I'm sorry," I said to Ken.

"Forget it. When hospitals tell you not to bring valuables, that includes your dignity."

"Good point." I sighed. "Anyway, care to tell me how this whole thing happened?"

"Not really." He maneuvered in bed. "The whole thing was so stupid. I couldn't remember where I left my cell phone, so I was calling it from the cordless phone. But just when I heard it ringing on the terrace, you rang the bell. I buzzed you in, ran to the terrace, and I guess tripped on the table leg, crashed into the chair, hit the pavement and blacked out."

"At least it wasn't a wrong number."

"No kidding." His room phone rang. "Hello? Hi Mom . . . Yes, I'm fine . . . They're just keeping me overnight for observation . . . Yes, I have someone to help me get home . . . no, not her . . . no, not her . . . it's someone you don't know . . . it's not even someone I know . . . Yes, she'll take care of Rookie . . .

Mom . . . Mom . . . The doctor just walked in. Can I call you back?"

"Do you always lie to your mother?"

"Trust me, if I told her I was back on crutches, my face had to be stitched, and I was shopping for new teeth, she'd jump on the next plane from Florida and I'd never get rid of her."

"Gotcha . . ."

"Besides, my dad isn't doing that great right now. He needs her more than I do."

"I hear ya." But Ken's words hit me hard. What if my dad got sick and my mom wouldn't help him because she was too busy running around Phoenix in search of her long-lost fiancé?

"So wait." I shuddered. "Tomorrow you want me to go back to your place, walk Rookie, come get you, then take you home?"

"No, to a funeral. Which reminds me. I need a suit and tie when you pick me up."

"I'm sorry. I know I'm tired, but did I recently go to work for you?"

"You're right. I should have asked you first."

"Or maybe someone you know for more than an hour."

"Well, I figured anyone who's seen my penis knows me well enough."

"Does that include Nurse Rambo?"

"Hell no. He scares me. He reminds me of Bo Bice."

"You watch *American Idol*?" I squealed.

"Sadly, I not only watch it, I work my whole Tuesday and Wednesday nights around it."

"Aren't you so sick of Paula?" I imitated her penguin clap. "And Randy with his 'Yo Dog, you're in the dogpound man' . . . They could all use some new material."

"Agreed . . . Okay now that we've bonded, can you help me out tomorrow?"

"Are you sure they're going to discharge you?"

"Believe me, my insurance company wants me out of here."

"Right . . . Anyway, not that it really matters, but who died?"

"My boss at Showtime . . . A great lady . . . Breast cancer . . . Left a husband and two little kids . . . but she'd been sick for a long time . . . at least now she's out of pain."

The way he spoke of death as being the better of the two evils saddened me. What if my mother's breast cancer ended the same way? Now, the idea of going to a funeral in connection with a disease that was possibly eating away at her was freaky. But how could I say no?

"One problem." I cleared my throat, "We're doing 'round-the-clock coverage on the pope's funeral, so I really have to be at the studio, like, all the time. Could you maybe ask Seth? Or a friend?"

"To be honest, I'm tapped out on eager beavers," he said. "I don't know how much of the story Madeline told you, but I've been out of commission for so long, Rookie brings *me* treats."

"Okay, that's it. I'll ask for time off. What time is the funeral?"

"No, don't worry about it. I'll figure something out."

"It's okay. I'd like to help. So far we've done ambulances and hospitals. Tomorrow is a funeral. Maybe next we can attend a cremation."

"Hey fella!" The man in the other bed laughed. "Your girl is pretty funny. If you don't keep her around, maybe I will."

"Thankyouverymuch." I bowed. "I'll be here all week . . . What's your name?"

"Eddie Fisher. Like the singer . . . You know, you remind me of my wife. She was funny like you." He pointed upward. "God gave us forty-seven beautiful years . . . Veronica could drive me nuts, but she always made me laugh . . ."

"Then you were a very lucky man, Eddie." I sighed. "Give

me a minute and you can tell me all about her . . . So wait. Where's the funeral?"

"Not sure yet . . . Oh. And don't forget. Won't Brie and Triscuit need a sitter?"

"You mean Breanna and Tristan." I laughed. "They're babies, not appetizers."

"Exactly. Kids' names should not sound like cheese and crackers."

"Oh, but it's okay to be called the Three Stooges?"

The color drained from his face. "I'm going to kill my brother."

"Nah. Save the jailtime for something good. He didn't tell me. I already knew."

"Yeah right."

"I swear." I reached into my bag for the photo of the three boys. "Because I took this."

"Of all the things you could have ripped off from my apartment, that's what you picked?"

"I don't mean I stole it. I mean I'm the one who took the picture."

"What?" He studied me. "Who are you?"

"You go first." I placed the picture on his lap. "Which one are you?"

He didn't have to look. "I'm in the middle."

"Oh my God," I screamed. "It is you. I don't believe this."

"What's going on?" His eyes teared. "Have we met?"

"Not officially."

"Then how . . . when . . . ?"

"I took this my first semester at school . . . We are . . . Penn State!" I cheered. "I was living in Bigler, and one Saturday, I think it was the weekend before winter break, I was about to leave when one of you threw a camera at me and said, "Hey chickie. Take our picture." So I did, and then I asked your names and somebody said Larry, Mo, and Curly."

"God. I'll never forget that day." Ken looked down. "Were you Robyn Fortune then?"

"Robyn Holtz."

He studied my face. "The name sounds so familiar. Had we ever talked?"

"No, but I was dying to because I had this major crush on you. Unfortunately, back then, so did everyone else."

"Yeah. Those were the days."

"I didn't mean it that way."

"Sure you did. But it's okay. I don't even recognize myself anymore."

"Sorry, but if I can't pity you, you can't either . . . Anyway, I used to spend every day in the Commons waiting for you to show up to eat. But after I took the picture, it was like you vanished."

Ken looked out the window.

"And since I didn't know your name, I couldn't just go up to people and say, 'Have you seen that tall guy with the brown curly hair who used to sit over there and eat nothing but Froot Loops and bananas?"

Ken smiled.

"But that was you? Froot Loop guy?"

He nodded.

"This is unbelievable . . . I always wondered what happened to you."

"Long story," he mumbled. "And I'm pretty wiped out now . . . I'd like to get some rest."

"Sure." *What did I say?* "I should be getting home anyway . . . Way past my bedtime. Oh. Speaking of that. I couldn't find any pajamas so I threw in a pair of sweats and a T-shirt, and I put your cell in the outside pocket . . ."

"Thanks," he said. "You're terrific."

"I know."

"Wait. Do me one last favor? The way they bandaged my face, I can't wear my glasses. Can you check my phone for messages?"

"Sure." I rummaged through his bag. "Okay, yours is nothing like mine. Gimme a sec to figure it out . . . Is this a TV too . . . Wow. Mr. Sharper Image over here. I'm happy if my text messages come through . . . hmmm. This is strange."

"What?"

"It doesn't look like there are any voice mails, but there was one missed call at four-twenty, which was about the time I got to your apartment. Thing is, there's no phone number. It's just three digits . . . must be an area code. Where is 827?"

"I don't know. Let me see."

Ken squinted, but couldn't make anything out.

"It's weird." I said. "Even on mine, which is like a hundred years old, it shows you the whole phone number."

"Oh Christ." He lay back.

"What?"

"He is unbelievable."

"Who?"

"Mo."

"Yeah. How did he leave just an area code?"

"It's not an area code. It's his birthday."

"You can do that?"

"You can if you're dead."

"What?" I got a chill.

"He did this once before . . . totally freaked me out."

What was Ken talking about? Who was dead? Oh wait. Madeline said that his best friend died in the World Trade Center. How devastating to be part of a trio and suddenly be one down.

"Check your cell phone," Ken said.

"What?"

"Check your cell phone. I want to see if he left you the same message."

"Are you kidding me?"

"Just do it. Please?"

I was in such a state, I tripped trying to grab my bag, and landed ass first. By the way Ken stared, it was like he was thinking, Oh great, she's as bad as me, which made me sweat more.

"You okay?" he asked.

"Still good. Still good." I dusted myself off and searched for my phone. "Floor was slippery." I coughed.

"Exactly."

I opened my flip phone and did a double take. "What is 1–2–2–2?"

"Son of a bitch . . . I don't know how he does it, but it's definitely from him."

"Are you kidding me?" I got a chill. "I can't even get service in my apartment. Now I'm getting calls from heaven?"

"It's the day he died," he choked. "December twenty-second."

"No, the World Trade Center was on nine eleven."

"Not the day Larry died. Mo. The day Mo died."

"Oh my God." I started to weep. "They're both . . . ?"

Ken looked at me, one eye bandaged, the other wet with tears. I wanted to wrap my arms around him and tell him how sorry I was, but he had been ever so clear about his feelings about pity. And yet, what could be worse than to be this young and the last man standing?

"I don't know what to say." I sighed.

"I do," Eddie Fisher called out. "It means I need one of them cellular phones. My kids are always telling me, Dad you gotta get one, but I said what for? Who's gonna call me? The bill collectors? But maybe it's a way my Veronica can reach me . . ."

Ken and I looked at each other. Who here had a decent explanation? Even a wild-ass guess.

"I frankly don't know what to say, either." Ken squeezed my hand. "But obviously there is plenty to think about." He smiled.

Chapter 12

I NEVER UNDERSTOOD the concept of paying to have the crap scared out of you at the movies. Frankly, life was surreal enough. And yet, somehow, without my expressed, written consent, I had inadvertently walked onto the set of a Fellini film, where confusing and improbable scenes were being shot in real time, with me playing the lead role. Please. Somebody yell, "Cut."

Think I'm being a drama queen? Not after the day I had. And it wasn't over. In the cab on the way home from the hospital, Phillip called for a Mom update, and when I said, once again that day, that I had no idea where she was, he went nuts. "Then get her a goddamn cell phone already!"

"I don't want to get her a goddamn cell phone. I want her to go home so she can't read my mail and listen to my messages and hock me every morning about brushing my gums and taking my vitamins and ask me ten times a day where I'm going and when I'm coming home and who I'm going out with and is he from a good family and what do his parents do . . . I'm not kidding. By next week I'll be up on murder one."

"Then I promise to represent you."

"You're a bankruptcy lawyer!"

"Exactly. You need to protect your assets during your incarceration."

"I *have* no assets."

"Even better. Then you won't interfere with my paying clients."

"I know where you live, Phillip. Be afraid. Be very afraid."

"I'm sorry, but I'm under a lot of stress right now."

"Oh that's right. You work for a living, unlike me who raises sheep and lives off the land."

"You're just pissed that I didn't tell you about the cancer."

"Damn right. That was unforgivable."

"Tough. I still think we did the right thing. Anyway, what did she say when you told her?"

"That she's fine and to leave her the hell alone."

"Yeah right. Like she'd ever let us ignore her. That would be a story for *Daybreak*."

"Actually, the late-breaking story is she wants to fly to Phoenix."

"For what? She hates the heat."

"Oh right. I didn't get to tell you her other big secret."

"Save it for later. I have to go get Max at hockey practice and pick up dinner."

"Okay, but don't say I didn't try to tell you about Marvin Teitlebaum."

"Who?"

"The man Mom was engaged to until he got cold feet and married some Asian girl. Now she wants to hunt him down in Phoenix and ask him if had any regrets."

"You're making that up."

"Yes, because that's what I do in my spare time. I dream up stories to try to fool you."

"Wait . . . What did you say the guy's name was?"

"Marvin Teitlebaum."

"Really? That's strange. A few weeks ago I did a favor for a new client, Alan Teitlebaum. He asked me to set up the estate plan for his father in Phoenix . . . and I think his name was Marvin."

"Interesting . . . By any chance was Alan half Asian?"

"No, but come to think of it, I met his sister. She came up to the office to sign some papers, and she was one of those. Korean, Filipino. I don't know. Something."

"Wow. Hard to believe you're not a UN ambassador."

"Funny . . . You think it's the same guy? Wait. Maybe his name was Alan Teitleberg . . ."

"Tell you what, chief. How about I get right on it and do a thorough investigation?"

"Fuck you."

"I'm telling Mom you cursed."

Two minutes later, the gypsy mother herself checked in. Seems she hadn't enjoyed her day with Aileen because breast reduction and tummy tuck aside, the woman hadn't changed a bit from her self-absorbed days when she drove to the annual block party, just to show off her new car.

And what good was it having money to eat in nice restaurants if your idea of a decent meal was one of those *ferkakteh* "shooshi" places where they served nothing but squid and seaweed (and no cake and coffee)! Oh, and would I mind if Sierrapaigemather stayed at our apartment tonight because the poor kid would rather sleep on the floor than go home.

Did she just say OUR apartment? No, she couldn't bring her home. It wasn't Noah's Ark, where runaways lined up two by two. "By the way, whose phone are you using?"

"Hers. We're in a cab on the way back to Brooklyn."

Then while I was on the phone, Ken left a voice mail. I seemed like a very nice person, but he hoped he hadn't given me the wrong impression when he held my hand. Obviously his life was too crazy to get involved right now. As for the funeral, it was at Riverside Memorial at two and could I please look for the navy suit that just came back from the cleaner's and pick out a shirt and tie I thought looked good with it? "And don't forget dress shoes, even though I can only wear one."

Was it too soon to ask for a raise?

I swear I was home maybe five minutes when my work cell and my beeper went off at the same time. My cue to hightail it back to the studio. So like a firefighter who had been trained to slide down the pole, I headed out the door after stuffing a bag with clean clothes, two apples, and a bag of Fritos. What I wouldn't have given for some delicious "shooshi."

"Yo yo homie Joe." My mother laughed as she and Sierra got out of a taxi. "Now where are you going?

"Hold the cab." I flew down the stoop. "I have to go back to the studio. Gretchen's nose must be shiny. Did you just say yo yo homie Joe?"

"Isn't that the cutest expression? It means . . ."

"I know what it means . . . See you guys later. Don't touch my ice cream."

"You want to go back with her?" my mom asked Sierra.

"What the fuck?" She shrugged.

"No. Uh uh." I slipped past them into the cab. "We'll manage without you . . . The Century Building in Columbus Circle."

"How kin I go nowhere, ma'am?" The driver sobbed. "I sad for the pope. He with God now . . . I go to my church for Mass . . ."

"My condolences, sir . . . Really. He was the best pope ever . . . But could you maybe drop me off first?"

"Why can't we go with you?" my mother whined. "I bet they could use some extra help."

"Would you stop? I have to get to work. Gretchen will literally go on the air the second I finish her makeup."

"Iz she thi news lady?" The driver blinked. "Que lindo!"

"Yes. Yes. That's her. Do you like her?"

"Si. My daughter. She watch her every morning. She going to be big TV star one day, too."

Lucky for me, Gretchen called. Yes, I was on my way as soon as I could convince the cabbie to take me back to midtown . . . Unless, wait a minute, would she be willing to march in the Puerto Rican day parade as a favor to my friend, Juan Carlos?

"Hell no," she yelled.

"She'd love to," I told him.

"Okay." He clapped. "We go."

"We go too." My mother and Sierra pushed their way into the cab.

"Oh my God." I shoved over. "Why are you doing this to me?"

"You'll see." She slammed the door. "You'll be glad we're there."

"Plus, it's a free country," Sierra said. "We can go whereever we want. Right, Sheil?"

I really need to find out the penalty for murder in New York. I ate my apple.

"Don't eat with your eyes closed," my mother said. "You could choke."

"That's the idea."

"What's gotten into you, Toots?" she asked, as if I'd come home from school with a puss.

"Nothing. I'm great. Couldn't be better . . . did you two spend the whole day together?"

"Yes, and Sierrapaigemather couldn't believe how awful Aileen behaved. Ordering this one around and that one around. P.S. She gained all her weight back. What did you call her, dear?"

"A fugly crap weasel." She burped.

"All these new words I never knew . . . it's marvelous."

"Maybe you'd like to hear some of my favorites . . . Did you call Daddy today?"

"Why should I?"

"Don't you want to know if he's eating? If he's taking his blood pressure medication?"

"If he's hungry, he'll eat. If he doesn't want to get sick, he'll take his pills . . . What about you? Did you speak to that poor fellow who needs a laugh?"

"Actually, we met."

"And?"

"And there were all these odd coincidences. Like he started out Penn State and maybe went to Lohikan . . . and Rachel met him once before . . . but I don't know. He wasn't very nice."

"But you'll see him again because maybe he's one of those who needs time to warm up?"

"I just said I didn't like him. But yes, I'm seeing him tomorrow. We're going to a funeral."

"A funeral? What kind of date is that?"

"It's not a date. I'm doing him a favor."

"I never go to funerals," Sierra blurted. "They're a total crock."

"You're kidding," I replied. "What if there's a death in the family?"

"It's not like the dead guy takes attendance."

"Exactly. A funeral is to comfort the living, not the dead."

"I'm sure Sierrapaigemather has her reasons," my mother chimed in.

"Like she does for making people call her Sierrapaige-mather? What is the deal with that?"

"I think it's because her dad and grandmother died when she was so young," my mother whispered. "Now every time you say her name, you honor their memories."

"Mom," I whispered back. "She's not in the next room. She can hear you."

But from the way Sierra peered out the window without uttering a nasty retort, perhaps Detective Mom had found the key that unlocked this girl's troubled psyche. The what-the-fuck bravado was simply the deadbolt she'd installed as a kid to prevent any more sorrow and disappointment from breaking and entering her heart.

And if it was also true that she insisted on being called Sierra-paigemather as a way to keep alive the memories of two loved ones, I had to admit it was one of the sweetest things ever.

As the cab whizzed past street lights dotting the night sky, I studied my own pained reflection in the window and wondered how so much unhappiness and misfortune could inhabit my tiny world. Could I name even one person who thought life was good?

Within the confines of this car alone sat four burdened souls. A grieving man who feared for his future without the spiritual guidance of Pope John Paul II. A resentful wife who questioned why it was incumbent upon her to make a marriage work if her partner lacked interest. A young woman who came from wealth but was emotionally impoverished. And me, a thirty-three-year-old divorcee whose view of love had been tainted by high levels of broken promises.

And what of the men I knew? My father could look at a globe and point to the tiniest country in the Western Hemisphere. But when it came to finding his way back to his wife's heart, he was hopelessly lost.

David was squandering his life in a men's penitentiary, unable to see the irony of devoting his day to hacking the prison's computer system so he could still gamble on line.

My brother was also imprisoned, but at the hands of his ungrateful, they-have-more-than-us family. Every year he worked his ass off to provide for them, yet lived in fear that should he for any reason step down, Patti would take the kids and dump him for the first runner-up.

And now there was Ken, Mr. I-Once-Had-It-All. A cynical, sad man who had essentially admitted that after investing heavily in relationships, he had given up believing in the return of a bull market. Love was a cursed commodity.

My WFs were faring no better. In spite of her frequent consults with psychics, Rachel was so exhausted from juggling between the single mommy trap and the lawyer-partner trap, even she had lost hope that her load would ever lighten.

Julia had all the trappings of happiness; beauty, wealth, and fame, but gave about as much thought to her relationships as she did the purchase of a new pair of boots. She chose what looked good, but if they made her miserable after one wearing, off they went to the donate pile.

And finally, there was Gretchen, the grande dame of misery. No matter that she earned the gross national product of a small country. A happy girl did not have to befriend the twins Zoloft and Zinfandel, or prey on married men to assuage her fear that with the crops of young, beautiful TV journalists being delivered fresh to the networks each year, her sell-by date had expired.

So in spite of health, wealth, and the chance to live better than ninety-nine percent of the world, the people in my immediate circle were miserable. And from the likes of the tragic stories we broadcast every day, we were hardly alone. Most everyone, it seemed, felt not only deprived in some way, but incredibly gypped about something.

We expected a perfect marriage. A bigger paycheck. A better body. A newer car. A nicer home. A second home. The smartest kids. The right college. Championship teams. Prosperity. And anything they sold at Best Buy.

Where was I going with this? Oh yes. Maybe the problem

wasn't so much that we had such high expectations, because we were born hardwired to dream. It was that we all felt entitled to whatever was on our wish list.

Unfortunately, when we put up our lives as collateral for happiness, there was often a small hitch. The harder we pushed, the farther we got from the finish line.

I would love to tell you that these were my insights, except that they belonged to a priest and a rabbi who recently appeared on the show to discuss the universal teachings of the pope. Although up until now, I had given no more thought to their words than I had the next guest, who was a leading expert in the fight against unscrupulous car dealers.

But taking stock of my struggles, and that of everyone around me, it hit me hard. True happiness would not come from praying for that which had eluded us, but being thankful for that which was already in our midst.

I had family, friends, good health, talent, a job, a nice place to live, food to eat and nobody trying to kill me because Jon Stewart was my idol. I think they called this belief system Zen Judaism. Think of misfortune as a blessing. Or else what would you talk about?

"Oh. By the way." My mother nudged me. "I've decided to fly to Phoenix on Friday. All you gotta do is show me how to get one of those cheapy air fares from the computer."

"No," I said.

"Can I go with you?" Sierra asked.

"Sure," my mom said. "Do you know how to do that Internet business?"

"Duh." She yawned.

"You are not going to Phoenix," I said. "Either of you."

"You're not the boss of me." Sierra glared.

"Actually, I am . . . That's why tomorrow after the show, I want you to go over to Chanel and invest in the best set of brushes Simon can buy. Then get yourself some nice black pants and tops, maybe a good pair of shoes because you'll be on your feet a lot, then show up at five A.M. every day ready to learn whatever I can teach you."

"Maybe after I come back from Phoenix."

"You tell her." My mother patted her hand. "And just so you know, you're not the boss of me either."

"I am as long as you live under my roof. You want to go to Phoenix on some wild-goose chase, then first you have to talk to Daddy and explain yourself . . . believe me, I've just figured out the key to happiness and I'm doing this for your own good . . . Hello?" I picked up my cell. "No, I haven't heard from Kevin. He's your . . . coanchor . . . Well, have Simon call his house and his cell. Maybe try his driver . . . Gretchen, I'm sure he's on the way in . . . What do you mean he left a note?"

Chapter 13

I'M JEWISH, but what little I'd retained about my heritage from my years attending Hebrew school could fit on a Post-it note. And ever since my parents stopped going to their temple because they didn't care for the new rabbi, it was as if I too had become an occasional Jew.

I still lit the menorah on Hanukkah, attended Passover Seders, and fasted on Yom Kippur. But put to the test, could I actually explain the significance of these holidays? Frankly, it all boiled down to this: They tried to kill us. We won. Let's eat.

And yet, I had always appreciated the Jewish laws pertaining to death, for our rituals are not only humane but smart. We quickly bury our dead in a simple pine box. We gather at the mourner's home for a week to share their grief. And together we recite the kaddish, the beautiful mourner's prayer that reminds the living to live, and not to die with the loved one who was buried.

And though it normally made no sense to compare religious practices with work rituals, I did notice a similarity when crisis struck. Petty tiffs were put on hold. Union nitpickers stopped threatening to report minor infractions. Producers, writers, and crew, fueled by adrenaline, worked without a break. And somehow the anchors maintained their buoyancy, managing not only to look good but to sound good, even when there was little new to say.

But never had I experienced the flawless synchronization of religion and reporting as when the pope died, and these two monoliths, the Vatican and the press, did what they did best. Carry on with tradition. In fact, there was so much beauty in the pageantry and prayers, the profound loss was felt by people of all faiths.

That's why I was never more proud to be a part of this news team, though my efforts had no bearing on the success of the broadcasts. In fact, my even being there went largely unnoticed, except, interestingly enough, by Gretchen.

Each time I powdered her face, she would clasp my hand and thank me for being there. I suspected, however, that her gratitude had more to do with the fact that I had opted not to humiliate her when I found her naked and on all fours yelling, "Giddyup little doggy."

But mostly she was clinging to me because she was in shock, as was the entire network, that Kevin O'Shea was missing in action.

Not that there wasn't a bullpen full of weekend anchors available to fill the void. Yet none who could erase his boyish glee, like that of a young pitcher who was getting his first shot in the big leagues, and it was in the ninth inning of the last game of the World Series.

Unfortunately, their overanxious zeal was unbefitting this somber time, leaving Simon in the untenable position of having to walk to the mound to calm the rookie relievers while simultaneously screaming at producers to go find his fucking ace.

Rumors were thrown like curveballs. He was headed to Vatican City. He was passed out at a bar. And my favorite, he was getting hair extensions and couldn't leave until the glue dried.

Meanwhile, Simon instructed Gretchen to tell viewers that Kevin was en route to Rome, which prompted calls from his counterparts at *Today* and *Good Morning America*. "Rome my ass!" they teased. "You've got three guys on assignment there now. Where is he really?"

With suspicions up, Simon had to inform Kevin's wife, Anne, who was generally clueless. Sure enough, she suggested that Simon call the gym. Sometimes he lost track of time in the sauna.

What neither Simon nor Anne knew, nor I until that day, was that there was no gym. Only a hotel down on Thirty-fourth and Lex where he and Gretchen apparently "worked out."

Gretchen, mindful that her mic was hot, scribbled a message during a commercial break:

AFFINA DUMONT HOTEL. ASK FOR ANTONIO. ROOM UNDER DR. GLEN SMITH.

I covered her mic and whispered. "What did his note say?"

HE'S FREAKED OUT THAT YOU KNOW.

"Fortune! Off the set. We're trying to check Gretchen's lighting and you're blocking her."

"Go." She pushed me.

"Why me?"

She answered with her eyes. How can I leave in the middle of the year's biggest story to hunt down a man I supposedly despise?

I was dazed, starved, exhausted, and desperate for my alarm

to ring so the nightmare would be over. But when I turned around, it was just beginning. My mother was flirting with a cameraman, while a now braless Sierra sat on a stage manager's lap. Where were the cute little summer interns when you needed them most?

"Getting some fresh air." I waved good-bye. *And never coming back.*

If anyone had a reason to run away, it was me. But just as Gretchen suspected, Kevin had beat me to it, holing up at their hideaway hotel. According to Antonio, the coconspirator, housekeeping had found him passed out in his room after dining on scotch and Sleep-Eze. Which explained how he missed the eleven calls to his cell.

Apparently he was showering and had assured Simon he would be at the studio in an hour. Now all Simon had to do was pray that Kevin was not only sober enough to read the teleprompter, but that Antonio didn't keep the tabloid reporters on speed dial. A "Just Asking" blurb in tomorrow's Page Six would be disastrous:

> What bickering news duo is actually engaged in a torrid affair at a midtown hotel, weekdays at three? They'll need the luck of the Irish when the little wife finds out.

When I reported in to Gretchen, I couldn't help but ask if she trusted Antonio not to alert the gossip mongers. "Damn right we trust him. The little douche bag is taking his family to Italy on what we pay him."

Then, generous soul that she was, she gave me the rest of the night off, except it was now almost eleven, and I had to be back at work by five A.M. But shlep back to Brooklyn? I couldn't bear the thought. Not when that's where my mother and Sierra were headed. "Don't worry, darling. Sierra Paige Mather doesn't mind sleeping on the couch."

She doesn't mind? I mind! I might as well spend the night in Kevin and Gretchen's already paid-for room, and hope he hadn't finished the scotch. But just as I headed back into the hotel, it hit me that I did have a place to hide. An excellent place.

"Shhh." I pet a barking Rookie as I let myself in. "Remember me? The nice girl who fed you? Let's make a deal. You don't tell Ken I was here, and I'll give you an extra green treat."

Smart doggy. He wagged in favor, which was good because I wasn't leaving. I was now only a few blocks from the studio, so I could sleep until 4:30. Heaven! A few blissful hours alone in a king-sized bed with five hundred-thread-count Egyptian cotton sheets.

I threw my bag on Ken's couch and scouted out the place for, let's see, the third time that day. And each time it was a self-tour. So why not continue the stroll and check out the fridge? God willing there was real food, and enough of it not to notice Goldilocks helped herself.

Rookie followed, barking when I opened the refrigerator door. "I'll share. I promise." He wagged his tail. "Wow! Three kinds of beer, spare ribs, is that a tomato . . . gross, an apple, no thanks, I'm stuffed from the last one. Ah! The bag of goodies Ken was carrying when I spotted him on the street . . . cheese, stuffed mushrooms, prosciutto . . . Yum! And since it was intended for me in the first place, how could he mind?"

I was breaking into the Gouda when I saw his answering machine blinking. "Should we see who it is?" I asked an even happier Rookie, who was gnawing at a spare rib. "He'll never know."

"Ken? Hi. I don't know if you'll remember me. We were on a panel discussion together a few years back . . . This is Rachel Waldman . . ."

Rachel Waldman? My Rachel Waldman?

"It's the funniest thing. I just heard through the grapevine that you're single again, and amazingly enough, haha, so am I . . . I was wondering . . . would you like to meet for drinks? Talk old times? We were quite a team on Torts-R-Us. Haha."

"That bitch!" I grabbed a spare rib for myself. "Can you believe her?" I asked Rookie.

I played the message again to make sure I'd heard right, and she sounded like an even bigger backstabber the second time. But now what? Call her back and tell her friends didn't let other friends call drunk?

"It's like being sixteen again," I said to Rookie as I crawled into Ken's bed. "You'd like a guy, then your friend decides she likes him too, and makes her move. Jeez! Grow up already."

A confused Rookie stared up at me and barked.

"Come here boy." I patted the bed. "It's you and me against the world."

Then I realized he wasn't waiting for an engraved invitation. He was too small to jump. I picked him up and watched him circle the bed, sniff for the best spot, lick himself, lay his head on my feet, and, I swear, sneeze like my grandfather.

"Are we happy now? Damn. You don't suppose Ken keeps makeup remover around . . . Didn't think so. Okay. Night, Rookie. Sweet dreams."

I'm not sure what woke me. The erotic dream or the sound of the phone ringing. But the dream might explain why I was in a sweat. Damn whoever was calling for interrupting the best sex I'd had in . . . ever.

I lay there trying to figure out who had been on top of me. I'd e-mailed Derek Jeter, but he'd yet to reply. All I knew was that this guy smelled of cognac and cologne, had swimmer abs and these dazzling, rum-colored eyes.

Rookie barked and I looked at the clock. Twelve goddamn thirty. Who would call now?

I walked into the kitchen as a woman was taping a message. It was probably his ex-wife. They were notorious for calling at all hours. But no, Nina's voice wouldn't sound this familiar.

"Anyway, sorry to be calling so late, sweetie. I'm still on the coast . . . Call me back . . . It's very important that we talk . . ."

Oh my God. It was Mira Darryl. And though I met celebrities all the time, it was still a thrill. "Hello?" I picked up.

"Who is this?" she asked.

"Who is this?" I replied.

"I asked you first."

"It's . . . Sierra."

"Sierra Paige Mather?"

Oh my God! You know her? "Who?" I shivered.

"A friend of mine from LA . . . Her daughter's name is . . . oh never mind."

"Can I help you?"

"Yes. Is Ken there?"

"Um . . . he's asleep." *Not lying yet . . .* "He had a rough day." *Also true.*

"Well, this is quite important. Can you tell him that Mira is on the phone?"

"How about I take a message?"

"Do you know who I am?"

"Someone named Mira who is a little pushy?"

"This is Mira Darryl."

"Wait. Let me get a pen . . . How do you spell that?" *Couldn't deny it. Having fun.*

"You don't recognize my name?"

"Uh, no. Sorry. Are you the lady who comes to clean on Fridays?"

"Jesus Christ. Is he dating twelve-year-olds now . . . Look . . . This matter cannot wait, and since he's not answering his cell . . ."

"Okay. Okay . . . Rookie, go get Daddy . . . Tell him he's got a phone call . . . Thatta boy."

"Hi Rookie," she oozed. "It's Mira? Remember me?"

"What's wrong?" Pause. "He won't wake up? I guess the sleeping pills knocked him out."

"Fine!" She snorted. "I'll leave a message. Do you think you can get it right?"

"Not usually." *This call may be monitored for quality assurance.*

"Tell Ken that Kyle has asked me to marry him and . . . I don't know how to answer."

"Ken. Kyle. Maybe it's time to start with the Ls?"

"What?"

"Nothing . . . Okay. I've got it . . . Kyle wants to marry you . . . what should you do?" *Hello, Page Six. How much do you pay for exclusives?*

"Good. Now continue . . . Kyle is wonderful, but so are you, and I know I told you that we were through, but I think about you a lot . . . I worry about you . . . I'm so confused and you understand me so well . . ."

"Whoa, slow down. I graduated from Penn State, not Katharine Gibbs . . . Okay, let's see . . . He's really wonderful . . . but so are you . . ."

"Oh fuck! Just tell him to call me first thing in the morning. I don't care how early."

"Good-bye?" I said to a dial tone. "She is not a nice lady." I turned to Rookie.

He barked in agreement. Good doggy.

Now I was torn between not wanting to waste another precious minute of sleep and wanting to return to our regularly scheduled fantasy, in which I was being made love to by a man who was getting me so hot, I would never change the channel.

Unfortunately, too much time had elapsed and the images were mere fragments. But I didn't need Freud for the analysis. Yesterday I'd had two accidental penis sightings, Kevin's and Ken's. I was sleeping on pillows with traces of a wooded scent, and feeling pent-up demand for the mornings I would arouse David, then playfully climb aboard for a steamy wake-up call.

If only I could replay this dream on demand, like an HBO movie. And not have to focus on the clock's loud ticking, Rookie's scratching, and my own self-loathing.

How could I have interfered in Ken's personal life when I didn't know or even like him? It was his business if he wanted to go out with a two-faced lawyer who would urge her best friend to hook up with him and then go behind her back to do the same. Ditto for getting back with a fickle Hollywood star who would drop him again as soon as the wind blew east.

So why was I feeling possessive, like a dog marking his territory? Maybe other women chasing him upped his value, though that wasn't what normally inspired me . . . It had to be something else that was drawing me to Ken. His testy bedside manner? His presumptuous demands? His extreme negativity?

Of course! I was destined to cure the emotionally disabled, one sorry dude at a time . . . provided they were irresistibly sexy and had a goose down comforter with sumptuous sheets . . . But who was I kidding? I was so conflicted about my feelings. Time for the old list of pros and cons. Luckily, Ken kept paper and pen at his bedside.

Pro: (1) We have a history even if we don't know what it is. (2) He is sooooo hot oh my God what a body I love his hands. (3) Smart, successful, not in bankruptcy. (4) Weird sense of humor but at least he has one. (5) Contacted by his dead friend to pay attention to him.

Con: (1) He needs Rookie's distemper shots. (2) Not his type/only stunning girls need apply.

Pro: What if it's fate we met now?

Fate? Really?

I erased Rachel's phone message and decided to mention nothing to Ken about Mira Darryl's call. It was the least I could do to honor the memory of his beloved friends Mo and Larry.

Chapter 14

TURNS OUT I couldn't live with myself unless I confessed my crimes.

"I slept in your bed, I ate your food, I erased a phone message, and I pretended to be your girlfriend."

"Yesterday you were my wife." Ken took the clothes I'd brought him."Do you ever just pose as yourself?"

"Only on payday . . . Did you hear what I just said?"

"Yeah. It's fine. Whatever. I need help getting dressed."

"Me?"

"Yes. You try balancing on one foot. Besides, the nurses all think you're my wife."

"Right . . . but they do plan on giving you crutches?"

"No, roller skates. Yes I'm getting crutches." He looked at the time. "We're late. I thought you'd be here sooner."

"Oh my God. I have a job, remember? And maybe you didn't hear, but it's Pope week at the networks. I'm lucky my boss gave me any time off."

"Sorry. You're right . . . Let's get moving. First stop is the john."

"Oh no. No, no, no . . . I'll get a nurse."

"Why? So we can take a vote? I just have to pee. And it's not like you haven't seen my—"

"Why are you being so mean?"

"I'm not. This is my normal, pleasant self . . . Here. Grab my waist and I'll hop."

"Where's Eddie Fisher?" We slowly maneuvered to the bathroom.

"In surgery. A hip replacement I think. Nice guy, but too much of a talker . . . you shouldn't have encouraged him."

"I swear I'm going to drop you right on your head."

"No don't." He laughed. "I'll be nice."

"Is that possible?" I flipped on the bathroom light. "Oooh. Gross. Don't they ever clean these? This is a job for Mira Darryl."

"What?" Ken stopped so we were wedged in the doorway face to face.

"Nothing," I gulped. "Why don't you hold on to that rail and I'll turn around and . . ."

He didn't budge. "What did you mean by what you just said?"

"Okay. See. That's what I was trying to tell you before. I was too tired to go home last night so I stayed at your place." *You are very cute.* "And your friend Mira called." *It's very hard standing this close . . .* "I kind of let her think I was your girlfriend . . . and she was your cleaning lady." *Are you feeling the electricity?*

"YOU WHAT?"

Apparently not. I turned my head. "Just . . . you know. Do your thing and I'll tell you the whole story."

"Oh my God. You're a menace."

"I'm sorry. I didn't think you'd be this mad."

"Mad? Who's mad? You slept in my bed, you ate my food, you listened to my phone messages . . . You're like a stunt double for Goldilocks!"

My, what a big penis you have. Although technically, Goldilocks didn't have to confess details of her bad-girl behavior while trying to help Papa Bear into a Brooks Brothers suit.

Trust me, it was a delicate operation—dressing a naked stranger who was pissed at you. But at least I didn't have to wait long to solve the new-guy mystery. Boxers or briefs? Briefs!

And to my surprise, the more he lectured me, the more turned on I got. Yes, yes, I should have respected his privacy, I said as I pulled the curtain around us, wondering if it was against hospital policy to use their beds for nonmedical procedures. Yes, it was wrong of me to misrepresent myself, I said as I buttoned his shirt and helped him wriggle into his pants, wondering if maybe we had time for a quickie before the funeral.

Unfortunately he wasn't thinking about sex. At least with me.

"Was she in New York or California?" He tightened his belt.

"California. Definitely."

"Did she seem upset?" He held up the shirt and tie and looked stumped.

"You could say that . . . What's wrong?"

"This is one bizarre combination. I never would have picked it out."

"I'm sorry. I don't know your taste."

"But I like it." He checked out his reflection in the window. "It's sharp-looking."

"Thank you." I blushed. "I have a good eye for color . . ."

"Yeah. Too bad you're not as good at minding your own business . . ."

"I really am sorry. I guess it freaked me out that my good friend Rachel Waldman would go behind my back to try to hook up with you. Incidentally, hers is the message I erased. And then you get this call from Mira, and it's really late, and she doesn't seem to care that she might have woken you, plus you could tell she was just jerkin' your chain . . ."

"You know me for one day but you already have keen insight into my relationships?"

"Am I wrong?"

"Dead wrong."

"Really? Did you know that Kyle proposed to her?"

"What?"

"Yes. And she wants your advice on what to tell him since lately she's been worried about you and she wanted to know what you made of that . . . Excuse me, but what an asshole."

"Did she leave a number?" His breathing was uneven.

"No . . . I assumed you knew it. Are you really going to call her back?"

He grabbed my arm. "Did she say . . . do you think . . . where do I stand?"

"Well, I'm no expert. But if she didn't still care about you, why bother calling? She'd just go get married, and you'd see the photo spread of the wedding in *People* like the rest of us."

"Good point . . . Let's stop at my place so I can get her number off the caller ID."

"You don't have it?"

"Not after she dumped me. I deleted it from my cell and blocked her on line."

"Gee. That does sound like someone you should stay in touch with."

"You don't understand. If there's any chance of us getting back together, I'm going for it. Thanks Robyn." He hugged me. "You've been great."

Thanks Robyn. I like you but I'm not inspired to offer you monogamy.

* * *

I am sure Sharon Horowitz was a loving wife and mother. A devoted daughter. A cherished friend and colleague. A whip-smart attorney. But not for one second could I focus on the rabbi's eulogy, for my mind was racing like a lawyer's, trying to grapple with the facts of this case.

Fact: I couldn't sit this close to Ken, inhale his cologne, and still be able to focus on her life story. I was too engaged in a lusty daydream that was most inappropriate for a funeral.

Fact: Ken had no reason to fall for me when he was being lured by a beautiful actress.

Fact: He was self-centered, insensitive, and behaved as if he was taking emotional anaesthetics.

On the other hand: If he really was such an ogre, how come when we got to the funeral, he was swarmed by coworkers who were begging him to come back? "We miss you so much," I heard over and over. And didn't he ask this older lady about her husband's heart condition? And what about the young girl he promised to take to the ballet because he hadn't forgotten their bet?

I glanced at his chiseled jaw and rum-colored eyes for a sign that I wasn't crazy to want to hook up with him, and then felt this unexplainable rush. Ken was not only the guy I'd loved from afar in college, he was the one in my hot-hot-hot dream last night. And though the cautious fairy said, "He's nothing but trouble," the little princess in me said, "Don't care. No one's perfect . . . and have you noticed how cute he is?"

"Let's go," he whispered.

"What? Why? The funeral just started."

"I'm tired and in pain. Plus everyone saw me, I signed the guest book . . . we can go."

Bullshit, everything hurt. While I'd been thinking of nothing but him, he'd been thinking of nothing but *her*. He just wanted to leave so he could get Mira's number and make plans to see her. No wonder we'd sat in a back aisle. Damn! This getaway was premeditated.

How quickly the silent treatment becomes the third wheel in a relationship. Frankly, on the cab ride back to his place, what was there to say? His only thoughts were of the case he'd make to convince Judge Mira that he was the man for her, while I dwelled on the fact that this little twenty-four hour rendezvous had been a nice diversion, but the commercial break was over, and it was time to resume to our regularly scheduled broadcast, *The Shit Hits the Fan*.

"Want to grab some lunch?" Ken asked.

"Now? I thought you were tired and in pain."

"I am. I must have an exposed nerve where my teeth fell out, but I'm also starving."

"Oh. Sorry to hear that, but I should get back to work."

"Are you sure? It's the least I could do."

"Positive, thanks."

"I hate eating alone."

"Take Rookie. He loves ribs."

"Are you pissed at me?"

"Yes. You didn't have any makeup remover in your bathroom. I believe that's a violation of the 1994 Estée Lauder Agreement."

"This is about Mira, right?"

"Yes. Ding, ding, ding. Tell him what he's won, Johnny!"

"I wouldn't expect you to understand."

"I'll let you in on a little secret I learned from working around the rich and famous. There are two kinds of people in this world. Assholes and those who are blown away by them."

"And which one are you?"

"Depends on the day. Same as you."

"I really think she loves me. She just needed time . . ."

"She's an actor. A very good one. But see, I don't believe for a minute that Kyle proposed. In fact I bet he started shopping around and she was just trying to make him jealous."

"You think I'm that much of a schmuck?"

I shrugged.

"Fine. But what does that have to do with lunch?"

"Son. Do you hear the words coming out of my mouth?"

"Okay, but don't say I didn't try to repay you for your kindness. Especially after you accused me of needing distemper shots."

"What?" I shivered.

"At least I think it was you who left that very insightful note by my bed . . . the pros and cons of Ken? Unless, of course, Rookie's penmanship miraculously improved."

"Oh my God. I am so lame. Wait. How did *you* find it? You haven't even been home yet."

"I didn't. Madeline did. She ran over to take care of Rookie, and I guess decided to straighten up the place."

"Oh. Look, I'm really sorry."

"No need to apologize. Always good to learn where you stand two hours after you meet someone."

"I didn't mean anything by it."

"Sure you did. Every woman I know does the same thing. One little date that doesn't go badly and here comes the phone blitz. 'I met someone,'" he mimicked a high-pitched voice. "'And he's soooooo cute.'"

"Excuse me, but I wouldn't say our little date was a rousing success."

"So then why the list?"

"Because . . ."

"Exactly. Which is why you should have lunch with me . . . I can tell you how cute *you* are."

"You think I'm cute?"

"I think you're beautiful."

"Really?"

"And funny. And very good at lists. Which incidentally, for the record, I am up to date on my shots."

"Do you like sushi?" I laughed.

"Namo Gachi on Fifty-ninth?"

"L14. Triple maki combo."

Stop, stop, stop. That last part never happened. What do you think? This is a Danielle Steel novel? Ken did not tell me I was beautiful and funny. I had no idea if he ate sushi. I did know that although he needed a lunch buddy, it was a temporary fix until he could reach a woman who was capable of destroying whatever hope he had of finding love again.

Which is why I helped him up to his apartment, wished him good luck, and kissed Rookie good-bye. I was many things, but not a one-meal deal.

Luckily, it was only a short walk to the studio. But en route, I stopped to stare at a woman standing in the second-floor window of her apartment, as if I was studying a breed of orangutan. Rude as this was, I was gripped by the image, for it catapulted me back to my childhood.

Like my mother, she had smoke billowing from her nose as she stood in a mindless gaze in a pink seersucker housedress that I bet smelled of Tide and tobacco. But that's not what threw me. It was that she stood with her hand burrowed in a pocket, probably clutching a mint or a lighter.

My mother's hands were forever in pockets. Bathrobes, blazers, slacks, even bathing suit cover-ups. Where else to hide her secret stash of cigarettes, lighters, Coffee Nips, diet pills, to do lists, and occasionally a comic from the paper?

Now I knew why. She was a pathological hider. A person who claimed to be an open book, except for a few missing chapters she was loath to reveal. A previous engagement. A lifelong yearning for her first fiancé . . . Breast cancer.

Of all the shocking events of the past few days, the one that I could not reconcile was the possibility that my mother was not only dying, but in denial. Didn't she want to live to see me become a famous comedian with a hit TV series? Maybe even married with kids, a nanny, homes on both coasts, and a frequent guest of Jon Stewart. ("I tell you, I can't get enough of Robyn Fortune. Sorry, honey. She just does it for me.")

Before I reached the studio, I stopped at a card store. Not to look for some sort of sentimental mush to tell her what she meant to me, but to splurge on a coffee mug in the window that said, "Avenge Yourself. Live Long Enough to Be a Burden to Your Children."

"Thanks for coming back." Gretchen pulled me into her dressing room.

"You said I could take a few hours off to—"

"Jesus Frank Christ. Can't you tell when I'm being sincere? I know you're tired too . . . I just wanted to be the one to tell you. I'm going to Rome. You're not."

"Oh no." *YES!!!* "How come?"

"It's a budget thing. You know Simon, the cheap bastard. He said it's more efficient to use the Rome bureau's staff . . . like he gives a crap how I look on the air."

"No, I mean why are you going to Rome now? The funeral will be over."

"Exactly. Every other network will be packed and gone and *Daybreak* will still be covering the story. The search for the next pope, how parishioners are managing . . ."

"Good thinking . . . of course I'm disappointed," I pouted. "But I understand."

"Now see? I said to Kevin, Robyn will probably freak out and do her usual crying bit."

The only reason I cry is 'cause you treat me like a servant. "No, it's fine. Simon is right. It's an added expense to bring me. I'll just pack a bag of your favorite things. I'm sure they'll do a great job."

Gretchen just stared at me like I'd said no thanks to a winning lottery ticket. But what I hadn't forgotten from our last trip to Rome was that I might as well be in Rome, New York, for as much free time as I'd get to explore.

"Oh, I get it." Gretchen eyed me. "You want the few days off so you can go to Phoenix with your mother and that awful Sienna."

"Sierra . . . And no one is going to Phoenix," I insisted. "How do you know about that?"

"Because Simon is doing the happy dance that she's leaving town . . . I heard he's even paying for your mom's ticket too."

"No!"

"Yes!"

"But why does he care where Sierra is? He'll be in Rome."

"Yes, but he's coming back. If it all goes down according to plan, she's not."

Chapter 15

WHAT DID GRETCHEN MEAN, if it all went down according to plan? Had Simple Simon talked my mother into becoming a paid assassin? What a lovely exclusive that would make. *Daybreak*'s executive producer hires makeup artist's mother to kill new wife's daughter.

Damn right we would be discussing this when I got home. Except that the future convict was busy when I walked in, as she had converted my apartment into the Sheila Holtz Center for Mah-Jongg Mavens.

"Okay. Listen up, kiddies." My mother tapped a tiny baton on the card table as if she were still conducting a string quartet. "There are three suits that go from one to nine and a fourth suit called Winds. Are you listening, Sierra? . . . No, each player starts with three double stacks of four, plus one tile unless you're east, and then you get two extras."

"Oh good. You're in time." She clapped when she spotted me standing at my front door. "Grab a chair from the kitchen and join the fun."

"Who are these people?" I yelled over the familiar din of tiles clicking.

"Well, Sierrapaigemather you know of course . . . Say hello to her," she whispered as she stuck my bag in the closet. "She thinks you don't like her. And the rest of these nice folks are your neighbors . . . No Kaneesha, the bird tile is one bam . . . remember. Four suits. Dots, bams, cracks, and winds."

"I don't believe you. I haven't slept, I haven't eaten . . ."

"Go wash up and make a sandwich. You look like you could use some fun."

"I don't want to have fun." I dragged her to a quiet corner. "I want to open a bottle of wine and put a straw in it."

"What's gotten into you, Toots? You used to be a lotta laughs . . . I think maybe you've come down with a case of psy-chosclerosis."

"What?"

"Hardening of the attitudes . . . Correcto, Mrs. Schnecken-berg. If you don't like the tile thrown, then pick from the wall. Maybe you'll be lucky and get a joker."

"Mom. I'm talking to you. This was a crappy idea. Tell everyone to leave."

"But they're having such a good time. And I was trying to figure out. Which night do you think is better for a standing game? I like Mondays but if it's a three-day holiday, then—"

"Stop, stop, stop . . . Is that the weird guy from downstairs with the six cats?"

"Who? Jack Greenberg? Yeah. Nice man. Lost his wife last year. A massive stroke and boom, adios Evelyn . . . He brought up a fruit platter with kiwis. Love those . . . I'll introduce you."

"No. I'm begging you. Just move the party someplace else."

"But I bought coffee cake. Can't play mahj without it, al-though I shouldn't have bought all those low-fat ones. Is it me, or do the boxes taste better . . ."

"I don't care what you give them," I said.

Imagine walking into your home to find strangers playing a game whose main requirement was that you sat for hours while talking, snacking, and exchanging ivory tiles with their three opponents who, like you, had no life.

"You know what I think?" My mother gave me the maternal eye. "I think you're all worked up because it reminds you of when your idiot husband had his buddies over to gamble."

If not for the company of strangers, I would have strangled her. The unmitigated nerve to invade my home, insult my marriage, and once again, possibly be right.

Still, I was tempted to hurl the next grenade. If she was such an expert on marriage, why was she living with me instead of her husband, why was she plotting to find an old lover, and did she really think teaching strangers to play mah-jongg was the sign of a happy life?

Instead, I ran past her, slamming my bedroom door for good measure. Then with one hard-hitting swipe, the pile of dirty clothes on my bed fell to the floor and I collapsed. Just as one of my old *Mad* magazines mysteriously dropped from the bookshelf.

Whoa! Third time this week that that had happened. Was it a sign that I should stop slamming my door until I got new, less warped shelves? Or was there some mystical phenomenon at work?

Ever since getting those cell phone messages from the spirit world, it wasn't that much of a stretch to think I could receive other supernatural communications. Maybe I was hearing from my faithful childhood companion Alfred E. Neuman, who wanted to remind me that my being angry with my over-bearing, meddlesome, clean-obsessed mother was nothing new. Maybe he was venting his own anger with her for throwing out my cherished collection of *Mad* magazines while I was away at camp. Only to defend her indefensible act by accusing me of being a slob who should have been thrilled to have a mother willing to clean her ungrateful daughter's room so it was spotless and organized.

Thrilled? Are you kidding? I was so devastated I didn't speak to her for weeks, not even to accept her offer to renew my subscription. In fact, the only reason I forgave her was because Julia found a stack of back issues I'd lent her that she'd never gotten around to returning.

If not for those few issues being spared, I might never have talked to my mother again.

Oh fine. I was being over dramatic. Which made me laugh, for lying there reminded me of the many times my mother stood over my bed playing Vivaldi's Concerto in A minor, her surefire method for cajoling me to wash my face and make a sandwich (the cure for whatever ailed you).

Ah. Time for the old Robyn Holtz self-pity pie.

Start with one cup of resentment.
Add in heaping dose of paranoia.
Mix well with anger.
Slowly blend in fear and loathing.
Cook until the whole damn mess blows up in your face.

Actually what scared me more than feeling sorry for myself was realizing how much I was starting to sound like the people for whom I held the least respect. Those who, through their own words and actions, created chaos and dissension, then bitched that life was so hard.

My ex: Lived for illegal activities, then wondered why the cops showed up.

My dad: Ignored his wife for thirty years, then wondered why she left him.

My mom: Insisted she was always right, then wondered why her relationships went wrong.

Phillip: Overindulged his family, then wondered why they wouldn't let him rest.

Gretchen: Stepped on toes all the way up the ladder, then wondered why she was alone.

So just how many mirrors did one have to hold up in order to see one's own reflection?

Me: Married David in spite of all the trouble signs, then wondered why the marriage never had a chance.

Oh for those innocent days when Julia Volkman and I could attribute everything bad that happened to us to something we called sucky luck.

Sucky luck was when you had to walk around school all day with your jacket tied around your waist because your period surprised you. Or when you had to go to the prom with a boy six inches shorter than you because his father was your father's client.

But real sucky luck was having your locker next to Josh Vogel's for four years of high school because they were assigned alphabetically. Poor Julia could only open hers when Josh wasn't there. "No room for the three of us," she'd groan. "He's so fat, his ass is in front."

It was an unfortunate pairing, but at least Julia's sucky luck ended in high school, while mine seemed to be just warming up.

"Where are you going?" my mother asked when I flew past her without saying a word.

"For pizza."

"Get me a few pepperoni slices, wouldya?" Sierra, she of supersonic hearing when it came to free delivery, said. "Anyone else want?"

"And when I get back, everyone had better be gone."

"No," Sheila replied.

"No?"

"Who invites friends over and then tells them to leave?"

"See, and I thought, who invites strangers into a home that isn't theirs?"

I rushed down three flights of stairs, colliding with a man who was just buzzed in. "Excuse me. Sorry."

"Robyn?"

"Yes?" I turned around, steam still pouring out of my eyes.

"Hi." He hugged me. "It's me . . . Josh."

I blinked. "Josh who?"

"Vogel . . . From Hebrew school? Fair Lawn High? Go Cutters?"

"Oh my God!" Fellini films my ass. This was *Twilight Zone* right down to the Rod Serling shiver. Until twenty seconds ago, I hadn't seen or thought of this kid in decades, and now he was standing in my vestibule? It had to be the punishment for cruelty to fat boys. The six-letter word for premonition. Doomed!

"Are you okay?" He steadied me. "You look like you just saw a ghost."

"I'm sorry. This is so bizarre. Not two seconds ago I was thinking about you, and now here you are."

"I guess your mom told you I called."

"Huh?"

"She didn't tell you I called before? I was leaving a message and she picked up . . . Then she invited me over for your big mah-jongg party. How could I miss that?"

"You like mah-jongg?"

"Are you kidding? I grew up on it. My grandmother used to drag me down to her beach club every summer and make me her fourth . . . Where do you think I learned to pig out on cake?"

"And for this you shlepped all the way from Fair Lawn?"

"Actually I live a few blocks from here. Over on Garfield Street . . . I just moved back to New York."

"What happened to the rest of you?" I blurted. "Oh my God! I'm sorry. You look great."

"You too." He laughed. "I guess I shouldn't be surprised by people's reaction. I did grow six inches since high school and dropped a hundred and fourteen pounds."

"Amazing . . . And I love your glasses. You look—"

"Like someone you wouldn't want to pull a chair out from under in chem lab?"

"Hey. That wasn't me, I swear. It was Craig what's-his-name with the twitchy eye."

Josh smiled. "Yeah right."

"So wait. How did you know I lived in Brooklyn?"

"Mom talk. What else? I think they ran into each other at Shop Rite and it came out we both were in Park Slope."

I still couldn't get over the eerie fact that a name had popped into my head, and thirty seconds later I was talking to the very person, let alone that this was the same Josh Vogel who was so overweight, he needed two seats in the lunchroom.

I half listened to his tale as I sized up the new and improved packaging. He wasn't quite in the handsome, ripped, Ken Danziger category. But he was tall and husky like David, and he had that whole Clint Eastwood, I'm-not-your-victim-anymore look. The gelled hair. Sexy black glasses. The leather jacket and Rolex watch.

". . . After I graduated from Colorado State, I worked for a bunch of different guys in Silicon Valley. Then I opened my own consulting firm in Seattle. But after six years I got burned out and realized I missed my family. So this January I moved back and found a place down here."

"I don't know what to say."

"Shocking, right? That I might become a not half bad-looking, successful guy?"

"No. That you missed your family so much you came home."

"Well, it's not the whole story." He laughed. "I had a pretty bad breakup too."

"Hey. That line forms to the left . . . Care to order the team jacket?"

"Sure . . . See, I was living with this woman, Rebecca . . . I really thought she was it. Then this friend of hers from work turned her on to Orthodox Judaism, and all of a sudden I wasn't kosher enough. Which really pissed me off because I had gotten so good at davening."

"That happened to a cousin of mine," I said. "It's not a religion, it's a cult."

"Exactly. And call me a sloth, but I still like bacon cheeseburgers. And I'll drive all day Saturday to find a good one."

"Me too! By any chance do you gamble?"

"Gamble? Not really. I think it's a stupid hobby. I work too hard for my money . . ."

"Good answer! I know the place for the perfect burger. Do you want to go have dinner?"

"Sure."

"And then spend the rest of the night holding me naked in bed?"

His eyes popped.

Wait until I called Julia. She was not going to believe I not only slept with Josh Vogel but tried to have sex, and *he* turned *me* down!

What guy said he'd rather just talk? Although his brain might have been saying no, I could see beneath the Jockey boxers that his boys were pacing like prisoners, waiting to be released on their own recognizance.

Still, it was nice to be lying naked in a man's arms, talking the night away as he stroked my back. Occasionally he'd kiss my forehead, but I swear, his Orthodox ex must have brainwashed him into thinking he had to save himself for marriage.

Finally, after a night of drinking and filling each other in on the past fifteen years, up to and including these past few days, I couldn't hold out. I needed to get laid, Ken was a lost cause, and if Josh felt as sorry for me as he said, then he would do right by me.

Can you believe it? In spite of the beer buzz, he still said no. He liked me too much to do this on impulse; every time he'd given in, the girl lost interest in him; he'd had a crush on me since seventh grade and now that I had become this beautiful, funny, and interesting woman, he wasn't going to screw up a possible relationship due to quick sex.

"I don't want quick sex. I want the kind that takes a long time."

"If we do this, one of us will be sorry, and it's probably going to be me," he said.

"Who turns down a freebie? I'll do anything you ask."

"Believe me, I can think of six things I'm going to do to you when the time is right."

"Oh come on. Do them now. Please? I might get hit by the D train tomorrow and miss out . . . What's so funny?"

"Who could I call who would believe me? Robyn Holtz is begging me for sex."

"I swear I'll let you be the one to tell Julia if you just do it already." I stroked him.

"You're not playing fair."

"No, you aren't. You can't wave that thing at me at full staff and say, Sorry, it's off duty . . . Do you have condoms?"

"Somewhere."

"Somewhere? Do you even like sex?"

"I love sex. But I also love the idea that it's with the right person at the right time."

"Well could you at least do something to relieve my tension?"

"That I can help you with." He rolled me over and kissed me.

"Lower," I whispered. "The tension is much lower."

"Sorry. Can't order me around like in chem lab anymore." He laughed. "Besides, I've discovered the secret formula that turns air into fire . . ."

The secret formula that turned air into fire? Time to go back to the drawing board, my friend, 'cause all it did was make me fall asleep. I hope . . .

Thankfully, I awoke before Josh and tiptoed to the bathroom, praying my beating heart didn't rouse him. Not that it was beating from being turned on. It was from waking in a panic that I'd overslept for work . . . until I remembered, among other things, that I had the next few days off.

That was the good news. The bad news? When I looked in the vanity mirror, I saw a selfish girl who had forced herself on a vulnerable guy who had begged not to be that night's boy toy for fear he would be summarily dismissed in the morning.

As for how far we'd actually gone? It remained a mystery. What I did remember wasn't pretty. Josh's idea of heavy breathing was less porn than pig in heat. And his secret formula for making women crazy had nothing to do with being turned on. More like being turned over, like a roast that needed basting.

What to do now? Grab my clothes and go? Take him to breakfast and hope he had a good enough sense of humor? Check my cell and discover they *did* need me in Rome! Ciao baby . . .

I wandered through his apartment, realizing that in my haste to get the party started, I hadn't taken the grand tour. Only to feel worse. Josh had created a safe space of warm touches with plants, pillows, and seating, all blended to match the rich moldings and grand arches . . . Damn! He was a nice guy, with a nice home. So why couldn't I wait to leave?

"You are so beautiful." He kissed my neck.

"Thanks." I shivered. *Naked girl. Naked guy. No screaming kids. Not good.*

"Are you okay? Do you want a robe?"

"Um, no. I'm good. I really should be getting home . . ."

"I knew it." He stepped back. "Here comes the brushoff. Thanks for the burgers and sex, Josh, but I have to get back to my real life now."

"No. It's nothing like that . . . It's just that I'm sure my mom is wondering what happened to me and then . . . I'm sorry I have to ask . . . Did we do it?"

"Must have been memorable . . . No, we didn't. But not because you didn't finally wear me down . . . I went to get condoms and when I came back, you were lights out . . ."

Thank you God. "I am so sorry for throwing myself at you . . . Remember Mrs. Heilman's health class? All those warnings about drinking and sex being a dangerous combination and—"

"Told you," he moped. "It always ends like this for me . . . I'm the fool who never learns . . ."

"I like you." I touched his face. "I do. You're very sweet . . ."

"So do you want to go out again?"

"Definitely."

"You're full of it. You'll never take my call, so just answer this. Why were you thinking about me?"

"What?"

"When we first ran into each other in your building. You said you had just been thinking of me even though you had no idea I called . . . Why was I on your mind?"

"Oh. That." I cleared my throat. "Actually I was thinking about Julia Volkman and how I really needed to give her a call. And then it was the strangest thing. I was thinking about high school and lockers and—"

"—whatever happened to that fat, ugly kid she was stuck next to?"

"Not at all. I was thinking, whatever happened to all those nice guys like Josh Vogel?"

"That's what you were thinking."

"Yes."

"I happen to have a portable polygraph machine. Mind if I get it?"

"I'm telling the truth." I kissed his cheek and went to fetch my clothes.

"You really have a great ass." He sighed. "Which I'll probably never see again."

"That is not true. We're going to have dinner again very soon."

"Really?" His face lit up.

"Absolutely." *With a friend from work who would love you.*

Chapter 16

My mother was a big fan of letting her badly behaved children choose their own punishments, thinking guilt would force them to be harsher on themselves than she would ever have the heart to be.

Phillip would opt for a television ban, then cry about his great sacrifice. Meanwhile, he'd be up in his room jerking off while listening to the Mets on the radio. And me? I'd go the food deprivation route. No candy for a week unless I had a party, a craving, or a sudden memory lapse.

But how to atone for having taken advantage of the still vulnerable Josh Vogel? A written apology? Watch *Mean Girls* for the next month? Maybe write a hundred times on the blackboard I WILL NOT SEDUCE FORMER FAT BOYS?

He deserved better. I would invite him for an evening of dinner and mah-jongg, then explain why he'd be a fool to get involved with me. Maybe ask if he was willing to be fixed up. Anything but date him, for as was common to my species, I had a natural predilection for guys with a basic understanding of the female anatomy. Or at least the parts that liked attention.

Exactly. Irrational fool that I was, I was wondering about Ken. As I trudged the few blocks from Josh's place to mine, I checked for missed calls, and although there were several Manhattan Man was not among them. But no surprise. I got the karma thing. This was payback time. I was being blown off because I'd done the same thing to Josh.

Uh. I hated turnabout, I thought, as I sidestepped two jogger-mommies pushing their Rolls Royce stroller babies down Seventh Avenue. But having to jump the curb did make me realize that it was the first time since moving to Brooklyn that I was getting a look at my neighborhood in all its early weekday glory.

Power walkers, commuters, young moms, and retirees were out enjoying the best of both worlds. An urban dwelling in close proximity to Manhattan, but suburban in the vast choices for shopping without ever having to beat someone to a spot in the parking lot.

Park Slope was especially desirous, with its stately brownstones, trendy restaurants, and a lush, safe park at your doorstep. "But it's not Central Park," I had cried to Rachel on moving day. "There's no zoo, no ice rink, no directors rushing over here to shoot scenes for their films."

I guess until now I hadn't realized that I was still in mourning for my short-lived marriage and the luxury life that came with it. Still in shock how quickly I'd had to unload our beautiful co-op, only to discover David had already borrowed against the equity, and what little profits were left were needed to cover legal fees and credit card debts.

So it was hardly a celebration when I arrived in this borough. No fun when I installed my new phone line, and the first people to greet me were the courtesy callers from Visa with a reminder that I was late on my payments. "No!" I said. "Are you sure you have the right number?"

Seriously, what did the back office folks living in North

Dakota know from Manhattan? Had they ever resided within minutes of the five Bs: Bloomie's, Bendel's, Bergdorf's, Barney's and Broadway? Or catered small dinner parties that cost more than a flight to London? Or watched a football game knowing income was riding on the outcome, then heard their husband confide that the thrill of gambling was still better than the best sex he'd ever had?

But now in this moment of clarity, I had to admit how nice a community this was. And a hell of a lot less pretentious, even with five-dollar lattes, Gucci-clad nannies, and million-dollar co-ops selling like Nathan's hot dogs.

Nobody ogled my pocketbook to see if it was, sniff, last season's (though they did eye the stitching to see if it was a fake). Nobody tried sizing up my net worth in an elevator, wondering if I was just another a Wall Street bonus baby, or a descendant from a venerable New York family.

This was my home now. Time to embrace my surroundings. May it be ever so humble . . .

Have you ever noticed confidence is that feeling you have right before you understand the problem?

"That musta been a helluva long line for pizza." My mother stood outside my back door, one hand in her seersucker pocket, the other clutching a cigarette. "Where were you all night?"

"At a friend's . . . I can't believe you're not even trying to quit."

"Says who? I'm already down to a pack a day . . ."

"You shouldn't be smoking at all. You have cancer."

"You say potato, I say potato . . . I'm doing fine." She took a last puff and came inside.

"You know this may come as a shock to you, but I don't want you to die."

"Good to know . . . let's go shopping. I heard you got some time off."

"I don't want to go shopping. I want to talk to you about what the hell you're doing." I poured water into the coffeemaker.

"What's to discuss? However much time I have, I don't want to spend it with a husband who grunts in the morning, farts in the afternoon, and snores at night."

"Fine. But that doesn't give you carte blanche to walk all over us . . ."

"Who's walking over anyone? . . . You gotta use more coffee than that or it'll taste like water . . . Other than stay here for a few nights, what have I asked you for? And how am I supposed to feel knowing my own daughter doesn't give one hootenanny that her mother is lonely?"

"I'm not saying you don't have a right to be happy. I'm saying, can you at least think logically about this before you destroy a good thing?"

"I've done nothing but think, and believe me, it's time to bail . . . Here. Let me show you how to do that." She took the coffee scoop.

"Would you stop?" I pushed her away. "I can't stand the fact that you think you're always right about everything."

"Because I am."

"Not about love. You're acting like a fool."

"So buttons? Now tell me what you were so worked up about last night. We were all having fun until little Merry Sunshine walked in."

"Well excuse me, but I didn't appreciate strangers dropping cake crumbs on my floor."

"Are you kiddin' me? Thanks to me, this joint is cleaner than ever."

"Thanks to you, my life is crazy again."

"If you don't want to see the negative, stay out of the darkroom."

"What?"

"I don't know. It sounded good in a fortune cookie . . . Sierra left a little while ago."

"Good."

"But Friday we're flying to Phoenix."

"Fine."

"All of a sudden, fine?"

"Yeah. I don't care anymore. You want to chase some crazy pipe dream and turn into an assassin, be my guest."

"An assassin?" She sat down. "You honestly think I'm going there to kill Marv?"

"No. Sierra."

"Sierra? Why would I do that? She's a sweet kid. Just needs a little attention."

"Then how come I heard Simon's paying your way to make sure she doesn't come back?"

"And you call that place a newsroom!" she snorted. "Get the facts straight, Toots . . . Sierra told me she was thinking about seeing Arizona State. Maybe transfer and start over . . . Then that Simon fellow said if I chaperoned her, we could use his condo in Scottsdale."

"Oh. That does sound good. Except the part where you try to find the man who got away . . . Have you even spoken to Daddy?"

"Did you call your idiot husband every day after you left him?"

"That was different. He was in trouble with the law."

"Well your father's in trouble with me! Why don't you call him?"

"I did a few minutes ago. He's fine."

"See? He's fine, I'm fine. No hits, no runs, no errors . . . oh . . . before I forget. You got an interesting call yesterday, but you ran out of here before I could tell you."

Here it comes. "From who?"

"Remember that Joshua Vogel from high school? I used to bowl with his mother?"

"Oooh gross. Why would he be calling me?"

"What? You never heard of a frog turning into a prince?"

"Oh, so suddenly he's royalty?"

"Just about! He dropped over a hundred pounds, sold his business, and now he's this big-deal millionaire . . . bought a whole building right around the corner from here."

"A whole building?" I stared at the coffee dripping into the pot.

"Yes ma'am. Plus he's still got a big house in Seattle, horses in Florida, and . . . he's single!"

And will be for the foreseeable future unless he buys a farm and marries a pig.

"It's up to you of course." She coughed. "But what would it hurt to see him?"

"You know you're right? Then maybe we'll start going out, we'll get engaged, I'll become the wife of a rich tycoon, we'll have a bunch of kids, you'll complain that they're too spoiled and fat and they're not reading enough books, and I don't know the first thing about raising children, and you can't stand his mother and why do you have to share the holidays with her . . ."

"She is a yenta, that's for sure. Has her nose in everyone's business . . . telephone, telegraph and tell Helene Vogel . . . Come to think of it, don't call him back . . . Oy. The coffee looks so weak."

Josh Vogel was rich enough to buy a building in Park Slope? I lay in bed pondering if that changed my feelings about him. Not if he was the next Donald Trump. He was a sweet guy, but I was hornier than I was broke, and a man who slobbered and slithered and thought Shake N Bake was an erotic sex act would need more than a huge portfolio to keep me happy.

And then I laughed, for if nothing else, here was some new material to mine.

I threw the covers off and raced to my computer. Thankfully, Sheil was in the shower and heading out to buy some books to read on the plane. That meant I could get right to it without having to explain the intricacies of how the comedic mind worked. Not that I had a clue myself.

Every stand-up I knew had their unique approach to developing a routine, and about the only bond we shared was the one that centered around angst. *I'm not funny. I'm pathetic. And ugly too. But where else can I work where they let you drink on the job?*

Not to mention our best material was born out of our most painful experiences. And given how many I was having all at once, that should explain my sudden inspiration. I had an idea for a bit I could add to this one-woman show I'd written all about dating.

So yeah. I love the whole dating scene. All the anticipation. The daydreaming. Will I like him, will he like me? Will he turn me on? Will he pay . . .

And getting ready for that first date is the best. You buy something new . . . and leave the tags on so you can return it the next day. You shave . . . I'm not kidding. If it wasn't for dating, I'd be a target during bear hunting season.

And what about that first long conversation? Easy. You just act natural. Like at a job interview. Only there's no need to lie on your résumé:

2002–present, Executive vice president, United States Marines, Fifth Battalion, third floor, second door on the left. I type eighty words a minute. Some are actually right.

Yeah. The worst time to lie is on a first date. There's plenty of time for that when you're engaged.

[man's deep voice] "Do you like football?"

"Are you kidding? I love football. Never miss a game."

"Awesome. Who's your favorite team?

"Oh. The ones with those blue and orange costumes?"

"Uniforms."

"Exactly."

"You mean the Mets?"

"Yeah. The Mets. They're the best. Especially that Latino guy . . . what's his name . . ."

"The Mets are a baseball team . . . and the whole team is Latino."

Apparently the routine was so stellar, I dozed at the computer and was woken by the phone.

"Did you say your father's a dentist?"

"What?" My heart raced at the sound of the familiar voice.

"It's Ken . . . Danziger . . . Isn't your dad a dentist?"

"Yes." I wiped the drool from my face. "Although he's semi-retired."

"Which means what?"

"That he drives halfway to work and then goes home."

Ken laughed. "No really. I mean is he still licensed?"

"Yes, but he sold his practice and only goes in once a week to help with the overflow . . . I thought you said you were covered on that front."

"I was, until I found out my dentist is out on maternity leave and I can't stand her partner. She's awful."

"Bad hands?"

"Yes. They end up in my lap instead of my mouth . . . long story. We used to go out."

"Oh. Uh huh . . . okay. So yes, my dad is a dentist. A great one. But how would you get there? His office is in New Jersey."

"I thought you could take me. I have a car. I just can't drive it yet because it's a stick."

"Well then that makes two of us. My brother once tried to teach me to drive a stick and after I made a left turn going fifty in neutral, he was so mad I had to walk home."

"Yeah okay. Forget that. You're not touching my car . . . It's a brand-new M3."

"Oh. My brother has that. No wait. He has a 767."

"Really? He drives a Boeing jet? Doesn't he have a hard time parking in midtown?"

"Good point. Shows you what I know . . . Anyway, are you sure you want to shlep to Jersey?"

"I can afford the tolls."

"I know. But wouldn't it be easier if you started with someone in the city? You'll probably need several visits."

"It would be a lot easier, but then I wouldn't get to spend time with you."

"Oh." My pulse raced.

"Yeah. I was thinking I was pretty rough on you the other day and you've been such a good sport. I'd like to make it up to you."

"By letting me drive you to my dad's office."

"What dentist doesn't want more business?"

"True. And then maybe he won't have to stand out on Route Four with a sandwich board."

"Exactly. The only thing is, I'm in kind of a hurry to get this done."

"Are you in pain?"

"A lot. But also, Mira is coming in and I really want to get rid of the Captain Hook look."

"Oh." *I hate you!*

"Plus . . . I'd like to see you again."

"Oh?" *I take it back.*

". . . I want to talk to you about the picture you took of me and my friends . . . I don't know. Maybe it would help me . . . It's been a long time since this came up, but if this is too much of an imposition, I understand . . . Besides, there's always plan B."

"Which is . . ."

"Move in with my parents in Florida and spend my entire day going to doctors."

"Great idea . . . And Florida is perfect for single guys. You can have your pick of lonely widows, and boy do they love to cook!"

"Eddie Fisher was right." He laughed. "You are funny."

"I know. But seriously, I think I can help you. There's a lot of stuff going on that I need to talk to my dad about. Plus, it turns out I not only have my mom's car, I have the next four days off."

"Really? And you'd be willing to do this for me?"

"What are make-believe wives for?"

Let me tell you, it elicits real excitement when your father is a dentist. Oooh. Can he can get us samples of Crest? No, not the same as having a dad who is a titan of business and so well connected, he can score front-row seats to Aerosmith.

But finally Harvey Holtz's occupation was going to serve me well. It was going to make me a hero to a prospective suitor in need of teeth, and give me uninterrupted quality time with Ken to explore our shared pasts. Maybe even open his eyes to the possibility of a relationship with me instead of an actress who was clearly more interested in finding a pawn than a partner.

But have you ever noticed that daydreams rarely come true? Not that it stops us from fantasizing.

In fact, I would have never survived high school without my vivid imagination. Particularly my senior year when I convinced myself that my psych teacher was honestly and truly in love with me but couldn't compete with the affections of the class president who was desperate to ask me to the prom but feared the rejection because I was rumored to be dating a college freshman whose father owned the Jets.

Which is why it wasn't much of a stretch at all to envision spending a day with Ken . . . a nice car ride, a lot of laughs, the beginning of something . . .

So what happens? It turns into a full court nightmare due to an offhand comment made by a guy riding shotgun who wasn't even supposed to be there . . . If only I'd hadn't taken Josh Vogel's call.

Chapter 17

RIGHT BEFORE TAKING an eighth grade science test, I remember telling Julia that I had solved the mystery of how she never got caught ditching gym, while if I was two minutes late, I got detention. She was born under a lucky star and I was the Sucky Luck Queen.

She claimed there was no such thing as a lucky star. But I wondered. I studied all night for that stupid exam and got an A. She forgot that there was a test and not only got an A, but the extra credit points and Mr. Wrobleski's recommendation to speak at our junior high graduation.

In high school, she never so much as stuck a paper carnation in a class float, but got voted on to homecoming court every year. She would get high in the girls' bathroom and walk out smelling like a daisy. The one time I smoked a cigarette in the school parking lot, it cost me the right to go on the class trip to Williamsburg, Virginia.

Eventually my mother saw the light. After losing a student council election to a kid who got caught stealing projectors from the AV lab, and after not getting a call back for a part in the musical, even though my mother volunteered to conduct the orchestra, I overheard her tell my dad, "What can we do? The kid has no *mazel*."

Exactly. Luck wasn't something you bought, borrowed or stole, like twenties from your dad's wallet while he napped on the hammock (although in deference to that old trick, it sure felt lucky to hit the Bergen mall without having to beg for an advance).

No. Luck, like beauty and brains, was one of those intangible assets they assigned before you were born. You. Good luck. You. Amazing luck. You. Sorry. Outaluck . . . You. Bing bing bing, we have a winner . . . Then it was my turn. Robyn Holtz? Oy. Don't ask.

Funny thing? Even though David was doing time in an upstate prison, he still contended he was one lucky guy. He'd won hundreds of thousands of dollars gambling and had a blast in the process. As for all the money he lost, say nothing of his wife, his home, and his future, he could still point to lady luck and think, maybe tomorrow.

Meanwhile, I sat in a near-empty co-op, wondering when, if ever, a memo would circulate that said, "Robyn's been through hell. Next victim." It couldn't happen soon enough.

Just after I made arrangements to pick up Ken the next morning, Josh called. At first it was empowering to stand over an answering machine and not answer, even though it was sweet to hear him say he had a great time the other night, and would I like to make good on my promise to see him again by having dinner tomorrow?

When I realized I had the perfect out, I picked up and said sorry, I'd love to see him but not tomorrow because I was driving home so my friend Ken could see my dad.

My luck being what it was, however, Josh was thrilled that I was headed to Fair Lawn, as it so happened that his new car had just come in and the dealer wanted him to take delivery on it before the rebate offer ended.

Fast forward to the next morning when I helped a hobbling Ken downstairs to my mother's car, Rookie in my one arm, a pillow and their bag of meds in the other.

Did I know Josh would jump out of the front seat and yell, "Kenny? Kenny Danziger?"

Ken removed his sunglasses, squinting in the daylight.

"It's Josh. Josh Vogel." Josh hugged him. "From Ocean-side . . . nursery school, Little League, Boy Scouts . . ."

Oceanside? Wait. What? Him too?

"Oh my God." Kenny laughed. "Are you serious?" He nearly tripped on his crutches trying to hug him back. "How did you recognize me? It's been forever."

"I don't know, man. You look like hell, but you still look like you."

"Hold on." Ken looked at me. "This is the guy who was your terrible first date? How could you not have fun with Josh? Josh, next time you gotta bring the Transformers."

"I'm a terrible first date?" Josh looked like his ice cream dropped.

"No, of course not," I said. "Ken is teasing . . . You're a dead man." I whispered as I helped him into the backseat, delighted that his knees would be up to his nose . . . "So hold on you guys . . . Is this crazy or what? We're all from Oceanside, Long Island . . ."

They didn't care. It was their personal reunion and my job was to shut up and drive. Until a still miffed Josh turned to current events.

"Yeah, so I thought Robyn and I had a great time the other night. It took her like thirty seconds to jump into bed naked and beg me to—"

"Stop!" I said. "Don't be an asshole."

"Robyn did that?" Ken laughed. "No way. She's not the type . . ."

"Oh yeah. She is. Put on a little Duran Duran and out comes a wild woman."

My luck, we were sitting in bumper-to-bumper traffic on the Cross Bronx Expressway so I couldn't drive off a bridge.

"She slept in my bed the other night too, but I wasn't there . . . Rookie . . . Was Robyn naked?"

Rookie barked.

"Man . . . I missed it?"

"I swear I'm pulling over and throwing you two out . . . good luck catching a cab."

"Oh come on. It's funny," Josh teased. "And it's not like it's going to stop you from applying to rabbinical school. We'll never tell."

"Exactly. We're all consenting, horny adults," Ken piped up. "You know, when you stop short like that, the seatbelt cuts my neck . . . and by the way, the gas pedal is the one on the right . . ."

"Really?" I jammed on the brakes again. " 'Cause I wasn't sure . . . Now let's see. Who among us is the good soul? I'm playing nursemaid to an ingrate and chauffeur to a big mouth."

"Takes one to know one." Josh winked. "You told Ken I was a terrible date . . . and he's right. You are the world's slowest driver . . . I feel like we left in the winter of '02."

"Joke all you want. I've never gotten a speeding ticket."

"No kidding. I've been in funeral processions that went faster."

"Josh, c'mon man. Don't make her nervous. We want her to pass her road test."

"Say your good-byes," I said. "When we cross the GW Bridge, you both must die."

"We're just playing with you." Josh stroked my cheek.

"Yeah, you've saved my life. Right Rookie? Robyn's our hero . . . Can you roll down the window so he can stick his head out?"

"How about I open the doors and you can all jump out?"

"Uh oh, Josh. I think I lost my ride. You may have to drive me back."

"Nah . . . Don't worry. Robyn's easy."

"I never liked you, Josh . . . As for you, Super Klutz, I'm telling my dad to pull out his biggest drill and that it's against your religion to use lidocaine."

So fine. They were having fun at my expense. Do you really think I would have thrown caution and my clothes to the wind, and gotten into bed with a kid who used to drink five milks at lunch, if I thought I'd be outed like Lori Schumacher who everyone knew the Sunday after homecoming had done it under the bleachers with Craig Abernathy?

This is what I'm saying. I have no luck.

"Josh used to have the best birthday parties," Ken said. Apparently after they'd discussed my small breasts and round ass, I was now allowed back in the conversation . "His mom would make these forts out of Rice Krispies Treats . . . and I'm not talking the little ones that fit on a plate. She'd build these amazing fortresses with marshmallow moats . . . Does she still make them?"

"No."

"Oh come on. Really? You're never too old for—"

"She, um . . . she died." Josh cracked his knuckles.

"Oh my God," I said.

"I'm sorry, Josh. I didn't know." Ken leaned over to pat him.

"Yeah. It was a long time ago now, but . . . Remember when I moved to Florida?"

"Sure. Your dad took us to Hooters for a good-bye party and we got autographs. That was huge at ten."

"We had just moved down there . . . One night she got lost

coming home from the supermarket . . . went down a one-way street the wrong way . . . But at least it was quick. They said she probably never realized the other car hit her."

"I'm in shock," I said. "I had no idea. I always thought your mom was Helene."

"No." He drummed on the dashboard.

"So wait," I said. "You moved from Oceanside to Florida . . . How did you get to Fair Lawn?"

"We flew."

"Funny. I mean what brought you there?"

"I guess it was about a year after my mom died, my dad met Helene at a wedding in Boca. She was from somewhere in Jersey, they started going back and forth . . . then when they decided to get married, she wanted to be near her sister who lived in Fair Lawn, and that's where we ended up."

"You know? I'm starting to remember when you moved in," I said. "Wait. Were you the one who had the open house bar mitzvah?"

"That was me." He leaned back and closed his eyes.

"Oh come on. My driving isn't that bad."

"Actually it is. Are you aware that even old ladies are giving you the finger?"

"Fine. I'll go faster, but I'm warning you. The Cross Bronx is a speed trap."

"I've never seen them pull over a car that's already on the shoulder," Ken mused.

"Anyway," Josh continued, "so yeah. The open house was Helene's idea. We moved in in August and my bar mitzvah was in October. I had no friends, hardly any family, so she said, Let's just have a big party in the backyard and invite the whole town."

"You know? I think we went to that . . . it was a carnival, right? Big tents . . . a guy on stilts . . ."

"Yep." he winced.

"Not a good memory?"

"Nope . . . not a good memory. I was miserable . . . I missed my mom so much I spent most of the day in my room crying . . . I think my sister had more people there than me . . ."

It wasn't hard to feel his anguish. Who couldn't relate to reliving painful childhood memories which played in your head like old home videos. "See? Didn't we tell you that you pooped in the pool at Phillip's birthday party?"

But, of course, Josh's memories were far more devastating. I couldn't imagine losing my mother as a child, though was there any age at which death did not feel like abandonment?

Frankly, all this recent talk of dying was getting too close for comfort. My mother was stubborn and irascible. But the prospect of her leaving this world was too daunting to consider. Not that it would stop me from strangling her one day.

And ditto for these two why-chromosomes for making fun of me, although it was nice to hear Ken laugh. But when he suddenly changed the subject and brought up his nursery school teacher, I went from annoyed to stunned.

"Did you just say Mrs. Abramowitz?" I looked in my rearview mirror. "I had her too."

"When?" Ken replied. "What year?"

"I don't know. I was four, so that would have been . . . what? 1975?"

"That's when I went there," Josh added. "A.M. or P.M.?"

"Beats me." I shrugged. "I'd have to ask my mom. Not that she'd remember. She used to forget to bring me altogether."

"I know I went in the mornings," Ken said. "Because I remember waiting for Seth to get home from school and it would feel like hours."

"Me too." Josh nodded. "I'd come home, have lunch, take a nap, watch cartoons, and then my sister Brittany would finally walk in."

"Hey. Does anyone remember Jason Horowitz?" I asked. "What a crybaby. He's probably still crying."

"Actually he's a plastic surgeon in Santa Monica," Ken said. "I think he stopped crying."

I thought Josh would try to impress Ken with his success, but he resisted. Impressive!

"Yeah, I remember that kid," Josh said. "That's how I got chicken pox . . . he was always stealing my juice and next thing I know I'm covered in spots . . . so wait. Were we all in the same class?"

"I looked at my watch and what did it say?" I sang.

"Time to put the toys away." They laughed.

"This is unbelievable," Josh said. "What are the odds? Three people end up in a car thirty years after they played in a sandbox together . . . Hey Ken. Are you still in touch with those two other kids? Larry somebody and I can't remember the other one's name . . ."

"No."

"The three of you were like glue. I remember you'd cry if they tried to separate you."

I caught Ken's sad face in my rearview mirror. Was Josh talking about Mo and Larry? Oh God. They were in our class too?

"I guess you never know where your life is going to take you," Josh said. "I would have thought for sure you guys would still be tight."

"Yeah, me too." Ken peered out the window.

"I remember this one time you kicked a soccer ball so far it went into the temple parking lot and the three of you ran like hell to chase it, and the teachers were screaming, 'Come back here,' and nobody's listening . . ."

". . . They're both gone now."

"You mean they moved?"

"No . . . they're dead."

"They're dead?" Josh turned around. "You mean they were still together . . . Were they gay?"

"No, they weren't gay. Richie Morris got drunk at a party, then got hit by a car . . . Larry Gerber was a bond trader for Cantor Fitzgerald . . ."

"Holy shit. I don't believe it . . . I had no idea . . . But you stayed friends until the end?"

"Yeah. Friends till the end." He held Rookie to his chest.

Good God. How did the fun of catching up suddenly morph into the pain of looking back? As they retreated to their corners like stunned boxers, now I wished they were dissing me again.

"I gotta tell you," Josh finally said. "I'm in shock . . . First I run into a girl I haven't seen since high school, then a boy who used to come over to play Transformers. Then we find out we all started out together and look how much has happened to us . . ."

"Yeah, it's crazy," Ken said. "But what makes this even more bizarre for me is I hadn't thought about nursery school since nursery school. I mean I'd occasionally run into some of the kids when my folks still lived in Oceanside, but after they moved to Florida, I never went back.

"But a couple of months ago my mom calls and says she's sending two boxes. One to me, one to Seth. She doesn't care what we do with them, she just wants them out of the garage. So Seth gets his, sees all this crap he can't believe she saved, like report cards and haiku poems and camper awards, and tosses the whole thing . . . Then he calls me and says it's all a bunch of a junk, don't even bother opening it. So I didn't . . . It sat on a shelf in my closet. Until last week . . ."

Oh no. The box in his closet . . .

"I don't know. I had this like nagging feeling I should see what was in it. So I go and take it down and I call Seth back and I say, 'Shmuck! How could you throw this stuff out?' "

"What was in it?" I asked. *Nice. Sound innocent so he doesn't suspect you ransacked it.*

"Well, a very important report I wrote in fourth grade on the mating rituals of fruit flies . . . I guess just stuff that was fun to see again. My Nolan Ryan rookie card . . . I am gonna be rich . . . oh, and, then believe it or not, there were even a few things left from nursery school."

"My mom was a pack rat like that too." Josh smiled. "Anything I did, she loved."

"Not my mom," I said. "The first thing she did when I got home from school was dump my book bag . . . God forbid excess cookie crumbs found their way into the house."

"Anyway," Ken said, "there's this letter to my mom from Mrs. Abramowitz."

"Great lady," Josh said. "She was the only one who didn't send notes saying, 'Your son can't cut for shit and he needs a tutor to teach him to skip.' "

"Yeah, I loved her. But listen. It's a letter about what a great boy I was because I was so nice to this girl in the class whose brother died, and she went on and on about how I made it my job to take care of her, and carry her everywhere and make her tea in the playhouse . . . and I'm thinking, what girl whose brother died? I don't remember anything like that? Do you?"

"No." Josh shrugged.

"I do." I stopped driving. Right in the middle of busy Route Four.

"What the hell are you doing?" Josh grabbed the wheel. "You can't stop in the middle of the road. Freakin' drive! We're gonna get hit!"

"I remember her." I clutched my heart as cars sped past us, honking in fury.

"You do?" Ken asked. "Who was it?"

"Me." I burst into tears. "Oh my God. It was me."

Chapter 18

COMEDY IS BORN FROM TRAGEDY. Not much of a news story there. Every stand-up I ever saw perform came to the party armed with my-life-was-insane material that they had learned to mine for laughs in lieu of seeking professional help.

And yet, if you asked me why I wanted to be a comic, I would tell you how much I loved observational humor and the cathartic feel of poking fun at our struggles. I would be loath to admit I was an in-disguise patient who was attempting to rationalize my inner turmoil.

But I would be lying. In spite of our stately, colonial half-acre home with the greenest lawn on the block, what went on behind the doors at the Holtz house teetered between serious dysfunction and a sitcom writer's dream.

We were two parents, two kids, and a dog, but don't let the Weber grill fool you. We were a family in crisis, and no matter how well we fit the mold, with our annual timeshare vacations in Orlando and our frolicking block parties turned toga parties, we were scarred. Our past, mired in an almost Shakespearean tragedy that was but a tiny chapter, yet forever defined the rest of the book.

I never met my two-year old brother, Todd, as he died before I was born. I did know from stories and pictures that unlike our brother, Phillip, whose dark coloring foreshadowed his solemn demeanor, Todd was a cherubic blond known for his hugs around your neck.

I knew from my aunt Marilyn that his nickname was Magellan, due to his mysterious and unlikely fascination with my father's maps, and that he was already a great collector, stashing precious finds beneath the stuffed animals in his crib.

I knew from accounts from family members willing to talk that he was kidnapped from Lido Beach on a steamy, summer Sunday in August 1971, exactly six weeks before I was born. Only to have his remains discovered four years later, less than a mile from the concession stand where my father had bought him a lime Popsicle.

To say that guilt and agony were the sentiments greeting me when I was brought home from the hospital that late September didn't begin to describe it. Phillip, then five, said he remembered having to tell our inconsolable mother that I was crying, to which she said, "Me too."

It was not a home that could celebrate gurgles and coos, for day and night, my parents and neighbors were focused on police investigations, media coverage, and ear-shattering cries about how something this tragic could have happened on Long Island.

If only my father, a man ill prepared for the challenge of parenting two young, active little boys, hadn't offered to bring them to the beach that day, giving my mother and her swollen ankles time to rest before entering the home stretch of pregnancy.

Though she had warned him repeatedly about not taking his eyes off them, he was a trusting sort, certain her overprotective pleas were caused more by her fears of her children drowning than disappearing.

So when a whiny Phillip insisted on going back into the water, though Todd was asleep in his stroller, he saw nothing wrong with asking the young couple lying next to them if they would please keep an eye on the baby.

They turned down their radio, admired the adorable little boy in his Winnie-the-Pooh bathing trunks, said they would love to watch him and was there a bottle in case he cried?

To this day, my father swore there was nothing suspect about them in either manner or dress. They were well spoken and polite, not having had so much as a cigarette or a beer since arriving. The girl even swooned that one day she hoped to have a son just like him.

Only to have my father and Phillip return to their chairs and discover, in horror, that the couple had vanished, as had Todd and his belongings.

Four years later, when a group of high school students, examining igneous rock in preparation for their New York State Earth Science Regents exam, came upon a skull and a toddler-two bathing suit, the unsolved case was reopened, causing my family's anguish to resurface.

It was then that I was attending nursery school at the Oceanside Jewish Center, learning to read, write, and count to a hundred like the other children, yet feeling inherently different because the one thing I had not yet learned was how to be silly.

I remember trying to fit in by laughing too loud and pretending to be uncooperative when Mrs. Abramowitz said it was circle time. But I was bad at being bad, much preferring to play alone in the corner.

So when a boy in the class learned the reason I was always sad was that my brother died, I was thrilled when he befriended me, carrying me from the classroom to the playground to the sanctuary where we sang with the rabbi.

During playtime, he brought me toys and tea, pushing away those who would dare disturb me. But mostly I remembered him kissing my hands, as if that might make my boo-boos go away.

Now to discover that my childhood hero was seated in the back of my car, and that, unbeknownst to me, he had reappeared in my life so many times since then, left me breathless. Why were we being thrown together under the oddest of circumstances, weaving pain and suffering in between moments of childhood bliss? Why?

I looked up to see that Josh had jumped out of the car and was directing traffic away from our disabled vehicle. Disabled because the driver had shut down. Gently, he buckled me into the passenger side, then eased back into traffic, getting us to Fair Lawn without incident.

And all I could think was, God bless these boys for their endless courage and compassion.

In all the haste to make arrangements for my dad to examine Ken, I had failed to share one important matter. The name of the patient. So when he came out to help me pull Ken and Rookie from the backseat, and I quickly said, "Dad, this is Ken Danziger. Ken, this is my dad, Harvey Holtz," I didn't expect for him to nearly let go as Ken struggled with his crutches.

"Ken Danziger?" My father took a step back. "From Oceanside?"

Not you too!

"Yes." Ken wobbled.

"Howard and Judy's boy?"

"Yes?" He looked up.

"Oh for God's sake. I don't believe it." He kissed his cheek. "Robyn didn't tell me she was bringing home an old friend of the family."

"Because Robyn didn't know," I said.

"Yeah, we actually just figured out in the car we went to OJC together . . . we're in shock."

"Isn't that something?" My dad watched Rookie jump like mad. "Who's your friend?"

"This is Rookie." I tried to get him to stop. "I've never seen him like this."

"Discipline's just not the same since his tutor quit," Ken quipped.

"Rookie, huh," my dad said. "Mets or Yankees?"

"What's a Yankee?"

"Bingo! You just earned yourself a nice discount . . . So how are your folks? Are they still in Oceanside?"

"No, they moved to Sarasota, Florida, about three years ago."

"Wonderful. Who needs the crowded East Coast? And they're both in good health I hope?"

"Actually my mom is doing great. Still whips my ass at tennis, but my dad is having a hard time right now. Prostate cancer."

Really? My mom has breast cancer, but shhh. It's a big secret.

"Uch. God. It's all I hear," my dad replied. "But he's going to be okay?"

"Yeah. They think they caught it early enough. It's just the treatments are rough on him . . ."

"You send them my best . . . and how is your brother? Steven, was it?"

"Seth. Yeah. He's great. Married now, having a baby . . ."

"Glad to hear it."

"So wait, Daddy. How do you know his family?"

"Long story, sweetheart. Too long to go into now. Let's get Ken in the chair and see about fixing him up. Are you in pain, son?"

"I'm not going to lie. Hot and cold kill me . . ."

"That's nerve damage. Might need a quickie root canal. But

let's go take a look. Robyn, how about you head home and straighten things up for me?"

"Well wait." Ken hesitated. "Who's going to hold my hand?"

"You've spent months in a hospital, but you're afraid of dentists?" I teased.

"They have to give me sweet air in the waiting room."

"Don't worry." My dad winked. "We just hired a new assistant with big knockers . . . I hear she's an excellent hand holder."

"Daddy! This isn't 1956 . . . and how bad is bad at the house?"

"Remember when your mother won that contest and went to California for a week?"

"You put Tide in the dishwasher again?"

"No, I had a tiny fire in the kitchen after the microwave blew up . . . maybe later you can help me shop for wallpaper."

Say what you would about my dad being a great dentist. He had learned nothing from my mother about housekeeping. In fact, I was tempted to take pictures so she could see what had become of her once immaculate, three-Dustbuster home.

Take-out containers in the living room, bath towels hanging from the dining room chairs, and evidence of the said fire, no doubt because Harvey wasn't housebroken and forgot that microwaves were no place for metal objects.

"Daddy-o's been having one helluva good time," I called Phillip. "The house is a mess."

"Well whatever you do, don't let Mom get on that plane to Phoenix or we're screwed."

"Me? I'm sorry. What is your job exactly? Air traffic control?"

"Oh, give it up. I'm doing as much as you."

"Is that right? Well I know for a fact you haven't been here or you'd know there was a new big-screen TV in the den and that dad is using the box to throw out all of Mom's clothes."

"Really? What kind? HD or rear-screen projection? I hope he didn't just walk into Best Buy and get the first thing they tried to sell him."

"Focus, Phillip. Focus. Mom has only been gone for five days and the fridge is filled with a cardiologist's don't list."

"Relax, okay? Just do the best you can cleaning up, and next week I'll have Patti . . . call a maid service."

"You're so kind. Maybe you should apply for that job opening at the Vatican."

By the time the garage door opened, I couldn't believe five hours had passed. Time flies when you're cleaning what looked like a frat house, taking care of a spoiled city dog, and answering the phone every five minutes.

Neighbor friends of my mom had spotted her car in the driveway and called to hear about her great escape, only to hear my voice, and my ultimatum. "I swear if I hear you're trying to set my dad up, I'll teach your husbands how to meet girls on MySpace."

A concerned Josh called to see how Ken and I were feeling, and would I please keep my promise to see him again? "Yes," I said. "Unless I find out you were the one who always looked up my dress."

Rachel begged my forgiveness after learning I'd heard the message she left on Ken's machine, and to show her remorse, offered to pay for a reading with her favorite new psychic. "Deal," I said. "But she better not tell me my mother's getting remarried before me."

Madeline and Seth both called for updates on Ken and my honest opinion if I thought we had hit it off. "Hard to tell," I said. "At this point it's a doctor-patient relationship."

But the best call was from my mother. She wanted me to be

the first to know she bought a cell phone, and could I tell her how to send a picture so she could show me this beautiful rocking chair she bought for our living room?

What to react to first? That she kept using "our" in the most literal sense, or that someone who couldn't figure out how to answer a call, let alone take a picture, had a nicer phone than me?

"But I'm not sending any of those sex messages," she said.

"You mean text messages?" I laughed.

"Yeah. Whose got time to push a hundred buttons just to say nice ass?"

I was about to suggest that we swap phones so she didn't have to worry about high-tech features when my dad walked in with an ashen-looking Ken. "Mom, I gotta go."

"He'll be fine." My father saw me flinch. "He needed an emergency root canal, a temporary bridge, plus he's got a fistula in the bottom left . . . you don't want to ignore a draining abscess . . ."

"Can I get you something?" I asked him as Rookie rushed over, his tail wagging.

"A gun would be good . . . Hey boy. How are you?"

"I was thinking more in the line of an ice tea . . . You know what? Come sit down in the den and hold the new controller. That seems to have a strong, medicinal effect on men."

But he was going to need more than a remote to recover. He was in such agony from his multiple injuries, he wanted enough pain killers to be knocked out until the next presidential election.

"Daddy, what did you do to him?"

"What do you mean what did I do to him? He had the start of a raging infection, he couldn't eat or drink, he was in terrific pain . . . He'll be fine in the morning. Good as new."

Rookie growled, as if to say, He'd better be.

Ken finally conked out on the couch in the den, giving me some much needed alone time with my dad. But typical Harvey, no discussion was complete without a meal. As I whipped up some omelettes and toast while begging him to stop noshing on leftovers in the fridge, I thought of how little both the kitchen and its inhabitants had changed over the years.

Especially the heavy maple kitchen set, circa 1967. Though it had lost its Pledge luster, the chairs had managed to survive forty years of holding up my father's girth and Phillip's futile attempts to lean back on two back legs without falling.

About the only noticeable change now that my mother wasn't on the scene was the absence of two strong scents, cigarette smell and roses in bloom. The latter of which was intended to mask the former, though not even fragrant flowers could disguise tobacco smell, absorbed for decades into the shag carpets as my mother paced the halls, her cigarettes her only beacon of light.

It dawned on me how hard it must have been for her to keep up appearances, like the roses she raised to perfection, only to discover that like her garden, happiness could wither at the hands of nature's clock.

As for my dad, I had to laugh as I gazed at his familiar, I'm-eating-don't-disturb-me face. How many times had I sat in these chairs, waiting patiently to talk, knowing I couldn't start until he stretched, rubbed his belly, and examined the fridge to see what goodies my mother had hidden from him.

"Mommy's going to Phoenix tomorrow," I blurted.

My father nodded with a mouthful of egg. "It's about time."

"You know about him?"

"Of course. He's been hanging over my head from the beginning."

"She said you didn't know."

"She said a lot of things." He licked his fingers. "But it's fine. Let her go chase after the poor shlemiel. Finally get the answers she thinks she's been missing . . . It won't bring him back."

"Who? Marvin?"

"No. Todd. It won't bring the baby back . . . All these years she's tortured me, hounded me . . . if God had just let her marry him instead of me, she never would have suffered like this . . ."

"You poor thing . . . Rookie, stop kvetching. Come here. I'll give you some pie."

"Don't pity me, sweetheart. I've spent a lifetime fixing things and here's what I know. Teeth can be restored, but not always the heart."

"But what happens, you know, if she gets there, and he actually wants her back?"

"Believe me, if he's got the stomach to deal with her *meshugass*, be my guest."

"Are you serious? You're just willing to give up on your marriage like that?"

"She gave up on it years ago. Let her try to make a new life for herself if that's what she wants. I'll be fine."

"I don't know." I looked around. "You're not exactly running things like a captain."

"Funny you should say that." He rinsed his plate. "For the first time, I feel like a captain."

"You don't even miss her?"

"The truth?" He pulled the pie from the fridge and grabbed two forks. "You want?"

"No thanks . . . just tell me your life insurance policy is still in force."

"Leave me alone . . . I'm havin' a ball. Nobody telling me what to eat, what to wear . . . To be honest, she's been so unhappy for so long, it's like the fog lifted and I can see land . . . If she comes back, and I suspect she will, she's going to have to get used to some big changes around here."

"You mean like the big-screen TV? She's going to freak when she sees that."

"I'm telling you, if she says one damn word about it, we're through!"

"God, what is it with men and TV? It's like it's the one thing they know they can turn on."

"Never mind, young lady . . . Just make sure your mother goes to the bank and takes out enough money before she leaves. She can't dig through my pants pockets anymore if she forgets."

"I can't believe how nice you're being."

"What nice? This is like a vacation for me."

"Now you're scaring me."

"Then we're even . . . Now tell me about you and Kenny. Why didn't you tell me you were seeing someone nice?"

"Because I'm not. I met him three days ago on a blind date, which only happened because a guy came up to me at Brandon's bar mitzvah after hearing my act and asked if I was willing to be fixed up. And guess who that guy was? Seth!"

"No."

"Yes. But that's only one of like a hundred coincidences . . . It turns out Ken not only was in my nursery school class, but I think he and Seth went to Lohikan, and Ken went to Penn State."

"Is that right?"

"Yes."

"I tell you, Robyn. Every day I hear things that make me wonder. What's a coincidence, what's not? What does it all mean?"

"I know. Now tell me how you know the family? What's our connection?"

"How much time do you got?"

Chapter 19

Working in the news business, I heard stories every day that sounded so improbable, they had to be dreamed up by some acid-dropping Hollywood writer. But who, I wanted to know, was writing my insane tale, and what was the point? Because there had to be a point. Right?

God, please tell me that some greater good was supposed to come from learning more about my past in five days than I had in years. And that the seeming randomness of the events was actually part of some master plan to get me to what? Be a better daughter? Wife? Dog-sitter?

"You want to know how we met Judy and Howie?" My father stabbed at the pie. "It was at one of those crazy childbirth classes . . . what a bunch of crap that was . . . breathe in, breathe out. Like otherwise the baby won't come out.

"Anyway, your mother was pregnant with Todd, and Judy was having Seth, and they got to talking in class one night and found out they're using the same practice, but they both hated this one doctor, and next thing I know, they're good friends.

Especially after the boys were born. They'd meet at the park, they'd babysit for each other . . ."

"Cool." I watched him inhale the pie.

"Then, wouldn't you know it? The week your mother found out she was pregnant with you, Judy calls to say she's expecting too. You never heard such excitement . . . You sure you don't want?" He looked up. "The bananas are fresh."

"No, Daddy. One of us should be able to pass a physical."

"Fine. Let it be you."

"You're going to weigh three hundred pounds if you keep this up."

"More of me to love . . . Anyway, Judy and your mom were thinking now they'd have two kids the same age, we could go on trips together, share a cabana at the beach . . ."

"And then Todd . . . the tragedy."

"Yeah." He stopped eating. "The tragedy . . . I tell you, the day you were born should have been the greatest ever. I always wanted a little daughter to spoil, and there you were. But we were in bad shape by then. They hadn't found the baby's body, the phone stopped ringing with leads . . ."

"I can't even imagine what it was like. How you survived."

"What choice did we have? We had a helpless newborn to take care of, and Phillip was having nightmares every night that someone was coming to take him away next . . . Between the two of you, we never slept. Then right before your second birthday Phillip says, 'Instead of going to Disney World, can we go visit Todd in heaven? I miss my brudder so much.' Can you imagine?"

"No." Poor Phillip. I'd never really thought about what it must have been like for him. One day you had a brother, the next thing you know he's gone and there's a baby sister instead . . . Old enough to remember the pain, too young to understand. No wonder he was such a tortured soul.

"Speaking of birthdays, did you know Ken and you were born on the same day?"

"You're forgetting I didn't even know there was a Ken . . . but that's crazy."

"Yeah. Judy was two weeks late, and your mother was two weeks early . . . Go figure you'd both be born on September 27 . . . I think he maybe beat you by an hour. And oy. That poor doctor. Running back and forth between the labor rooms because the girls refused to use his partner. Somewhere there's a picture of the both of you in the nursery right after you were born."

"Unbelievable . . . So you guys were really close?"

"Well, Judy and your mother became good friends, but I didn't care too much for Howie. Nice guy, but we had nothing in common. He worked in the garment district, played golf, he liked the horses . . . Occasionally we'd go out to dinner, then take bets on who'd call the sitter more.

"But when the whole thing with Toddy happened, Howie was unbelievable . . . I don't have to tell you the pain we were in. And the house was in chaos with all the neighbors coming over to bring dinner, make phone calls, put up flyers, you name it . . .

"Judy couldn't come over because she was busy with her new baby, and your mother couldn't face her. Too hard because they still had Seth. But Howie was with me every night . . . He'd get off the train from the city, go home and change, then pick me up to meet the search party . . .

"This went on for weeks . . . We covered every inch of beach, the Dumpsters, donation bins . . . I'll never forget the stench, and the rats as big as cats, and you're praying with all your heart that this isn't where you find your precious, little baby . . .

"So anyway, every night before we'd call it off, Howie would say to me, 'Don't give up hope, Harvey. If we didn't find the body, maybe it means Todd is still alive somewhere,' . . . and I believed him. I did. On account of him, I didn't give up . . ."

"I had no idea." I reached for the tissue. "This is so devastating . . . Then what happened?"

"Well, one night we realized we'd reached the end . . . we assumed the worst . . . I tell you, heartbroken is just the beginning . . . but somehow we kept going. Not that you ever forget the baby you lost, but by then I was working for one dentist in Queens, and another fellow way the hell out in Smithtown somewhere . . .

"Then one day from out of nowhere, we get a call that this group of high school kids found the remains of a little boy. Not a mile from where we were that day . . . And instead of your mother feeling relief that at least now we'd have closure, she got worse. She couldn't eat, couldn't sleep . . ."

"Oh my God." I took his hand.

"I was scared she might kill herself.

"So, naturally, I got her help . . . even had a neighbor try hypnotherapy so we could get her off the mental meds, which were making her even more cuckoo than before.

"Meanwhile, as luck would have it, the same week we got the news from the police, I got an offer to buy a practice from a New Jersey dentist retiring to Florida. And before I could even read the buy-out agreement, your mother was calling the real estate people . . . I said, 'Sheila. Slow down. I don't know if this is even a good deal for me. He's askin' for a lot of money.' And she says she doesn't care what he's asking. She wants out of Oceanside, couldn't live there another day facing these memories. And that was that. When your mother says she's doing something, she's doing something.

"One day I come home from work and there's a For Sale sign on the house. And boom. We sold the house in two days, bought this place a week later, and here we are."

"I'm in shock . . . How did I grow up and not know any of this?"

"We told you what we could . . . the rest . . . did you really need to know?"

"Maybe not. But tell me this. If you were so close with the Danzigers, why didn't you stay in touch? It's not like we moved to California."

"Good question . . . Judy tried, but your mother wasn't interested. She said if she talked to her, all she'd do is think about Todd and the life we once had. So what could I do? Force her?"

"I guess not. So wait. Mommy had no idea Seth would be at the bar mitzvah?"

"How would she know? It's going on thirty years ago since we were in touch with the family and it's not like we'd recognize him . . . Who even knows why he was there?"

"He said he grew up with Rhonda's brother and was still close with her family."

"See? Total coincidence."

"It's nuts. A guy comes up to me at a bar mitzvah and asks if he can fix me up with his brother, and a few days later I find out that our families had this whole history together . . . Our mothers were friends, we were born on the same day in the same hospital, we went to the same nursery school, the same camp, the same college, and yet we never knew each other . . . Seriously. Who is writing this script? You can't tell me there's not a grand plan."

"Oh, there's a grand plan all right. But hell if I know what it is . . . Last chance on the pie." He stood and stretched.

"No thanks. I should wake Ken . . . It's eight o'clock already. Doesn't he need to get up and take his meds?"

"Yeah, but feed him first . . . If you need me I'm in the bedroom. The Mets are on."

"No way! You've got a TV in there?"

"A hundred and twenty seven channels . . . Your mother will flip, but tough noogies on her." He twirled me around. "I not only watch television in bed, I eat in bed! This is the life!"

Unbelievable. My parents were apart for five days and both behaving as if they were free on bail. Frankly, I could understand my father being ecstatic about experiencing a life unrestricted by my mother's iron-fisted fetishes, especially her insistence that food and television be forbidden in the bedrooms.

"It's not a house, it's a jail," he would yell, especially after the advent of twenty-four-hour sports on cable. But to no avail. My mother's rules were the law of the land and now I knew why. The more time she obsessed about keeping a clean house, the less time she'd have to obsess about losing her baby.

In fact, so fearful was my dad of a trauma causing her to go off the deep end again, he paid the guilty piper by giving in to her craziness. And no more so than this past year after she was diagnosed with breast cancer. Whatever she did was fine, even if it meant flying the coop.

Now that was love.

I found Rookie snuggled next to Ken on the couch in the den and wondered if it was a federal mandate that men had to keep ESPN on when they slept in the event of a national emergency (Pedro Martinez going to the Mets?).

I tried shaking him and calling his name but he didn't budge. Finally I had to resort to the tickle torture my father used to get me up for school.

"Go away."

"No. You have to eat something and take your antibiotics."

"Stop being my mother."

You should only know what I know about your mother. "C'mon. Be nice. If your condition doesn't improve, I'll lose my job."

He opened one eye. "You can always go back to being a stripper."

"Sic 'im, Rookie. Go on. Bite hard."

"Yeah, because it's not like I don't already feel like I've been hit by a semi . . . My ankle is throbbing, my back is killing me, my mouth is on fire . . ."

"Well, if it's any consolation, you look awful too. C'mon, Hopalong. Let's get moving."

"First help me to the john. I'm woozy."

"What great skills you have, Goldilocks. You're so good at holding men while they pee."

"Funny . . . I bet Rookie has to go too . . . Is your backyard fenced?"

"Yes." We hopped down the hall. "But when I let him out before, he saw our next door neighbor's German shepherd and ran back in."

"Rookie, you wuss! And after all that money I spent on karate lessons . . . Damn. My phone."

"It's been ringing all night. Didn't it wake you?"

"No. Who called? Because I'm sure you know . . . Let's see. Who were you this time? You've already been my wife, my girlfriend . . ."

"For your information, smart ass, I was talking to my dad the whole time and he told me the most unbelievable story about our—"

"Sorry . . . hold on . . . Hi Mom . . . Yes, I'm fine. I got teeth . . . Yes, they gave me painkillers . . . Yes, I know I have to eat first . . . Yes, I'm not driving . . . Can I call you back in a little while?"

Wait until she hears who your dentist is and whose house you're at. She'll plotz. "Mothers," I said. "Can't live with them, can't leave 'em in the trunk."

"Exactly." He laughed. "Hey. This looks just like our old bathroom. The shiny wallpaper, the shag toilet seat cover . . . I guess our moms used the same decorator."

"You have no idea how much they have in common . . . Do you need help?"

"I'm not stable yet. Would you mind?"

"Sure." *Never have I spent this much time with a penis not intended for recreational use.*

"Were you crying before?" Ken asked as we hobbled to the kitchen.

"Always."

"Madeline told me your parents split up. That's a shame . . . my father would fold like a house of cards if my mom walked out on him."

"Go figure. Mine is having a blast."

"So why the tears?"

"My dad finally told me the story about my baby brother." I helped him into a kitchen chair and iced his ankle. "And about how our families became friends . . . I'll tell you everything, but first you have to eat. Care for some banana cream pie?"

"I love pie." He looked. "But I don't want to take the last piece."

"Don't worry. If I know my dad, there are three more just like it in the fridge downstairs."

By the time I finished retelling the tale, tears were streaming down our cheeks and it looked like a shivah call more than a midnight snack. Ken was stunned that his parents had never said a word about our families' history, though we were babies when we moved away. What would have been the point?

And yet what caused Ken to break down was hearing of the generous spirit in which his father volunteered to help search for the missing baby.

"That's my dad. Always there for others. Which is why the letter from Mrs. Abramowitz about me carrying you around hit me so hard. It reminded me of how much I used to be like him."

"So what happened?"

"What happened?" he repeated. "You make two rights and a left and suddenly your life falls apart and who can think about being a good guy? Your only thought is survival."

"I hear ya, brother."

"But see, your dad is just like mine. You know how much he charged me today? Zilch . . . Had me in the chair for five hours and wouldn't even take my insurance card . . . Then he called a dentist he likes in the city, made all the arrangements for my follow-up visits including working it out with the lab to send everything to the other office so none of it would be a hassle . . ."

"Doesn't surprise me. He took care of everyone like that."

"Oh, and then he tells the other dentist I'm family so maybe the guy gives me a break . . . How can I possibly repay him?"

"You can't. But for guys like our dads, all they want is to get to heaven and say, 'Okay God, how did I do down there? Now can I play catch with the Babe?' "

"What about the Babe?" My dad walked in. "Hey, how's the patient?"

"Much better, actually. Your daughter is taking excellent care of Rookie and me."

"She's the best . . . You'd be lucky to have her around on a permanent basis."

"Yes," I said. "And if you call before midnight, you'll get the three-carat, tanzanite engagement ring."

"What did I say?" He shrugged. "I'm just suggesting—"

"Daddy. Stop. I don't need an infomercial."

"No, you need a good man who appreciates you." He kissed me.

"Just in case you missed it, he's talking to you." I winked.

"Well, he's right. You do deserve a great guy. But I'm not the best candidate right now."

"Are you kiddin'?" My dad laughed. "Who needs her more than a guy who can't pee by himself?"

One would think that after so many intimate exchanges with Ken, say nothing of our shared history, that he would understand that something rare was unfolding, and so what if the detour took thirty-three years, all signs were pointing to us getting together.

But no. When we said good-bye the next day, about the most personal thing he could think of to say was that Josh was right, I did have a cute ass.

Not that he didn't thank me for helping him, or relay the message from his mother that she was thrilled that we met, and next time she was in New York, she wanted to meet me and to please send her regards to my parents, whom she thought of often.

Bite me, I thought. That's what you said to a homely girl with acne who you had to be nice to because she was your best friend's cousin.

And yet my relationship expert, Rachel, thought maybe the reason he wasn't hinting at a future was that he was in shock and would call when he had clarity. "Just don't lay any guilt trips on him. If you hook up, you'll have plenty of opportunities."

Madeline dittoed that but had to admit the unexpected Mira influence was a possible snag. "She's the reason I wanted him to find someone else. You'll never know how she messed with his head. I hate her."

But when I spoke to my mother, who was waiting to board the flight with Sierra, her first reaction to hearing that we'd become friends was jubilation. "It's a miracle."

"I don't get it. If you wanted us to meet, why didn't you stay in touch with his family?"

"Don't you get it, Toots?" she cried. "It's my fault we

stopped talking. I tell you, one of my greatest regrets is that I turned my back on these people after they were so good to us . . . Judy was one of the nicest friends I ever had, but so much time had passed. What was I supposed to do? Call her up and say, Hi, I don't know if you remember me? We used to be neighbors in Oceanside? The family whose son was kidnapped?"

"I guess not."

"But see? What did I tell you? Fate stepped in and now things are right again."

"No, he's a user . . . I think fate knocked at the wrong door."

"Fate never knocks at the wrong door, dear. You just may not be ready to answer."

Chapter 20

I HAD THIS CONVERSATION with Rachel so many times, even I was sick of it:

Me: *Psychics are full of shit. They make everything up.*
Rachel: *No they don't. They get messages from spirit guides that are amazingly accurate.*
Me: *And the tooth fairy is straight.*
Rachel: *Just try it. It's better than therapy. You don't waste time blaming all your problems on the fact that your mother toilet-trained you too early.*
Me: *Never.*

But you know what they say about saying never. When life bites you in the ass, there go your beliefs. Which is how I ended up shlepping to Massapequa, Long Island, for a reading with Rachel's new favorite medium, Annette the Magnificent.

Oh fine. She didn't call herself magnificent. And though the reading with Annette was a gift from Rachel, and I was desperate for answers, I remained skeptical that this lady would be able to tell me anything other than how to get back to the Southern State Parkway.

And yet, it might be the only way to learn if Ken was in my future. Or even my present.

An entire week had passed since dropping him off at his apartment, and not a peep from the scoundrel, as if the whole encounter had been a hallucination.

Seriously. Who did that? Who took advantage of a stranger's generous nature, then disappeared like a magician's rabbit without properly thanking them? The least he could have done was pull flowers out of his hat, or, I don't know, an engagement ring.

Call me crazy, but I actually believed that five minutes after we said good-bye, he'd call to thank me for rescuing him. Or at least by the time I got home, there would be a message on my machine. Or the next day, a dinner invitation.

But when none of that materialized, I became obsessed, checking my voice mail every twenty minutes and my e-mails in between that. Only to be crushed when the lone male voice leaving messages was Josh.

Then call Ken, you're thinking. A casual hi, how are you managing? Couldn't. I had my pride. And a seemingly high tolerance for martyrdom. The key was to throw myself back into my old life, like finding a pair of jeans I'd shoved in the back of my drawer and forgotten were there. I didn't love them anymore, but at least they still fit.

I went back to work, pretending to know nothing of Gretchen and Kevin's daily dalliances. Back to teaching my makeup class at the New School. Back to worrying about money and my comedy career and whether my family would still be intact after my mother returned from Hurricane Marvin.

Only to decide in the middle of another sleepless night to

take Rachel up on her offer to see a psychic. Lucky me, Annette had a cancellation for Saturday, giving me enough time to teach my class, have the reading, and pick up my mother at the airport.

Yep. Sheil was on her way back, and though we had spoken several times and I knew she had found Marvin, she'd refused to discuss their reunion. So it was good I was seeing a psychic. Maybe she would give me a heads-up on whether to greet my mother with handcuffs or a hug.

Then again, as I sat on a beat-up couch in the basement of a single mom living in her ex-in-laws tiny Cape, I asked myself, how good could this lady be at predicting the future if she couldn't even predict that her own marriage would blow up after her daughter was born?

Not to mention, the longer it took for her to go through her spiel about how her spirit guide would come through but maybe not my dead aunt Joyce, the more I found the situation laughable. This was already such a waste of gas.

"Make a wish," Annette said. "Then tell me to begin."

"Okay." *I wish I was getting a pedicure instead of being here.* "I guess you can start."

"First thing I will ask is, is there anything you do not wish to hear?"

"Yeah. Bad news."

She laughed. "I meant, if I see that a family member might pass, do you want to know?"

"No." I shivered. "Definitely not. Unless maybe it's my aunt Fran."

"Fine . . . Now tell me your full name, your age, date of birth, where you live, and the first name and ages of anyone you're currently living with."

Why don't I just tell you my life's story so it cuts down on the guesswork. "My name is Robyn Fortune, I'm thirty-three, my birthday is September 27, 1971, I live in Brooklyn, and as of late, my roommate is my mother, Sheila, whose true age is unlisted."

Apparently Annette didn't get jokes when she was in her trance state, which didn't throw me as I was accustomed to playing to audiences who were too out of it to appreciate my humor.

"Now what will happen is both you and I will be silent for a few minutes while we ask that the white light of the holy spirit be around you. I want you to imagine that whatever questions you could possibly have, the answers will come, and I also want you to imagine that at the end of the reading you will feel that it was a wonderful union between you, me and my spirit. And the last thing I want is for you to imagine a place or a situation that gives you great pleasure so that you can feel that positive energy coming through."

And I want you to imagine me leaving because that pedicure really sounds good.

"To start, I'll ask you some questions, and you just need to say yes or no."

"Okay." *Do you think this is all a crock? Yes. Do you want to take notes? No.*

"Oh wow," she finally started. "This has really been a crazy year for you."

"Yes." *Duh. Why else would anyone come to you?*

"Do you . . . who is Daniel? I think he's on your father's side. He's showing me the heart area . . . which means that is how he probably passed . . ."

Big deal. She got my grandfather's name right. Rachel was at his funeral and heard the whole story about his heart attack in the middle of taking an eye test at the DMV.

"Do you know who I'm speaking of?"

"My grandfather."

"He's telling me about your work . . . Are you a painter? Because I see your arm making these little sweeping motions with a brush . . . it looks like you paint eyes and faces . . ."

"I'm not a painter." *It is so obvious you talked to Rachel.*

"Well, is painting a hobby? Because I see you . . . it looks like you're holding these little brushes, dabbing here, dabbing there, then you stand back and see if you like it."

"Surprise! I'm a makeup artist."

"Oh. Well that's the same idea. Right?" she laughed. "Forgive me. I see the images but I need help interpreting them . . . Now this isn't your only job, right? You do something else?"

"Yes." *Maybe if I leave now, I can find a Korean shop that takes walk-ins.*

"Because I see you standing in front of people and they're laughing. Do you teach?"

"Yes." *I might even have time for a manicure. Are my nails long enough for a French?*

"But it's funny. It's not like a regular classroom. I don't see desks. I see tables and chairs, almost like a restaurant . . . but that doesn't make sense. Who teaches a class at a restaurant?"

"I do stand-up comedy at clubs." I yawned.

"Okay. Yes. That makes sense because everyone is laughing and having a good time . . . So do you write your own material?"

"Yes . . . Look, I don't mean to be rude, but this is really starting to sound like my friend Rachel told you my entire life story . . . I'd ask for a refund, but she paid for the reading."

"It's okay. I get accused all the time of making this stuff up, or being a spy. But I have hundreds of clients . . . I don't even think it would be possible to know all their friends, bosses, neighbors, doctors, husbands, lovers . . . let alone remember a thing they said. Now who is Rachel?"

"You saw her a few weeks ago. Petite brunette . . . a lawyer . . . divorced . . . twin boys . . ."

"I know this sounds terrible, but I wouldn't remember her

if she were standing right next to you . . . Do you still want me to continue?"

"I guess."

"Because I'm hearing about your work being transferred to another medium. Are you trying to sell something?"

"Yes." I felt my arm tingle.

"Well it's definitely going to happen. And I don't know why, but I see a connection with you and that blond actress with the big boobs."

"Okay, that describes everyone in Hollywood."

"No, I know." She laughed. "Wait. Is it Pamela Anderson? But that makes no sense? She's not a comedian, is she?"

"Oh my God! She's not a comedian but the show is about her. How did you do that?"

"It's magic." She laughed. "No. I just heard her name. So wait. You wrote this for her?"

"Actually it's a one-woman comedy special called " 'When I See Pamela Anderson It's Like Looking in the Mirror.' "

"That sounds hilarious."

"You just gave me chills. I haven't told a soul what the title is or what it's about."

"Well, good. Start shivering, because I definitely see it being on TV."

"Really? When? Who buys it?"

"I would say by the end of the summer you'll have a deal . . . I'm hearing a cable channel hears about it through some kind of connection . . . Somebody who knows somebody who knows somebody . . . does this make sense to you?"

"Yes." *OHMYGOD! Seth knows Ken who knows all the people at Showtime.*

"So congratulations. This will be great . . . But let's move on because I'm hearing something about marriage and money . . . It's funny. The feeling I get is you have it, you don't have it, you have it again . . . Is your husband on Wall Street, because

it's like he's one of those who takes big chances with invest-
ments? A gambler type . . . Wow. I'm shocked you married
him. You're so different."

"That's why I married him."

"I get it." She laughed. "But are you separated now? I feel
like there's been a breakup."

"We're divorced."

"Unfortunately it needed to happen . . . He was a sweet guy,
but very troubled . . . Now why are they showing me two
rings? One of them looks like it's from the crown jewels of En-
gland, and the other one is huge too. Just more traditional-
looking."

"Oh my God." I shook.

"They were stolen from you?"

I nodded.

"Well I'm sorry to tell you this, but I don't believe you'll get
either of them back."

I started to cry, for Annette had just touched a wound I
thought was buried like an underground cable. A wound
known only to David.

After he'd proposed, my future father-in-law was so thrilled
that his son was fulfilling his promise to his mother, Essie, to
marry a Jewish girl, he presented me with one of Essie's rings,
which not only held great sentimental value to the family, but
could be guarded by Brinks.

With its burst of rubies, diamonds, and emeralds, it looked
like a miniature fireworks display. I doubted I would ever wear
something so ostentatious, but I was touched by the magnan-
imous gesture and the validation that I was worthy of owning
a family heirloom.

It was also worth more than my car. Which explains why
David pawned it. Anything not to have his car, a vintage red
Porsche, be repossessed in the middle of the night.

When I confronted him, he was so underwhelmed by my

tears, so sure that in a few months he could get it back because he had an "understanding" with the pawnshop, it was a turning point.

But it was the disappearance of my engagement ring, my perfect three-and-a-half-carat Tiffany diamond in a Legacy setting with graduated side stones, that caused me to call a lawyer.

At first I'd panicked when it wasn't in the pretty Wedgwood dish above the kitchen sink. I had searched for two days before telling David I couldn't find it, all prepared with my speech about how I was sure it had to be in the apartment because I distinctly remembered taking it off before showering the night before, and at least, thank God, it was insured.

Only to peer in his eyes and know I was looking at the thief and that our claiming the loss was not only his plan, but one of which he was quite proud, as it gave him enough money to cover his latest losses. All we had to do was call the police, report it missing, accuse the cleaning lady, and voilà, the insurance money was ours.

In the end, the police were called, but by our neighbors who heard David's loud screams as I beat him with a floor lamp and a broom . . . It was the only time I saw him cower and cry, but his tears had less to do with his remorse than the fact that his life had no meaning if he didn't have the money to bet on the World Series.

A pathetic story, but not one I had ever shared, not even with my parents. So there was no way Annette could have knowledge of these details unless she was really hearing, God help me, from some other dimension . . .

"Oh my God." I could barely talk when I called Rachel on my cell in the car.

"What did I say?" Rachel clapped. "She's amazing, right?"

"I can't breathe."

"So tell me."

"Well, first thing she said is, ditch the friend who sent you here. You can't trust her."

"She did not."

"Fine. But she did say that you are insanely jealous of me."

"Don't I tell you all the time I'd give anything for your ivory complexion?"

"Rach, I don't think I can drive now . . . I am so blown away."

"Oh my God. Pull over then. I didn't know you were in the car. Where are you?"

"Still in Massapequa . . . oh wait, there's a Dunkin' Donuts . . . Two toasted coconuts and one of those six-thousand-calorie lattes, and I should have enough gas to get to JFK."

"Do it later. Toby and Devin have friends over, another set of twins, only girls, and I have to keep my eye on them so they don't start looking down each other's underpants again."

"Are you kidding me? They're not even four."

"It's perfectly normal . . . That whole penis envy stage . . . Mine are so in love with theirs I have to bribe them to put it away . . . Now c'mon. Spill it."

"Okay." I turned off the car. "Basically she said that my parents will work things out but that my brother and Patti are going to split, which shocked me because they fight like crazy, but it's been that way from the beginning, so who would suspect? But according to her—"

"I don't care about Patti and Phillip. Tell me about you . . . are you going to be okay?"

"Yes. In fact she said things would be amazing for me . . . I'm definitely getting a TV deal."

"Fabulous. What did she say about Ken?"

"Wow. Let's cut to the chase. If I'm not ending up with him, maybe there's hope for you."

"I didn't say that . . . Look, I told you. I called him on a whim, but he's not my type."

"He's not?"

"No. He's perfect. I prefer men who are deeply flawed."

"Oh believe me, then Kenny's your boy. He has more flaws than a Fendi knock off."

"But does she see you hooking up with him?"

"Not sure. She saw me with a guy who sounded so great I wanted to run out and buy monogrammed towels."

"But it wasn't him?"

"I don't know. She just described him as someone from my past who suddenly comes back into my life, and our families know each other . . ."

"Oh. Then that's him."

"No, because she also described him as this really sweet guy who you liked as soon as you met, which is definitely not Ken . . . Oh my God . . ."

"What?"

"I bet she was talking about Josh."

"Who?"

"Nooo. I don't want to marry Josh."

"I repeat. Who is Josh? Wait. Was he the one who lived on his boat and wouldn't date you until you passed your deep water test?"

"No. That was Justin. Josh is someone I went to high school with, and now it turns out, nursery school too, and the other night, he suddenly showed up at my door and he looked great . . ."

"He sounds perfect."

"Would you stop? I know what you're doing, okay?"

"I'm sorry, sweetie. Ken is so cute. And we have so much in common. We're both attorneys, we both love to ski and travel and—"

"I'm hanging up now. I very much appreciated your gift. I'll have my thank you note in the mail by Tuesday . . . Please don't ever call me again."

"Stop. Don't be like that."

"Remember before when I told you Annette said to ditch you because I couldn't trust you?"

"Yeah."

"She really said that."

But as I drove to the airport, it wasn't Annette's advice about Rachel that kept repeating on me, it was her remarks about my unlucky streak.

"I can't believe you think you're unlucky," she said. "You grew up in a nice house in a nice neighborhood with parents who loved you. You had friends, got to take great vacations, you went away to camp, to college, you got an education, a job, you're beautiful, smart, talented. Don't you get it? You've been blessed with everything you needed to have a great life."

"Except for a husband who broke my heart and left me with more bills than a session of Congress."

"And you've come out of it smarter and tougher . . . Are you the same person anymore?"

"No. I used to be happy. Now I'm lonely and depressed and I don't trust people."

"You will trust again. You just need to think about your role in all of this. You knew he was a gambler, yet you convinced your self that once you were settled, you'd make him so happy, he wouldn't need his addictions."

Exactly.

"Then you thought if you handled the money, he couldn't spend it without your knowing."

I started to cry.

"Then you thought if you threatened to leave him or turn him into the authorities, he'd have no choice but to straighten out."

"He said that's why he married me." I reached for the tissues.

"I know. He thought you would be his savior, only he didn't want to be saved . . . You just have to remember next time you're in a bad situation like this, don't wait to be rescued. Get in there and fix it yourself . . . There is no AAA for life. It's up to us to repair what's broken. Which doesn't mean you can't ask for help, it just means you're in charge of making sure you get it."

"I tried so hard with David, but so what? When it was all over, we were in worse shape than when I left him alone."

"Don't you get it? You suffered a tremendous loss, and I don't just mean financially. But now you have to decide. Do you want to be miserable for the rest of your life and blame him? Or do you say, Well, that really blew, but I'm going to learn from it and move on?"

"I get it. I was an enabler. But what about my brother? He died before I was born and my parents never recovered. How was I supposed to fix that?"

"Things don't have to necessarily be our fault in order to learn from them. Sometimes, it's just enough to figure out how to survive . . . but don't you see? You saved their lives."

"Um, no. They didn't even notice me until I was five."

"Which is why you're so funny. You had to get their attention and you did it with your great humor . . . and because of that, you brought all this laughter back into the house."

"I guess."

"No, I mean it. You were blessed with an incredible gift . . . It's got to be the greatest feeling to make people laugh, and you are so good at it. I promise your life will turn around once you put all of this in perspective."

Of course I knew Annette had given me wonderful advice, but it wasn't her wise counsel that almost caused me to have an accident on the Grand Central Parkway. It was an offhand

comment she made about Ken and me having been thrown together over the years.

"You mean it was fate?" I asked.

"Partly," she said. "Which was helped along by a little plan.
Ask your mom what I'm talking about."

Chapter 21

DON'T YOU LOVE the days when things are going great? Nobody pisses you off at work, your hair looks good, you find a twenty in your raincoat? And then one little thing happens that freaks you out and you're banging on the vending machine so the Hostess Cupcakes come out faster.

Annette's vision of my future was so positive, I should have left her house floating on a cloud. Instead, I was so thrown by her last comment, I stuffed my face with Dunkin' Donuts.

She had said that it wasn't pure fate that had brought Ken and me together, it was a plan I should ask my mom about. Ask her what? Did she intentionally send me to the same nursery school, camp, and college as Ken?

No way. When I was little, my mother was so out of sorts, she couldn't even remember to take me to nursery school, let alone orchestrate a strategy that would guarantee Ken and I would be in the same place at the same time.

Sadly, Annette had to be mistaken, which meant that the rest of her predictions were bogus too. And yet there were so many details she'd nailed. The story of my wedding rings. The details of my divorce. The fact that I was an artist and a performer. The Pamela Anderson connection with my comedy special.

I was so bewildered thinking about the reading, I didn't recognize the woman who was waving to me in baggage claim. Good God. She was wearing so many different colors it looked like she had a run in with a Sherwin-Williams truck. Only to realize "she" was my mother.

You had to see this getup. A tight, pink peasant top that screamed, *They ran out of larges.* A long skirt with bright, neon flowers. High-heeled silver sandals in search of a maid of honor. Turquoise jewelry that could seat four, and the straw hat the Queen Mother wore to meet friends for lunch.

And get this. Her traveling companion wore a matching outfit, so that you weren't sure if they were gay or just a dysfunctional mother/daughter duo who still thought it was adorable to dress alike.

Yep. Sierra. Minus the oversized sweats, the purple hair, the piercings, and the painted black lips. It was Godzilla meets Pretty Woman.

"Yoo hoo! Toots!" My mother blew a kiss. "Over here."

"Look at you guys." I hugged her. "What did you do? Strip the mannequins at the mall?"

Sierra stopped smiling.

"What's the matter with you?" my mother scolded me. "I think Sierrapaigemather looks classy now."

Yeah. The Class of '46. "You do look great, Sierrapaigemather." I coughed. "Love the skirt. Hope you brought me one."

"Oh, can it, blondie." She glared. "You're so full of shit I don't know how you sit down."

Yep. It was her.

"I'm serious. You look very together." *For a retired teacher. What? No brooch?* "Did you like Phoenix?"

"She loved it!" My mother clapped. "And we had a ball, didn't we?"

"Definitely." Sierra gave a thumbs-up. "Your mom is a piss."

"Oh I know."

"No, I mean it." She took my arm. "Your mom is a very cool lady. You should treat her better . . . Hey Sheil, you still got the cookies from the plane? I'm starvin' . . ."

"I treat her fine," I said. "But it's nice that you got along so well." *Normal people want to strangle her after a day. You lasted an entire week. It's like the miracle of Hanukkah.*

"How come you didn't answer my e-mail?" My mother gave Sierra the cookies while searching for the right baggage carousel.

"You sent me an e-mail?" I tried to keep pace.

"Yes-sir-ee bob. You shoulda told me it was so easy."

"Hmm. I wonder if I deleted it not knowing it was from you. What's your screen name?"

"I gotta remember that too? First the cell phone number, then my e-mail name, then your address in Brooklyn so I can get my regular mail . . ."

"You're staying?"

"Sure I'm staying. What did you do? Rent the room already?"

"No. I just thought that maybe once you had time to think, you'd reconsider . . ."

"She's not going home." Sierra spit out her gum. "You gotta problemo with that?"

"I have a big problemo." I gave her a look. "It's where she lives."

"Sheilbethere@aol.com," my mother shouted. "Wasn't that it?"

"Yeah." Sierra burped.

"That's sweet, Mom." I ignored Sierra. "What screen name did you use for me?"

"Oh for Christ's sake. I sent a lousy e-mail, not took over as secretary-general."

"Fine. Then what did the e-mail say?"

Sierra pulled me aside. "This is what she wrote: Dear Barbie, Please hook up with Ken so you can buy a pink house, drive a pink convertible, and live happily ever after with your pink kids."

"Is that true?" I looked at my mom. "Was it about Ken?"

"You betcha, Toots. I think it's great that you two finally met."

"You mean you're glad that your little scheme finally worked . . ."

"What little scheme? All I said was I would be so happy if you two got together."

"He's an asshole, okay? He took advantage of my generosity and Daddy's time and didn't so much as send a token of his—"

"What did you mean by a scheme?" my mother interrupted. "You think I had something to do with fixing you up?"

"I don't know. I just found out about all these amazing coincidences which sound awfully fishy . . . How do I know you and his mom didn't conspire to—"

"You've said a lot of stupid things in your day, but that takes the cake."

"Yeah." Sierra yawned. "Really stupid."

"For your information," Sheil said, "I haven't been friendly with his mother in thirty years. Furthermore, I am sick and tired of hearing all these crazy accusations that I interfere in your life."

"Really. You swear you had nothing to do with this?"

"Not me," she said. "Your father!"

My father? The guy who couldn't assemble a simple toy if the manufacturer sent over the guy who designed it? He was the mastermind behind some cockamamie plan to keep two kids in the line of sight of each other? No way. She was lying. But on a positive note, maybe this was the sign that Annette wasn't a crock after all.

Thank God Sierra agreed to be dropped off at her mother and Simon's Upper East Side apartment. I needed to speak to Sheil in private, and hell if I wanted the goo girl putting in her two cents, which she'd probably borrow from me anyway.

Only to get home and have the ordinarily chatty Sheila claim to be too tired to talk. But not too tired to see if our neighbors were up for a last-minute game of mahj, and to ask what I had in the freezer to serve, and didn't I know I was running low on napkins?

Finally we reached a compromise. She would rest for an hour, then we would talk over dinner, then she could do whatever the hell she wanted. Which was fine, as it gave me time to check my messages, return phone calls, and get my dad, Dr. Brainiac, on the phone.

He was happy to hear that my mother had arrived safely, but not happy to hear that Ken hadn't called me since I took him home. Still, it gave me the perfect opening to pose the question. Had he been in cahoots with Ken's family so that we'd go to the same camp and schools?

No, absolutely not, what would ever possess me to ask such a ridiculous thing? But if I'd learned anything from watching Gretchen all these years, it was how to get a source to talk.

"I know you're hiding something, Daddy. You're breathing extra hard."

"I'm not hiding anything."

"Do you swear on my life that you never made special arrangements with the Danzigers?"

Silence.

"Daddy?"

"Why did you have to say swear on your life? Never say that to a parent who lost a child."

"Sorry. I'll rephrase the question."

"What are you? A lawyer?"

"No, a lawyer's sister . . . Now I know you're not telling me something and if I have to, I'll—"

"Fine. You caught me. Yes, I had a plan. Are you happy now?"

"Are you serious? Oh my God. No, I'm not happy. What do you mean you had a plan? Were you so afraid I'd never find a guy on my own?"

"What are you talking about? This had nothing to do with you."

"What are *you* talking about? Why else would you do this?"

"For your mother."

"What?"

"Because it's like I told you. She was in very bad shape after we lost the baby. She refused to see a psychiatrist, she barely spoke to Aunt Marilyn, me she couldn't even look at . . . It got so bad, she stopped leaving the house.

"So one day I'm telling Howie how bad things are getting and he says to me how much Judy misses her, and maybe if you and Kenny were in the same nursery school class, then your mother would run into her again, and Judy could try to reach out to her."

"Oh my God." I burst into tears. "He sounds like such a nice man." *Unlike his son.*

"Only it didn't help. Your mother would drop you off without getting out of the car. Any time the parents were invited to school, she'd make me go. The teachers would ask her to chaperone a field trip, she'd first ask who else had volunteered."

"But you said they were such good friends."

"That's what happens when you're in a deep depression . . . I couldn't even mention Judy's name without her getting all worked up . . . didn't I know how hard it was to see Judy and have to hear all about Seth's accomplishments, or see how big he was getting. All it did was remind her that Todd was gone . . ."

"This is so sad." I sniffed. "But why keep trying?"

"Because Howie kept saying how Judy was still hoping that Sheila would talk to her again if they found something new in common."

"But then we moved."

"Right. And little by little, things did get better. She started to come out of her depression. She started teaching violin again . . . But God forbid I should ever bring up Judy and Howie's names? Don't ask . . ."

"So then how did we end up at Lohikan together?"

"Well, in spite of everything, Howie and I stayed in touch. One day we got on the subject of sleepaway camps and he suggested I send Phillip and you to the one his boys were going to because they loved it, and if you did go, then we could all bump into each other on visiting day."

"Are you serious? This sounds like the plot of an espionage film."

"Except no happy ending . . . At first I thought, this is a bad idea. What am I doing stirring the pot again? We had finally settled into a comfortable life, you and Phillip were happy, we had friends and neighbors . . . just leave well enough alone.

"But one day, out of the blue, your mother tells me how she was looking in the basement for her tennis racket and found the fondue set that Howie and Judy gave us, and she wondered how they were doing. So I said pick up the phone and call her. But no, she can't do that. She was afraid Judy would think too many years had gone by . . . Of course I didn't dare tell her I was still in touch with Howie and I knew Judy would love to hear from her.

"Anyway, it got me thinking, maybe it was a sign. Send all the kids to the same camp, we'll run into each other on visiting day, and the girls might start talking again."

"And?" It was like being glued to a radio broadcast.

"And . . . we made arrangements to meet at such and such a time, but they never showed up. So the next day Howie calls all apologetic. All of a sudden, Judy didn't want to have anything to do with us. Sheila hurt her terribly and what did she need this for?"

"So they never saw each other?"

"No. And that was the only year you were all together."

"Wow. What a story . . . and Mommy didn't know about any of this?"

"Not until Penn State."

"Are you serious? You were still at this ten years later."

"No. Howie and I had lost touch by then . . . We had nothing to do with the fact you both ended up there. That was pure coincidence."

"No way."

"Well, I don't know why Kenny went there, but you went because your mother insisted."

"Believe me, that I remember. I hated it the first time we visited. It was too big, it was in the middle of nowhere . . . but she kept pushing."

"Well, you had a good four years there."

"Yes, but I didn't know that when I started. So wait. Why was it so important . . . Oh my God. Did she know that Ken was going too?"

"How would she know? No. It's crazier than that . . . The reason she pushed so hard was because some *meshuganeh* psychic on Long Island told her it was your destiny."

"I'm sorry?"

"Can you imagine? I'm working night and day to earn a good living, and she's throwing away money on gypsies who sit around and make up these cock-and-bull stories."

"No way!" *Please God. Don't let this be the first sign I'm turning into my mother.* "How did she even find her?"

"I think she used to listen to her on some radio program, and then a neighbor went to see her, came home raving how she was so amazing, she got this right and that right, and next thing I know, your mother's driving to Long Island and she doesn't care that I think it's a stupid idea."

"Wait. Do you remember the psychic's name?"

"No. All I know is she comes home all pumped up that you have to go to Penn State because that's where you're going to meet your husband."

"Oh my God."

"But we all know that was a bunch of crap because you didn't meet David at school. You met him on that cruise."

"I don't believe it. She made me go there so I'd end up with an MRS degree?'

"Believe me, I thought the whole idea was crazy. You got a nice scholarship at Lehigh and what did we need to spend that kind of money for if you weren't excited to go? I said to her, Robyn can find a fella after she graduates."

"Wow. Talk about having no faith . . . but wait. What happened at Penn State? You said that's when Mommy found out you had been going behind her back."

"Well, of all things, she ran into Judy in the elevator in your dorm on moving day."

"You're kidding? All that work and the way it finally happens is a chance meeting?"

"Only I didn't know. I was helping you unpack and she went down to smoke. I remember she came back white as a ghost, but said nothing. We go home, she says nothing. A few weeks later, she decides to tell me the story. She ran into Judy, they hug and kiss, have a nice conversation. Then Judy starts talking about how funny fate is and tells her the whole story. How many times we tried arranging a meeting that looked coincidental, but it was only after we stopped trying that it happened."

"That's crazy. Was she mad?"

"No . . . She said she knew all along and how could I ever think I could outsmart her? Hadn't I ever heard of picking up the extension and eavesdropping?"

"Sounds just like her." I laughed. "She used to do that to me all the time. Don't you remember when Adam Gellner called to ask me to the prom and I said, Mom can I go? Click . . ."

"No, but anyway. Turns out she was very happy you were at the same school."

"Then how come she never mentioned his name or told me to look him up?"

"Are you kiddin'? Back then she couldn't give you a weather report without you trying to start a fight."

"I remember . . . It's just so bizarre . . . A psychic says one thing and my life is changed forever. Remember how badly I wanted to go to Maryland, but Mommy carried on that I'd be so much happier at Penn State? I swear, if I had known it was because she wanted me to find a husband . . . That is sick . . . Are you listening, Daddy?"

"I'm listening . . . I was just thinking. Wouldn't it be something if that psychic turned out to be right and you did end up marrying Kenny?"

"Don't put money on it. I can't even get him to call me."

"Well, I understand he's a little *farblandzhet* right now. But one thing I've learned in life . . . Every day brings something unexpected . . ." His voice trailed off.

Amazing. Thirty years later, one little thing could still trigger memories of that fateful day.

"Look," I said. "If Ken and I are supposed to be together, then it will happen. But I'm sure as hell not going calling that ungrateful putz."

"It's your life." He sighed. "Besides, I just remembered you never met Kenny at college, so it turns out that that psychic lady was wrong about everything."

"Wait. That's not true. It turns out I did meet Ken at school . . . we just didn't *know* it until now . . ." *Hello Annette? I know I doubted you, but help me out here. How does this whole destiny thing work exactly?*

Chapter 22

I PUT UP A POT of coffee (the way I liked it!) and checked in on my mother, who was still dozing. How innocent she looked when she wasn't plotting to change the course of my life. And how neat this room could be kept when it wasn't doubling as a shipping department for items I needed to sell on Craigslist.

We're so different, I thought. If I had a room the size of Madison Square Garden, I would still be tripping over shoes and searching under piles of clothes for clean bras.

But what did Grandma Rita always say? The cleaner the room, the crazier the tenant?

That was certainly true of my mother, though I could see where in her distraught state, she might have convinced herself that keeping a tidy home would allow her to think she had control over her life.

Yet studying her peaceful expression, I wondered what troubled me more. That I was clueless to the extent she had struggled with depression, that I had been kept in the dark about our ties to a family with whom we shared a tragedy, or that my future had been tampered with, like a lavatory smoke detector, just to fulfill a psychic prophecy?

It was none of the above. Something else was breaking my heart.

"Go away." My mother swatted me. "I'm not done resting."

"Oh, trust me. You are." I kept shaking her.

I had questions, I told her. Dozens of them. But one that mattered the most. How could she live with herself knowing how unfair she'd been to my father? All these years he'd struggled to keep their marriage alive, knowing his angry wife didn't share the same desire.

"You want to know how much he loves you?" I cried. "You walked out on him and he still wanted me to make sure you had enough money for your trip to Phoenix . . . So what if he wasn't your dream date? He turned into a wonderful husband. A fantastic father . . . He worked his ass off so we had everything we needed . . . And look how hard he tried to get you back on friendly terms with Judy Danziger so you'd have a good friend again."

"Fine." She sat up and yawned. "I'll join his fan club. When are the meetings?"

"This isn't funny, Mommy. I'm tired of listening to you bitch about him, when you've been so mean to him, and he never complained."

"Oh. So he's Saint Harvey and I'm Sheila the Shrew?"

"I'm saying you weren't the only one who lost a child. Daddy suffered as much as you. Maybe even more because he felt all the blame. But did you ever reach out to him? Tell him you loved him and you'd get through this together?"

"Why are you attacking me?" She waved her finger in my face. "You have no idea what went on between us . . . What did he do? Take out my violin and tell you his sob story?"

"All I'm saying is it's so unfair that you never forgave him or stopped punishing him."

When I was acting fresh as a kid, she was very fast with her slapping hand. But as this was my home, and I was taller, now her only defense was to reach for her cigarettes.

"Don't you dare light that in here!"

"Uch! So many damn rules." She grabbed her lighter and headed out the kitchen door.

"You mean like at our house?" I trailed behind. "Name a food I was allowed to have in my room . . . The answer is none. What time did I have to turn off the TV, even when I got to high school? Ten o'clock. What did you do if my laundry wasn't sitting on the washing machine by Sunday night? You threw it on my bed . . ."

"This is what you want to fight about? The laundry?"

"I don't want to fight. I want to tell you how I feel because if you think I'm going to support you when you walk out on Daddy for some man who—"

"Go to hell. The only reason you're on his side is because you need his money."

"Oh my God. That was so mean . . . You know how hard I've tried to handle everything on my own. I'm working three jobs, I sold my furniture and my car . . . Wait. Hold on. David used to do this to me, too. Turn everything around so it becomes about me and then you're off the hook—"

"Oh, stop your bellyachin' . . . This is my life and my marriage." She puffed. "If I want to make changes, I sure as hell don't need your permission. Furthermore, your father and I had an understanding that you wouldn't know about."

"Really? You mean that he was to blame and you were never going to let him forget it?"

"Now you're talking nonsense. Of course I forgave him . . . Not that it made a damn bit of difference . . . He still couldn't get it up if his hoo-ha was attached to a forklift."

"Mommy. Stop! I don't want to hear that stuff."

"No ma'am. Too late. You brought it up and if it's the truth you're after, then start openin' your ears and shuttin' your trap." Smoke billowed from her nostrils.

"Fine. Tell me your side of the story. Just . . . you know . . . leave the bedroom out of it."

"Fine. 'Cause here is all you need to know . . . You're damn right we both lived this nightmare. But you're wrong about how it was. It wasn't me who wouldn't forgive your father. He wouldn't forgive himself . . . He'd cry himself to sleep every night telling me he didn't deserve to live, and why did God spare Abraham's son, but not his own . . .

"You don't know what I went through with his drinking, and then his heart problems, and then that lunatic partner he brought in from Chicago who cooked the books and nearly ran the practice into the ground, leaving us with a hundred grand in bills and a lawsuit that could have cost your father his license altogether.

"And I didn't even get to the part where he was such a basket case, we couldn't have sex . . . there I am. A woman in her prime with a husband who can't even pee straight."

I studied her through the mesh screen, trying to let some of what she was saying register, but not really comprehending the enormity of it because I was so focused on her skin, which despite her smoking, was remarkably creamy, and her almond-shaped eyes, which against all odds, remained lustrous after a lifetime of grief.

"What are you looking at?" She snuffed out her butt.

"Sorry. I was trying to let everything sink in. Your story is very different than Daddy's."

"Of course it's different. He's lying."

"Maybe." I laughed. "But it's like Grandma always said. There's your side and his side, and somewhere in between is the truth."

"I suppose." She came back inside and peered inside the

coffeepot. "Again with the weak coffee. Why don't you just boil water, add food coloring, and call it even?"

"Why don't you just settle the score with Daddy and go home?"

"No. I'm thinking of moving over to Phillip and Patti's house."

"Really? So you're not running away to Phoenix?"

"Nah. It didn't work out so good. Besides, who the hell wants to live in the desert? You spend two seconds outside and get baked like a potato."

"But what about Marvin? And how come you never told me about the Danzigers? And did you really make me go to Penn State to find a husband? And what was the name of the psychic you went to on Long Island?"

"I can't discuss this without real coffee."

"Fine." I dumped the pot. "Make it however you like . . . When are you going to tell Phillip the good news?"

"I'll call him tonight."

"Oh no." I clapped. "Let me. Please let me."

Forget giving a mouse a cookie. Give my mother Starbucks and she'll tell you anything you want to know, and plenty you don't. As we sat in my kitchen, interrupted only by phone calls and bathroom breaks, I learned more about my life in two hours than I had in two decades.

Seems my father's closest companion was Jack Daniel's, while my mom was on so many different antidepressants, Merck bought stock in her. He once thought about taking his life, she thought about helping him.

No wonder the house was like a quiet hotel with guests who kept to themselves. Every night my dad retreated to the basement and his map collection, while my mom holed up in the converted attic and her violin studio.

Meanwhile, the mutual threat of abandonment hovered like a slow-moving tropical depression. My father would reach a low point and tell my mother he put a deposit on a condo in Florida for himself, while she would wave the Marvin Teitlebaum flag in his face, claiming he would take her back in a heartbeat if he knew she was single.

But as with most threats, when all was said and done, more was said than done. And in their case, with good reason. They knew in their hearts that who but each other would understand their private hell? Not to mention, my father would wilt in Florida's heat, while my mom had no idea if Marvin remembered her.

As it turned out, he did. Though it being forty years and a heart condition later, he could not remember why. What Marv did recall, however, was that he had several lady friends to whom he professed true love, so that upon his return from his tour of duty, at least one or two would still be interested in settling down with him.

Sheil did not take kindly to learning of this cruel deception, and made sure her good-bye included the wish that his pacemaker was made by the company that knew the wiring was faulty.

Frankly, hearing her recant these tales stunned me, not for the judicious retelling, but for the eye-opening revelations (so rare for secret agent mom). She had insisted on my attending Penn State because of a psychic's prediction, though not the one having to do with meeting my future husband (it turned out the woman only mentioned this in passing). Instead Sheil banked on the omen that I would have a great college experience and leave with a diploma.

Naturally, I was grateful that my mother had managed to make good decisions on my behalf in spite of her troubles. Yet how disconcerting to realize I had grown up with such a myopic view of my world and that it took a psychic to bring reality into focus.

But what really irked me was how it was one thing to have a mother who shared nothing when you were a child. It was quite another to be a grown woman and still not qualify to be her confidante.

"Why didn't you ever tell me how much you suffered after Todd?" I dumped the last of my coffee down the sink.

"Why? So you could turn around and blame me for screwing up your childhood?" She peered out the kitchen door as if the cigarette fairy was beckoning.

"I never said you screwed up my childhood . . . Can we please have one conversation where you don't light up? I'm saying I would have appreciated some honesty. But God forbid anyone should ever know the truth about Sheila Holtz."

"I'm plenty honest. I just think a person has a right to their privacy." She fondled the cigarette pack on the kitchen table as if to say, "Mama's comin'."

"That's right. You don't show your tax returns to your neighbors, but it's perfectly acceptable to discuss a family tragedy with your family."

"It was no secret we lost a baby."

"Only because Aunt Marilyn told me. It would have been better hearing it from you."

"Oh please. What would have changed if I'd burdened you with my nightmare?"

"Are you kidding? It would have changed everything. I would have been more understanding. More sympathetic . . . All I remember is Daddy constantly worrying about you going off the deep end. I just never knew why . . . And what about me and Phillip? We couldn't even fight without hearing, 'Cut it out. Do you want your mother to end up in the hospital?' "

"That's what you're angry about? That you couldn't deck Phillip? Believe me, Toots. Nothing I said would have made you do anything different. You were totally self-centered."

"I was self-centered because you never let me in. And what's changed? Nada! Did you really think it was fair to keep it from me that you had cancer? And how should I feel knowing you didn't want me to be there for you after your surgery? That's what daughters are for."

"Oh for Christ's sake. It had nothing to do with not wanting you there. I just didn't want to burden you because I was afraid *you* would go off the deep end. That's what a mother is for. To protect her children."

"When they're little, fine. But hello. I'm an adult, which means I get to decide what I can and cannot handle . . . God, what is it with people who take advantage of you, then push you away when the relationship isn't convenient?"

"When did I ever take advantage?"

"Forget it." I looked out the window. "It's pointless trying to talk to you . . . I just wish someone would explain to me how I always end up on the wait-and-see side of the relationship . . . why no one gives a damn about my feelings . . . I really have to stop putting up with this crap . . . I'm either in your life or out of your life, so don't expect me to jump for joy every time you decide to show up after your little disappearing act."

"Slow down, Toots. You lost me. I never disappeared on you."

"And what did I ever do to deserve being treated like a servant? Do this for me and that for me. Run here, watch my dog, take in my mail . . ."

"Sounds to me like you got your wires crossed. Like that time I tried to jump my car battery and almost blew myself up . . . Who are you mad at exactly? Him or me?"

"What?"

"You're going on and on about things I never did . . . I think you're just getting out your anger with Kenny Boy."

"I guess."

"So is it safe to come out now?"

"No. I'm mad at both of you. In fact I'm mad at everyone . . . Have I ever told you how much I hate people?"

"Every day. Time to take the civil service exam."

"Go have your cigarette." I sighed. "This is getting me nowhere."

"Well maybe not . . . It's good to get angry. That's the only way we ever vow to change."

"Does that mean you're going to change?"

"Hell no. Too late for me. But no reason you can't go find fly boy, yank 'im by the ear like I used to do to Phillip, sit 'im down, tell 'im what's what, and threaten to ban dessert for a year if he doesn't shape up."

"That's the solution to my love life? Deny the guy pie?"

"It worked for your father."

At the urging of my friend Dante Ferrete, a fellow stand-up, I was being dragged out of retirement. It had been a week since my mother had returned, but almost a month since I'd last performed. Had I forgotten that I'd been on a roll and was messing with my momentum?

Dante was right, of course. And it's not that I didn't want to get back out there. But I still had so much on my mind, namely that my mother had yet to pack her bags. Something to do with Phillip screaming that it would be a huge imposition, and she made them all nuts, and he was sick of this stupid game already and why didn't she just go home where she belonged?

But I also knew that Patti, the Agenda Queen, had called back to say it would be fine if Sheila was there temporarily, as long as she was willing to help with the three Cs: cooking, cleaning, and carpooling.

Meanwhile, with my mother still circling like a flight at JFK, I just hadn't felt comedic enough to even try an open-mic night. Until Dante called and said we were going to go on at a new club on the Lower East Side called Busted.

It was an unusual venue in that it was housed in a former police station, and audiences voted which acts were so bad, the comics had to serve time in a slammer. But a gig was a gig, and this one even paid. Only hitch was that the owner expected you to bring your own entourage.

Good-hearted Josh had volunteered to come as a reward for me having gone out with him. And now if I could get Julia to come, she could not only whistle through her teeth, but reminisce with him and hopefully keep him occupied.

"Fine, I'll go," she said. "But I'm only doing this for you . . . So he's really sexy now?"

"Well, don't come expecting Antonio Banderas, but yeah, he's got that certain look."

"I don't know why he'd even want to talk to me. You're forgetting I'm the one who used to tape Twinkies to his locker."

"I didn't forget. Just bring your checkbook. You might have to reimburse him for therapy."

"Haha . . . so who else is coming?"

"Rachel if she can get her nanny to switch her night off, a few people from work maybe . . ."

"Did you ask Ken?"

"Who?"

"Oh God. He hasn't called you yet?"

"Nope."

"He sucks! But better to find out they're dirtbags before you've had sex."

"Exactly."

"So you're over him?"

"Totally." I cleared my throat.

"Then why are you doing that throat thing you do when you're lying?"

"Because I can't get him out of my head, okay? Julia, he's everything I want."

"Except a decent human being who knows how to express sincere gratitude."

"It's just an act. He can be very nice. You should have seen him at this funeral we were at."

"Oh please. Everyone's nice at a funeral."

"No, it was more than that. Everyone from work was there and they were so happy to see him, and then this one chick started crying because he looked like his old self again and this other lady kept saying to me, 'He's such a sweetheart, isn't he?'"

"Fine. He's a big hit at work. But take off the blinders, babe. He's trying to piss you off so you don't get any ideas."

"Too late. I have more ideas than a Google search. And there's something else, and don't laugh. I think maybe it's fate that we were brought together now."

"Good old fate. The single girl's number one defense . . . It was so meant to be . . ."

"I mean it. We've got this whole history together and his friend who died keeps sending me signs to stick around."

"You want signs? I'll buy a billboard on Broadway. 'Wake up Robyn. He's using you.' . . . Just let me come up with something to get back at him and you'll feel a hundred percent better."

Little did I know Julia would move so fast.

I had started to do this bit in my routine where I brought my cell phone up on stage, and if it rang, I took the call, then milked it for everything it was worth.

One time it was a wrong number, and the poor kid who thought he was ordering in Chinese couldn't understand why I recommended the house special, Sum Dum Fuck. I got huge laughs, and the best part was that the routine was all off the cuff, eliminating the need for memorization.

So you bet I brought my cell up on stage with me that night at Busted. And to make sure it rang, I made Josh the setup man. He would wait four minutes, then call. Only when I looked out, I saw that he and Julia seemed wrapped up in more than just conversation.

Yoo hoo? Up here. Remember me? Josh, stop touching her . . . Julia . . . don't toy with him. It'll be the worst sex you ever had . . .

"Yeah, so, how does it feel knowing your tax dollars are paying for all these scientific studies trying to prove that men and women are hardwired differently . . . Really? Because unless some fat-ass professor in Kansas with patches on his jacket can prove it, I'm thinking, what differences? You, sir. The guy with the Hooters shirt . . . did you bring one for me, because I would be so proud to wear it? [turns to crowd] Jesus loves him, but everyone else thinks he's an asshole . . .

"Look, it's simple. We are different. To make a girl happy, compliment her, encourage her, laugh with her, cry with her, hold her, smile at her . . . And to make a man happy? Show up naked, bring food. Don't block the TV. [audience applauds]

"Quick. What's the difference between a girlfriend and a wife? Forty-five pounds. What's the difference between a boyfriend and a husband? Forty-five minutes. [laughter]

"But here's the biggest difference. Men are the happier species. Wanna know why? The garage is all theirs. Wedding plans just take care of themselves. Chocolate is just another snack. They can wear a white T-shirt to a water park. Car mechanics don't lie to them. One mood, all day long . . . [heckler: Underwear is six bucks for a three-pack!] Exactly!" I clapped.

It was great. The crowd was eating it up. Then my cell rang, right on cue. *Nice work, Josh.*

"Sorry. Hold on. Let me just see who this is." I put it on speaker phone. "I've been waiting for the results of my eye test and I forgot to study . . . Hello?"

"Robyn?" A man says.

"Yes?"

"Hi . . . It's, um . . . Ken."

"Ken?" I give the audience a look that says, Oh, this is going to be good . . . Now, of course, I'm thinking that Josh and Julia, bless their hearts, set him up for revenge and I'm so happy.

"Nice to hear from you, Ken. Been a while . . . I wondered what happened to you because after you had your accident and I took care of you, babysat your dog, ran your errands, took you to a funeral, drove you to Jersey so you could see a dentist, put you up at my parents' house . . . Call me crazy . . . but I thought you might call."

"I'm sorry. I—"

"No, but really. It's fine. I like dating inconsiderate assholes. Good for character building. Plus it gave me time to think about converting to Catholicism and becoming a nun."

"Robyn . . . stop. Please."

"Sorry. I shouldn't tease. But it's funny. I was just sitting around and saying how—"

"Robyn! My father died."

"What?" I gasped, but not as loud as the crowd. "Oh my God. When?"

"Yesterday . . . He played eighteen holes in the hot sun . . . on all this medication . . . drowsy . . . fell asleep at the wheel . . . maybe if the ambulance got there sooner . . ."

Talk about dead silence.

Chapter 23

WHAT A NIGHTMARE to go from feeling the crowd's love to feeling they would stone me if they ever saw my face in public again. Didn't matter that I was as taken by surprise as them, I still wanted to crawl into one of those tiny golf holes.

As for Ken's reaction, he sounded so numb, I'm not sure he realized his voice had been piped through the club's sound system. Thank God. For if he knew that I had just ridiculed him in front of a live audience, there would be no forgiving me.

Still, when he asked me to attend the funeral and to please bring my parents, I felt so guilty, I was tempted to confess so that he at least had the option to rescind the offer, then changed my mind for both our sakes. There would be plenty of time to hate me afterward.

But imagine my angst on the way to Long Island the next afternoon. What if Ken had somehow figured out that our private conversation wasn't very private? What would I say to Seth and Madeline if Ken told them about my mean trick? How would Ken's mother react to seeing my mother? More important, after three weeks apart, how would my *father* react to seeing my mother?

I really wish I smoked.

"What are you going to say to Daddy when you see him?" I asked Sheil in the car.

"What do you mean what am I going to say? I'll say hello."

"I know that . . . but are you going to be nice to him?"

"Of course I'll be nice. I'm always nice . . . but I don't want to discuss this. Next subject."

"Fine . . . Do you remember the name of that psychic you went to?"

"Why do you keep hocking me about this? It was a hundred years ago . . . Oy, I always get so *farmisht* when I have to come back to the South Shore . . . it must be mental. Are you paying attention? We want Peninsula Boulevard."

"I'm paying attention. The last sign said Valley Stream."

The good thing about my mother being behind the wheel was that I didn't have to listen to her wisecrack remarks that I was a great driver except for starting and stopping. The bad thing about her driving was that for someone who was married all these years to a guy who loved maps, she couldn't even open one, let alone read it. She was forever getting lost.

"I just was curious if you remembered her name." I read the directions again.

"Why?"

"Because I had a reading with a psychic, and I was just thinking how weird it would be if it was the same person."

"You think there's only one in New York? Today there's one on every block . . . And what do you gotta see a psychic for? You want to know your future? I'll tell you your future. Get married again. Have a few kids. Learn how to bake. You'll live happily ever after."

"That's your key to true happiness? Get married? Have a cookie."

"Helen something Polish."

"What?"

"The psychic . . . it's coming back to me. She gave me a little tape when we were done and she wrote her name on it . . . But she was an old lady back then, and that was twenty years ago. She wouldn't still be at it today."

"What else do you remember?"

"Not much. I was in a bad mental state and her little granddaughter kept interrupting . . . I think maybe she had the gift too, because instead of the old lady telling her to go play in traffic, she listened to whatever the kid said. And now that I think of it, she did say one interesting thing.

"She said, 'Don't you get it, lady? Your baby is safe. He's with God now. You don't have to worry about him no more.' "

"Pretty profound for a child."

"I didn't think so then, but I guess it must have sunk in because see? That I remembered."

"It's funny that she said, 'Don't you get it, lady?' The one I went to kept using the same exact expression . . . they must teach it at psychic school."

And here is what they must teach at the Jewish funeral school. When mourners arrive, make sure there are two goons in dark suits stationed by the door to the chapel looking somber, as if they were close, personal friends of the deceased. Then have them ask everyone to sign the guest book, and wait quietly in the hall until the immediate family is ready to receive them in the parlor.

That's why I was surprised to see Seth and Madeline greeting everyone at the entrance like anxious hosts. Had an overwhelmed mom sent them out to play until company came?

I surprised them back by tripping over Seth's foot and

knocking over the little basket of yarmulkes. Then, as I scooped them up, it was Sheil's turn. She introduced herself to him and started sobbing in his arms. How wonderful to see Todd's first playmate looking so grown up and handsome. How tragic that her son had never reached this stage. Oh, the injustice of it all.

After that masterful entrance, I didn't expect Madeline to squeeze my hand and thank me for coming. Or tell me that she and Seth had to talk Kenny out of asking Mira Darryl because they thought with her being a big celebrity she would make too much of a scene, and now that everyone knew we grew up together, it just made more sense to ask me.

Thank you for sharing. It's every girl's dream to be first runner-up.

"If you want, I'll sneak you in now so you can have a few minutes alone." She sniffed.

"How is he?"

"A total mess . . . Robyn, we are all in such shock."

"I know . . . He was just telling me how great his dad was doing."

"It's so sad . . . Now we have to change the baby's name to begin with an H, and we had one all picked out we really liked and H is so hard. We were thinking maybe Harlan or Hershel, but oh my God, I just love the name Montgomery. Don't you?"

Are you serious? Your father-in-law drops dead and your biggest concern is that you have to name your son in his memory?

"It's a great name. Oh look," I said. "My dad just got here . . . We'll talk later. I am so sorry for your loss." *And your stupidity.*

I was glad I spotted him before my mother, who had managed to compose herself and reunite with what looked like former neighbors from Oceanside.

"Daddy, you don't look so good." I kissed him. "Are you okay?"

"I'll be honest," he said. "I'm not feeling great . . . the traffic was unbelievable . . . and being here? So hard."

"I know." I hugged him. "Mommy broke down when she saw Seth . . ."

". . . This is where we would have had Todd's funeral . . . if we'd have found the body in time."

"Oh my God."

"Yeah . . . you think there's someplace I can get a little nosh? I'm feeling kind of—"

And with that he collapsed.

Say what you will about the Holtzes. We sure know how to get a funeral started.

Fortunately, my dad was fine after drinking some orange juice, getting a little fresh air and a hug from my mom. She, of course, accused him of fainting to get her attention, but I could tell she was concerned, as his last fainting spell was followed by his first heart attack. That would not look good on her permanent record.

More important, the two walked into the parlor together to express their condolences to the family. I learned later that Judy had been holding up beautifully until then, but upon seeing her dear friends from her young married days, she cried uncontrollably.

As for seeing Ken, I was so stunned by his haggard face and still broken body, I nearly forgot that he had good reason to be even more angry with me than I was with him.

But at least for that moment there was no ill will, just the need for him to hold someone who cared and be able to cry without shame.

He introduced me to his mother, who kissed me and said she was so happy to meet me and of course she always knew I'd be pretty, but not this pretty. I loved her.

Ken and I were only able to chat briefly, as a roomful of people were there to pay their respects. But I at least got a moment to ask about Rookie and if he thought it would ever be possible for us to spend time doing something other than going to hospitals and funerals.

Thank God he laughed.

For the second time in as many weeks that I was at a funeral, I could not focus on the rabbi's words, meaningful as I'm sure they were. For every time the chapel doors opened, I had to turn to see if Mira Darryl had showed up uninvited.

But mostly my attention was directed to my parents, who were seated next to me and wept quietly in the name of all that was lost. A baby son. A beloved old friend. A marriage.

Though they hadn't exchanged a single cross word, to me it was a sign it was all over except for the lawyers. For if it was business as usual, the insults, the criticisms, and the what's-the-matter-with-you accusations would have been argued in rapid succession.

As they wiped their eyes, I sensed that the last vestige of their bond was grief, and it could no longer sustain them. Too many years and too many tears had chipped away at their marital bridge, so now all that remained was a worn foundation and a thin layer of love. The time had come to look for new crossings.

I don't know how I held it together myself, but I did. Until Ken and Seth approached the podium and shifted the microphone. Before they could utter a word, my hands were wet with tears.

The prospect of losing your father as these boys had, or your mother, as Josh had, was unimaginable. I wondered how a child of any age carried on without the unconditional love and support that had been a driving force from their first moment of life.

Seth, the elder statesman now, spoke first. "I've heard it said that a funeral is the one place you don't want to have a front-row seat. So true."

To his credit, he was eloquent and funny and shared such wonderful memories, I felt as though I knew his father well, and it was my great loss that I had never had the privilege.

Then it was Ken's turn. At first there was a slight crackle to his voice as he swayed like a skyscraper on a gusty day. Yet somehow he maintained his composure. Even cracked a joke about having to clean out the garage, along with everyone else's on the block, as punishment for driving his dad's car before he had his license . . . four years before he had his license.

Everyone laughed and it seemed to propel him, until realization hit. This wasn't a speech at an industry seminar. He was speaking at his beloved father's funeral.

It started as a sniffling and a pause. Seth slapped his back, the he-man gesture to tough it out. But the levee was breached and the tears had to flow. And rather than allow this drama to unfold, Mama Bear popped up, said a few quiet words to her son, and said, "Now go sit down. There isn't a soul here who doesn't know how much you loved and worshipped your father."

"But you let Seth talk," he whined.

"We love you, Kenny," an old woman yelled. "But listen to your mother."

Wow, even funerals had hecklers now. But he took the woman's advice and sat down.

"I wasn't planning to speak." Judy repositioned the microphone, as her tiny frame squeezed between her strapping sons. "I didn't think I could . . . but I've changed my mind . . . I know Howie would feel slighted if I didn't share with you the things that only a wife would know . . . In fact, this is vintage Howie. When he first got the cancer diagnosis, he sat down and wrote his own eulogy . . . he said he wanted to make sure we didn't forget anything . . .

"My husband was an extraordinary man. Kind, generous, thoughtful, and no one made me laugh as much as him . . . And

I'm not just saying that because I know he can hear me . . . In fact, honey, where did you leave the key to the shed?" She looked up. "You never took out my bike like I asked and it's going to be a beautiful week."

Of all the anecdotes Judy shared, my favorite was about Howie's love of music. When he found a CD he enjoyed, he'd buy extra copies to give to her, Ken, Seth, and Madeline. Judy complained it was a waste of money to have duplicate collections, but he never wanted her to have to wait to hear a beautiful song. "Of course he had no problem with me waiting to get into the bathroom in the morning."

I was in awe of this tiny wisp of a woman who was better at doing stand-up than some veteran comics I'd seen perform, no less at her own husband's funeral. But it wasn't only her humor that moved me, it was the proof that two people could share a lifetime of happiness.

"It is so fitting that only last week, Howie added to my collection with a new CD by this young girl from Long Island, Alex something or other. Anyway, I reminded him that I already had more music than I could listen to in a lifetime and to please not waste the money, and like usual, he ignored me and told me to listen to this one song called 'Before the Last Dance.'

"Well, it took me a few days and wouldn't you know it? I finally listened to it Wednesday morning when I was out walking the dog . . . only a few short hours before Howie passed away . . . You have to hear the words . . . It so happens I brought them along."

Some things come easy, you get it right from the start
but heaven this isn't, life's gonna break your heart
askin' why the road turns when you're just findin' your way
ain't gonna matter if you don't get up every day
and take one more chance
you gotta do it or die before the last dance

Everyone's got their stories, their reasons for believin'
the hard times are chasin' 'em, their fate's just gettin' even
But if a darkened path fills you with doubt
Use your head and your heart to lead the way out
Give unto others, help them realize their dreams
That's your salvation, your reason for bein'

Gotta go out there and take
Just one more chance
Gotta do it or die
before the last dance

"Now if those words don't sum up my husband"—Judy
wiped her eyes—"nothing will. No matter what his problems,
Howie believed that the only way to make his troubles seem
smaller was to give back and help others. And that's what he
did. He gave his time, his money, his love, his guidance . . .
every day of his beautiful life."

When she finished I looked around, for as a stand-up, it was
an automatic reflex to study crowd reaction. And no surprise,
there wasn't a dry eye in the house.

We hadn't intended to join the procession to the cemetery, or
even decided about paying a *shivah* call, as we had no idea
where it would be held. Judy no longer had a home in New
York, Ken was in no position to entertain, and Seth and Madeline were living in a tiny studio near the UN until their co-op
was ready.

But once Judy had the three of us in her possession, she
wasn't letting go.

And so it was that we spent the most difficult day of the
Danziger family's lives with them, and oddly, didn't feel like
outsiders. Howie's brother and sister-in-law, Dave and Andrea,

were especially gracious, insisting we come for dinner as the *shivah* would be held at their home in nearby Bellmore.

It seemed that most of the day was a blur of tears, hand holding, reminiscing, the occasional laugh, and as any Jew knows, food, and lots of it. And it was during one of those familiar, comfortable moments around the dining room table, when hungry guests piled their plates and talked about sports, weather, or anything that didn't dwell on death, that I noticed Ken smiling at me with tears in his eyes.

It was the first time I felt hopeful that he thought of me as the winner and Mira, the runner-up.

Chapter 24

"So what's the latest with your parents?" Ken punched up the pillows to find a comfortable position on the couch, though just being back home made it good enough.

"I wish I knew." I collapsed next to him. "The funeral was the first time they were together in three weeks."

"How was it?"

"I guess okay. They stuck together the whole time, but it had to be hard. Being back near Oceanside and seeing the old neighbors, knowing it was your dad's funeral . . ."

"Hopefully they'll work things out."

"No kidding . . . if my mother doesn't move out soon, I'm looking at a lifetime sentence."

"Why? She wouldn't eventually get her own place?"

"No, I'd have to kill her and end up behind bars."

Ken laughed.

"Although she did go home yesterday . . . She said it was to pick up more clothes and check her mail, but she's still there, so who knows?"

Rookie barked as if to say, Hey, don't leave me out. I want to hang too.

"So we meet again, Bond." I imitated Sean Connery.

"I can't believe how much he likes you." Ken watched him snuggle on my lap.

"You would too if I gave you extra green treats."

"I like you fine." He tousled my hair.

"Really? You'd never know it."

"And here it comes. The lecture."

"Nope. Not gonna tell you how low rent it was not to call me. I'm just gonna sit here and feel sorry for you because I know how much it pisses you off!"

Rookie growled at Ken.

"Thatta boy." I kissed his wet nose. "Who's your daddy?"

It was Sunday evening, nearly a week since Ken's father passed, and in that time, we'd had many similar-sounding exchanges.

They began after the funeral, when Ken would call from his uncle's house to chat, perhaps because he needed a breather from hovering family and friends, or because I was already familiar with his no-pity policy.

How ironic though. After I'd waited all those weeks for him to pick up the goddamn phone, now he was calling daily, which made me wonder. Was he sincerely trying to build on a friendship or did he have an agenda? Sure enough, he asked my help in making a shivah in the city for him, and my stomach turned.

Shivah was just another name for long, loud, all-day open houses where your nearest and dearest paid their respects by gathering for cake and coffee while keeping an eye on the score of the Knicks game.

But the real issue wasn't the prep work, it was that he had already played his user card. Was I that gullible that I would jump in and be Ms. Fix-It again, only to never be properly thanked? I was so conflicted, I consulted with my panel of experts:

Rachel: "Who cares what his motives are for asking? Half of Showtime will be there."

Julia: "I feel bad for him, but I wouldn't do it. You're not a caterer, you're a date. Well not a date yet, but how are you ever going to be one if he thinks of you as a caterer?"

My mom: "How many kugels should I make? Oh and should I make my fancy Jell-O mold?"

Even Gretchen weighed in with an opinion: "Do it . . . Just borrow my Versace jeans and that little pink Dolce sweater so you're the hottest chick there."

"Thanks, but isn't it kind of slutty for me? All you'll see are boobs."

"Robyn, darlin'. Name two things that are wrong with that?"

As it turned out, I was glad I took Gretchen's advice, for it didn't take long to realize that this wasn't going to be an ordinary shivah. Not when a ten-tier fruit basket sent by Billy and Janice Crystal was delivered. Not when twenty-three women showed up within the first hour, all with bakery boxes and an agenda: Find out who Ken was dating and if it was serious.

"Do you know all of these people?" I whispered to him as I passed by.

"Some are from work, two I know from physical therapy, the rest I have no idea."

Just then he was hugged by a tall redhead in tears who was so sorry to hear about his grandfather. And a tiny blond in leopard pants who introduced herself as a Kabbalist and said he needed a red string to protect him from the Evil Eye, and any time he wanted to learn where he came from and why he was here, she would help him unravel the mystery of life.

"That is so neat." I handed her a wineglass. "Do you know Madonna?"

This wasn't a shivah call. It was Jewish speed dating. Grab a bagel and a boy and give him five minutes to impress you or move on.

I guess by virtue of the fact that I was working the kitchen, no one suspected me as competition, though if they'd paid closer attention, they might have wondered how a server living on hourly wages could afford Versace and a professional makeup job.

On the other hand, at least I could eavesdrop:

"Wonder if Ken heard the rumors about Mira Darryl's hot weekend with Kyle in Cancun."

"See that girl in the corner? Isn't she the *Dateline* producer he was dating? God, she is so not his type."

I slunk back into the kitchen, broke open a tray of brownies and stuffed my mouth. Welcome to the Josh Vogel School of Painful Realizations . . . I probably wasn't Ken's type either.

"There you are." He walked in with one of the few male visitors, a heavyset fellow with the world's most obvious hairpiece.

"*Is that a toupee?*"

"*Yes.*"

"*Wow. It's a good one. You could never tell.*"

"Robyn!" Ken had caught me with a cookie in each hand and bulging, brownie cheeks. "Are you hoarding the good stuff?"

"Sorry," I said, blowing crumbs as I spoke. "I was starving."

"She doesn't get out much." Ken took a napkin to wipe his friend's jacket. "She's so busy writing and doing her stand-up act . . . Honey, this is Mitch Kaplan from Showtime."

Honey? Showtime? Oh my God. "Pleased to meet you." I shook his hand. "Sorry about that . . . I was just . . ."

"It's fine . . . So Ken tells me you're one of the funniest ladies he's ever met."

Yes, but did he say I was his type? "Thanks." I smiled. "It's just not a funny day today."

"Right." He nodded. "Of course . . . Well maybe after you polish off the babkah, you can tell me what you're working on."

Ken laughed and left the room, but not before giving me a wink, which warmed my heart. But no time for sentiment. This was my once-in-a-lifetime chance to pitch my script and hope that Mitch didn't hold it against me that I had the eating habits of a chimp.

To his credit, he listened attentively, and though he wasn't sure my ideas were linear and high-concept enough, whatever the hell that meant, he was willing to let me come in and pitch it to the programming people.

I was so excited, I handed him a rugeleh instead of my business card, then ran into Ken's room to call Rachel. Only to realize that this was one of Annette's predictions : . . . a cable channel would buy my script because of someone who knew someone who knew someone.

Frankly, I was running out of fingers to keep track of how much she had gotten right.

"That was nice of Josh to come." Ken lay back on the couch.

"He's a good guy. He came to the funeral too."

"I didn't know that. Then again, I had no idea who was there . . . except for my ex."

"Really? That was brave. Doesn't your whole family hate her?" I rubbed his leg.

"No. Why? Is that what Madeline told you?"

"No. I guess I just assumed . . ."

"It's not like that. There was more than enough blame to go around . . . Anyway, I'm happy for her. She married a nice neurosurgeon, they have one kid and another in the oven . . ."

"You mean she came to gloat?"

"No . . . she and my dad were pretty close. I'm sure she meant well . . . I don't know. The whole day was a blur . . . Anyway, how did Josh know about my dad?"

"Yeah. About that . . . He was with me when you called."

"Where were you? It sounded like a party or something."

"Of sorts." I coughed.

"So what's the story?"

"If I tell you what happened do you promise not to be mad?"

"Let me guess . . . This time you impersonated my accountant so you could find out my net worth."

"I was pissed that you never called, and when I heard it was you, I put you on speaker phone . . . while I was on stage doing my act. I do this improv bit where I work unsuspecting callers into my routine."

"Robyn! You are incorrigible!"

"Believe me, if I knew why you were calling, you think I would have done it? And if it's any consolation, the audience was so mad, they booed me off stage."

Ken snorted.

"What . . ."

"My dad would have laughed his ass off and told that story forever."

"Oh thank God, because I thought for sure when you found out, you'd hate me."

"I couldn't hate you. Besides, even I think I had it coming. But you have to understand, after you dropped me off, I was in so much pain I slept for two straight days. And I really did intend to send flowers or do something nice, but the time got away from me, and the more that went by, the stupider I felt . . . and then Mira came. And she just confuses the hell out of me."

Rookie growled.

"See?" I said. "Even he knows a bitch when he sees one."

"C'mon. You've never even met her."

"Never met Saddam Hussein either, but I'm pretty sure I've pegged him right."

"Well whatever. If it makes you feel any better, I felt awful about what I did, and then Madeline was going nuts on me, e-mailing me every day with gift ideas, but I didn't think a spa treatment was any big deal to you. You're probably comped all the time."

"No I'm not . . . I'd love a glycolic triple-action vitamin C facial at Georgette Klinger."

"Done! Now tell me the deal with Josh and that chick he came with today . . . She looked very familiar . . ."

"I'll tell you after your hard-on goes away . . ."

"I'm just curious."

"Yeah . . . if I can get her number for you."

"Can you?"

"Yes. I can also tell you her entire life story because she's my oldest and dearest friend. Her name is Julia Volkman, and the reason she looks familiar is because she was a top model at Ralph Lauren. Now she's an executive there, but for years she was in every ad campaign.

"As for her and Josh? I have no idea. I mean the three of us all went to high school together, but she hasn't seen him since we graduated, and I don't know what he looked like when he was little, but he was one hell of a fat teenager . . . I'm talking huge . . . And follow me here . . . His last name is Vogel, hers is Volkman . . . their lockers were next to each other . . . She used to poke him to see if he'd deflate . . . it was so mean, but it was high school. Everyone was an asshole.

"Anyway, a few weeks ago, Josh found out he'd moved a few blocks from me, we got together, don't you dare say a word about that, and then I called her and said he'd lost all this weight and he looked amazing, and he was coming to see me do my act and she should come too.

"At first she was like no way, I'm happy he's doing so great but I could care less. Then next thing I know, they're sitting together at the comedy club and they're touching and laughing . . . and I'm like . . . hello? You do realize that is Josh Vogel you're coming on to . . ."

"So you didn't know he was bringing her today?"

"I would have been less surprised if Bill showed up with Monica."

Ken laughed. "You think they're sleeping together?"

"God I hope not."

"Oh come on. It would be great. Joshy gettin' it on with a super model."

"Not this one . . . I just don't want to see him get hurt . . . Julia doesn't so much dump guys as she donates them to worthy charities."

Maybe two minutes went by. Maybe ten. All I know is that we opted for silence over banter, and contemplation over kissing, though the pressure was building. Even Rookie was barking at us, as if to say, Do it already, I haven't got all night.

But hell if I was going to make the first move, not after Josh told Ken about my naked-in-bed adventure. Did I really need him thinking all customers were entitled to the same service? Besides, a long kiss might lead to sex, and our first time was not going to happen before I'd had a chance to exfoliate.

"You were right, you know." He broke the silence.

"Yay." I clapped. "I love being right. It's so rare . . . About what?"

"About Mira wanting to make Kyle jealous . . . about her using me for that."

"Oh. Sorry to hear it."

"Yeah right. Help me move the furniture so you can do cartwheels."

"Well aren't we all full of ourselves . . . So how did you leave it with her?"

"I didn't . . . I couldn't . . . With everything going on . . . and you . . ."

"Me?" I sat up. "Really? You were thinking about me? But I'm not your type."

"I know."

I swatted him with a pillow. "I guess when you've got your pick of the litter like today . . ."

"Oh please. I didn't even know half those girls . . . It was crazy . . . The people I expected to come didn't show up, and ones I never met were telling me how sorry they were for my loss. And that Kabbala kook with the red string? Thank God that's over."

"Except for the food. Did you see how much was left?"

"It's fine. Rookie and I live for leftovers . . . anyway, if I didn't already tell you, thank you for doing this today. Every time I turned around you were running the whole show. It was amazing. You mingled, you served, you—"

"—ate all the desserts."

"Yeah. Next time I'm hiding the brownies. That was tonight's dinner . . . Rookie, enough with the barking already!" he yelled into the bedroom.

He tried putting his arm around me and winced.

I tried lying on his chest. "Does that hurt?"

"Only when you breathe."

"Sorry." I sat up. "Now go back to the part where you couldn't stop thinking of me because I have to get home. Believe it or not I have to get up for work in a few hours."

"Then stay here. You're perfectly safe. I can't even lift my leg without cringing."

"Can't. My set kit is home and I can't show up for work without it. Every makeup product I own is in that bag."

"Got it . . . It's just that . . . Look, I still need help getting dressed . . . Rookie pitches in, and he's got the whole fetch-the-socks thing down, but shirt buttoning is for the more advanced dogs . . . I don't want to hurt his feelings. Plus, you've already seen the merchandise."

"I liked the merchandise." I kissed him and he answered with passion, pulling me nearer.

Maybe two minutes went by. Maybe ten. All I remember is that we started in neutral and ended in drive, and there was no mistaking his desire as he overpowered me with affection while his hands slowly sought refuge on my body.

"Wow." I pulled away. "That was amazing."

He nodded with tears in his eyes.

"I swear you are worse than me." I wiped his face. "I may have to give you some of my shares in Kimberly-Clark."

"Sold! . . . Rookie! Pipe down," he yelled into the bedroom. "What is with him tonight?"

"Want me to see what he keeps barking at?"

"I'm sure it's nothing. Probably a magazine fell off the bookshelf. It makes him crazy."

"That's so weird. I had the same thing happen in my room. I had a stack of these old *Mad* magazines that—"

"*Mad* magazines?" Ken sat up so fast we nearly knocked heads.

"Yeah. Remember those?"

"Are you kidding? We lived for those, especially Mo. He was a total *Mad* freak. He had every issue. No, he memorized every issue. He had the lunch box, the board game, he was Al-fred E. Neuman every Halloween . . ."

"Yeah, well I once had a huge collection too, until my

mother decided to throw them all out. Thank God Julia saved the day because she had a bunch of issues she never gave back and—"

"Did you say that's what was falling off your shelf?"

"Yeah. In fact, I'd forgotten that's where I put them until—"

"I bet that was Mo."

"Oh stop. That's just creepy."

"Well how would you explain it? All of a sudden *his* favorite magazine starts falling off *your* bookcase? . . . I gotta go see what's going on in there. Help me up."

We hopped to the bedroom to find Rookie sniffing a magazine on the floor beside Ken's desk.

"Did you leave *Road and Track* on the floor?" I picked it up.

"No, it was definitely on my desk."

We looked around the room. Did we have company? Then Rookie started barking at the air and our eyes widened.

"Do you remember the other night at my uncle's house when we were sitting around the dining room?" Ken asked. "And I was staring at you . . ."

"Uh huh."

"It was the strangest thing then too. I felt like Mo was there with me and it hit me that I was looking at the girl who took my favorite picture of us . . . I was in shock."

"Why?"

"Because it was the last one of us together . . . Two weeks later, Mo was dead."

I shivered. "So . . . do you think . . . are you feeling . . . is he here?"

Rookie barked again, and we both knew the answer was yes.

I did not make it home that night. Or the next. In fact, for the first time in all the years I worked for Gretchen, I called in sick when I wasn't. For in spite of my fear about losing my job, now there was something that frightened me more . . . witnessing a nervous breakdown.

This is what happens when someone is haunted by a story that begins with these words:

"At least my dad's death wasn't my fault. Not like Mo and Larry's . . . If it wasn't for me, they'd both still be alive."

Chapter 25

OH, TO BE ABLE to choose our defining moments, for they would surely be a reflection of our greatest virtues. Grace under pressure and wise resolve in the face of adversity.

But all too often, the experiences that shape us come at an age when we have neither the acumen to make good choices, nor the maturity to accept what lies in the wake of foolishness.

Mostly what defines us are the dates with destiny no one sees coming.

Kenny Danziger, Larry Gerber, and Richie Morris were energetic toddlers drawn to one another at Oceanside Park in the spring of 1974 by a connection their mothers could only describe as instinctual. How else to explain a bond that formed with language intelligible only to them?

If only their mothers found one another as engaging.

Judy Danziger called Larry's mom, Terry, the queen of show-and-tell. In between broadcasting her latest vacation and home improvement plans, she made sure you took notice of her jewelry and pocketbooks, the prices of which she was happy to share.

"What does she think? We're all on the G.I. Plan (generous in-laws)?"

In turn, Terry didn't appreciate that Richie's mom, Carol, was so self-absorbed that she would drop off her son for play dates, but rarely reciprocate. And if she did, the play date was short and timed to coincide with her having to leave for other, more important commitments.

Judy thought they were both meshuggenehs, and urged Kenny to broaden his social circle. "Why don't you play with that nice Joshua Vogel?" she'd say. "He's got a big pool in the backyard and his mom I like!"

But by kindergarten, the mothers resigned themselves to the fact that their sons were glued to the hip for good, and it made sense for them to try to become friends as well.

In fact, it was over lunch at Twenty-four Hour Bagel that Judy told Terry and Carol about walking into Kenny's room and discovering the boys had taken every tie from Howie's closet and were trying to tie them together so they could climb down the side of the house through a window.

"I knew something was up when they were being so quiet," she said. "I tell you, they're like the Three Stooges."

"You know?" Terry laughed. "Even their names are the same. Kenny's got that big head of ringlets, so he's Curly. Richie Morris is Moe, and Larry, is, well, Larry."

And so they became known, and not only by family and friends. Teachers, camp counselors, and coaches were quick to discover that when there were pranks, pratfalls, and anything resembling trouble, one of those boys, if not all, was responsible.

Even Maureen at Dr. Glatt's office knew if she was making an appointment for one checkup, she'd better make them for all three. Especially if Richie was due for a booster shot, for without his two best friends holding his hands, it would take half the staff to restrain him.

Holiday dinners, vacations, Hebrew school, Little League games . . . Where one went, the other two followed, and it was a natural assumption that nothing would keep them apart. Until they reached high school and Richie's mom, Carol, found proof in her pharmaceutical rep husband's briefcase that he was cheating on her with a radiologist in Connecticut whose code name was Babycakes.

It was the decisive blow to an already maladjusted, we-know-people-talk family, what with money problems and Mo's older sister, Jennifer, home from college, pregnant and chain smoking.

The boys were worried. Mo wasn't one of those resilient kids who bounced back easily, particularly since adolescence. Like his Three Stooges namesake, Moe, he also didn't need much provocation to become agitated. Or to drink.

At first it was amateur stuff. A few beers behind the garage. Then it was vodka binges. Then alcohol wasn't his only substance of choice. Then he didn't wait for the weekends.

Larry and Kenny finally confided in their guidance counselor, but when the school intervened, a now separated Carol and Michael rebuked the administration's efforts, and at least in this instance, maintained a unified front.

As long as their son's conduct in school was fine, they had no right to interfere in what was a personal family matter and if the district pursued this, they would be hearing from their lawyer.

Judy and Howie also tried reasoning with them, only to run head on into the blame game. Michael said the only reason Richie couldn't function was that Carol had coddled him for so damn long, and it was too late to try to make a man out of him. Meanwhile, Carol claimed if Michael had paid enough attention to Richie as a kid, he wouldn't have a need to rebel, but she was sure he would eventually straighten himself out.

"His parents sounded like assholes," I said. "How could they not get him help?"

"I agree," Ken said. "But in Mo's case, he really did do it on his own. He got himself into rehab, started college at Nassau Community, and then he met this girl he really liked whose dad gave him a job at the gym he managed . . .

"Which is why that weekend he and Larry came to see me at school was the best. He was sober the whole time. It was like the old Mo . . ."

I sighed, knowing that no matter how nice a time they had then, the story ended tragically.

I got up from the kitchen table to pour us coffee and peek at *Daybreak* and did a double take. I had been trying for months to convince Gretchen to let me experiment with her eyes, but she was so resistant to change. Now a sub was in for one day, and boom, suddenly she was open to the more playful violet tones.

Normally, professional jealousy would lead to a slow burn. But how riled could I get, for I was guilty of something far more unthinkable. It was eight o'clock on a Monday morning and there I was playing hooky with Rookie and Ken, devouring rugeleh and reading the *Times*.

In an act of faith, but mostly fulfillment, I had spent the night there. And though the most intimate thing Ken and I did was kiss intermittently, we spent hours talking through tears.

Ken, of course, having just buried his father, had reasonable cause. But it was his dance around the divorce question that sprung the big leak. Nina was amazing. Beautiful and brilliant. An accomplished tennis player and skier. A wonderful cook.

She just had this thing about emotional baggage. It had to be either checked at the door or thrown overboard, for why dwell on the past when you could be having lovely lunches with friends and shopping for country homes in Nantucket?

So when Ken learned on the morning of September 11 that he had lost his only remaining best friend, she was sympathetic, but determined not to let it affect their future happiness. Sadly, counseling did not provide a rapid enough cure for Ken's depression, and rather than helping row the boat ashore with love and support, she jumped ship.

At first I was flattered, and frankly surprised, that he was being so forthcoming in divulging these painful details, as up until now, he had been as impenetrable as a detective who never removed his bulletproof vest. Piercing questions bounced off him, preventing possible injury to his heart.

But when he began spinning words in a verbal free fall about the night he lost Mo, I realized he wasn't talking because I was a good listener. He was talking because with the loss of his father came the loss of his resolve. He could simply hold back no longer.

"Things fell apart that first Christmas break from school." Ken picked up Rookie. "Larry was up at Binghamton and had gotten home a few days before me. I remember because I was still studying for finals when he called to say he thought Mo was back to his old tricks.

"Then when I got home, I took one look at Mo and knew Larry was right because he'd do this thing where he rocked his head like he was listening to music, only there was no music. And I was pissed because I didn't want to deal with this crap anymore. The babysitting, the puking . . . I mean I loved Mo like a brother . . . I just couldn't watch him self-destruct again . . ."

"I know where this is going," I said. "He was driving drunk and he died . . ."

"No." Ken looked down. "I wish that's what happened . . ."

"What?"

"You know what?" Ken stretched. "Forget it. I don't need to do this."

"Are you sure? Sometimes talking—"

"Believe me, I've talked my ass off . . . been in and out of therapy since I'm eighteen."

"But obviously you're still in pain."

"I'm fine."

"Okay. Well, at least it solves the mystery of what happened to you. The reason you didn't come back to school the next semester . . . Thing about it is, what happened was a terrible tragedy. Beyond awful. But, and I know I sound like Robin Williams in *Good Will Hunting*—"

"It wasn't my fault. Right? That's your best shot? Let it go, it was God's will . . ."

"I don't mean to sound cliché. I just—"

"Don't."

"Wait. I'm just saying, the reality is you weren't the one who made him drink, you didn't make him drive . . ."

"The reality is," Ken yelled, "I fucking hit him with my car, okay?"

"Oh my God!"

"Yeah. I hit him with my car and he died."

"I'm sorry." I took his hand. "I'm so sorry."

"I hit him with my car and he died." He rocked back and forth. "I killed my best friend."

"On purpose?"

"What?"

"I didn't mean it like that . . . how . . . what happened?"

Rookie barked at me for making Ken cry, and I felt so ashamed I wanted to flee. Then he started talking about a party.

"Forget it," I whispered. "You don't have to do this."

"What the hell?" He wiped his eyes on a napkin. "I've already told you more than I've told ten people and you didn't leave . . . It doesn't even faze you when I cry."

"Hey. I'm Miss Waterworks . . . So is my dad. To me it's not a sign of weakness . . . In fact when you were talking before, I was thinking about him . . . I remember he'd be sitting at the kitchen table reading the paper and I could hear him sniffing so I knew he was trying to hide . . . I was little then, and I'd say, Daddy why do you read the paper if it makes you sad?"

Ken smiled. We were partners in pain. Surely I would not judge him as had Nina.

"Larry's roommate at Binghamton was this kid from Merrick . . . lived in this huge house on the water . . . you had to see it . . . the Jag in the driveway, the twenty-foot speedboat in the canal . . . His parents were out of town so he was having this big blowout party . . . Larry wanted to go but he'd just had his wisdom teeth out and didn't feel up to driving, so he said to come with him so I could meet his new friends and I was like yeah, great, but let's not tell Mo . . . he'll get totally wasted.

"So what does Larry do? He tells Mo to come after he gets off work so he wouldn't feel left out . . . Sure enough, Mo shows up with a joint in one hand and a beer in the other, and I'm like c'mon man, don't. You were doing so great . . . So now he's all pissed at me, so I go fine, then give me your keys and he's like stop being my fucking mother, and that was it. I walked away . . . I told Larry to hell with him, you invited him, he's your problem . . . But Larry's mouth was killing him from the surgery and he said he was leaving but not to worry about driving him home because this girl he knew was going to give him a ride and to just keep an eye on Mo . . . He must have said it six times. Keep an eye on Mo."

"You didn't want to leave with Larry?"

"Leave? Not after I'd met this really cute girl . . . So hot . . . Jordie Cohen . . . Legs up to here . . . amazing body. A sophomore at Cornell . . . lived a few blocks from this kid's house and I'm thinking, this is going to be one hell of a great vacation."

"I get the picture." I laughed.

"Anyway, maybe an hour goes by and we're having a great time getting it on in one of the bedrooms and all of a sudden I remember Mo . . ."

"So I tell Jordie to hold on, I just have to make sure my friend is okay and I'll be right back . . . and I'm so mad because I really didn't want to have to get up to go look for him . . . but there's no way now that I'd thought about him that I could go back to . . . you know . . . anyway, I'm searching the whole house and nothing . . . And it was weird, it was right before Christmas but it wasn't freezing and a lot of the kids were outside . . . so I go out and I'm asking everyone have you seen a short little guy, answers to the name of Mo, and they're all like no, he's not here, so now I'm scared and I run to the front of the house, praying his car is still there . . . and I'm trying to keep it together by reminding myself this guy's been driving drunk since he was sixteen and somehow he always made it home and it's not that far to Oceanside.

"But you know how you just know when something's not right? So I get in my car, and Merrick down by the water is all these real narrow streets and a million stop signs every thirty seconds . . . and I'm thinking I'll never find him . . . Mo was one of those guys who'd go down ten different streets to avoid two lights . . .

"Then all of a sudden I see this guy running . . . but it's so dark, and I'd had a few beers myself, and I'm thinking, Wait that can't be Mo. So I roll down the window and start yelling his name and I'm honking the horn . . . and the closer I'm getting I'm realizing . . . I'm realizing—" Ken stopped.

"I'm realizing . . . son of a bitch. That's his car rolled over on the sidewalk . . . a dog is barking . . . there's a man just lying there . . . or what's left of him . . . and I'm so blown away looking at the most God awful thing I've ever seen in my life that I don't see Mo running in front of my car."

"Oh my God."

"And I'm screaming, Stop, what the hell are you doing? But I can't brake fast enough . . ."

"Oh my God."

"And that was it." Ken muttered. "He threw himself in front of my goddamn car so I could have the honor of killing him . . ."

"You don't know that," I cried. "He was probably just running for help and he was scared."

"Believe me, he didn't want help. He wanted to die . . . he always wanted to die . . ."

"I can't even imagine . . ." I reached for the tissue box. "What a nightmare . . ."

"Oh, it gets even better."

"What?"

"Yeah. The man Mo ran over? It turned out to be Jordie's father . . ."

I gasped.

"How's that for bad Karma? A guy goes out to walk his dog, he's a block from his house, and then gets hit by a drunk driver who was just partying with his daughter, and now it's all over. Your life is over . . .

"Of course, everything would have been fine if I'd kept my promise and made sure Mo wasn't doing anything stupid. But no, I had to be a schmuck and try to get into Jordie's pants . . . and look at the price of admission for that fuckup . . . She loses her dad, who she loved to pieces, they were so close, and I lost Mo . . .

"Pretty hard to go back to school after that, don't you think?"

Just as there are twelve steps to recovery and seven phases of mourning, being around the news business, I'd discovered that there were also stages of processing a shocking story.

First, of course, is total disbelief, accompanied by all its subsequent questions. How could anything so awful happen? Where was God? Why do innocent people have to die so violently?

Then comes realization. It doesn't matter whether you believe that something has just happened, it did, and though the fallout is devastating, denial creates even more victims.

Finally there is resolution and acceptance. It is not for us to question why life unfolds as it does. Our job is to carry on, learn from the experience, do what is in our power to prevent this type of tragedy from reoccurring and somehow regain faith in God and the future.

As Ken stared out the kitchen window, clutching Rookie, clearly in spite of all the time that had passed, and all the therapy money could buy, it appeared that he hadn't reached this final stage.

How could there be resolution when guilt and remorse were still on board the pain train? The only reason I recognized the symptoms was because I'd been an eyewitness to a similar fate. By outward appearances my dad, like Ken, had carried on after facing great tragedy, but he too had managed to sidestep the path to forgiveness.

What I did not know, nor did any other living soul, was that Ken was doubly burdened.

"Want to hear another good story?" he asked.

We had moved out to the terrace, as it was sunny with a cool breeze. I had hoped the fresh air and change of scenery would brighten his mood, but from his grim look, not yet.

"How about we recover from the first one first?"

"But I'm on a roll now . . . and this one's short."

"Is it helping . . . talking about it?"

"Not sure. Maybe. I never realized what a good listener Rookie was." He kissed him.

"Go figure." I laughed, elated that he had made a joke.

"And you're pretty amazing yourself." He stared at me. "I don't know why, but I've never felt this comfortable talking to a stranger."

"I'm not a stranger." I smiled. "We've known each other our whole lives."

"Good point . . . Anyway, I was thinking I would tell you about the day Larry died."

"Are you sure?"

"No. The only thing I'm sure about is that my dad wanted me to talk about it . . . I never told him the truth, I never told anyone, but he knew there was more to the story . . . Who knows. Maybe he can hear me . . ."

"I believe he can."

Ken pulled a blanket over him and Rookie. "On the morning of September eleventh, Larry was at his desk at Cantor Fitzgerald, already working the phones. Except he wasn't supposed to be there . . . he was supposed to be with me. We had made plans a few days before to meet for breakfast because he had some great news to tell me and he wanted to do it in person.

"I had a feeling I knew what it was . . . He'd been dating this girl, Michelle, and I'm sure he was going to tell me he was going to propose . . . But hey. I'll never know because, great friend that I am, I canceled on him the night before. Just blew him off. Made up some bullshit excuse about some last-minute meeting I had to go to. Only the truth was, a guy from the office needed a sub for an early racquetball game and I said, What the hell? I can see Larry any time . . ."

I held him until the tears stopped, though I doubted that either the confession or the embrace had liberated his soul, for guilt was a merciless jailer that did not take kindly to redemption. Only when a prisoner insisted on freedom did a key magically unlock the cell.

Chapter 26

GIVEN HIS DESPONDENCE, I was afraid to leave Ken for even a few hours. But what's a girl to do when she needs clean clothes? Then it hit me that good-neighbor Josh could come to my aid.

Luckily he was too wealthy to need work, giving him ample free time to break into my apartment, only to discover Sheil had left the back door open when she went out to smoke. But no time to dwell. I had to conduct a virtual tour of my drawers and medicine chest so he could pack a bag, while reminding him my bra size and panty choices were not acceptable discussion points.

"Thanks for coming." I hugged him. "You're a lifesaver. I didn't know what else to do."

"Sure. Where is he?"

"Out on the terrace . . . He hasn't moved in like two hours."

"What happened?"

"Basically he divulged some deep, dark secrets . . . I felt like Barbra Streisand in *Prince of Tides* . . . only she played a professional. All I could really do was listen."

"I'm sure that's what he needed the most . . . what can I do?"

"I don't know. I guess just go out there and hang with him."

"Does he know you called me?"

"I told him, but who knows if it registered? He hasn't answered his phone all morning, he hasn't eaten anything . . ."

"Been there . . . the total mess stage . . . Okay, I'll just sit with him. See if he feels like talking."

"You're the best." I kissed him.

"That's what all the girls say. Until I ask them out."

"Hey. C'mon. Don't do this."

"Fine. But before I go out there, will you at least tell me if you two—"

"—hooked up?"

"Just curious."

"Honestly, I don't think there's a name for what we have . . . It's not your normal boy-meets-girl, boy-screws-everything-up relationship . . ."

"But you like him?"

"A lot." I smiled. "Sorry."

"No, don't apologize. I could definitely see you together. You're both funny and smart and look how much history you have."

"Um, hello. I could say the same about you and Julia . . . I saw what you two were doing at Busted the other night. And then you asked her to come to the shivah with you yesterday."

"A shocker, right? Someone finds me irresistible."

"Well, just be careful. We both know her entire playbook. She's a heartbreaker."

"Are you jealous?"

"No. I'd just hate to see you get hurt. She's got a long history of dumping guys when the moon is in the seventh house."

"I'm a big boy and I know the score. She's gorgeous and I'm the former fat kid who shouldn't be playing in her league."

"I didn't say that."

"You didn't have to . . . it's all over your face. She's a winner, I'm a loser."

"No, she's a bitch and you're a sweetheart . . . just . . . you know . . . don't get so wrapped up in her that you can't walk away if you have to."

"Okay, but if I'm such a sweetheart, how come I can't get anywhere with you?"

"Because it's like we learned in chem. Nothing happens without internal combustion."

I wasn't sure how Ken would react to having company, especially when I brought Josh out to the terrace and found him and Rookie staring into space. But testimony to what a great guy Josh was, he simply pulled up a chair and stared right along with his friend and his dog.

I found out later that they never exchanged a single word, until in a unanimous vote, they decided it was time for me to make them lunch. And nothing like a fridge full of leftovers to give two hungry guys a common bond.

In fact, it was over a plate of cold cuts that Josh asked Ken an innocent question. Wasn't this the last day for his family to sit shivah?

"I sort of lost track, but maybe," Ken replied. "Why?"

"Because there's this nice tradition you do to end it. You take a walk around the block and when you come back, you basically agree to start your life over."

"Whoa," I said. "Someone paid attention in Hebrew school."

"Not even a little bit." He chomped on a giant corned beef sandwich. "Remember I told you about Rebecca, my all-of-a-sudden-Orthodox girlfriend? She was always talking about the meaning behind Jewish rituals and customs . . . and it so happened I liked this one. In fact, she used to get a whole group to join the families in mourning, even if they didn't know the person who died."

"Why?" I stole his pickle.

"Well, first off, the walk gives the family a way to acknowledge the end of the mourning period and to accept that their loved one is gone."

"That's a terrible idea." Ken stopped eating. "Who's ready to stop grieving after a week?"

"No. Not stop grieving. Start living. Go back to work. Go back to doing the things they did before. But then when Rebecca started having a bunch of people come along, it was more like a symbolic gesture for anyone who needed to put the past behind them . . . Let's say you'd been feeling guilty about something, so you'd do the walk around the block, make your peace with it, and then when you got back, the deal was you had to give yourself permission to let it go."

God bless your cunning soul, Josh. You are a genius.

"Well that may work in Oregon or wherever the hell you were." Ken sniffed. "But it's too hokey for here."

"No it's not," I chimed in. "Now that I think of it, my grandmother in Florida did the walk when my grandfather died. But in the middle they all got so knocked out from the heat, they stopped for lunch, did a little shopping . . ."

"Nice story. Thanks for sharing . . . By the way, do either of you know how to say the Kaddish?"

"I do." Josh raised his hand. "It's tricky with all the *yis-gadals* and *yis-kadashes* . . . but if you want, I can teach it to you. The English transliteration is pretty good."

"Great, because I'm supposed to say it every day for a year."

"Actually, eleven months and one day for a parent."

"Thank you Rabbi Vogel," I said. "But don't you need ten men to say it with you?"

"You'd love ten men," Josh teased. "Right Ken?"

"You're never going to let this rest, are you?" I laughed, so happy to see Ken smile.

"Never . . . but in answer to your question, yes, technically, you need ten Jewish adults, but that's more to keep the mourner company than to impress God. He listens no matter what."

"That's the spirit," I said. "Now tell me again about this walk-around-the-block thing. I think that's the coolest idea I ever heard. Don't you, Ken?"

"Would you stop talking to me like I'm a retard? I get what you're up to, but I'm not into symbolic gestures. Besides, I'm barely off crutches."

"Then I'll drive you while everyone else walks." I clapped. "I'll just go real slow."

"That is your specialty," Josh mumbled.

"Yeah, and it would be totally humiliating," Ken grunted. "They'll all beat us."

"What beat us? It's not the running of the Indy 500."

"Sorry, but the way you drive, everyone will be back and gone by the time we show up."

"Fine. Josh can drive you . . . just don't come crying to me when you get a ticket."

It's funny how a little, innocent idea can capture people's imagination and completely take on a life of its own. But Josh's suggestion to end shivah with a walk not only struck Ken's family as fitting and wonderful, everyone I called said they wanted to come, and could they invite others?

We called it for the next afternoon so everyone could arrange their schedules and I could go to work in the morning, though technically, it would no longer be the seventh and final day. But Josh, Keeper of Important Jewish Information, said there was something called halacha, for just these instances. Translated, it meant that the laws were open to interpretation, as long as the person doing the reasoning was making good sense, like an umpire rendering his view of the strike zone.

And as far as Josh was concerned, a walk around the block

on the eighth day was as meaningful as the seventh, which clearly was the consensus, for when Seth peeked through Ken's living room window, he counted a hundred people waiting.

This had to be testimony to the fact that there were either a lot of compassionate souls in Manhattan, or a lot of troubled ones who thought that this walk promised the miracle of redemption.

Seth hugged me so hard I thought my lungs would collapse. Madeline too was grateful, although she planned to stay back, lest her second-trimester legs swell in the seventy-degree heat. Ken's mom, Judy, along with family and friends, marveled that Josh and I had pulled this off literally overnight, and hoped that Howie would see us because it was exactly the sort of thing he would have loved, which made me cry.

My parents drove in from Jersey, which was a very good sign. Then Julia arrived, and while in the middle of telling me she would always be there for me, off she went to find Josh. Finally, Rachel showed up with two friends from work, but from the way they were dressed, clearly this was less about paying respects than paying attention to the date bait in the shivah pond.

Several of Ken's coworkers arrived, armed with water bottles and Gatorade, as if this was a 5K race. Pet-walking neighbors were also in force, setting a new standard for multitasking. And then came Sierra, minus the old lady clothes, bitching that since New York City blocks were so big, we should only have to go halfway around. Oh, and could she bum a cigarette?

"Thanks for coming," I said.

"Whatever."

"So let's do it." I hooked Rookie to his leash.

"Well wait." Ken stopped. "Aren't they going to expect me to say a few words? I didn't prepare anything."

"It's not a fund-raiser, dear," Judy said. "Maybe just thank everyone."

"I'll get it started," Josh offered. "Rebecca e-mailed me this short prayer she uses."

"Okay." Ken hesitated. "But now I'm going to feel really stupid being in the car when there are all these people walking."

"Do you still have your wheelchair?" Judy asked.

"I am not going in a wheelchair, Mother. That's pathetic."

"Actually, it's not," I said. "You and Rookie will get the fresh air, we'll take turns pushing, and then we don't have to worry about the car getting stuck at a red light."

Ken looked around and he knew he was outvoted. Nobody cared about him being embarrassed. They just wanted to get the show on the road. And so it was that we assembled in front of his building on that sunny, warm May afternoon, each person with his own personal goal.

From the gaggle of girls who greeted Ken with hugs and kisses, clearly they had come to score points. Each one looked in his eyes, like Monica Lewinsky on the rope line, hoping for a sign of desire, which, God, how low could you go? The man just buried his father, did they honestly think he was thinking about hooking up? Yes.

Then Rachel whispered that she just saw Nina get out of her car, pregnant and glowing, and sure enough Ken and family greeted her as though royalty had arrived. I tried to pick up on Ken's reaction to her, but there was such a swarm, I couldn't see his face.

But that was nothing compared to the buzz when a black stretch limo pulled up to the curb and out popped, say it ain't so, Mira Darryl. Who else could afford the new forty-eight-hundred-dollar Fendi spy bag?

"Oh my God." Rachel grabbed my arm. "Check out the pocketbook. It cost more than my mortgage payment."

"You poor thing." Julia came up to me. "This must be a nightmare for you."

"I'm fine." I tried to remember David's best poker face.

"The nerve of her!" Madeline came over. "How did she find out about this?"

"It was in the paper," I said.

"Really?"

"No, of course not. He obviously asked her to come."

But what really hurt was that El Schmucko didn't even bother trying to introduce me, as if I was the event coordinator, too busy handling the logistics to have time for socializing.

Didn't I get it? Every time I thought we were connecting, I got slammed by reality. I was no better than Josh, thinking I could join relationshipland with one of the perfect people. Especially when membership required five-thousand-dollar pocketbooks and chauffeur-driven limousines.

I felt like Little Sally Saucer. Cry Sally cry. Turn to the east, and turn to the west, and turn to the one who Ken loves best. Given that he seemed elated to have Mira hovering, it sure wasn't me.

"Come, dear." Judy grabbed my hand and pulled me in their direction. "This was your idea, and you are going to lead the way."

"No wait. Stop. What are you doing?"

Before I knew it, she was introducing me to Mira. "This is Ken's dear friend, Robyn Fortune, who has been taking such wonderful care of him."

Ken coughed. "I think you two spoke on the phone when I was in the hospital."

"We did?" Mira sniffed.

Uh oh. That was the time I said my name was Sierra and now the real one was here . . . God help me if they start chatting.

"I don't recall the conversation." She stroked Ken's arm.

"But Ken might have mentioned you in passing. Aren't you his little friend from nursery school?"

"Yes, but she's a big girl now." Judy grabbed Ken's wheelchair. "Robyn, you push."

"I'll do it." Mira reached for the handles.

"Not necessary." Judy practically stepped on her toe.

"Why don't they each take a side?" Ken begged.

"Because it's dangerous if too many people steer." She cued me to take over. "Do you want to end up on the ground?"

Nothing like feeling like the nurse's aide walking beside the patient's beautiful lover. And though Mira seemed equally uncomfortable, it didn't stop her from continually leaning over to pet Rookie and ask Ken if he was comfortable.

Hardly the warm, emotional outing I'd expected, but it did confirm one thing. God and the spirit of Howie were on my side, for just then, a cab sped by, splashing Mira's new, creamy beige Emilio Ungaro trousers and Gucci flats, which was such a Carrie Bradshaw, in-the-tutu moment. Only this time, the actress freaked and raced back to her limo.

"Ding dong, the witch is dead." I whispered to my parents. "Can you see if she melted?"

Ken probably thought about rescuing her, but Josh spotted the opening and tore through the pack like a Giants linebacker, grabbing hold of his wheelchair.

"What the hell?" My dad looked back to see if the quarterback was coming through next.

"I always liked that kid," my mom added as we watched them take off.

"What is he doing?" Julia jogged up to join us. "What happened to Mira?"

"Nothing." Sheil laughed. "She got a little *shmutz* on her pants and had to leave."

"Did he ask her to come?"

"Looks that way." I shrugged. "I sure didn't call her."

"Are you mad?" Julia put her arm around me.

"I'm hurt, but what can I do? He obviously wants to be with her . . . His whole face lit up when she got out of the limo . . . I don't know. Maybe she did me a favor by showing up . . . Now I don't have to stick around to see how the story ends. Because for me it just did."

Chapter 27

AWK-WARD. That was the only possible word to describe the scene when family and friends returned to Ken's apartment and stared at me, waiting for my reaction to the humiliation of being upstaged by Mira Darryl.

Everyone knew she was a famous actress who had perfected the art of scene stealing, but no one knew what came next in the script. Would I break down and cry, would I carry on as though I hadn't noticed she was there, or would I confront him and ask, What the hell were you thinking?

In the interest of not causing myself further embarrassment, I chose b, the polite chitchat route. Wasn't it such a nice day for a walk, and had anyone else thought it was hysterical that a cop thought we were protestors and tried to stop us because we were marching without a permit?

My parents and Judy followed my lead by marveling at how many people had come, while Seth and Madeline focused on the enormous fruit basket sent by the Crystals. Josh and Julia headed for the kitchen to make coffee and put out the leftover pastry trays, the remaining family and friends remained silent, sorry that there was no TV in the living room to distract them.

Ah, but the focus of group disdain ignored them all by collapsing on the couch with Rookie and yawning. He was wiped out, he said, but agreed that the walk had been a great idea because it did revitalize him knowing his father would have loved the effort.

Nobody cared. They just wanted to know why he invited the loathsome Mira to this private, family event. Didn't he think that the friend who put it all together, the friend who had been caring for him for weeks and who obviously had feelings for him, would be hurt by the insensitive gesture?

Didn't he know that Mira's presence would turn this from a solemn, spiritual time into a circus? But when no explanation or apology was forthcoming, Mother Hen did what only she could.

"So tell me, dear." She sat next to him on the couch and patted his leg. "What's up with you and Mira? Are you an item again?"

"Discreet as always, Mom," Ken replied. "Now I really miss Dad . . . Who else will tell you to butt out of my affairs?"

"I'm sorry. Am I prying?"

"Could we do this later?" he whispered. "When we don't have a live studio audience?"

"Of course. I was just trying to figure out whether it was safe to go back home yet or if I should stick around in case she leaves you again and you have another nervous breakdown."

"What are you doing?"

"I was going to ask you the same thing. Why did you invite her today of all days?"

"I didn't. She called me this morning to say she was heading back to the coast tonight, and happened to ask what I was doing today, so I told her, and next thing I know she shows up . . ."

"Well, you can only imagine how embarrassing it was for Robyn."

"Why? We're just friends. I mean, yes, I owe her my life. She's been amazing. But she knows how I feel about Mira, and that I still think we have a chance, so please stop harassing me."

My parents looked around to see if I'd heard, which I had, and since I couldn't possibly feel any more mortified, what did I have to lose by packing? "Tell them I have to get back to the studio," I said. "And wrap up some of the rugeleh."

Now if this was a novel, this would be the part where Ken chased after Robyn and begged forgiveness for being such an inconsiderate oaf who didn't deserve her friendship let alone the hopes of anything more.

But this was my life, and that sort of gooey-in-the-middle stuff never happened. Guys in my dreams never loved me enough to crawl back to my heart. Not that it stopped their families.

Judy and Madeline ran into Ken's bedroom to beg me to stop packing, hitting me with what sounded like prepared albeit lame remarks, as if they'd made this speech before.

He was just under a lot of stress right now and he didn't mean the things he'd said and it wouldn't take him long at all to finally realize how perfect we were together and to just give him some time because once he saw the light, this would never happen again.

"I appreciate your support," I said. "But he's right. We're just friends. He doesn't owe me an apology . . . I saw the look on his face when her limo pulled up and he was ecstatic . . . you can't fake that stuff. He loves her, he wants to be with her . . . he doesn't feel the same way about me and it doesn't matter how awful she is to him, he's going to take it."

"But I know he has feelings for you too." Madeline took my hand. "He just doesn't, you know, totally understand them yet."

"He'll eventually come to his senses." Judy took my other hand so I'd stop packing. "He always does. He's just stubborn like his dad."

"Look, I get what you're doing but I am not going to push myself on a guy who clearly knows what he wants, and I sure as hell don't want his family trying to strongarm either."

"But you love him, Robyn." Madeline started to cry. "I can tell."

"It turns out I've always loved him. Unfortunately for me, fate and fortune don't mix."

Aw-ful. That was the only possible way to describe the days that followed.

My mother, having returned to Fair Lawn for the weekend under the guise of being ready to talk to my father about their future, but really to clean the house because it was making her ill to think that it was ready to be condemned, was now back at my place.

Her issue now was that since my father clearly didn't need her, as evidenced by the fact that he had purchased so many televisions, what was the point of talking to the old fart? "He seems plenty happy on his own. A hundred-fifty channels is all the company he wants."

But she couldn't fool me. The real reason she came back was to be able to keep coaxing me not to give up on Ken. And who was she in cahoots with? Her new best friend, Judy.

Oh yes. Now that they had resumed talking, they were making up for lost time. But not in person, not even by phone. She and my mom were suddenly online warriors, burning up the minutes as if AOL was awarding prizes for most e-mails sent in a day.

Yep. Not only had my mom gone and hooked up her computer in my living room for high-speed Internet access, she had joined the legions for whom online communication was an all-day, everyday affair, setting up a buddy list, icons, instant messaging, and forwarding dirty jokes.

Trust me, nothing gives a daughter pause more than receiving an e-mail from her mom that was forwarded from her never-gonna-be-your lover's mom stating how sure she was that this little falling out between Ken and me was surely temporary. To which I replied to my mother, who I suspected would forward it to Judy, "Trust me. It's the end of the line. If it wasn't, I would have heard from him by now."

Just like old times, Kenny boy was doing his famed magic trick, the disappearing act.

Well, not totally. At least this time I knew where he was. At his mother's urging, he had gone back to Florida with her so she didn't have to walk back into her house alone for the first time. Which had merit, but I suspected it was a ruse. She just wanted time alone with her son to talk some sense into him, and if she had to do it while sorting through her deceased husband's personal effects, so be it.

Except that as testimony to how stubborn he was, or how much he was in love with Mira, he didn't call me, write me, send flowers, or make good on his promise to buy me a spa package.

But get this. You know the fifteen hundred Madeline offered if I would just call Ken? *She* made good on her promise and mailed me a check. Which I promptly deposited and then used to pay Seth, who I asked to represent me at my bankruptcy hearing.

He couldn't understand why I wouldn't use my brother, but I said that was only because he didn't remember my brother. Besides, it turned out Phillip was preoccupied with his own problems, as his eighteen-year marriage to Patti the Whip was mysteriously unraveling.

There were two sides to the story, as there always is, but according to Phillip, Patti claimed that he had made golf his entire life and didn't seem to care whether she and the kids were around, and frankly at this stage in their life, she had assumed they would be much more financially comfortable than they were, and maybe if he'd focused more on the partnership track instead of the country club track, they wouldn't always be fighting about money and they could have done a bathroom renovation at the same time as the kitchen.

Different story according to Patti. Phillip wasn't playing golf. He was playing around, and for that he would pay dearly.

Naturally this freaked the hell out of me because not only had Annette predicted this, and it was one of the more preposterous things she'd said, now I was afraid Phillip would pressure my mom to get the hell back to Fair Lawn so he could move into my spare room.

There were some bright spots, however. Guess who the bankruptcy judge was? The widower of Sharon Horowitz, Ken's boss who died of cancer. Remember? Her funeral was our first "date," but we left early so I never heard her husband speak, not that it would have mattered. Sharon had retained her maiden name for business so I never would have made the connection.

But once Seth did, he introduced himself as Ken's brother, and mentioned that I was Ken's fiancée ("Do you still have a diamond ring you can wear to the hearing?") and the entire tone of the proceedings changed. I would only be responsible for ten cents on the dollar and have practically a lifetime to pay them off.

Best fifteen hundred dollars that wasn't mine to begin with that I ever spent.

And now for the grandfather of all ironies. The same day I got my "get out of jail almost free" card from bankruptcy court, I heard from Mitch Kaplan, the program chief at Showtime who I'd sprayed with cookie crumbs at the shivah.

He was over that now, and over the top in love with the

script I'd sent him. In fact, he told me it was one of the most original comedy concepts he'd read in long time, a combination of Tracy Ullman über-smart and Carol Burnett hilarious, and when could I come in for a meeting and had I submitted this anywhere else?

Not bad for Robyn, Queen of Misfortune. My luck, however, it was all part of some cruel hoax to lull me into thinking the tide was finally turning in my favor, only to discover it was a tsunami in disguise, ready to drown me with totally insurmountable problems.

"Why do you have so little faith?" Annette the Magnificent asked me as I sat on her lumpy couch in her basement for the second time in a month.

"Sorry. That's right. You walked in late. You missed the first thirty-three years of my life."

"I told you things were going to work out great." She laughed. "Just be patient."

"Look, don't get me wrong. I'm thrilled that now I don't have to sell my co-op to pay down my debts like last time. And it's a dream come true to have written a comedy pilot that might make it to television. And my gut tells me that even though my parents are still fighting, they'll somehow figure out a way to work out their problems because, frankly, no one else would want them."

"Okay I know there's a but coming." Annette laughed. "Because otherwise you wouldn't have taken two trains and a cab to get here."

"I don't know if it's a but . . . I guess it is. When I was here last time, you kept talking about this great guy I would marry who was such a sweetheart, and there is this man I really care about but the feelings aren't mutual. He's still hung up on this actress, and thinks of me as a good friend, although he's not been very nice to me. So that can't be him, right?"

"Sounds like you answered your own question."

"But what should I do? I can't stop thinking about him. And it's not like he's some guy I met at a bar . . . We were born on the same day in the same hospital, our families were friends, we went to nursery school together, camp, college . . ."

"Are you going out west? I see a trip out west."

"Huh? No. I'm lucky I can afford to cross the bridges and tunnels in New York."

"Because I see something with . . . It looks like they're showing me a map of California."

Is this a reading or a geography lesson? "But what does that have to do with this guy?"

"Are his initials LMC?"

"No."

"Okay, but I do see you making a trip and it's more for business than pleasure."

"Well wait. Maybe it has to do with Showtime. They loved my script and I have a meeting in New York next week . . . Do you think maybe they'll send me out to the coast to meet with someone and maybe that person is this LMC guy and we really hit it off . . ."

"Hold on." Annette laughed. "I need help interpreting. Not the pilot for a TV show . . . Does it make any sense that you'd be with this LMC person at the airport?"

"You mean like he'd fly out to LA with me?"

"Maybe . . . I see you two laughing like you're watching the Three Stooges or W. C. Fields."

"What did you say?"

"Old movies? The Three Stooges?"

"Oh my God! That's it. The initials LMC . . . I know who that is now. Larry, Mo, and Curly."

"No, I doubt I'm predicting you'll marry one of them. They're all dead."

"Only two . . ." I could barely speak. "Curly is still alive."

"But wouldn't he be like ninety-five by now?"

"No, no. Not the real Three Stooges. I'm talking about nicknames for these three boys who were best friends since they were babies . . . and two of them have already died."

"Now you're giving me the chills," Annette said. "What a sad story."

"You have no idea. But here's the freaky part. The day I met Ken, we each got these weird text messages on our cell phones from his deceased friend, Mo. Ken's was his birthday, the one on mine was the day he died . . . 1–2–2–2 . . . December twenty-second."

"And so you think what I heard now were the first letters of their nicknames?"

"Yes. But what does it mean?"

"Well, it means to me that Mo wanted you to know that you're supposed to be together."

"That's what Eddie Fisher said."

"The singer who married Liz Taylor? You channeled him too? Impressive!"

"No." I laughed. "He was Ken's roommate in the hospital the day we got the text messages. We were freaking out and Eddie said, 'I think it means you two should be together.' "

"See? Prophecies everywhere you look. And you started out such a skeptic."

"No, but really. Can spirits or ghosts or whoever they are actually come through like that?"

"It's an everyday occurrence. It's just that most people aren't making the connection when it happens. They think they're imagining things like the lights going on and off."

"Because it's so out there, like the *Twilight Zone*. How do they do it?"

"Basically spirits are just these huge energy fields, which is why it's so easy for them to come through either bodies of water or anything electrical. TVs, radios, even cell phones."

"This is creepy."

"Really? I think it's comforting when loved ones from the other side try to let us know they're okay."

"But I never met his friend Mo. Why would he want to reach me?"

"It sounds like he was trying to tell you to pay attention because something important was happening and he did it in a way that your friend would understand and then have to explain. Was there some unfinished business between them?"

"Big time. Mo was driving drunk and hit and killed a man who was out walking his dog. Then he got out of the car and ran in front of Ken's car so he would die too . . . It's been a lot of years but Ken still hasn't forgiven himself . . . All he kept saying was I killed my best friend. I killed my best friend . . ."

"What a tragedy."

"Wait. It gets worse. Their other friend, Larry? He died at the World Trade Center because Ken canceled having breakfast with him . . . Until last week, he hadn't told a soul."

"I can't even imagine what it's been like for him . . . Did it help him to finally talk about it?"

"Who knows." I sighed. "He left for Florida right after because his dad died and his mom didn't want to be alone."

"Oh my God. This poor man . . . it sounds like he could use a good friend right now."

"Lord knows I've tried, but every time I think we're getting close, he leaves. That's why I want to know . . . do you see . . . do you think . . . will it ever be more than that?"

I waited for what felt like an eternity for Annette's answer. And then I cried.

Chapter 28

THERE IS AN OLD SAYING in politics that every campaign comes down to a battle between hope and fear. And perhaps the same is true of relationships. We pray to meet the one who will bring meaning to our lives, and when they appear, we panic if the feelings aren't mutual.

For nothing is worse than obsessing over a person's face, body, walk, smell, laugh, kiss. Or thinking of ways to change so we are more to their liking. Or stalking them with text messages, e-mails and IMs in the hopes of finally, one day, hearing them profess words of love.

I kept telling Josh I wasn't worth this much energy. That he was a great guy, but not right for me, and was he crazy to turn away Julia's advances?

On the other hand, I could relate, for I too was traveling down the road of obsession, and it was getting awfully congested. Julia wanted Josh, Josh wanted me, I wanted Ken, Ken wanted Mira, and Mira wanted Kyle. Would any of us get our heart's desire?

Julia told me no one was more shocked than she that she

was attracted to Josh, given the ingrained image of him as an obese teen with glasses and crater-skin. But what a difference fifteen years made. He was taller than her, of great importance to a statuesque girl who loved stiletto heels. He was also funny, sweet, an amazing cook, wealthy by his own right and baby-faced handsome, preferable to her other men who were as gold-medal gorgeous as she.

"We're like Albert and Allegra in *Hitch*," she said. "Nobody expected them to hook up, but they were great together."

"Yeah, but movies are different," I said. "Parking spots are always right in front too, and how often does that happen in real life?"

"Why are you so down on this? You told me you weren't interested in him."

"I'm not. I just don't trust you not to hurt the poor guy."

"I won't. I promise . . . Wait . . . This is revenge, isn't it? You're getting back at me for making out with Andrew Stein at Corey Blumberg's bar mitzvah."

"Yes. I've been harboring resentment all these years because my life would have turned out so much different if you hadn't stuck your tongue down his throat."

"What could I say? He liked me better."

"They always did."

But not this time. To my amazement, Josh actually told her that although she was a great girl and beyond gorgeous, he'd had a crush on me forever and would love to finally have the chance to build a relationship. And timing was everything.

With Ken still in Florida, his plan was to seize the moment. He would capitalize on the brief time he had me to himself so that he could sell me on his attributes without interference from his biggest competitor. And I'll give him that he made a strong case.

If I said I was too tired to have dinner with him, he came over and made eggs Benedict. If I mentioned a DVD, he brought it over with popcorn. When my shelf in the kitchen fell down, he replaced it with one that was stronger and then fixed the faucet handles so they didn't drip.

Except that while he was doting on me, I was going on line to see if Ken had answered my e-mails. While he was running to the store for me, I was calling my mother to see if she'd spoken to Ken's mother to see what was new on the Mira front ("He wants to fly to LA? Damn. When?")

Not that Ken was ignoring me this time. We spoke by phone and exchanged e-mails, though the tone was never anything but casual (translated: I did not beg). Instead, I reread his messages to see if I could decipher any hidden meanings, like passages from the *Bible Code*.

Did "You're such a great listener" mean he was starting to see he couldn't live without my love, wisdom, and guidance? Did "Your friends are lucky to have you" mean he was thinking about me much more than expected?

Of course whenever Rachel got this overanalytical, I would be sympathetic but firm. Sure there was always hope the guy would change his mind, but time was a-wastin'. Which is why when she gave me the same speech, I understood the intent. I just didn't appreciate the distraction.

"Yes, Ken is a great catch," she said over lunch. "I was the first one to tell you that. But as they say over at the Democratic National Headquarters, the best candidate doesn't always win."

"I know." I stole a walnut from her salad. "But how can Ken not see Mira is using him?"

"Oh, he knows. He just doesn't care. Just like you can't see that you and Josh would be amazing together."

"Only if I was neutered first."

"Hey, if I stopped seeing guys every time the first time sucked."

"Oh please. You don't even wait for the first time to end.

You call from the bathroom to tell me to call in five minutes hysterical crying so you can say there's an emergency at home."

"Fine. You need chemistry. Just give him another chance because right now with Ken you're at the intersection of nowhere and really fucking nowhere."

"I know . . . I just want to give him a little more time."

"Why? Can't you see he's a gambler like David?"

"He is not."

"Is too. He'd rather risk everything on the big prize than go home with the sure thing."

I hoped she was wrong. I feared she was right. But why wait to find out? I finally conceded to everyone who had been telling me all along. Josh was the man for me.

Don't you just want to gag when a friend is in a new relationship and goes on and on about the guy? "Tomorrow is our one-month anniversary of the first time we kissed." Or when they are clueless how nauseating they sound? "He drove all the way to East Hampton to get those crab cakes I love and then he stopped at my favorite winery to pick up this amazing Chardonnay."

Oh shut up and die is what you want to say. Six months from now you'll be calling my cousin Vinny to get the going rate for breaking the guy's legs. Until then, you have to feign excitement and tell them you are insanely jealous.

Meanwhile, I started seeing Josh, and though he was knocking himself out to make it a special time for us, I wasn't up to the gush stage yet. Not that I didn't feel affection for him. I was just waiting for him to do something, anything, that turned me on.

Rachel said to give it time because some men had to grow on you (like fungus?). Julia said to let her know if I planned to dump him because she didn't mind playing second fiddle, she liked how he kissed (really?). And my mother said she was thrilled I had a good man to take my mind off Ken (um, no).

"So you'll bring him for your father's party on Sunday?" She called me at home.

"Oh my God. Daddy's birthday. I completely forgot. Wait. You're making him a party?"

"Don't I always?"

"Yes, but with everything going on, I wasn't exactly looking for the invitation in the mail."

"Well, I realized I'm stuck with the old fart. Nobody else wants him."

"That's great, Mom. What made you finally see the light?"

"Not what. Who. It was something Sierra said. Turns out she is one smart, little cookie."

"Sierra?"

"Is there an echo? Yes, Sierra. You never gave her a chance, but she is a very bright young lady who understands people a hell of a lot better than any of those good-for-nothin' therapists."

"Who knew? So what did she say about Daddy that made you change your mind?"

"It's not what she said about him. It's what she said about me."

"That you're a pain in the ass and where are you going to find another saint at your age?"

"You got it."

"Hey, I said the same thing. Several times in fact. How come you didn't believe me?"

"It's not what she said, it's how she said it. She said, 'Sheil, what the fuck? You know you love 'im. You know he loves you. Soon you'll be dead and then you can party like hell.' "

"Those are the profound words that gave you a new lease on life?"

"Do you want me to move back in with you?"

"Sierra is brilliant. Didn't I always say that?"

"Exactly. Then I made a deal with her. I said I would give my marriage another try if she would give school another try. I'm thinking she should go for a degree in psychology."

"That's great. And she agreed?"

"Yes. In fact, Simon got her into NYU for the fall and until then, she'll do volunteer work."

"Amazing. Where?"

"At *Daybreak*. She's going to be Gretchen's personal assistant."

"I'm sorry?"

"Yeah. She just called me. Simon also made a deal with her."

"With who? Gretchen? No way. Gretchen doesn't make deals."

"She does when she doesn't want it leaked to the papers that she's having a whoop-dee-do affair with a married man . . . Sierra's main job is to babysit to make sure she stays out of trouble."

"Oh my God. Go Simon!"

"I thought you'd like that news up date . . . Now tell me what is going on with you and Josh."

"Oh. Um. Things are really good. He's very sweet . . ."

"So you'll bring him on Sunday to Daddy's party?"

"Can I get back to you on that?"

"No. I already invited his parents."

I was starting to get so nervous about my upcoming meeting with Showtime, Josh suggested I call Ken for advice. Who better to guide me through the television wilderness, with its mumbo-jumbo talk of options, royalties, and syndication rights, than a man who did this in his sleep?

Which is why when I dialed his number, I swear I was only dreaming about the possible offer, not the memory of Ken's aftershave, which once almost made me steal his pillowcase.

But when I heard his voice, and he sounded so happy to hear from me, and he said he'd just gotten back from Florida and was going to call me because he and Rookie missed me, and I should come over for sushi and yes, we should absolutely talk about the Showtime deal, I'm not going to lie. My mind ventured.

It did not help that when he opened the door, he appeared tan, relaxed, and healthy, the antithesis of the bent and broken man I'd first met. It did not help that he was sweet in a way I'd never experienced. It did not help that when we talked about my script, I was fantasizing not about making money but about making love. It did help that he said nothing about Mira.

"Are you okay?" He lifted my chin. "You're like a million miles away."

"I was just thinking how great you look and how happy I am that you're doing better."

"I am a thousand times better thanks to you . . . I don't know what I would have done without your help."

"Great. Would you like to repay me?"

"Right. I promised you a trip to a spa."

"Yes, but now I'd like to trade that for what's behind door number one." I led him to his bedroom.

A sad Rookie barked when I closed the door.

"Don't you want to hear my suggestions for the meeting?" He laughed as I removed his collared T-shirt and threw it on the floor.

"Later." I kissed him.

"They're really good."

"So am I."

"No wait." He pulled away. "What about Josh? He's crazy about you."

"We have an understanding." I ran my hands over his chest.

"What kind of understanding?"

"You're right." I kissed him again. "This is all wrong. People could get hurt."

"And there's enough pain in the world." He unzipped my sweatshirt.

"Exactly." I unbuckled his belt and forced off his jeans.

He went for my bra. I yanked off his briefs. We stared at the best show-and-tell we ever had, fondled everything forbidden until the anticipation was too great, then hopped aboard for what I thought would be a short joyride, only to discover my ticket was good for the please-don't-stop-you-are-amazing Kenny Coaster.

Slowly we climbed, teasing and pleasing, until finally we plummeted into a delirious corkscrew spin, in and out, upside down, around and around . . . And just when I thought I could catch my breath, the ride started over. Exactly as I'd dreamed that night in his bed. Only this time it was for real.

"No wonder the line forms around the block," I said as we lay in bed, mangled and mashed.

"Thanks, but I only did half the work."

"Yeah, but you were . . . I've never . . . when you did . . . how much is an all-day pass?"

"I think I can get you a discount."

"Good. Because I'm coming back tomorrow so I can go on again."

"Great."

But it was a hesitant "great" and my heart sank. After committing body and soul to him, it should have been a resounding, damn-right-you're-coming-back reply. And though he tried to erase my pained expression by kissing my hand, it made me sicker, as that was the casual gesture of a man who had been in it purely for the sex.

Then I remembered the trouble with great rides. As soon as they were over, someone else was waiting to get on the second you got off . . . Or waiting to go again . . . like Mira.

*   *   *

Every December when family and friends were picking out their new calendars for the coming year, my mother would remind them that if Harvey's annual birthday barbecue wasn't listed on the Sunday of Memorial Day weekend, they'd bought the wrong calendar. For your presence was not only expected, you'd better have a note from your doctor if you weren't coming.

Even God had it marked down, for no one could remember it ever being rained out. Until this year, when it not only poured, the streets flooded. And nothing was sadder than watching my dad look out the window like a little boy, praying for the sun to appear.

Naturally, most everyone but family canceled. And as I looked around at those of us who had no choice but to come, I knew what they were thinking. No skirt steak à la Sheila? No bloomin' onions? The Mets aren't on until four? Are we actually going to have to talk to each other?

Meanwhile, I tried to estimate the retail value of what was on my niece Marissa's back. The Seven Jeans. The Coach belt. The Louis bag. "Can I go shopping in your closet one day?"

"No. Then my mom would have nothing to wear."

"Good point. Where is she anyway?"

"Duh. Where do you think she is? She doesn't have to come to this stupid thing anymore."

"Don't let Grandma hear you say that or she'll smack you . . . So how bad is it at home?"

She shrugged. "Em and Max are freaked out but I'm kinda glad it happened."

"No way. What kid wants their parents to split?"

"Beats having to listen to them scream all day long . . . God I wish I could drive already so I could get the hell out of the house whenever I wanted."

Phillip walked over to prevent me from pumping his daughter for more details, only to have Marissa glare at him and head for my bedroom where she could check out my old yearbooks and memorabilia. "God, I so don't get what you saw in Davy Jones. What a dork."

"How's it going?" I asked.

"Couldn't be better." He gulped his vodka tonic. "You?"

"I'm hanging in there . . . Do you feel like talking?"

"No."

"Me either."

Then we realized if we didn't talk to each other, we'd be stuck listening to Aunt Marilyn go on and on about her diverticulitis and the difficulty of finding a good gluten-free bread.

"Guess what Mom's giving Dad for his birthday?" he asked. "A satellite dish."

"Sweet! So I guess she's not making him get rid of all the TVs."

"Are you kidding? She's loving the HD. Next week she's ordering TiVo."

"Once again TV comes to the rescue. Another relationship saved."

"Speaking of which, what's the deal with you and Josh? God, I can't believe that's the same kid they had to sew two graduation gowns together for."

"Maybe you could remind him of that because I'm sure it's a fond memory."

"Sorry . . . But he doesn't exactly look like he's cheered up much since then."

"Well, he is at one of our family functions."

"No, I think he can tell you're not into him."

"Wow. I must be a bad actress if it's obvious to even you."

"Why do people always say that to me? I'm Princeton educated, a successful lawyer . . ."

"A major putz . . . Nice job playing around on Patti."

"Is that what she told you?" He chugged the last of his drink.

"Is it true?"

"Let's just say the score is even at one all."

"Oh. Sorry. I had no idea . . ."

"Neither did I . . . Studies show the husband is always the last to know."

"I thought you were cheating on her."

"Yeah. Ten years ago. A one-night stand with Marcy Mann at our class reunion."

"And that's it?"

"That's it. Of course when Patti got wind of it, she milked it for everything it was worth, and now I find out she's been screwing the contractor . . . which explains all those free upgrades."

"And the long delays."

"Yeah. According to her, he takes forever in bed too. Unlike me who takes Viagra and gets a cowlick."

I spit out my soda. "We are one hell of a messed-up family. First me and David split, then Mom and Dad, now you and Patti . . . you think we're cursed?"

"Who the hell knows? All I can say is, if you ever get married again, make damn sure you're crazy about the guy. It sucks when one of you starts out with one foot out the door."

"Like you?"

"No. Patti."

"I'm sorry, Phillip." I hugged him. "I really am."

Chapter 29

Robyn's Rules of Break-ups

Rule # 1. Don't say, "It's not you, it's me." Everyone knows it's crap because they've used the same line themselves.

Rule # 2. Don't do it on an empty stomach. Otherwise all you'll think about is food and if the dumpee is just as hungry, you'll end up at a diner listening to why you should stay together.

Rule # 3. Do the break-up on neutral territory, like Switzerland or a place with easy-offs, like the New York State Thruway. The key is a quick getaway.

Rule # 4. Don't ask for a loan.

Rule # 5. Don't have sex because it leaves the door open and you're not coming back, unless it's to see about that loan.

So what did I do when I broke up with Josh (which should have been easy since we were a couple for less time than it takes to get a reservation at Nobu)? I broke the rules.

I swore to him the problem was me. That I was too stressed out from my crazy life to dedicate myself to a serious relationship. I did it at his place before dinner and happened to mention needing a small amount of cash to tide me over until payday. I even told him not to give up on me because when I got back from LA, I would probably want to try again.

Lucky for me, he didn't buy a word of it. In fact, he started yelling that he couldn't understand how I could do this when I'd hardly given us a chance, and if I was so sure this wasn't going to work, why had I agreed to see Paris with him in August?

Easy. I'd never been there . . . and it was proof of my good intentions.

Then came his scorpion dagger. If I thought I could dump him so I'd be able to chase Ken, I was wasting my time because he knew for a fact that Ken was going to try to win Mira back.

"He told you that?" I gulped.

"Yeah. We agreed on a secret plan that day at the shivah walk. He would go after her, and I would go after you."

"You had a secret plan? Why wasn't I consulted?"

"Thus the name. Secret plan."

"Well, then here's a little secret for you. I went to this psychic who said she saw me married to Ken."

"You went to a psychic?"

"Yes." *Uh oh. What if predictions were like birthday wishes? If you told anyone, the wishes wouldn't come true.*

"You had so little faith in me?" Josh pouted.

"No, I had so little faith in me." *There's that pesky Rule #1 again.*

"Oh, that's crap and you know it. It's bad enough you're walking away from a great thing. Don't lie on top of that."

"Fine. I'm sorry. The truth is I have been in love with Ken since I ran into him in college."

"And I've had a mad crush on you since junior high."

"Well, I know deep down, no matter what he says about Mira, he has a crush on me too."

"Really? How?"

"Because you can just tell the way someone makes love to you." *You idiot!*

"You guys had sex? Damn him! When?"

"Last week."

"I can't believe he did that. He promised he wouldn't."

"Are you serious? You made a pact that involved my not having sex? How dare you?"

"Oh you could have sex. Just not with him . . . God, this pisses me off . . . The only reason you're dumping me is because you think now he's going to forget about Mira."

"No . . . yes . . . maybe." I started to cry.

"Not the tears, Robyn. Please. I can't handle the tears . . ."

"I'm sorry . . . You have every right to hate me. I am being such an asshole."

"I don't hate you. I'm just jealous as hell . . . So now what's the deal with you two?"

I shrugged.

"He disappeared on you again?"

"Like the great Houdini." I sighed. "I mean we talk on line all the time, but we haven't seen each other since we . . . Oh my God. I am such a putz."

"I know. Maybe you should go."

"Really?"

"No." He kissed me so sweetly I felt aroused. "I think you should let me fool around with you. Like a consolation prize . . . 'Sorry, Josh. You don't go home tonight's winner, but enjoy this brand new washer/dryer and a farewell fling with Robyn!' "

"Don't," I said as he kissed my neck. "You deserve better."

"And so do you . . . Ken is not worthy of you."

I kissed him back for being so nice. Maybe this would be

like a wine tasting. The second sip would be more satisfying. On the other hand, did I really want to break Rule #5?

No, I did not. I would limit this little good-bye party to kissing and groping, which was a good thing. For when I was leaving, we mutually agreed to face the inevitable. I was in love with Ken and though Josh still had feelings for me, he couldn't deny that dating the very desirable Julia might be very exciting.

Wouldn't you know it? The next day he seized the moment and hooked up with her, only to later learn that they were having so much fun together, they both warned me not to even think of changing my mind about Josh as their relationship had potential. A merger of horses and houses and a passion for travel.

Good for them, I thought. Now if only I could be that lucky. But no. My love interest only thought of us as friends. No wonder I couldn't sleep, eat, or focus. Hell. I was so depressed, I couldn't even remember the sequence of steps to apply Gretchen's foundation.

Which was why the last thing I expected was good news to interrupt the broadcast. But there it was. An out-of-the-blue phone call from a development guy at Showtime who said that my pilot script was so original and hilarious, they were willing to pay my way to the coast so I could interview agents who could represent me at the negotiations (in real life, this *Never* happens).

Only deal was, I had to jump on this within the next week because they wanted to announce the deal at the upcoming cable convention. Within the week? It would take me a month to find the nerve to tell Gretchen I needed a few days off.

"The hell with that dame," my mother scoffed. "Talk to Simple Simon. He owes us big time for saving Sierra."

Sure enough, Simon was so appreciative of my mother's intervention (another first), he approved a one-month leave to see if I could make a go of my new career. Even Gretchen wished me well and thanked me for my years of service with a new set of luggage filled with designer clothes (so what if they were property of the show, how often does someone give you Dior?).

But the best send-off came from Julia and Josh, who planned a surprise dinner at Josh's place the night before I was to leave. And though the guest list was an eclectic mix of family and friends, and the good luck gifts were amazing (I scored an iPoD *and* a new cell phone), pitiful me spent half the night with my eyes on the front door.

"I invited him." The intuitive Josh handed me a drink. "It's just that this was kind of last minute and he had physical therapy at seven. I'm sure he'll try to stop by."

"No, he won't." I sighed. "We're obviously just friends with benefits. He doesn't have to do any of the obligatory stuff."

"Ten bucks says you're wrong."

"Save your money. You'll need it to keep Julia in fur."

My head said don't, but in the game of love, a heart beats the head. Even though I was only a few blocks from home, I was feeling the need to invest big bucks in a cab ride to Ken's, though I had no idea what I'd say when I got there.

Only to discover my expensive joyride might be joyless in the end. It wasn't even ten-thirty but from outside his building I could see that his apartment was dark. Was he asleep? Or worse yet, asleep with another?

Ring the bell . . . No don't . . . You're a coward . . . You're a fool . . . You spent all this money to get here. Ah, but what is the price of pride? What a time for my head and my heart to declare war. If not for the need to pee, I would have left. Then I heard a voice behind me.

"Sorry, little girl. The ride's closed."

"Oh my God!" I jumped. "You scared me. I didn't even hear you."

"I know. Everyone but me misses my cane."

"I'm sorry. I should have called you," we said in unison. Then, "Great minds think alike."

"Ladies first." He dug his hands into his jean jacket.

"No, it's okay. I was just stopping by because . . . actually, I don't know."

"It's okay. I'm glad you did. I wanted to wish you good luck and also you left a bra here."

"I did? And you know it's mine because it's a La Perla?"

"No, because it's a training bra."

"You are so mean." I smacked his arm.

"So they say." He laughed. "Anyway . . . I really am sorry I missed your party . . . I planned to go. Then everything got messed up."

"What else is new?"

"What does that mean?"

"Nothing. It means that shit happens. I get it."

"Tell me about it. Physical therapy ran late, then I had to come back here, pick up Rookie, take him over to Seth's, and just when I was leaving for the party, Madeline started heaving and she was out of her nausea medication and Seth didn't want to leave her alone while he went to the drugstore and by the time he got back it was late and I was starving so we brought in Thai, then—"

"You left Rookie there?"

"Yeah. I have to fly to Chicago tomorrow. Showtime wants me to attend this conference—"

"What did you mean before when you said the ride's closed? I loved that ride . . ."

"Come in and we'll talk."

"No . . . Not the talk." I shivered. "Although I do have to pee."

"And you want your bra back."

"Exactly. But wait. Did I leave it here? I thought I left it at Josh's."

Ken flinched.

"Oh that's right." I winked. "You thought you had a secret plan with him."

"We really have to talk."

I listened to his whole spiel about how he thought I was beautiful and fantastic and funny and sweet, but he was doing me a favor by not hooking up with me because he was such a mess and while I'd never know how much I'd helped him, it came down to this. My life was complicated enough. The last thing I needed was extra baggage to carry around.

Why did this all sound so familiar? Exactly. Rule #1 of breaking up. I'd just given the same speech to Josh. Now it was payback time, along with the game of twenty questions.

"How could you make a deal with Josh not to sleep with me?"

"Well hold on. It's not really what happened. All I said to him was that you were getting a chance to turn your life around now and you didn't need either of us getting in the way."

"Well aren't you thoughtful? You still had no right making decisions on my behalf."

"You're right. It was stupid. I'm sorry . . . The truth is, I didn't want him sleeping with you . . . in case of anything."

"You mean like an emergency at thirty thousand feet?"

"You know what I mean . . . I didn't want Josh to get hurt if there was any chance the two of us could make it work."

"You're an idiot. Of course we could make it work. Just say pretty please."

"It's not that simple. It turns out . . . look, the truth is . . . I know that Mira and I are very different and long term it wouldn't have worked. But you and me are very different, too."

"Oh bullshit. The problem isn't that we're different, it's that you're a coward. You think because you've had your share of misfortune, that it entitles you to spend the rest of your life running away from everyone. But don't you see? You've convinced yourself that you were dealt a lousy hand at birth and your life was supposed to be this bad and voilà, self-fulfilling prophecy come true."

"That is not at all what I think. In fact, quite the opposite. First off, I don't believe in self fulfilling prophecies or any of that other karmic crap you always talk about. I'm an attorney. I go by the facts of the case, not some mindless, arbitrary assumptions that stem from the moon rising in Libra or any of those other way-out-there theories you have about destiny and fate."

"So I'm living in a dream world?"

"I'm just saying we don't share the same values. I could never base a serious relationship on anything that isn't black and white. I need hard evidence."

"Really? You want hard evidence? Then here are the facts. Since the moment I met you, I have been rescuing you, caring for you and looking out for your every need. I have been here to listen to you, hold you, comfort you, and advise you. I have shown you that I am trusting, loyal, and compassionate. And in spite of your often rude and boorish behavior, your presumptions about my role in your life, and your total lack of sensitivity, I have given of myself in every way possible.

"So you want tangible proof of a connection between us? I'm still here, which is more than you can say for Nina or Mira. And as for your feelings that there is no such thing as fate? Well here's a fact. Nothing could be more certain than someone destiny brought to your door."

Ken couldn't look me in the eye. And though I could tell he wanted to respond by the way he'd opened his mouth to say something, for the first time, words failed him. After a minute of deadly silence, I grabbed my pocketbook and left.

*   *   *

Of all things, I made the mistake of calling another lawyer on the way home, only to hear Rachel's closing arguments. It wasn't fair to be mad at Ken for having lost interest in me after sex since (a) I offered it to him no strings attached and all he did was cooperate, (b) if it wasn't for him, Showtime wouldn't have even acknowledged I existed and I wouldn't be on my way to California, and (c) Annette may have been great, but sometimes she was wrong. He obviously wasn't the man for me.

To which I added (d) Ken would be like my mother's Marvin Teitlebaum. The man who would remain in my heart and on my mind . . . but not in my life.

Chapter 30

GOOD THING ABOUT being an adult traveling solo? You could eat all the candy bars you wanted and no one could hound you about ruining your appetite or your teeth. But as I waited in the gate area and bit into a Mars bar, I spotted a couple who was staring at me for longer than was polite. I stared back and then it hit me. They weren't a couple, they were twins and my dearest friends in college.

"Oh my God!" I swallowed my candy and raced over. "Gabs?" I shouted. "Lane?"

"Robyn?" they sang in unison.

We locked arms in a three-way hug, just as we did before every theatrical production at Penn State. Gabrielle and Lane Cohen were my best friends in the department, and it was my fault that we'd lost touch after a small rivalry I had with Gabs during *The Fantastiks*, over which one of us was going to bed El Gallo.

"I kept saying to Lane, I think that girl eating candy is Robyn Holtz," Gabs cried. "But it's been forever so who knows?" She hugged me again. "God, you look amazing. How are you?"

"Still eating candy." I laughed. "What about you guys? Tell me everything."

We did our best to exchange the *Reader's Digest* condensed versions of our lives in between shrieks. Gabs was married to an architect, had a one-year old daughter, lived in the Village, and, bless her hardworking soul, was still acting. In fact, she was waiting to hear about a call back for the lead in for, ready, a limited revival of *The Fantastiks*.

"Oh my God. You were the best Luisa." I squeezed her hand. "I hope you get it . . . You have to let me know so I can come see the show. And what about you, Lane Michael Cohen?"

"Wow. Nobody has called me that in years." He laughed. "I'm great. I'm a documentary film producer."

"Last year he was nominated for an Academy Award." Gabs bragged. "And the reason we're going to LA is he was offered the chance to produce a series for the Discovery Channel and they're going to let me do the narration."

"Awesome! I am so proud of both of you."

But it wasn't their professional accomplishments that gave me a chill. Or the wistful way Lane looked at me, as he had in college. Or the fact that his now tall, sturdy frame and blue eyes were sexy in a way I didn't remember. No. What blew me away was hearing a voice in my head that said, Do you realize his initials are LMC? And you are in an airport laughing hysterically? Wasn't this another Annette prediction?

No way. Was everything that had happened to me a total setup so that I would have this date with fate? Just as the door to a relationship with Ken closed, another would open? And hold on. Hadn't the psychic my mother saw said that if I went to Penn State I would meet my husband?

No wonder I missed the announcement about the flight delay due to weather. I also missed the fact that for the second time that day, someone was staring at me.

"Don't turn around," Gabs warned. "But there's a guy over by the desk who's checking you out and he is so hot!"

"Really?" I started to peek, but she stopped me.

"Fine. What does he look like?"

"Well, if *Playgirl* was still around and they were doing centerfolds, he'd get my vote."

"He's tall, dark, and handsome," Lane offered, but glumly.

Two good signs, I thought. Lane seemed interested in me and he wasn't wearing a ring.

"I don't care." I took his hand. "Tell me all about you . . . I have so thought about you."

"Really?" He beamed. "Me too . . . Are you . . . with anyone?"

"Actually I'm DAA. Divorced and available."

"Perfect." He hugged me. "Same with me."

"Oh shit," Gabs said. "He saw us looking. Now he's coming over here . . ."

But before I could turn around, two strong hands were stroking my shoulders, and my heart stopped, for I knew that unmistakable touch.

"Got room at this table for one more?" Ken asked.

"What are you doing here?" I glared.

"I thought I was going to LA, but I think they just said the flight may be canceled."

"Why?"

"Because the whole eastern seaboard is under fog."

"No. I mean why aren't you going to Chicago? I thought you had a conference."

"I did. But LA is so much nicer this time of year. And then I thought, how can I let you handle these meetings by yourself? You'll be lost."

"Don't you think after last night you should have asked me first?"

"I'm sorry. I thought you'd appreciate the help. I know how these agents in LA think, and you're no match for them."

"I'll be fine . . . oh wait. Now I get it. Josh made you come, right?"

"No, Robyn. I'm here by choice . . . Besides, you of all people should know by now that I can't be talked into anything I don't want to do. Just please say it's okay for me to come with you."

I bit my lip.

After an awkward silence, Lane broke the ice. "Lane Cohen." He shook hands. "This is my sister, Gabrielle Pearlman."

"Oh hey." Ken shook it hard. "Ken Danziger. Nice to meet you."

"You know him?" Gabs whispered to me. "Yikes. Lucky girl."

Lane gave his twin the thanks-a-lot look.

"So it looked like you were having a reunion," Ken said. "How do you know each other?"

"The theater department at Penn State," Gabs answered. "Four years of hell but we were stoned the whole time so who cared?"

We all laughed.

"Do you want to maybe get some coffee while we wait this out?" Lane rubbed my arm.

"Love to." I picked up my things. "Let us know if you hear anything about the flight."

"Well wait," Ken said. "I could use some coffee too. You?" he asked Gabs.

"No, I'm good," she replied. "I have to call home and check on my husband. It's the first time he's alone with the baby for more than a few hours."

"Oh. Sure." With his eyes he asked what I was doing. I answered back, Talking to a man who likes me.

"Shall we?" I took Lane's hand.

"Robyn, stop. Please. I am so sorry about last night. I've thought about everything you said . . . I just need for you to listen."

"Do you two . . ." Lane mumbled. "It's fine. We can catch up on the flight."

"No. It's you I want to catch up with. I already know his story."

It was empowering to walk away holding the hand of a man whose initials were LMC who I'd met in college who obviously was not gay as I once suspected and who was very much in like with me.

So why was it so hard to focus on what he was saying? Because dumbass that I was, I was thinking about Ken. He looked distraught when I blew him off, which he deserved, and yet I couldn't stop wondering if I'd made a big mistake by turning down his help. I knew nothing about the business and now maybe I'd screwed myself.

"So were you a fan of the Three Stooges?"

"What?" I jumped back into my skin, then watched coffee blow out of my mouth. Hardly ladylike, but it made Lane laugh.

"You haven't changed a bit."

"I know. But wait. That's what you're working on for the Discovery Channel?"

"Great listening skills. Yes. That's what we've been talking about for the past half hour."

"I'm sorry." I rubbed his arm. "I'm here and I'm not."

"No kidding," he sighed.

"But it's not what you think. I'm just in shock."

"Me too. I can't believe we let all these years go by without getting in touch and then by sheer coincidence, we end up on the same flight."

"I know, but there is more to the story . . . I had a psychic reading a few weeks ago and I tell you, word for word, this is what she predicted. That I'd be in an airport with someone with your initials and that we'd be laughing like we were watching, and I quote, the Three Stooges."

"Whoa. She's good. Don't lose her number. What else did she say?"

"A bunch of things . . . and something about Ken."

"Of course . . . Look, you don't owe me any explanations, but obviously whatever it is that's going on with you and him is important. And as much as I am happy to see you again, and you are as beautiful and funny and hot as I remember, it's okay if you want to go back to the gate and find him . . . I'm starting to feel pain in my back from all the voodoo pins."

"You're a sweetheart, but honestly, there is nothing between us. He made that very clear."

"Are you sure? I saw his face when you walked away and he looked like he was about to puke. If that's not love, what is?"

Maybe Lane was right. I should at least hear Ken out. But when we returned to the gate, he was gone. Just as well, I thought. In spite of feeling tiny pangs of regret, I was still glad I hadn't allowed him to steamroll me with sentiment that would likely dissipate the second the landing gear hit the pavement at LAX.

"Where did he go?" I asked Gabs.

"I'm not sure. At first I thought he went to the men's room, but he never came back."

"Fine by me." I looked around the crowded gate.

"But he left you this." She handed me an envelope.

"Trust me. A Hallmark card is not going to do the job."

"And then he asked me to give you a message . . . Well, it's not your standard give-me-a-call-when-you-get-back type of thing. It's long."

"How long?" I laughed.

"It would have helped to have the script, but I'll give it my best shot." She cleared her throat. "Okay here goes. I'm not sure if I'm supposed to hold your hand, but you can pretend . . .

"Last night after you left, Josh called, and before he could tell me I was an ass for letting you go to LA alone when this would be the perfect way to pay you back for all your kindness, I told him to spare me the lecture because if you were willing to forgive me for the things I said last night, I wanted to go with you . . ."

"Oh my God." I burst into tears. "I love Josh. He is such a wonderful man."

"No." Gabs said. "The message wasn't from Josh. It was from Ken. Unless . . . oh my God. Did I completely screw that up?"

"No, you got it right." I hugged her. "But I'm sure the reason Josh called Ken was to yell at him, which was so nice because Josh has had a crush on me forever and still, his only thoughts were of my happiness."

"So I was right." Lane frowned. "Ken does love you."

"Maybe." I wiped my tears. "I just can't believe it. He's refused to admit it."

"Well then open the card," Gabs said.

I ripped open the envelope and found not a greeting card, but an index card on which a black and white picture was pasted. The very picture taken of Ken and me in our cribs in the hospital when we were only a few hours old. If you looked closely you could read the signs. Baby Girl Holtz. Baby Boy Danziger.

Underneath, Ken wrote: "Baby, we were born to be together. Please give me a chance."

I collapsed on the floor and cried.

"Don't worry." Ken appeared from out of nowhere, carried

me in his arms, and kissed me. "She does this all the time. Unfortunately the problem isn't treatable."

"What about being good to her?" Lane quipped. "Studies show that helps a lot."

The airfare? $379. The coffee? $2.60 The surprised look on Ken's face? Priceless.

One would think comedy was a funny business. It turned out to be anything but. In three days of meetings with agents, producers and network executives, the only time I laughed was when the waiter who delivered my room service tray tried to hit on me. He was my father's age, but with a lot less hair. And if this was the cosmos's idea of a joke, they should leave the writing to me.

What did work out great was having Ken by my side in my meetings as he was right that it took an experienced captain to navigate the rough, murky waters of development deals. I also could have used a glossary of terms, for other than the frequent cursing (are *fuck*, *fucked*, and *fucking* the only three words Hollywood agents know?) I didn't follow a whole lot that was being discussed.

Well, a few things. I got that Ben Stiller's new sketch comedy series deal had set a record for most money paid to a single comic, but I could bite myself if I had come here expecting to command those kind of bucks. "You have to be one funny Focker to be in that league," I was told.

And at least from having watched HBO's *Entourage* I knew that the ideal agent came off like Ari Gold, a guy who dressed like an assassin, talked like a navy SEAL, and could get a thirteen-episode commitment if he was hunting bear in Saskatchewan . . . as long as there was a cell tower in the wilds.

Fortunately, with Ken bludgeoning the BS with a hatchet, I was comfortable that I had the business affairs side covered. My job was to choose the agent I could live with, for as Ken explained, this relationship was like a marriage. There had to be mutual trust, respect, and understanding. (Good to know he was clear on that.)

When it was over, I signed with Steve Fisher, an agent I subconsciously chose because my dad would have loved him. He was supportive, head-of-the-class smart, and not a single vulgarity crossed his lips. Turns out he was Ken's first choice too, for he not only had more integrity than ten agents combined, he assured me his menschlike demeanor would not prevent him from slaying anyone who even thought about taking advantage of me. Including you? I wondered.

As for Ken? To his surprise, I insisted on separate hotel rooms. This was a business trip, I said, and as such, I did not want pleasure affecting his sharp edge.

He didn't buy it, of course. He just assumed I was still mad at him for having said he could never see us being together. But that wasn't it. It was that having thought about it, I should be the one who was afraid of getting further involved because of *his* history of abandonment.

We had experienced so many intimate moments together, yet it hadn't stopped him from disappearing on me. How could I let myself fall hopelessly in love, only to live in fear that he'd take off and not return?

And too, I had a slight agenda. What they refer to in the auto business as pent-up demand. The longer you had to wait to get your hands on your new car, the more you wanted it.

What harm could come from flirting with other men while keeping the thermostat on low with Ken? Why shouldn't I look my sexy best when we went to dinner (thanks, Gretchen, for all those amazing clothes, including the Theory pants, which called attention to my greatest ass-et)?

It worked. I saw him peering at me with the lecherous desire of a man who had found the car of his dreams and would not rest until he was behind the wheel. The downside was that watching him watch me made me want to stop the car, tear off my clothes, and do him until the mirrors fogged.

In fact, over breakfast at the hotel coffee shop, I was so wound up in fantasy, I buttered my hand and put a straw in my coffee.

"Are you okay?" Ken asked.

"I'm fine." I coughed. "I just have a lot on my mind."

"Well, I hope you're not worried about working with Steve. You're in great hands."

"I'm not worried about being in Steve's hands. I'm worried about being in yours."

"Meaning what? You don't think I'm doing a good job for you?"

"No, you're amazing. I'm saying that right now I am so horny for you, I—"

"Really?" His eyes lit up. "Waitress. Check please!"

"Not so fast, kemosabe. Because here's the problem . . . I've seen this movie already and I know how it ends. Every time we get close, you disappear on me."

"But that's what I've been trying to tell you . . . I have thought long and hard about this and—"

"Don't say long and hard . . . it gets me crazy."

"Our flight isn't until two . . ."

"Don't care. I need your assurance that you are going to stay by my side and not head for the hills, or to Mira's house, or wherever you go every time you feel like we're getting too close . . . I need to know you really care about me."

"I care a great deal. I always did."

"Well you have a funny way of showing it."

"Believe me, it wasn't because I didn't have feelings for you, it was because the feelings I had for you were starting to get so intense . . . The truth is, after Nina left me, I was destroyed. I couldn't fathom how something that started out so strong could literally fall apart overnight . . ."

"And why take the chance of being fooled again? You'd only get hurt."

"Exactly."

"Yet you had no problem chasing Mira."

"Exactly."

"But how could both things be true?"

"Because I never felt about Mira the way I feel about you . . ."

"Do you mean that?"

"Every word . . . I realized I was never in love with Mira. I was in love with the excitement, the boost to my career, which I needed after being out of commission for so long . . . When I was with her, I was back in *Variety*. And you have to admit she is a beautiful girl. She's the Ferrari every guy dreams of driving."

"And what am I? The '57 Chevy you take out on Sundays and then store in the garage?"

"No . . . you're the classic gem . . . the true beauty . . . the one who never disappoints."

"Then why did you practically have a nervous breakdown when she left you?"

"Because I was tired of being humiliated . . . After you've been dumped a bunch of times, everyone thinks it's you."

"Twice is hardly a trend."

"How about ten times?"

"No way. Ten times?"

"Eleven if you bail."

"What are you? Radioactive?"

"Actually, the woman I was engaged to before Nina did call me toxic."

"You were engaged before Nina? What happened to her?"

"She said it was cold feet. But it turns out they were just being warmed by someone else."

"It's like you've got a manufacturer's defect . . ."

"Thanks. I feel better now . . . The truth is, the only one who hasn't left me is Rookie . . . Maybe because I have him on a leash. Not that I blame anyone. I've been so moody and depressed all these years, I didn't want to be with me either . . . I wasn't a good partner. Not even a good friend . . . I don't know. Emotions would come over me that made it impossible to be there for anyone else . . . And when they'd call me on it, most times I wouldn't bother defending myself. I thought they were right."

"And therapy didn't help?"

"You have to want it to help. I had one shrink tell me she'd never had a patient as determined to sabotage himself as me and that I was secretly enjoying being a martyr . . . I didn't believe her, but then when you said the same thing, it hit me that maybe I was in denial. And then I started thinking about the minute I came to on the terrace and you were trying to rescue me and make me laugh at the same time . . . I thought I was dreaming because you looked like an angel."

Tears welled.

"And it was so weird because instead of thinking about how much pain I was in, all I could think about was that you must have been sent to me for a reason and I didn't need to be afraid. Then after we found out we had all these family connections and shared experiences, there was no doubt that your being there was no coincidence."

"Then what was all that bullshit last night about not believing in fate?"

"It's an ego thing. I hate sounding gullible. And more than that, I hate being wrong."

"It's funny. A few weeks ago, my mom said, 'Fate never knocks at the wrong door. You just have to be ready to answer.' "

Ken's eyes watered, and for that brief moment, the sounds

of clanking plates and clamoring silverware were drowned out by thoughts of love and hope.

"You do realize," I finally said, "that if everything works out, I may have to move here."

"I'm aware. But what kind of partner would I be if I got in your way? That's why if this does work out for you, and I have every reason to believe it will, maybe I'll join you. I hear there is an occasional opening for experienced entertainment lawyers . . . But only if you want me to."

"Are you serious?"

"Sure. Rookie and I love California."

"Oh my God. That would be amazing." I started to laugh.

"What's so funny?"

"Um, while we're being totally honest, I have a confession . . ."

"You mean about the fifteen hundred?"

"Madeline told you?"

"She had to. She needed me to give her the money before Seth found out."

"That's hilarious . . . But wait. Did you know that I used it to pay Seth's retainer for my bankruptcy hearing?"

"You're kidding. I paid my own brother for something he would have done for me for free? Damn . . . he better pay me back . . . Let's go upstairs and call him."

"Oooh. Very smooth." I laughed. "But hold on." I leaned in. "I need to know. Was it just me, or was the sex we had . . ."

". . . took me on a ride like no other."

"And do you promise to take me on that ride again and again?"

"You have my word." He pulled me to him and kissed me so hard I moaned.

"Hey, you two," a man at the counter said. "Get a room already."

"Excellent idea." Ken paid the check and took my hand. "Yours or mine?"

"Both." I clapped.

"Both?" His eyes lit up. "God, I love you. And I love you too." He kissed the man.

"Hey!" I said. "I didn't wait this long to have to share you."

"Right." He turned to the man. "Sorry. She saw me first."

"That's true." I laughed. "I know him since the day he's born."

In the End . . .

THE CONTRACT WITH my agent wasn't the only agreement I signed that week. Ken also drew up a contract that one might initially think was a prenup, though it mentioned nothing of assets. Instead, it stated in loving words his desire to share a lifetime together, and his promise that the only circumstances under which he would ever leave was if we needed milk.

Naturally, I was out-of-mind excited to get home and share my news. I had a real, live Hollywood agent, a possible deal with a cable network to produce my comedy special, and the man of my dreams with whom to share my life.

But instead of running to tell the usual list of suspects, my first call was to Annette. For she was the one who helped me understand the true meaning of fate. "Don't you get it?" she'd persisted.

Yes, I finally got it.

I got that fate may have been the unexpected guest at my cousin Brandon's bar mitzvah, but ultimately, it's what got the party started. For had it not been divined that I try my hand at comedy, I wouldn't have been asked to do my act. Had I not performed, Seth wouldn't have known I was there or had reason to talk to me about his brother. Had I not called his brother, I would never have known Ken Danziger existed, or learned the meaningful role he had played in my young life. Had I not called Rachel to tell her about Ken, I never would have gone to his apartment, or seen the photo I took of him with Larry and Mo. And had I given up on him when I felt he was emotionally unreachable, I would never have made it to a happy ending.

I got that what made marriage so empowering was not what it taught you about relationships, but what it taught you about destiny. That like a UPS package, you started out thinking you got exactly what you ordered, only to realize it could be nothing like you expected.

I married David, so sure he was the answer to my prayers, only to find out he was the beginning of my nightmares. Phillip married Patti, the shiksa goddess, only to discover that beauty did not age well when it didn't come from within. As for Sheil, she assumed when she married Harvey that she was settling, only to learn she had wed the one man who would love her more than she ever loved herself.

I got that when you thought you were a victim of difficult circumstances, it was in actuality the spin cycle of life. A cycle whose sole intent was to make sure you came out facing the right direction and ready to start clean.

I got that what you couldn't make happen was never meant to be.

But the one thing I didn't get was how I would find the time to start my new life.

I had to pack up my apartment and move to LA, begin work on a pilot for Showtime, return to New York to be Julia's maid of honor when she married Josh (talk about fate bringing two people together). Oh, and somehow I needed to start planning my own wedding.

It was an abundance of riches, though, as we are taught in the Jewish faith, sweetness and sorrow go hand in hand. For my parents' forty-second wedding anniversary, I sent them a card and inscribed this message: "Not even the best maps can prevent bumps in the road. But if you travel with the one you love, you will never be lost."

It was timely, for had I waited a week to send it, it would have been too late.

On a beautiful Sunday in October, Harvey Holtz suffered a fatal heart attack while tending to his wife's cherished garden. Only for her to discover him holding fresh roses in his hand that he had intended for her.

But eight months later, the cycle of life again brought joy to our door. For Ken and I celebrated the birth of our baby, the very round and silly-looking, Harris Todd Danziger.

What could be more perfect than to have a son to name in honor of three extraordinary souls? Harris for my father, Harvey; Todd, for my baby brother; and Danziger to carry on Ken's family name. Truly our boy was blessed with a legacy of goodness and the spirit of hope.

Ditto for his older cousin, Montgomery Howard Danziger, the rambunctious, talkative, two-year old son of Seth and Madeline who was the spitting image of his father.

At the bris, we prayed hard that Harry and Monty would grow up together and feel the kindred spirit of their grandfather guiding them through their hopefully blessed journey.

And oh yes. Remember the psychic my mother shlepped to Long Island to see? Her name was Helen Konieczka . . . grandmother to Annette. I kid you not. But how to explain that two generations of women from one family unknowingly consulted with two generations of women from another? Have I taught you nothing?

As for me? The former Ms. Fortune? I finally allowed fate to lead me to the road on which I was destined to travel. The road on which a comic lived happily ever after with one of the Three Stooges.

Talk about having the last laugh!

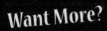

Want More?

Turn the page to enter
Avon's Little Black Book —

the dish, the scoop and the
cherry on top from
SARALEE ROSENBERG

I may be able to cook up good potboilers to read, but I am one crummy chef. Which explains why my son dreamed that our kitchen appliances were replaced with vending machines, while my daughters have always made sure the doorbell works. Cannot miss the delivery guy!

But even those who are pros in the kitchen will agree that when it comes to hosting a dinner or holiday party, the preparation can be overwhelming. Shlepping from store to store for the right ingredients, hauling in bags of groceries at the precise moment no one is around to help, putting away the food, straightening up the house, buying fresh flowers, digging out the good dishes and linens, setting a beautiful table, spending hours if not days cooking, and finally cleaning up the mess in the kitchen . . . at the precise moment no one is around to help.

Then in the blink of an eye, the meal is over and the men are up stretching, wondering what you made for dessert and can they eat it in the den so they don't miss the big game? Oh and how soon can they be invited back because they love coming over?

This is what it feels like to write a novel. By the time I've fully developed a fun, compelling story with memorable characters, and finished a rough draft that doesn't make me want to puke, the seasons have changed several times over. Add another few months for revisions, a year for the publisher to work its magic, and guess what? Readers gobble it up in the blink of an eye, stretch and say, "Loved it! Hopes she's got a new one coming out soon."

Naturally, it's inspiring knowing that people await your new book. It's just that as with hosting a dinner party, or especially a wedding or bar mitzvah, no one can appreciate how hard you worked to make it perfect because they didn't see the process, only the finished product.

That's why I thought it would be fun to take you behind the scenes. Share some of my earliest ideas, how I came up with the characters' names, and two scenes that were left on the cutting room floor. Or in my case, my bedroom floor, since that's where I do most of my writing.

In fact, let me set the stage, because so many readers assume that by virtue of being a published author, my jewelry is real, I have a beautiful office overlooking the water, and I party with Nora Roberts and Phillip Roth (because all of us "R" authors stick together, just like on bookstore shelves). Oh, and that I have an adorable assistant named Dylan who checks to see if I need fresh coffee or a massage. (This is why I love writing fiction. What other job pays you to sit home in your sweats while letting your imagination run wild?)

Reality check! I have neither an office nor an assistant, I've never met Nora or Phil, and only some of my jewelry is real. As for where I write, you'll find me in the master bedroom surrounded by laundry baskets and bills. And the people who check on me? They only want to know when I'll be done working because a toilet is overflowing and someone is at the door who wants me to sign a petition protesting the new Wal-Mart.

No respect, I think. Disrupting me when I'm slaving over a hot computer, toiling over plot and themes and character development. Um, no. I was probably just on line.

Did you know that there are over a hundred sites where you can check your horoscope for free (if Mercury is retrograde, oooh, not a good time to write)? And how I could start my day if I didn't read Page Six of the *New York Post* (I worry if Jennifer Aniston is holding up under the strain of the whole Brad and Angelina baby thing). Of course, there is always something to buy (No! I just saw that pocketbook for a hundred dollars more in the store), or something to comparison shop (They make washers and dryers in colors now?). And what's this? Two new e-mails and an instant message from my son at college? Could be important.

Eventually, guilt gets the better of me and it's back to work. Enough with the procrastination, I tell myself. I am a professional. The reading public is clamoring for this book (it's delusional, but it works). I won't get paid until I finish (this *really* works.)

When I'm in what I call the construction zone, I toy with ideas for storylines by sitting quietly with paper and pen. I put on a little Kenny G, maybe light a candle, and you guessed it. Naptime . . . The truth is, I get my best ideas in the shower, in the checkout lines at the supermarket, and while getting my teeth drilled because nitrous is so very stimulating.

But what really keeps my mind percolating is wondering not *what* this new book will be about, but *who*. For what I love best about writing fiction is exploring the human psyche and how we react to obstacles and challenges. And if by creating honest, heartfelt portrayals, I make readers connect with the characters' drama and quests, then I'm happy.

In the Beginning . . .

When I first conceived *Fate,* I knew that I wanted to examine, as I had in my previous novels, how destiny played a major role in our love lives, yet we were always the last to know. I also wanted to write about family relationships and how they too impacted us on levels we never imagined, and mostly how, for better or worse, money changed everything.

Here are just a few of the best (or worst) of my initial ideas:

First there were Hal and Jeannie Fortune, former hippies from the Bronx who never met a sit-in they didn't like, and who have tried for years to turn their adult daughter, Robyn, into an activist like them. Wouldn't she like to get people in the mall to sign petitions against the fascist/commie/pinko government? Not really. "Excuse me. Do you know if they moved the Coach store next to Bebe?"

Then I toyed with Robyn Fortune being a dutiful daughter of former antiwar protestors who had zero interest in conspicuous consumption or shallow pursuits. Until she married a Long Island boy, moved there, and won the lottery. Now they are rich, rich, rich and trading in the old Volvo for either a Mercedes or Porsche. "Which convertible comes in yellow?"

How abut this? Ken Gold meets Robyn Fortune at a family bar mitzvah and says that with their last names, they're a match made in heaven. Robyn is interested until learning that, good God, the man is a rabbi. Who would ever want to date one of those? They get traded like ballplayers without the huge paychecks . . . Then Rabbi Ken buys a winning lottery ticket and suddenly Robyn is lighting Sabbath candles.

This one was my favorite for a while: Chutes and Ladders, the suburban edition. The lives of two families are thrown into a tailspin when fate comes a-knockin'. One is unexpectedly bequeathed a huge inheritance and goes from being near bankruptcy to being able to buy a bank, while their neighbors, who were living beyond their means, get into serious legal troubles, and there goes the Jag, the house in the Hamptons, and "Hello Mom? We're movin' in."

How did I finally come to write about a young, divorced, stand-up comic from Fair Lawn, New Jersey, who gets fixed up with a down-on-his-luck attorney who turns out to be the boy in college she adored but knew only from afar? I don't remember. But from looking back at my notes, I clearly was aiming to write a love story that was rich in history and redemption. The details, the characters, the dialog . . . Seems I listened to an inner voice that was tuned to a great channel. And my hope is that I can find the same frequency for the next book.

What's in a Name?

Everyone asks how I come up with the names for my characters. Basically, I start by scanning yearbooks, phone books, synagogue bulletins, and *People* magazine. I consider the age and heritage of the characters, where they were born, and if I know somebody with the same name who would not appreciate being cast as a philandering shoplifter.

Sometimes I make lists of first and last names and do a Chinese menu routine. One from column A . . . Sometimes I do throw in the name of a family member or friend because I know they'll buy lots of copies of the book so they can brag, "Right here. That's me on page 114."

For instance, when Ken and Robyn meet, Ken is heartbroken because a famous actress (Darryl Hannah) had just dumped him for a famous actor (Keanu Reeves). Then I found out Keanu was married and Darryl was older than I thought, and why take the chance of pissing off real celebrities, especially if they weren't being portrayed in the most flattering light? In place of them, I made up the name Kyle Rider (to me that sounded like someone who starred in buddy pictures with Kevin Bacon) and "borrowed" Mira Darryl from my sister and brother-in-law because (1) they would be thrilled, (2) they would never sue me, and (3) book sales in Chicago would rock.

In most cases, however, my rule of thumb when creating characters' names is to go by instinct. What feels and sounds right usually is right. Robyn was initially Randi Sherman, and her ex-husband's name was Ira. Too Jewish, I thought. I didn't want this sounding like *Tales from the Temple*. But Robyn I liked. It just couldn't be Robin with an "i" because, well, her mother was going for the country club spelling.

And the last name, Fortune, of course, was an obvious play on words. How could someone with such a rich last name have such terrible luck and misfortune? I was also tempted to use the last names Gold, Silver, Diamond, Pearl, etc., but why go overboard with the irony?

Originally Robyn's parents were named Jack and Elaine Goodman, but after I wrote five chapters, their characters were stiffs. A dentist and a librarian. Yawn. Ah, but then I thought of Sheila and Harvey Holtz, and boom, I could just hear the bickering and kvetching.

Robyn also had an older sister at first. But since I had already done a tortured sister act in *A Little Help from Above,* I thought better of going there again too soon. But why not an older, pain-in-the-ass brother? Bruce maybe? Or Richard? Then I scribbled the name Phillip and could instantly envision the business suit, the BMW and the shiksa goddess wife.

Robyn's love interest, Ken, was initially Paul, then Stuart, then Bryan. But when I dabbled with the name Ken, I could actually hear his mother calling him Kenny, and having a hard time accepting him as a grown man who should be called Ken or Kenneth.

Oh, and about the locale? I decided to lay off Long Island for a while and choose a nice, middle-class town, Fairlawn, New Jersey. Now right up until I turned in the manuscript, I was spelling Fairlawn as one word. Fortunately, plans called for me to be on Route 208 in Jersey, and when I passed an exit sign, I noticed that it was spelled with two words. But instead of assuming I was wrong and the sign was right, I said to myself, What idiots. There's a typo on that sign . . . That would have been one, big oops.

The Cutting Room Floor

Sometimes, no matter how hard you try to shape a scene, it just doesn't work. Either the dialog is full of clichés, or there's not enough movement to progress the story, or the scene is just not true to life or the characters. And yet it's so hard to chuck scenes because, like your children, even if they disappoint you, you wouldn't dream of abandoning them.

So for fun, here are two deleted scenes I still like. This first one was the original start of Chapter One:

"I'm leaving your father." Elaine stared into her coffee cup.

"Leaving him where?" Robyn checked her cell for voice mails.

"Don't make jokes, dear. This isn't one of your comedy routines."

"What?" She looked up.

"Would you ladies care to take a look at the dessert menu?" The perky server sidled up to Elaine's chair.

"No thanks," mother and daughter stated for the record.

"Oh too bad. I'll bet you've never tried the chef's double chocolate . . ."

"And I'll bet you've never tried squeezing into jeans that were tight *before* they went in the dryer." Robyn chucked his shoulder.

"What my daughter is trying to say is that we're on the Weight Watchers program." Elaine smiled. "She's lost close to twenty pounds and I've dropped eleven. It works on points."

"Mom, it's okay. Really. He doesn't need to know this . . . Check please."

"Yes, and more coffee." Elaine smiled.

"Isn't that like your third cup?" Robyn asked.

"Have you quit smoking?"

"Absolutely." She coughed.

"When?"

"An hour ago."

"I thought so." Elaine frowned. "And why aren't you listening to me? You're just like your father. I said I'm leaving him."

"Damn! The one day I don't check my horoscope."

"I mean it this time." She leaned in. "I'm sexually bored. I'd practically have to be hypnotized to be attracted to—"

"This isn't happening." Robyn closed her eyes. "What did Daddy say?"

"How should I know? When does he ever listen? I thought maybe you could talk to him."

"Me? You want me to tell my father that his wife of almost forty years is planning to fly the coop?"

"You know, I thought you of all people would understand . . . because you're divorced and all.

"That was different. I was only married for three years. You and Daddy have been together for a lifetime."

"Exactly. And enough is enough. I was thinking that maybe you could teach me how to apply makeup and I could become your assistant at work."

"My assistant what? You mean like a caddy? I'll take the eyeliner brush now . . . No, I think you should use the number three sponge . . . It'll never work, Mom. I am the assistant."

"But you said you were going to be promoted soon."

"Well, it turns out it's like Passover. They keep passing me over."

And here is a scene I wrote to introduce Robyn's relationship with her father and brother:

Robyn had given her father every assurance that his wife's intentions were noble but ill conceived. That she didn't really want a legal separation, but a chance to be heard. It would only be a matter of days, a week tops, before Elaine realize that the life of a single girl was overrated and expensive. ("She'll freak when she sees what I pay for tomatoes.") Or that life without her flower garden wasn't worth living. Ditto for lunches with the girls, mah-jongg, and Wednesday matinees. Even her husband, creature of deplorable habits, would surely be missed.

And perhaps if said husband got off his neglectful butt and showed up with a dozen roses, preferably not ones purchased at Citgo, then offered to take his wife to dinner at a restaurant known for something other than two-for-one specials, everything could go back to normal.

Except that Jack Goodman refused to do his part for reasons Robyn found baseless. "She's been threatening for years. If she wants to leave, let her leave. I should go chase her?"

Yes, she thought. In fact, you should care a great deal that the mother of your children is so completely unhinged by the ravages of matrimony that abandonment is her only viable choice. You should care that your life partner, the woman you vowed to have and to hold, is checking out futons at IKEA because she lost interest in marital beds. At a minimum, you should be worried that in case of serious illness or injury, you'll be all alone in a rambling, two-story house in Fair Lawn, New Jersey, that is in even more need of repairs than your marriage.

"At least talk to her," Robyn pleaded. "Maybe there's an easy solution here. You pay more attention to her, she leaves you alone about your map collection."

"What's wrong with collecting maps? It's a nice, quiet hobby. Better than those silly card games your mother plays week in and week out. Oooh. I won twenty dollars," he mimicked.

Phillip, the older child, took aim with his usual legal babble, arguing what an outrage it was that his three innocent children were being subjected to the infantile bickering of their grandparents. Did the two of them honestly think Hailey, Jillian, and Max would forgive them if they didn't come over to light Hanukkah candles? Did they really expect the children to be happy about not going to Papa Jack's and Nana Elaine's for Passover? Who would hide the *afikomen*? "Did you think about that, Dad? Did you?"

And in Conclusion

I love the special features on DVDs, especially the one-on-ones with the actors and the director. It's always fascinating to hear about the screw-ups that turned into brilliant moves, the pivotal moments I totally missed, and of course, the behind-the-scenes dirt ("Really? She was five months' pregnant when they were filming?").

So I thought maybe I could do the same type of thing for *Fate*. Except that the only interesting thing that happened while I was writing this book was that I came up with an idea for a new one I've tentatively titled *Boredwalk*.

You see, most mornings I power walk on a boardwalk with my friend Susan. And because we've been doing this for years, we see the same group of people, including two middle-aged men who, like us, are giving it their best shot at keeping slim and trim. We don't know their names or what they do, but we say hi and they say hi back. End of story.

Until one morning it hit me. What if I wrote a story about two women and two men who do more than grunt as they pass? What if they noticed one another, especially in the spring when the heavy winter clothes get ditched? What if they started flirting and one thing led to the next . . .

No, no, no. Too predictable and *Desperate Housewives*-ish.

Okay, what about this? Rhonda, a suburban mom, is profoundly bored with tennis, carpools, and making lemon squares for PTA bake sales. But when her next-door neighbor moves away, and she loses the one friend with whom she could commiserate, all seems lost . . . Until a new mom moves in. Only this one ain't drivin' a minivan. Think Charo meets the Cat in the Hat! Did anyone say road trip?

Hmmm. I don't know. Maybe.

But stay tuned, as they say. I'm just warming up.

XOXOXOXOX,
Saralee

A Few Words About Compulsive Gambling

If through dumb luck I happened to win a few hundred bucks at a casino, I would head for the gift shop. Gambling isn't my thing. So when I began researching the problems associated with this addiction, I was naive. I didn't understand point spreads and vigs and the juice. I couldn't relate to the rush people said they felt every time they placed a bet. I had no idea that due to the proliferation of offshore and off-track betting, Internet gambling, casinos sprouting like weeds, and a seemingly unstoppable love of poker, every year hundreds of thousands of Americans are not only losing everything they own, they are losing everyone they love.

But the even bigger tragedy is that compulsive gambling has hooked children and college kids in epidemic numbers, and their parents are unaware until they are faced with insurmountable debts and legal problems.

As if this isn't bad enough, research indicates that many compulsive gamblers don't limit their addictions to betting. They are also addicted to sex, drugs, and alcohol, and in order to keep the rush going, resort to pathological lying and criminal activities until they are either caught, commit suicide, or are fortunate enough to be rescued and rehabilitated.

I am deeply indebted to Arnie Wexler, a recovering compulsive gambler, for taking the time to educate me and for sharing his harrowing experiences, as well as for giving other gamblers hope.

Arnie placed his last bet in April 1968. He, along with his wife, Sheila, have devoted the past thirty-seven years to helping gamblers break the habit through compassionate, confidential counseling and education.

If you or someone you care about are at risk due to a gambling addiction, please call the Wexlers at 1–888–LAST–BET. Or go to their website www.aswexler.com. Another excellent resource is the Gamblers Anonymous Hotline: 877–644–2469.

Friends, truth is stranger than fiction, but characters aren't the only ones who deserve a happy ending.

Photo by Glenmar

SARALEE ROSENBERG

This is **SARALEE ROSENBERG**'s third novel in her trilogy about destiny and love. Look for her other two Avon Books, *A Little Help from Above* and *Claire Voyant*. Please visit her website at www.saraleerosenberg.com.